DAVID ROBERTS was a publisher for thirty years before becoming a full-time writer. He is married and divides his time between London and Wiltshire.

Praise for David Roberts

'A most engaging pair of amateur sleuths whom I look forward to encountering again in future novels.'

Charles Osborne, author of
The Life and Crimes of Agatha Christie

'Roberts' use of period detail . . . gives the tale terrific texture. I recommend this one heartily to history-mystery devotees.'

Booklist

'The plots are exciting and the central characters are engaging, they offer a fresh, a more accurate and a more telling picture of those less than placid times.'

Sherlock

A GRAVE MAN

DAVID ROBERTS

ROBINSON
London

Constable & Robinson Ltd
3 The Lanchesters
162 Fulham Palace Road
London W6 9ER
www.constablerobinson.com

First published by Constable,
an imprint of Constable & Robinson Ltd 2005

This paperback edition published by Robinson,
an imprint of Constable & Robinson Ltd 2006

A copy of the British Library Cataloguing in
Publication Data is available from the British Library

ISBN-13: 978-1-84529-317-8 (pbk)
ISBN-10: 1-84529-317-7
ISBN-13: 978-1-84529-128-0 (hbk)
ISBN-10: 1-84529-128-X

Printed and bound in the EU

1 3 5 7 9 10 8 6 4 2

For Olly

Romeo: Courage, man; the hurt cannot be much.
Mercutio: No, 'tis not so deep as a well, nor so wide as a church
door; but 'tis enough, 'twill serve: ask for me tomorrow,
and you shall find me a grave man.

Shakespeare, *Romeo and Juliet*

———————————

Give me the daggers. The sleeping and the dead
Are but as pictures.

Shakespeare, *Macbeth*

August 1937 – February 1938

1

In England, when a great public servant dies, it is customary to hold a memorial service in Westminster Abbey at which his achievements are recalled and his sins forgiven if not forgotten. Death transforms a hated rival into a cherished colleague whose loss is genuinely felt, reminding the survivor of his own mortality. Like the Roman general enjoying his triumph, a slave whispers in his ear, *'Respice post te, hominem te memento!'* Look behind you and remember you are mortal. If called upon, the mourner composes a panegyric replete with platitudes.

At the Abbey, he removes his top hat with studied dignity, gives his name to the usher and wonders how far down the list it will appear in the following morning's report in *The Times* and the *Morning Post*. He sings an anthem and listens poker-faced to the eulogy. It is not a long service because the congregation is made up of busy and important men whose time is money. As the organ sounds in sombre magnificence he processes out, proud to be 'one of us'. He feels a stirring of excitement in the knowledge that soon he will be mingling with the high and mighty on equal terms. At the Abbey door, he whispers a few words of comfort in the widow's ear, gives the eldest boy a firm handshake and pats the youngest on the head and, his duty done, replaces his top hat. He raises his eyes and sees many friends and acquaintances whom he greets with a sad smile and a modest nod of the head. Gradually, back in the world of the living, spirits lighten and his smile broadens. He makes what he hopes are unnoticed efforts to put himself in the way of those higher in rank or in a more exalted office with whom he can speak a few words and be seen to be doing so. It is the way things are done, at least in England.

In the case of Lord Benyon, the economist, writer and government servant, who had been killed when the giant airship, the Hindenburg, had exploded in a ball of fire as it attempted to dock in New Jersey, the situation was a little different. For one thing there was the extraordinary nature of his passing. In the second place Benyon's only living relative was a sister married to a self-important stockbroker. There was no black-veiled widow or desolate children upon whom the mourners could focus their grief and, though no man is without enemies, Benyon had far fewer than most. Even Montagu Norman, the Governor of the Bank of England and an old sparring partner, admired Benyon's abilities and liked him as a man though he abhorred his ideas.

The Prime Minister and senior cabinet ministers filled the front pews along with the Court of the Bank of England, the American ambassador, the Provost and Fellows of King's College, Cambridge, leading British financiers and other dignitaries. There was a certain irony, which Benyon would have relished, that he should be mourned by a political class he had long derided and in a religious service he had been known to describe as 'hocus-pocus'. For all that, he would surely have been delighted to see so many friends gathered to say their fare-wells. These friends were a very mixed bag as his interests had extended far beyond politics, economics and business. His wife, Inna, who had died a year before, was a prima ballerina in her youth and had danced for Diaghilev. Many of her friends from the world of ballet had become his friends: dancers and choreographers such as Anton Dolin, George Balanchine and Lydia Lopukhova. His close friends included Sir Thomas Beecham, director of the Royal Opera House, writers and artists such as Virginia Woolf, Morgan Forster and Duncan Grant, as well as actors and theatre directors. Women had loved to confide in him despite his feeble physique, weak eyes hidden behind thick-lensed spectacles and balding head, so it was no surprise to find the Abbey filling up half an hour before the service was due to begin.

It was early August and the great church was almost hot and certainly stuffy. The Hindenburg had been destroyed in May when the Abbey was being decked out for the coronation; it was only now that it had regained its normal sober dignity and was

4

ready to give death its due. The House of Commons was about to rise for the summer recess, and politicians and civil servants were on the point of departing for the grouse moors or to take what many believed would be their final holidays on the Continent before the outbreak of a new European war.

Among the many hundreds who had gathered to pay their respects were Lord Edward Corinth and the journalist, Verity Browne. They had found seats way back in the nave where they could see nothing and hear very little. Verity, as a committed Communist and atheist, normally refused on principle to enter a church but on this occasion had swallowed her convictions out of affection for Benyon. In the short time they had known him, both Edward and Verity had come to look upon him as a dear friend. Edward had acted as his protection officer aboard the *Queen Mary* on a recent trip Benyon had made to the United States to try to persuade President Roosevelt to fund Britain's rearmament programme. Benyon had been unsuccessful, as he feared would be the case, but had at least survived an attempt on his life. Furthermore, he was a bad sailor and the ship had not been as stable as Cunard had promised. A storm in the Atlantic had prostrated him and he had declared that on the next occasion he had to visit the States he would travel by air. The Hindenburg had made several safe crossings and its only disadvantage seemed to be that, as an enemy of Fascism, Benyon hated to travel in an airship adorned with the swastika.

The service followed the normal pattern. The Prime Minister read the famous passage from Ecclesiasticus which includes, so aptly for Benyon, the words: 'Leaders of the people by their counsels, and by their knowledge of learning meet for the people, wise and eloquent . . .' The Archbishop of Canterbury called him 'a humane man genuinely devoted to the cause of the common good – radiant, brilliant, effervescent, full of impish jokes.' Verity found herself digging in her bag for her handkerchief and even Edward found his eyes prickling.

When the service ended, it was twenty minutes before they could even think of making their way to the West Door. Just as the crowd about them thinned and Edward had bent to retrieve his hat from underneath his chair, he heard a shrill cry which seemed to come from a woman who had been sitting a few rows in front of them on the extreme right, close to the entrance to the cloisters. Edward walked into the side aisle and saw that a woman was bending over a man slumped in one of the seats.

Verity had also heard the woman cry out but was too short to see who it was.

'I say, V, isn't that Maud Pitt-Messanger – the daughter of the archaeologist? Do you remember, we met her with Benyon once? I hope . . .'

Without finishing his sentence, he walked towards her, Verity in his wake. Two or three other people had also heard the cry and had turned to see what was the matter. Edward found her kneeling in the aisle, her arms around an elderly man half lying in the chair next to the one in which she had been sitting.

'Miss Pitt-Messanger . . . can I help? It's Edward Corinth. We met . . . is everything all right?'

'My father . . . he's . . . I think he's fainted.'

Edward saw at once that this was no faint. The old man's eyes were closed and his face was the colour of parchment. He raised Pitt-Messanger's limp hand and felt for a pulse. He looked up and saw Verity.

'Get one of the ushers, will you, V? Quick as you can. We need a doctor but I'm very much afraid . . .'

With the help of several of those who had crowded round, Edward laid the old man on the floor and loosened his collar. It was only then that he noticed the blood which had soaked through Pitt-Messanger's shirt and stained his coat and trousers. Gently, Edward pulled aside his coat to see where the blood was coming from. He saw with disbelief the handle of a knife sticking out from just below his ribs. The blade had been plunged into his body with such ferocity that it was too deeply embedded to be visible. There was a gasp of horror from those who could see what Edward had revealed.

'Everyone stand back. No one touch anything,' he said. He recognized one of those who had helped him move the dead man. 'Cardew, we need the police. Go to the West Door, will you? I noticed two or three constables on duty as we came in. If you can't see one immediately, find a telephone and ring Scotland Yard. Ask to speak to Chief Inspector Pride and tell him what has happened.'

The young man disappeared and Edward met the eyes of Miss Pitt-Messanger who had collapsed on to one of the chairs and was being comforted by a woman he did not recognize. As the young woman holding Miss Pitt-Messanger's hand turned to him, he saw one side of her face had been badly burned, perhaps when she was a child. He looked away, not wishing to embarrass her. Maud was sobbing into a handkerchief and making little moaning noises. He noticed a fleck of red on her glove. He hoped she had not seen the knife. To die in such a way, in such a place, at such a time, was grotesque.

'I'm afraid your father is dead, Miss Pitt-Messanger.'

'Has he . . . has he had a heart attack?' she managed to ask through her sobs.

Edward hesitated. It seemed cruel to tell her the truth but she would have to know what had happened. It could not be hidden from her. 'I am sorry to say I think your father has been murdered.'

'Murdered! Why do you say such a thing? It's not possible.'

'It ought not to be,' Edward said gravely, 'but I am afraid there can be no doubt of it. He has been stabbed and it can only have happened a few moments ago. He is still bleeding from his wound.'

Two days later Edward and Verity were poring over the newspapers which were spread out on the bed. Fenton, Edward's valet, was taking his annual holiday – in Margate, he had informed his master, where he had a sister who ran a boarding house. Taking advantage of his absence, Verity had ensconced herself in Edward's rooms in Albany. It was risky because the managers of the apartments would not have approved and nor would most of their friends and relatives. Edward shuddered to think what the Duke of Mersham would say if he knew his younger brother was living with a girl outside the bounds of matrimony. Or rather he would not have said anything. He would merely have harrumphed and looked at him with pained disapproval which would have been worse. Still, it was only for a week and it was fun to pretend to be married.

It was odd to love someone as much as Edward loved Verity and yet not be able to marry her. Neither of them was married to anyone else. There were no financial barriers to matrimony and, most important of all, they loved one another. It was simply that Verity was adamant that she could not feel free within the bonds of marriage. She said it would stifle their love, cause them much pain and would probably end in bitter parting. She once explained to him that marriage would mean being 'relegated to a camp behind the front'. She doth protest too much, Edward had once thought, but by now he was convinced she meant what she said. It was partly the fault of her job. She was not just a journalist but a foreign correspondent, though she disliked the phrase, thinking it pretentious. She had to be free to go anywhere in the world at a moment's notice. Domestic ties were incompatible with such an occupation which was why right-minded people believed it was a man's job. A woman ought to stay at home, look after her husband's comforts and carry his babies.

'It's a strange business, isn't it?' she said comfortably, reaching over him and taking buttered toast from his plate.

'What is? Hang on! You're dripping butter all over *The Times*. I was just looking to see who had died.'

'That's what I mean. Pitt-Messanger was stabbed to death in Westminster Abbey during one of the biggest memorial services in years and yet no one saw it happen and no one has been arrested.'

'Well, it's nothing to do with us,' Edward said with a shrug.

'Yes it is,' she protested. 'We found him. We called the police. Of course it's to do with us.'

'I'm not getting mixed up with it, V, if that's what you are hinting at. I've got enough on my plate as it is. Tomorrow I am going down to Chartwell to talk to Churchill about a job. I'm really feeling quite bucked.'

'Oh, him,' Verity said dismissively. 'I've told you, I don't like him and I wish you weren't getting so friendly with him. He's against everything I believe in from the rights of women to . . . the General Strike. He's not a friend of the people. I'm surprised you can't see that.'

'That's nonsense, V. Once you meet him you'll change your mind. He's not perfect – I'm not saying he is – but he's the only politician who can stand up to the dictators. I'm convinced of it.'

'Do what you want,' she said, half joking, half petulant. 'I don't care if you prefer a fat, over-the-hill politician to me. Leave me if you must but I thought only cads desert their mistresses when they are . . .'

'You're not going to tell me you're pregnant, are you? That would be wonderful!' Edward exclaimed in mock delight.

'Of course not, idiot! I was going to say "when they are in a mood – mistresses, that is – to give themselves to their paramours with wild abandon".'

'Sorry and all that,' Edward said annoyingly, 'but when my country calls . . .'

'Pompous ass,' she giggled, pinching him. 'Have you taken your Syrup of Figs this morning? You are sounding constipated. Anyway, I don't care. It so happens I too have an invitation. Do you remember my friend Ginny Waring?'

'Never heard of her.'

'She's my only school friend. She was head girl and I worshipped her.'

'Which school was that?' Verity had often told him she had attended a number of schools from most of which, it seemed, she had been expelled. One headmistress, exasperated by her having climbed to the top of the art school roof where she had got stuck – 'for a dare' she explained when the fire brigade brought her down – had called her 'a thoroughly bad influence on the younger girls, disruptive and impudent'. Edward had always thought this was a very fair description of Verity and had every sympathy with her many headmistresses.

'Grove House. I was there for almost three years. Ginny stood up for me when Miss Haddow wanted to throw me out.'

'Why did she wish to throw you out?' Edward inquired. 'Idleness, midnight feasts or was it boys?'

'If you must know, clever clogs, it was boys or rather one sweet, if spotty, lad from the local grammar. Not that I was doing anything wrong. He had lent me a pullover and I had forgotten to return it.'

'So you climbed out of the bathroom window and were caught?'

'Not at all,' Verity said haughtily. 'He came, without invitation, and climbed in at the dorm window. It was great fun but one of the girls sneaked. I was hauled up in front of the dragon, as we called Miss Haddow, and only Ginny's intervention prevented me from being shot out on my ear.'

'So Ginny what's-her-name has invited you to stay?'

'Ginny Waring – Virginia Castlewood as she is now. You must have heard of her. She's married to the millionaire. They built that house in Kent, just outside Tonbridge. Part of it is what remains of a castle and the rest is very modern. There was an article on it in *Country Life*. She has a pet mongoose – or do I mean a lemur?'

Edward did remember. Sir Simon Castlewood had inherited a fortune from his father who had supplied the army with uniforms during the war. The father had been one of those hard men who 'had done well out of the war', as the saying was, but the son had made a better name for himself as a patron of the arts and sciences. He was said to have a fine picture collection and an even finer library. He supported many charities, notably Earl Haig's fund for ex-soldiers. He had set up a medical foundation to develop cures for tuberculosis and polio. He had financed several expeditions to the North and South Poles and was something of an explorer and naturalist himself.

Verity never did anything without a purpose and Edward was suspicious. 'So why this sudden desire to look up an old school friend?'

'No reason except I haven't seen her for ages,' she replied airily, snuggling down beneath the sheets, her appetite for toast and marmalade temporarily sated.

'Hold on! I've just remembered. Didn't Castlewood under-write Pitt-Messanger's excavations in Egypt or somewhere?'

'That's right and, as it happens, Maud Pitt-Messanger is staying at Swifts Hill. Ginny has such a kind heart and, when she heard about her father's death, she scooped her up and took her there to recover and avoid the press.'

'Really, V, you are incorrigible. You want to investigate . . .'

'Chief Inspector Pride will never find out who murdered her father, now will he?'

'We may not like Pride but he is a very competent police officer,' Edward said sententiously. 'I have every confidence . . .'

'Well, I don't, so there.'

Edward pushed aside the breakfast tray and rolled over on Verity. 'Stop it, you bully. You're squashing me.'

'If only that were possible!' he retorted. They looked at each other with mutual indignation and then Verity was overtaken by

10

the giggles. 'Men look so absurd in striped pyjamas, particularly if they are trying to lay down the law.'

'Oh really? You have experience of men in pyjamas, do you? You jade, you juggler, you canker blossom, you thief of love!'

'How dare you call me a jade. I don't even know what it means. Are you calling me a horse?'

'I'm calling you a bad-tempered and disreputable woman and to prove it . . .'.

The plates and newspapers slid on to the floor as Edward caught Verity in his arms. She made inadequate attempts to escape but was soon overcome.

Panting, Edward released her. 'You've got jam on your nose,' he said, as he kneeled astride her.

'I surrender, I surrender,' she cried in mock alarm. 'Don't hurt me, you nasty, ugly man. I am thinking of getting another dog to protect me. Ouch! Remember, I'm still an invalid.'

Edward relaxed his grip. She had taken a bullet in her shoulder when the Spanish town of Guernica had been bombed and strafed by the Luftwaffe just a few months before. She had been lucky to survive. The photographer, Gerda Meyer, who was with her, had been killed. She was very much better but still not fully recovered – from the shock as much as from the wound itself. Gently, he turned her on her stomach and stroked the scar, still livid, where the bullet had pierced her. She twisted her head to look at him, for once almost meek. 'My scar . . . I can't even see it, damn it. Is it horrible? Does it . . . disgust you?'

He remembered the girl who had comforted Maud Pitt-Messanger in the Abbey. Her scar had spoilt her looks. 'No, my dearest,' he said, his voice thick with passion. 'I love every scar, every scratch on you.' He bent his head and kissed first her shoulder, feeling the wound with his tongue and then, rolling her over, the little scar on her forehead.

She put her hands to his face, pushing him back so she could look into his eyes. 'And I love you.' It went against all her instincts. She had held out against him as long as she could but she did love this man – she was almost sure of it. What was more, she trusted him absolutely, without reservation. She closed her eyes and gave a little cry, perhaps of pleasure, perhaps of protest. He needed no warning to treat her gently. With infinite tenderness he buried himself in her, his eyes never leaving her face. She threw her arms around him and held him to her fiercely as if he alone could protect her from the pain and blot out her memories of Spain.

Afterwards, they lay on their backs smoking until Edward suddenly remembered that they had an appointment with a house agent at eleven. Looking at his watch, he saw that it was already half past nine. Verity had been staying with her friends, the Hassels, in the King's Road since she had returned from Spain. She had sold her Knightsbridge flat before she left and owned no property in England. She had decided she needed a *pied-à-terre* in London, even though she was abroad for so much of the time. She did not want anything cosy. She had no wish to make a home for herself. She merely needed somewhere to leave the few possessions she did not want to carry about the world with her. She had settled on an anonymous-looking flat in a new, purpose-built block off Sloane Avenue called Cranmer Court. Before she made a final decision she wanted Edward to see it.

London was beginning to have the air of a forgotten city – Petra perhaps, Edward thought as they stepped out of Cranmer Court on to brown, balding grass. The flat had proved to be light and airy, though expensive. Edward wanted her to look at others but Verity was impatient. 'What is the point? It suits me and I've got the money.'

It was a slight embarrassment to Verity, as a Communist, that she was rich. Her father was a successful barrister renowned for his defence of left-wing causes. She had never liked spending his money but her resolve had weakened as the years passed and, anyway, she was earning herself now. Her employer, Lord Weaver, the owner of the *New Gazette*, saw her as one of his stars and paid her accordingly. The *Daily Worker*, for which she also wrote, paid her nothing but her book on Spain published by the Left Book Club had sold well and Victor Gollancz had been after her to write another.

The young man from the agency had been pleased and surprised that the flat had been such an easy sale. When he discovered to whom he had sold it, he had been fulsome. Edward was amused to see how Verity, in the face of frank admiration, managed to display irritation and pleasure at the same time.

It was hotter than ever and the dust spread over everything, painting the leaves on the trees grey and casting a grey veil over

Edward's Lagonda. London was emptying, so it was with some surprise that they bumped into Edmund Cardew whom they had last seen at the Abbey when Edward had dispatched him to summon the police. He was an MP – one of the youngest in the House – and was being talked of as a 'coming man'. The girl on his arm seemed almost a child. At first sight Edward did not recognize her but then, as she moved her head, he saw the burn scar which had transformed her cheek to rice paper, only partly concealed by the hair which fell about her face. It was she who had comforted Miss Pitt-Messanger in the Abbey.

She proved to be Cardew's sister Margaret – Maggie as her brother called her. Edward shook her gloved hand and they exchanged a few words about the murder. As they did so, it occurred to him to wonder if the handle of the knife which had killed the old man had been clean of fingerprints. All the ladies attending the memorial service would have been gloved of course but then it was not really a woman's crime. He reminded himself that the investigation was nothing to do with him. He introduced Verity and explained that she had been buying a flat.

'Excellent!' Cardew said. 'Then you must come and meet my mother. She bought one of the first flats three years ago and is quite the queen of Cranmer Court.'

It was impossible to refuse so Verity and Maggie walked ahead of the two men towards the other side of the block. Cardew said in a low voice so that his sister could not hear, 'When my father died, just after Maggie was born, my mother was left very badly off. She had to sell Molton – our house in Kent – and move into the gatekeeper's lodge. Then I began to make a little money and I was able to buy her this flat. She can come up to town and see her friends and I have a place to sleep when the House is sitting. I know she will love to meet Miss Browne. The truth is she gets a bit lonely. She says all her friends are dying off like flies and she loves the young. She was a great friend of Lord Benyon, you know. He was very kind to us when my father died. In fact, I owe him a great deal. When I left Rugby he got me a job with his stockbrokers, Thalberg and May. His brother-in-law, Horace Garton, was a partner in the firm. I don't know if you ever met him?'

'I met his sister, Mrs Garton, once very briefly. I liked her.'

'Between ourselves, she is worth two of him but I shouldn't

say so. Garton was always good to me and I am truly grateful. He has retired now.'

'And you are a partner?'

'I am but I may have to give it up. I spend so much time at the House. The Prime Minister has said ... but you don't want to hear about me, Lord Edward.'

In contrast to her brother, Maggie was silent. Verity, who had not noticed her in the Abbey, was shocked by her disfigurement and imagined she must be shy. She made up for it by talking rather wildly about her trip on the *Queen Mary* with Benyon but it was a relief to her when they reached Mrs Cardew's flat. Edmund's and Maggie's mother proved to be a woman of considerable charm who was clearly devoted to her children. She was rather stout and when she embraced Maggie the girl almost disappeared. She emerged laughing and adjusting her hat.

'Mother, please! This hat cost a fortune! Don't crush it.'

It was pleasant to see how affectionately they teased the old woman. Edward asked Mrs Cardew about Benyon, explaining his and Verity's connection.

'That's so like Inna,' she exclaimed when Verity described how Lady Benyon had helped her overcome her 'block' when she was writing her book on Spain. 'She was one of my closest friends but alas she is dead. As soon as Blackie brings me the *The Times* in the morning before I get up, I read the death notices. I expect to see my own there soon,' she smiled.

'Mother!' Cardew expostulated. 'You talk as if you are in your dotage. You are only as young as you feel. She has so many friends,' he said, turning to Verity. 'Tomorrow you are going down to Swifts Hill, aren't you, Mother? You always like going there. Do you know the Castlewoods, Lord Edward?'

'I don't but, as it happens, Verity will be staying with them at the same time as you are there, Mrs Cardew.'

'My dear, how wonderful,' the old lady said, smiling at her. 'Perhaps we can travel together. There's a train from Victoria at 3.28 that will get us to Swifts Hill in time for tea. But how silly of me ... you don't want to be lumbered with an old woman like me.'

'Not at all,' Verity said. 'I would very much like to come with you if I may. The truth is I haven't seen Ginny since we left school and I am a little scared of meeting her husband.'

'Oh, Simon's a charmer. You will get on very well with him. He has an eye for a pretty girl. Not that I am saying he is other than devoted to Virginia . . .'

'That's settled then,' Cardew said. 'It would be a weight off my mind, Miss Browne, if you *would* accompany my mother. It's a long journey and she has not been well . . .'

'Oh pish, Edmund. I have just had a summer cold which I have not been able fully to throw off. Dear Virginia swears that the air at Swifts Hill – so much cleaner than here in London – will clear it up in no time.'

'And I am sure she is right,' her son said. 'It will do you the world of good.'

Verity found his concern for his mother admirable but slightly suspect. She had never had a mother but imagined that she would be less patronizing than Edmund. She guessed Mrs Cardew must be seventy-three or four. She was hardly at death's door and why was Maggie so silent? Was it just shyness? She shook herself mentally. She was becoming cynical, she thought. 'I am staying with friends in the King's Road, Mrs Cardew. I will pick you up in a taxi . . .'

'Lord Edward, you are not accompanying us?'

'No, I was not invited and in any case I have another engagement.'

'Too bad,' Cardew said. 'You should know, Mother, that Miss Browne is a distinguished journalist. A foreign correspondent, I think they call it. Isn't that right, Miss Browne?'

'I don't know about that,' Verity said, reluctant to be flattered, 'but I certainly work for a newspaper – the *New Gazette*.'

'So you must know Lord Weaver?' Mrs Cardew inquired.

'He employed me. Is he a friend of yours, Mrs Cardew?'

'Edmund sees a lot of him, don't you, dear? He is one of the old monster's "young men".'

'Oh, Mother, where do you pick up those expressions? You have been reading the *Daily Express*. I am certainly not one of his "young men", Miss Browne, but he has been good to me. He, too, was kind to us when my father died. Lord Weaver sent many of his friends my way so I owe him what little success I have had as a stockbroker.'

Maggie seemed to want to change the subject because, to Verity's surprise, she broke her silence. 'Lord Edward, have you heard whether the police have caught the man who killed poor Mr Pitt-Messanger?'

'I know nothing more than I have read in the newspapers, Miss Cardew. As far as I know they have not charged anybody, but it's early days yet.'

'Quite terrible!' exclaimed Mrs Cardew. 'Sacrilege I call it, though I have to admit I could never stand him.'

'You knew Pitt-Messanger?' Edward asked in surprise.

'I knew him, yes, but not well. He was an obstinate old man and he led that poor daughter of his the most awful life. I hope you will tell me, Maggie, if I turn into a tyrant.'

'Mother!' the girl protested, taking her hand and squeezing it.

'He was a tyrant?' Verity asked.

'Maybe I am exaggerating but he was so obsessed with his work, he had no time to look to his children.'

'Children? I thought there was only Maud?' Edward queried.

'There was a son – Edwin, I think his name was. He ran away to sea when he was fourteen or fifteen and has never been seen since.'

'How romantic,' Verity sighed.

'Possibly, but to make a child run away from home, you have to have done "unromantic" things to him.' Mrs Cardew looked fierce. 'I don't know the ins and outs of it but I know something very unpleasant happened.'

'And now poor Maud is all alone in the world,' Maggie sighed.

'It's the best thing for her,' Mrs Cardew said sharply. 'If it is not too late for her, as I fear it may be, she can set about living her life.'

'Her father treated her badly?' Verity inquired.

'He made her his companion, secretary, housekeeper, dogsbody. He took her on all his digs.'

'That must have been interesting,' Edward put in. 'I remember reading he made some wonderful finds in Assyria.'

'He uncovered the grave of a great king,' Cardew said, 'but there were all sorts of problems. I can't remember the details. One of the young men who helped him on the dig claimed he, not Pitt-Messanger, had made the find and kicked up a bit of a stink about it. Fortunately for Pitt-Messanger, his accuser died fairly soon after – of cholera, I think – and the scandal died with him.'

16

'Yes,' Edward recalled, 'there were pictures of some of the treasures he had uncovered in the *Illustrated London News* ... a dagger and some jewellery. Amazing!'

Verity looked at him with surprise. 'I didn't know you were interested in archaeology?'

'I have a small collection of my own. Don't you remember that Etruscan vase I managed to smash?'

'But no body ... no skeleton,' Cardew said.

'What did you say, dear?'

'Sorry, Mother. I just said it was odd there was no body. I mean, usually an ancient grave is robbed of its treasures but they don't bother to disturb the corpse. On that occasion the opposite seems to have been the case.'

'I imagine the bones just turned to dust over the centuries,' Edward put in.

'Of course! Anyway, why am I talking about corpses?'

2

They were met at the station by the Castlewoods' chauffeur dressed, Verity thought, like von Stroheim, the film director – leather jacket and trousers, peaked cap and long, black boots. A porter rescued Mrs Cardew's two suitcases from the goods van and Blackie, her maid, who appeared to be even older than her mistress, appeared from third class with Mrs Cardew's jewellery bag, which was her special care and never left her sight. The chauffeur, who tipped his cap and said his name was Barry, relieved Verity of her new suitcase and she was glad to be able to look him in the eye. She knew from the *Queen Mary* that servants judged you by the quality and quantity of your luggage. She wondered if Barry was his first or last name but found herself unable to ask.

As she followed Mrs Cardew into the back of the Rolls, she began to worry that she might not have brought enough smart clothes. The Virginia she remembered from school had had no interest in clothes and wore her school uniform with such disregard for decency that she was frequently in trouble with the form mistress. Even the headmistress, meeting her once in a corridor, had sent her back to the dormitory for having holes in her stockings. However, Verity reminded herself, Virginia was now married to a millionaire and no doubt dressed with the help of a maid. She lay back on the soft leather and sniffed that delicious scent of wealth.

It was an odd inconsistency of Verity's that, though in principle she disapproved of chauffeurs, ladies' maids, Rolls-Royces and all the other appurtenances of wealth – and would not know what to do with a lady's maid if she had one – she enjoyed being the guest of those for whom all this was completely natural. As the car set off – so silently she was hardly aware they were moving – Mrs Cardew's Pekinese, Lulu, climbed on to her lap and she thought once again how nice it would be to have a dog. A delicious languor overtook her and, without meaning to, she slept.

It was little more than five miles to Swifts Hill and though the ancient Rolls travelled at a stately twenty-five miles an hour, it felt as if she had only closed her eyes for an instant when Mrs Cardew touched her on the arm and said, 'Do look, Miss Browne. Your first view of Swifts Hill . . . isn't it a dream?'

Mrs Cardew tapped on the glass partition and asked Barry to stop the car for a moment. Verity ought to have known what to expect because she had only recently been reading about it but the photograph in *Country Life* had not done it justice. Swifts Hill had originally been a medieval castle rebuilt for Henry VIII in the 1520s. Young Prince Edward was lodged there for a time but Queen Elizabeth had no use for it and it fell into disrepair. When Simon Castlewood bought it in 1933 nothing remained but the walls of the great hall. The Castlewoods began by rebuilding it as he and the Swedish architect imagined it must have looked in its first incarnation complete with minstrels' gallery. At huge cost the hall was capped with a magnificent oak roof – an elaborate 'false' hammerbeam construction. Then, in daring and powerful antithesis, the Castlewoods added a modern house attached to the hall by a low curved building surmounted by a cupola made of concrete and glass. The main part of the new house was circular and quite unlike anything yet built in England.

Thoroughly awake now, Verity could hardly wait as they crunched up the drive and crossed the bridge over the dry moat. As she walked through the glass doors into the triangular entrance hall she was struck by its airy simplicity. Light streamed through the glass roof and was absorbed by a huge circular carpet. On it several very modern-looking and possibly uncomfortable chairs were grouped around two small tables. A huge vase of flowers stood on a pedestal in the centre of the room reminding Verity, momentarily, of the foyer of the Ritz in Paris. The hall was lined in wood and decorated with marquetry panels showing scenes of Venice, clearly a favourite city of the owners. Two staircases led out of it up to a gallery which encircled the hall below it. Magnificent bronze-framed glass doors led through to rooms on the ground floor. Verity could not help noticing the coin-operated telephone booth and the cloakrooms to one side of the hall. It confirmed her impression of being in a hotel lobby and she had to smile.

As she looked around her there was a whooshing sound and in swept Virginia carrying in her arms a Pekinese which, Verity subsequently discovered, was called Halma. She dropped it on the carpet where it began to yap at Mrs Cardew's Lulu which, understandably, yapped back. The noise was deafening but Virginia seemed not to hear it. She kissed Mrs Cardew, calling her Emily, and then turned to Verity. Holding her first at arm's length, she studied her face and then embraced her. Just as Verity thought she would never be released, Virginia thrust her away but still held on to both her hands.

'My dear Crumbles – how wonderful to see you after all this time! And who would have thought you would be so famous. Let me look at you. Yes, I do believe you are the same devil-may-care rapscallion who gave poor Miss Haddow several nervous breakdowns before she finally gathered up enough courage to expel you. Your dear father was heartbroken. I remember him arriving in his green Rolls-Royce to take you home with him. I admired you so much, you know. You never shed a tear though I do believe your lip trembled when we said our goodbyes. You strode out with your chin in the air. Indignant – that's what you were. As though Miss Haddow had done you wrong when in fact she had gone to so much trouble to keep you on the straight and narrow. "That poor motherless girl," she said to me. "She needs all the love we can give her."'

Virginia paused for breath which enabled Mrs Cardew to say, 'Crumbles! Is that what they called you at school, Miss Browne?'

'I had quite forgotten,' Verity said, blushing, 'and, Ginny, I absolutely forbid you to use that name again.' In her imagination she saw Edward doubled up with laughter.

'But why Crumbles?' Mrs Cardew persisted.

'She used to take biscuits and cakes to bed with her. She was always hungry though she never got fat, which was so annoying.'

'You make me sound ungrateful, Ginny. How was I to know Miss Haddow was . . . doing her best for me? She never said so. I just thought she was a bully and an old fuss-pot.'

'I'm sorry, my dear! Here I am gossiping about old times and you are hardly in the house. Shall I show you to your rooms or would you like a cup of tea first?'

They opted for tea and were led through glass doors into the drawing-room. It was unlike any which Verity had seen before. It was entirely false and yet, for all its theatricality, conveyed Virginia's personality which was wholly sincere: exuberant, impetuous and enthusiastic. Verity looked about her in amazement. 'Ginny – what an extraordinary house! It's so light and . . . uncluttered . . .'

'What are you looking at, Crumbles?'

'Oh sorry, Ginny, but all these windows – wonderful in weather like this but surely in winter . . .'

'You might think so because, as you can see, we have no radiators, but I am very susceptible to the cold. Something to do with being always frozen at school, I expect. I said to Simon, "My darling, I don't mind what you do to the house but it must be warm." So the clever architect – who is Swedish and the Swedes know all about the cold – put in underfloor heating – hot pipes. I have to say, sometimes it is even *too* hot. In fact, everything that can be concealed is. The idea was to keep the inside absolutely pure: simple, smooth curves. I'll let Simon bore you with the full lecture. He will love to have someone new to talk to about Swifts Hill. It's his pride and joy.'

Verity walked over to a window to look more closely at the plaster panels depicting scenes from past civilizations, including fanciful evocations of ancient Greece and Rome. They were illuminated by spotlights housed in false beams in the ceiling.

'Who made these? They are beautifully done.'

'Gilbert Leward. Do you know of him? He's a genius and it was so clever of Simon to find him. Now, tea. You must be parched.'

Verity gazed about her fascinated. It was all false – down to the last Etruscan pot on the huge fake-marble fireplace in which an electric fire 'burned' fake logs. The floor was laid with imitation Turkish rugs and copies of Old Masters hung on the wall. Verity thought longingly of Edward's home, Mersham Castle, where nothing was false. Swifts Hill was too much like an hotel – or rather, it suddenly came to her, the interior of the *Queen Mary* – to be truly beautiful. Its saving grace was the abundance of flowers. Vases of roses, crimson, creamy white and yellow, stood on tables and in the windows scenting the air and giving life to the scene.

While she and Virginia discussed the house, Mrs Cardew had been talking to the two women sipping tea at the other end of the drawing-room. Verity knew one of them, Maud Pitt-Messanger, but it was the other girl who caught her eye. She was, Verity thought, in her late twenties. She had obviously been playing tennis – she wore a white shirt and skirt and white plimsolls – and exuded the healthy glow of an athlete. She was tall and strongly built but what made the word 'Viking' spring into Verity's mind was her flow of golden hair which framed an almost perfectly oval face. Her eyes were a startling violet and she was heartily glad Edward was not there to be tempted. She noted with relief that she wore on her finger a large diamond ring. No man who had wooed and won this beauty was going to let himself be easily deprived of her.

Maud looked dowdy by comparison. There was no other word for it. Despite making a valiant effort to smile, she wore an expression of profound misery. Her face was grey and un-healthy-looking and her pallor was emphasized by the harsh red with which she had unwisely coated her lips. There were dark pouches under her eyes and, though she could never have been a beauty, she now looked ill and much older than her forty years. In part this was due to the ugly woollen cardigan she wore over a cotton dress that might have looked well on a young girl but on Maud was frankly ridiculous. There could be no doubt that her father's death had left her distraught and desolate.

'Darlings,' Virginia said, 'I don't think you have met Verity Browne. Verity and I were at school together and she was always getting into scrapes and now she is a famous foreign corre-spondent – that's right, isn't it, dear? I checked with Simon who said I mustn't call you a journalist.'

'Oh no, Ginny, I am just a journalist who gets into scrapes,' Verity replied modestly.

'It's too, too shy-making meeting you, Miss Browne,' said the girl with the violet eyes leaping out of her chair as if she was about to serve for the match. 'I am such an admirer. You must be so brave and, you know . . . brave.'

'Verity, this is Isolde Swann. She has been longing to meet you.'

22

Verity shook the warm, powerful hand of the young Amazon and wondered if she could possibly be being satirical. 'Please, Miss Swann, there really is nothing to justify . . .'

'No, but really, I read your reports in the paper. You were wounded at that awful place with the ugly name – something like "hernia" . . .'

'Guernica. Yes, I was but I am quite better now.'

'And Maud Pitt-Messanger . . .' Virginia went on, almost dropping her Pekinese which was wriggling in her arms.

'Yes,' Verity said, stretching out her hand. 'You probably won't remember, Miss Pitt-Messanger, but we – Lord Edward Corinth and I – met you and your father with Lord Benyon some months ago. And then . . . well, I am very sorry indeed . . .'

Maud seemed to stir herself with an effort. She spoke in a low husky voice as though it came from deep inside her. 'You and Lord Edward were so kind . . .' she murmured. She fumbled in her bag and Verity, guessing what she was searching for, offered her one of her cigarettes.

'Oh, thank you, Miss Browne,' she muttered.

Verity lit the cigarette for her and had a strong desire to put out a hand to calm her. She was obviously very agitated, though whether from meeting her and being reminded of her father's death or because she was anxious and depressed Verity could not say.

'Where *are* the men?' Virginia inquired, as though trying to distract attention from the state Maud was in.

'They are sweating out London grime on the tennis court, Ginny,' Isolde told her. 'At least that's what Roddy said. He's my . . . my fiancé, Miss Browne.' She blushed and smiled. 'Dominic – that's who Roddy's playing – he's a doctor, or rather a surgeon, says we all ought to exercise more but I'm afraid he'll never get Ginny out on the court.'

'Quite right, too,' Mrs Cardew broke in. 'It's very bad for your skin – perspiring like that. And the sun – you're as brown as a nut, Izzy. It can't be good for you.'

Isolde blushed again. At that moment the glass door swung open and a footman entered bearing a tray with a silver teapot on it. Behind him, a maid carried a second tray with sandwiches and cakes on three silver dishes.

'Tea! I must have tea! And a sandwich. I'm dying for a sandwich!' It was a man's voice, low and attractive. Verity turned to see that they had been joined by two men still carrying tennis rackets. The young man who had spoken took a sandwich off the tray and made a grab at Isolde and tried to kiss her.

'Go away, Roddy darling.' Isolde turned her face away, perhaps to draw attention to her fiancé's ardour. 'You are all hot and . . . no, you can't kiss me till you've showered.'

'Who won?' Virginia inquired.

'Thrashed him!' Roddy replied, waving his sandwich above his head in triumph.

'What rot, Roddy! You're such a liar. I hope your inability to tell the truth isn't hereditary. It was 6-4 in the third set. Roddy's line-calls . . .! You believe me, don't you, Mrs Cardew?'

This was Dominic, Verity supposed.

'I am sure you were well matched,' Virginia said annoyingly. 'Now, leave Isolde alone and let me introduce you to Miss Browne. I have told them all about you, of course,' she added to Verity.

'Oh, I hope that doesn't mean . . .'

'I thought you would be a harridan – positively frightening,' Roddy said. 'I was terrified.' He raised his hands in an exaggerated gesture of surrender. 'Ginny, why didn't you tell me your old school chum was a beauty?'

'Roddy, behave yourself,' Isolde reprimanded, not altogether pleased, Verity thought, by her fiancé's readiness to appreciate another woman.

'Well, it's your fault, old girl. If you won't let me kiss you . . . I always behave badly when I'm thwarted. If I can't kiss you, Izzy, at least let me have another sandwich.' He smiled at Verity and then winked at the maid carrying the sandwiches. She blushed prettily as she passed him the plate. This was an attractive man, Verity thought, but didn't he just know it. 'Mrs Cardew!' he took her hand with exaggerated gallantry. 'How rude of me! I was so hungry . . .'

'Miss Browne,' Isolde said, 'I apologize for this greedy young man. Please forgive him for being a prize idiot. I certainly can't.' The adoring look she gave Roddy belied her words.

'Yes, please forgive me, Miss Browne,' he said, catching at her hand and carrying it to his lips. 'I do apologize. Truly, it is a great honour to meet you. I am Roddy Maitland and I am engaged to this wonderful girl who has just been so frightfully cross with me.' He furrowed his brow and pretended to look chastened before turning back to Mrs Cardew. 'It's very nice to see you again, Mrs Cardew. How was Le Touquet? I saw Teddy at the club the other night and he told me he had dropped a packet at the casino when he was visiting you.'

Mrs Cardew frowned and Roddy put a hand to his mouth. 'Oh, and I gave him my word not to let on. Please say you aren't angry, Mrs Cardew. I really don't think it was as much as he pretended.'

'Roddy, you talk such nonsense. Edmund isn't a gambler and I do wish you wouldn't call him Teddy. It's such a horrid name – so common, I always think.'

Verity smiled at the performance but she thought Mrs Cardew seemed genuinely upset and she had an idea that Roddy had annoyed her deliberately. Might this young man, despite his charm, turn out to be rather tiresome? She glanced at the older man who had also been watching her with amusement.

'May I introduce myself, Miss Browne? It is difficult to get a word in when Roddy is around. I am Dominic Montillo. Please believe me, I am honoured to meet you. I take the *New Gazette* solely to read your reports from Spain.'

Verity went a little pink. She knew she was being flattered but could not pretend it was not pleasurable. This handsome man with his white mane of hair, bright black eyes and fleshy lips was fascinating. He was not quite English, she thought, and then remembered his name. He must be Spanish or Portuguese but he spoke like any upper-class Englishman – clipped and rather nasal.

'Dom, come over here and pay me a compliment or I will be quite jealous,' Virginia called playfully. He strode over dutifully and kissed her cheek. 'There,' she said, 'I think you have met everyone now, Verity, except Simon of course. My husband had some urgent letters to finish off. Oh, here he comes now.'

A slightly stooped, distinguished-looking man in his early forties appeared with a thin woman dressed rather severely in brown.

'Emily, Miss Browne! I do apologize for not having been here to greet you but Miss Berners keeps my nose to the grindstone.'

'Oh really, Simon,' Virginia said crossly, 'you spend more time in Miss Berners' company than mine. I should be jealous but I'm not.'

To Verity's ears, this sounded like an insult. Was Miss Berners too plain to attract her husband? If that was the thrust of her remark, Miss Berners seemed not to mind or even to hear it. Verity looked at her. Dressed in a drab skirt and jacket over a blouse drawn tightly round her neck, she did look severe but she had good bones and, Verity guessed, a smile might transform her face and make her positively attractive. If Virginia was a little jealous perhaps she had, despite first impressions, a right to be.

Miss Berners disappeared. She was obviously not expected to have tea with the guests and Sir Simon, cup in hand, took Verity's arm and guided her over to a window seat where they perched uncomfortably. He might not be loquacious like his wife but he knew how to ask questions and listen to the replies. Verity found herself recounting the horrors of Guernica and was surprised to find that it was something of a relief to do so. The conversation then turned to the condition of the poor, about which Sir Simon seemed to feel almost as strongly as Verity.

'Did you know,' Verity was saying, unconsciously putting on her lecturing voice, 'that in our city slums malnutrition is killing more children than tuberculosis? Low-paid workers live on a diet of bread, margarine and tea, with a main meal of potatoes with a little stewed meat to give it flavour. Mothers seldom give their babies fresh milk, only condensed. Fruit and green vegetables are a luxury – and this isn't because of the ignorance of the working-class housewife but because she is too poor to buy fresh food.'

She glanced round and blushed, realizing that her tone had become strident. All the chatter in the room had ceased and even Virginia was silent, staring at Verity in horror.

'I'm sorry,' she said. 'I did not mean to harangue you, Sir Simon.'

He looked at her with a half-smile, which she could not interpret, but it was Dominic Montillo who came to her rescue.

'I do agree with you, Miss Browne. It is a scandal which needs to be addressed if we are not to be cursed by the next generation for having sat back and let them – the children of the poor – grow up stunted and weakened, morally and physically. You may not know it but Simon has invested heavily in the future by funding a foundation of which I am privileged to be the director. We are looking at ways to improve the health and physical well-being of our poor, particularly the children. We are well on our way to finding a cure for tuberculosis and we are demanding that the Government introduces compulsory vaccination against common child-killing diseases such as measles. In Germany they are already doing it. If we cannot breed healthy children, then our race will atrophy and we will deserve to give way to a better-fed, better-educated species from some other quarter of the globe. Our research shows that pauperism is hereditary. We have traced some pauper pedigrees which reach back four generations. There is no doubt there exists a hereditary class of persons who will not make any attempt to work.'

Verity was not sure she had quite meant all this when she had spoken about malnutrition.

'I don't think . . .' she began, but Montillo interrupted her, his eyes blazing.

'We must be like the Spartans and rear an elite breed. The best children should be taken from their mothers when they are six or seven and brought up in a special school – hardened and prepared for . . .'

'That's all very fine, Dominic,' Virginia stopped him calmly but firmly. 'When you men are drinking your port you can put the world to rights but now I am sure Emily and Verity want to go to their rooms and rest before dressing for dinner.'

Preceded by the butler, Lampton, and Virginia, they processed back into the hall and up a flight of stairs. Verity heard a strange mewing sound as she reached the landing. Virginia noticed her hesitate. 'That's Mah-Jongg. Come and see him. Lampton, take Mrs Cardew to her room. Emily already knows Jonggy, don't you?'

'Indeed I do, Ginny.' It was clear from the way she said it that Mrs Cardew was not one of the animal's admirers.

Virginia led Verity past the remains of the fourteenth-century windows and down a corridor to the lemur's quarters. They consisted of a large glass-fronted cage with a private upstairs section reached by a ladder in which the animal could sleep out of public view.

'I read about Mah-Jongg in *Country Life*,' Verity said. 'Did you bring him back with you from South America?'

'No. Simon bought him for me at Harrods,' Virginia replied, not seeming to think there was anything odd in this. 'Isn't he lovely? Jonggy, Jonggy, Jonggy . . .' she called, tapping the glass.

'How does he get his exercise?' Verity inquired.

'We let him run about the house.'

Verity was startled. Swifts Hill was even more rum than she had imagined. She had nothing against animals – she badly missed not having a dog – but she did not know if she relished the idea of being surprised by a lemur as she dressed for dinner or climbed into her bed at night.

After further endearments – Virginia certainly seemed to love her strange pet – she took Verity to her room. 'Here we are,' she said, throwing open the door with a dramatic flourish. 'I do hope you will be comfortable. It's called the Venetian Room. We are over there.' She gestured vaguely across to the other side of the gallery.

Verity entered one of the most lavish bedrooms she had ever seen. 'It's wonderful!' she exclaimed. Round the walls were intricately designed panels which Virginia said had come from a Venetian *palazzo*. She pulled at a glass handle on one of the panels and Verity found herself looking into a huge walk-in cupboard. Another panel, embellished with false book spines, proved to be the door to the bathroom. It was more like an Italian tomb than a bathroom, panelled in what looked like marble but was in fact, Virginia said, Vitrolite. The bath itself was on a raised dais and behind it, in an alcove, the goddess Psyche stood resplendent and aloof.

'Simon brought her home from Naples,' Virginia said airily. 'I have another god in my bathroom. Don't you love her?'

'I have never seen anything like it. It's too grand for me but I'll pretend I'm a *principessa*! May I have a bath now?'

'Of course! I made sure, when Simon built this house, that we could all have baths at the same time and the water would always be hot.'

'Even Mersham Castle, which is the grandest place I have ever stayed, only has one bath between three bedrooms and the water is *never* hot. Oh, Ginny, to have a bathroom for one's personal use without having to go out of one's room – this is bliss!'

Virginia looked pleased. 'It doesn't go against your political beliefs, Crumbles?'

'I am sorry about all that, downstairs. I don't know what came over me but Sir Simon is such a good listener.'

'I can see he has fallen for you. If he's bored by a woman – and he almost always is – he does not trouble to hide it. And just call him Simon. He thinks he's a democrat and hates being "sirred". I'll leave you now, Crumbles. Dinner at eight but we meet in the drawing-room at seven thirty for cocktails. You'll hear the gong.'

As Virginia left the room, Verity said, 'Ginny, would you mind not calling me Crumbles? I don't want to be more of a laughing stock than I am already.'

'Of course! I'm sorry, I forgot. But you are not a laughing stock. Dominic seems to want to impress you, and Simon, who usually can't stand my friends – well, as I said, I have never seen him so fascinated.'

When the door had closed Verity kicked off her shoes, threw herself down on the bed and whistled. This was some house! She thought she knew how the rich lived but Swifts Hill was a modern palace. She turned over and saw there was a telephone beside her bed. The only other time she had found a telephone by her bed was aboard the *Queen Mary*. Mersham Castle had only three telephones and the Duke would have had apoplexy if anyone had suggested putting one in his bedroom, let alone in the guest rooms. She wanted to call someone and the only person she could think of was Edward. There was a little notice telling her how to make a call and she soon found herself talking to the operator and placing a trunk call to London. It rang and rang until she remembered Edward was at Chartwell. She replaced the receiver disconsolately. It was no fun living in luxury if you had no one to discuss it with. She got up and turned on the bathtaps, which seemed to be gold-plated, and dropped bath salts from a coloured bottle into the steaming water. She had a hunch that Edward might wrinkle his beaky nose and call Swifts Hill vulgar but to hell with that, she loved it.

The Lagonda overtook the little black Austin and surged ahead with an arrogance and grace which did much to ease Edward's heart. Like Hamlet, he simply could not make up his mind. He was almost certain that Mr Churchill was going to offer him some sort of job which would make him responsible for his personal safety. He admired Churchill and when he was with him found his warmth and intelligence hard to resist. More importantly, he was convinced that Churchill was the only politician capable of leading the country if war came and the storm clouds were already visible on the horizon. The German Chancellor, Herr Hitler, was calling for *lebensraum* – living room – which appeared to mean colonies, and it was clearly only a matter of time before Germany united with Austria. Churchill had many enemies and if someone were to assassinate him – by no means an impossibility – Edward would blame himself if he had shirked the task of preventing it. On the other hand, Sir Robert Vansittart, the administrative head of the Foreign Office, had asked him to run a secret department keeping track of arms shipments and arms dealers. It was an important job and it was flattering to be offered it. If he did it well might he not be offered even more responsibility?

And yet, when it came down to it, neither option really attracted him. He knew his weaknesses: he was restless to a fault, impatient and easily bored. To be tied to a desk would be purgatory. To be tied to a man – even as fascinating a man as Churchill – might be as bad. As he took a corner at speed, almost blowing a bicyclist off his bike, he thought it might be more worthwhile to count his blessings – something his nanny had made him do when he was a child and fell into one of his sulks. The chief blessing was unquestionable: Verity was safe in England and not risking life and limb in Spain or on some other battlefield. He thought back to their love-making the previous day and, unconsciously, a grin lit up his face, sending deep creases from the corners of his mouth to his eyes. He let out a whoop and pressed his foot on the accelerator. If he was sure of only one thing it was that he loved Verity. He thought of her affectionately as a bantam – all flying feathers, fighting her corner and never surrendering. A Communist, a journalist and a woman who regarded bourgeois conventions such as marriage with suspicion and sometimes scorn. She never bored him.

Blessing number two was, of course, that he was wealthy enough to go his own way. He could perfectly well sit in his rooms in Albany and vegetate without having to worry about paying the bills, but he never even considered doing that. He wondered about giving up England and going to America or, better still, one of those countries on Europe's borders. He fancied he would not be bored in Czechoslovakia or Poland. As he swung into the Chartwell drive he remained undecided on all but one point: he would not accept a position with Mr Churchill which would effectively clip his wings.

Such was the cunning of the old man – Churchill was sixty-two – that he greeted Edward as an old friend and not as a dependant. He took him into his study and talked, as only he could talk, about his ancestor, the Duke of Marlborough, whose biography he was writing, about the new Prime Minister, Neville Chamberlain, and the 'jackal' Mussolini. He condemned the Government's craven acceptance of Italy's 'victories' in Abyssinia.

'I admit that in 1922 I had hopes that Mussolini might become a force for good in the world. Italy seemed ungovernable when he came to power. Look at it now,' he chuckled. 'It is said even the trains run on time.'

'What happened to change your mind?' Edward asked.

'I saw the violence with which he disposed of his enemies and his stupid pursuit of military glory. Dictators always need an external threat if they are to unite their people. Mussolini had to invent one. He promised them a new Roman Empire. What a shoddy thing it turned out to be.'

'But you admired his patriotism?'

'Patriotism is a dangerous sword which twists in the hand and often wounds the man who wields it but, I have to say, one may dislike Mussolini and yet admire his patriotic achievement. If our country were defeated, I hope we would find an equally indomitable champion to restore our courage and lead us back to our place among the nations.'

Churchill flattered Edward by taking him into his confidence and confessing his own weakness. 'You see, my boy, I had hoped Neville would offer me a place in the cabinet if only to shut me up, but I thank God he has not. I would have accepted an offer if it had been made and regretted it ever after. I would have done what I could to influence him in his dealings with the dictators but I fear I would only have compromised myself. I must remain free to warn and chivvy the Government without being tarred by their policy of appeasing the bullies that swagger across our world making life intolerable for so many thousands.' He turned on Edward his most solemn face. 'My sources tell me of a new so-called "labour camp" in Germany, even more horrible than the ones we already know of. It's at a place called Buchenwald near Weimar.'

He was interrupted by the butler, who announced a visitor.

'Leonard! How good to see you,' Churchill beamed, taking the visitor by the arm and guiding him into the room. 'I don't think you know Lord Edward Corinth? Lord Edward, this is Professor Blacker. He is a scientist attached to the War Office and of course he ought not to be talking to a reprobate like me,' he added gleefully.

Blacker was a short, balding man of about forty with spectacles and a small military moustache. He glanced at Edward keenly. 'That is your Lagonda in the drive, Lord Edward?'

'It is.'

'I thought as much. You passed me at great speed on the road.'

'I do apologize, sir. My only defence is to say that the Lagonda has a will of its own. I hope my recklessness did not frighten you.'

The Professor, with a bad-tempered twist to his mouth, snorted derisively.

Churchill quickly broke in. 'I have asked Lord Edward to join us because he has done some excellent undercover work for the Foreign Office while remaining quite detached from the department. You can trust him absolutely.'

'If you say so,' the Professor said, sounding unconvinced. 'Please be aware, Lord Edward, that what I have to say must on no account be repeated to anyone else. More than my career depends on you being secret.'

'You can count on it, Professor. You may not think it to look at me but I am accustomed to keeping secrets.' Edward wondered what this self-important little man had to say that was so significant.

'Very well then.' Blacker appeared satisfied. 'Mr Churchill is aware that I have wrestled with my conscience before coming here to talk to him.' He spoke with a slight Scottish accent – Glaswegian, Edward thought.

'I appreciate it, Leonard, and I can assure you that neither I nor Lord Edward will repeat a word of what you have to tell us.'

Blacker seemed to relax and sat himself down on the sofa beside Edward. Churchill paced about the room before coming to rest by the lectern he himself had designed and at which he wrote his books.

'No, thank you,' Blacker said brusquely when Churchill offered him a drink. 'I am a teetotaller. My father took a wee dram here and a wee dram there so that by the end of the day he hardly knew whether he was on his head or his heels. I took the pledge on my sixteenth birthday and I have never touched a drop since though I confess, just lately, I have been sorely tempted.'

Edward guiltily replaced his whisky glass on the table beside him.

'And I gather you cannot stay for luncheon, Leonard?'

'No, I must be back at my desk by three o'clock for a meeting with the Minister.'

'It's very good of you to come,' Churchill said, sounding subdued by this display of the Calvinist work ethic. 'Perhaps we should get straight down to business.'

'Indeed, sir.' Blacker seemed to hesitate and then, visibly bracing himself, began to unburden himself. 'If you will bear with me I shall begin with a little history. I assure you it is relevant. At the beginning of the century a German physician and socialist thinker by the name of Alfred Ploetz settled in Springfield, Massachusetts. He started a medical practice and began to breed chickens. He graduated to studying genealogy and human breeding. He coined the term *rassenhygiene* – racial hygiene. The name was changed soon after to eugenics, which somehow sounded less threatening. At the same time, quite independently, a German social theorist by the name of Alfred Jost was developing his theory that the state had an inherent right to kill the unfit and useless. He wrote an influential pamphlet entitled *The Right to Death*.'

'How chilling!' Churchill broke in. 'I have read something of this. The basic premise is, as I understand it, that the race should be purified and degenerates eliminated. Of course, who decides who is degenerate is crucial. If I understand rightly, Leonard, this is the so-called science which the Nazis have adopted with such enthusiasm.'

'The Nazis have, as you say, adopted this repellent philosophy to justify their persecution of the Jews. I have also had shocking reports that they are carrying out hideous experiments on the disabled and the mentally handicapped in their efforts to "purify" the race.'

Edward was deeply shocked. 'I simply cannot believe what you say, Professor. I have long recognized that the Nazis are gangsters but surely . . .'

'I only tell you what I have been told but my sources are reliable,' Blacker said grimly.

'At least we . . .' Edward began but was interrupted by Churchill.

'I wish our hands were clean, Lord Edward, but I very much fear they may not be. Tell him, Leonard.'

'In America,' Blacker continued remorselessly, 'the same ideas were developed independently without anyone taking them seriously. A key figure is an American – a zoologist by the name of Charles Davenport. He grew up in Brooklyn Heights and suffered under a tyrannical father imbued with an exaggerated respect for God's word as passed down to us in the Bible. As a young man he made a reputation of sorts as director of the Brooklyn Institute of Art and Science's biological laboratory on Long Island. At a place called Cold Spring Harbor on the coast he further developed his studies of what became known as eugenics. He became obsessed with race and came to the conclusion that Nordic types were far superior to southern peoples such as the Spanish, Italians and, in particular, people with black skins.'

'I have read about this kind of thing,' Edward said. 'These are the sort of madmen who gave Hitler the idea of the Aryan master race. I recall the fuss there was in Germany when Jesse Owens won four gold medals at the Olympic Games. Hitler was furious to see a black American beat his Nordic heroes and stormed out of the stadium.'

'Precisely. Davenport developed the idea that each racial type possesses not only its own physical characteristics but also moral and intellectual ones which are not visible to the naked eye. These are passed down from generation to generation. The Germans, according to Davenport, are thrifty, intelligent and honest while the southern peoples are lazy, feckless and . . . well, you get the idea.'

'So why is Davenport important? Surely he's just another madman?' Edward inquired.

'That would be true if he had not had the luck or the cleverness to get the backing of the Carnegie Institution. He persuaded it to fund a Biological Experiment Station at Cold Spring Harbor "to investigate the method of evolution". Davenport made it quite clear he would be studying ways of

34

purifying America's racial stock. He hoped to develop a race of super-Nordics and keep out what he called the "cheaper races".'

'That's disgusting,' Edward interjected, 'but, surely, that was all before the war. The Americans aren't still funding such research?'

'I am afraid they are. Davenport's ugly eugenic visions attracted Andrew Carnegie who flung money at him, as did John D. Rockefeller and the Ford Foundation. All of which gave Davenport not just the wherewithal to continue his "experiments" but a degree of respectability. He explained that America needed to "purge its blood" and "eliminate" the "feeble-minded", the poor, the crippled and the criminal. He offered up his theories as the "solution to America's negro problem".' Grimly, the Professor added, 'You won't be surprised to learn that he found much support, particularly in the Southern States. By the time America joined the war in 1918 several states had legalized eugenic sterilization. Before the war, German and American scientists worked closely together to refine eugenics into a "respectable" science. Schools were being taught eugenics illustrated with doctored photographs purporting to show children how to recognize "inferior" races. They invented the word "moron" to describe human beings regarded as being of sub-human intelligence. This led to further so-called scientific tests. By 1913 even the President, Teddy Roosevelt, was saying that "society has no business to permit degenerates to reproduce their kind".'

'I have never heard that English scientists got involved in this madness,' Edward said.

'That's why I am particularly interested in Leonard's story,' Churchill said, sounding very subdued. 'I have a confession to make to you, my boy. I was, for a short time, one of the deluded and I still feel guilty. Eugenics became very fashionable in the twenties. We had read about Darwin's theories of evolution and the survival of the fittest. Francis Galton had taught that you could measure character and produced graphs and charts to "prove" that most foreigners were inferior to us Anglo-Saxons and that women could never be scientists. Complete balderdash, of course.'

'But you opposed giving women the vote,' Edward could not resist pointing out.

'But not because they are inferior. They are often very much our superiors but their strengths and talents are different from ours. They can wield much more influence holding themselves above the political fray ... but I see you are laughing at me. I admit that I fought that battle and lost and it was probably a battle I ought not to have fought but it is easy to be wise after the event, young man, as you will discover.'

'I am sorry, sir – please, do go on.'

'Yes, well, where was I?' Churchill was obviously put out. He did not like to be interrupted when he was in full flow. 'In Galton, Darwin had a disciple who took his ideas much further than was justified by the science. He believed that mankind progressed through a constant struggle among nations with weaker races going to the wall, and his views were adopted by clever men like H.G. Wells and George Bernard Shaw.'

'Shaw!' Edward said contemptuously. 'I hear he praises Hitler as the greatest man of his time.'

Churchill went on with his apologia. 'We had heard of Gregor Mendel and his peas. If we could improve our maize, our wheat, our peas through selective breeding, surely we could improve our human beings? It seemed obvious to us that we had to improve our stock in order to provide strong, healthy young men to rule the empire. So many of the best of us had been killed in the war – like your brother, Lord Edward, and several young men close to me. My interpretation of eugenics was that we had to feed the population better and house working people in light, airy homes, not fetid slums. It seemed a democratic theory. The upper classes would have to justify their position in society or be replaced by fitter men.'

'But in fact it was a gift to the dictators,' Blacker put in.

'I still think it is right that we should improve the health of our people but, of course, we could not know how these common-sense ideas would be perverted.' Churchill sighed and hunched his shoulders. 'When I was Home Secretary, I was persuaded to put my trust in a man called Ernest Lidbetter who had worked in Bethnal Green with the Poor Law Authority but who, I later discovered, was neither a scientist nor a doctor. He was very convincing. He believed that pauperism was hereditary. I admit I fell into the trap and believed his claptrap, though I soon realized that this was a gross error. Poverty is only hereditary because society makes it so. It is almost impossible for people to hoist themselves out of it. Without education, with bad health and no money how can a man improve his lot? When he is young and fit he gets a manual job which, in time, takes its toll on his health. The moment a man's health begins to suffer from the rigours of his work, he can quickly become unemployable and quite useless to himself and to society. It seems ingrained in our society that the man who sits behind a desk as a clerk or, for that matter, a government minister looks down on the manual worker whereas we should respect him and improve the conditions under which he works.'

Edward wished Verity was here to listen to Churchill. She might not think he was the enemy of the people after all. 'Lidbetter is still publishing what he would call scientific books on the subject of race and how poverty should not be alleviated by charity as it merely encourages pauperism,' Blacker said indignantly. 'We thought the man had been laughed out of court but it appears that here and in America he still has a following. In Britain, he has been repudiated by all respectable scientists and starved of funds – we have seen to that. In the United States, the Carnegies and the Rockefellers have no wish to be seen to be bankrolling the Nazis and are very slowly seeing the error of their ways. However, their money has allowed Lidbetter and his like to go much further than they ought.'

'So if these people are being starved of money,' Edward rejoined, 'surely that means they won't be able continue with their "research" or whatever they call it?'

'That was what so alarmed me when I stumbled on this new "foundation",' Professor Blacker replied. 'It has refinanced the eugenics movement in Britain and we suspect it has close links with Nazi scientists doing the same sort of experiments in Germany.'

'So, just close it down,' Edward said.

'We can't without some solid evidence,' the Professor said in exasperation, 'and that we have not been able to find. Money has gone to perfectly respectable scientists interested in eugenics but, as far as I can find out, the main laboratories are in Hamburg and beyond our reach. One thing though, Sir Simon Castlewood – you know who I mean, Lord Edward? The millionaire – appears to own what I understand is called a "beauty institute" in the

South of France. It may all be above board. We don't know for sure but it might be worth investigating.'

'What do the French police say?'

'The French police are not interested in stirring things up,' Blacker said sourly.

'So who runs it – this beauty institute?'

'Its director is a plausible rogue called Dominic Montillo. He calls himself a cosmetic surgeon. To be fair, he has done some good work remodelling the faces of unfortunates with disfigurements. What else he does we do not know for sure but there is some suggestion that he carries out abortions, which are illegal in France as they are here, of course. Worse still, rumour has it that he has carried out castrations of the mentally retarded and even what the Nazis call "mercy killings". Simple murder, in other words.'

'He must be a monster! Montillo – is he English? He doesn't sound English.'

'He has a British passport, Lord Edward.'

'Who else is involved?'

'The Castlewood Foundation has the support of several MPs and at least one bishop but its driving force is Sir Simon. He makes all the important decisions himself. And why not? It's his money.'

'The authorities can do nothing?'

'No,' Churchill said decisively. 'Castlewood is a well-respected philanthropist. He has sponsored several expeditions to the North and South Poles as you probably know from the newspapers. He's popular with the public and there would be an outcry if he was accused of anything as disgusting as . . . well, you understand. We would have to have overwhelming evidence to take any action against him. He's seen as a force for good – someone who *does* something while others merely talk.'

'What else do we know about him?' Edward asked.

'He's a leading light in the Anglo-German Fellowship – Colonel Meinertzhagen's organization – which, encouraged by the German Embassy, leaps to the defence of Nazi Germany at every opportunity,' Churchill said, 'but there is no evidence that he has broken the law, at least here in England. In any case, the last thing the Government wants is a row about science. The PM has too much on his hands to open a new can of worms. We don't want any publicity about secret government laboratories and scientific establishments such as Bawdsey Manor or Porton Down. One question in the House about the Castlewood Foundation's financing scientific research and MPs would feel they could name any of our secret establishments.'

'Sir Simon lives at Swifts Hill in Kent, doesn't he?' Edward said meditatively.

'That's right,' Churchill said. 'Why, do you know him?'

'I don't but, as it happens, my friend Verity Browne is staying with the Castlewoods at this very moment.'

'The journalist, Verity Browne?' Churchill asked.

'Yes, sir.'

'I would very much like to meet her. I have admired her reporting from Spain though I don't always agree with her conclusions.'

'I fear she does not wholly approve of you, sir. She is a member of the Communist Party and is inclined to see you – if you will forgive me saying so – as the enemy.'

Churchill's brow furrowed and then his face cleared and he chuckled. 'What you tell me makes me even more interested in meeting her. Tell her I look forward to a spirited exchange of views.'

Blacker, impatient with this badinage, said roughly, 'I shall leave you now, Mr Churchill . . . Lord Edward.' He gave a stiff little bow. 'I have done what I can. It is now up to you to find out if there is anything . . . which needs seeing to. I confess I am relieved to have done what I believe is my duty but, as you appreciate, I can go no further while I am attached to the War Office.'

It was a pompous little speech and Edward expected Churchill to show irritation but in fact he could not have been more gracious and showed Blacker out to his car with many kind words. On his return to the study, Edward asked point blank what he thought of him.

'I do not presume to judge a man's character from a few minutes' conversation. I think you cannot understand what it means to the civil servants, Foreign Office officials and soldiers, airmen and sailors who make their way to Chartwell to air their concerns. They know they are right to follow their conscience but it nevertheless goes against everything they have been brought up to believe. It is very hard to betray a trust even if you are convinced that a greater trust is betrayed by keeping silent. You, Lord Edward, are lucky enough always to have been independent. I don't just mean financially, though of course that is a rare blessing, but also – if I may put it so – emotionally. You can say what you want and choose whom you wish to serve, though I don't doubt that when you do pledge your loyalty to an organization or person you are faithful to the end. Men like Leonard Blacker have less room for manoeuvre. They have served their superiors and their country faithfully. For them it is a very big step to come to an outsider such as myself, with what your Miss Browne would no doubt call an unsavoury reputation, to "spill the beans". Only the most overwhelming imperative makes it possible for them to do so.'

Edward felt rebuked and wondered if Churchill was warning him that he had a choice which, once made, was irrevocable. If he accepted a permanent position with the Foreign Office he would be bound to do what was asked of him without questioning the rights and wrongs. If he chose to work for Churchill he would, Edward was sure, rightly demand his absolute commitment. And yet so far, puzzlingly, Mr Churchill had made him no offer and he was certainly not going to raise the subject. Perhaps this business with the Castlewood Foundation was some sort of test. As it happened, he was not unwilling to take on the job of investigating it if that was what Churchill wanted. It would give him more time to think about what he wanted to do in the long term. In any case, what Leonard Blacker had said was horrifying. He was sure that Britain had clean hands when it came to this perverted science. It could not be denied that there was anti-Semitism in Britain. It pervaded society from top to bottom. He found it obnoxious but it was a long way from the institutionalized policies of 'racial hygiene' pursued by the Nazis which were utterly unworthy of a civilized country. It was ironic, as Churchill had pointed out, that this new prison camp, Buchenwald, was situated so close to Weimar, the city of Goethe and everything that was to be admired in German culture.

'Do I take it, sir, that you want me to do a bit of digging and find out what I can about this Foundation?'

'I would be grateful. It's not a police matter, at least not yet, but I don't doubt our country's enemies are behind it. If you can get me a few hard facts I can send a file to Special Branch and we can put a few spokes in some wheels.'

'Do you suspect Simon Castlewood of being one of those enemies?'

'I don't know. I have met him and he seemed a pleasant enough man. His father was a rogue, fortunate to have died before he was bought to book, but the son seems to be a different type. I don't want to jump to conclusions. He may be all right. I think he is probably an unwitting dupe of this man Montillo. These millionaires are surprisingly gullible, you know. He may not fully understand what he is financing.'

At Churchill's insistence, Edward stayed for lunch and they discussed his investigation of the two Foreign Office murders that he had brought to a successful conclusion.

'I have seen Sir Robert Vansittart only once recently,' Churchill said. 'As you know, he does not approve of me but I get the feeling that he is becoming disenchanted with the Government's conduct of foreign policy.'

'In what way, sir?' Edward asked.

'Neville Chamberlain, our new, energetic Prime Minister, and Lord Halifax have been circumventing the Foreign Office and making overtures to the Italians behind Anthony Eden's back. They hope to make some sort of "deal".' Churchill spoke with studied scorn. 'Lord Halifax sees Mussolini as an "honest broker" who will help bring about peace with Germany.'

'And you, sir?'

'It is a forlorn hope and probably a dangerous illusion which merely distracts us from facing reality. Mussolini is Herr Hitler's jackal, as I have already said. He snaps at his stronger partner's heels hoping to pick up scraps. I fear we are once again showing ourselves to be weak in the face of bullying.'

'And Mr Eden . . . Does he approve?'

'No, I was talking to him last evening and he was exasperated. Chamberlain and he will come to blows. You cannot have the Prime Minister pursuing his own foreign policy behind his Foreign Secretary's back. I have a great respect for the Prime Minister and I was glad to second his nomination as leader of the Conservative Party but, whereas we drifted to disaster under Stanley Baldwin, I believe we are now setting course for it with a determination that chills my blood.'

As he drove back through the peaceful countryside, Edward thought how difficult it was to believe that England might soon echo to the sound of falling bombs with the drone of enemy bombers drowning out the songs of the woodland birds. If Churchill was right, Britain would face a war with Germany for which it was ill prepared or, perhaps worse, a humiliating surrender without a fight. It did not bear thinking about. Instead he turned his thoughts to Verity. By a strange coincidence she was in a position to do some useful detective work, but how to get hold of her? She would be back in London on Tuesday so there was not much time if she was to find out anything at Swifts Hill. He was half-tempted simply to drive up there and ask to see her but that was too brazen. It would cause comment and he did not want to embarrass her. In any case, it might be better if, at this stage, he did not meet Castlewood and alert him to the interest he was taking in his affairs. He could write to her and she would receive his letter the next morning but, if for any reason it was delayed, it might fall into the wrong hands. A telegram would be too dramatic. Probably, after all, the best thing was to discuss it with her when she returned. If she suddenly started asking questions she might arouse Castlewood's suspicions and put him on his guard.

3

'Do tell us about him.' Virginia was being at her most annoying and Verity pretended not to know to whom she was referring.

'Tell you about whom?'

'Oh, Crumbles, don't pretend you don't know who I mean. Lord Edward, of course! Is he as good-looking as he appears in the picture papers? I would so love to meet him. Oh! I have just had the most wonderful idea. Next Saturday is the annual cricket match – Swifts Hill against the village. Simon was complaining only last night that he was having problems getting a side together. Simon! Come over here. I've just had a brilliant idea.'

When the 'brilliant idea' had been explained to him, Sir Simon was suitably enthusiastic and Roddy Maitland added his encouragement.

'Do you think you could ever persuade him to come?' Virginia asked Verity. 'It would be such fun and satisfy all our curiosity. Do say you'll ask him.'

'Yes do, Miss Browne,' Roddy chimed in and Isolde squeezed her arm and said it would be 'smashing'.

'I'll certainly ask him. I remember him telling me how good he was at cricket when he was at school,' she said, a touch sarcastically.

They were gathered in the drawing-room before dinner, sipping White Ladies, and Verity was wondering how she could get Maud Pitt-Messanger on her own and ask about her father's murder. She caught sight of herself in the mirror on the wall opposite her. She thought she looked all right and Simon Castlewood's interest in her seemed to bear this out. She was wearing a new dress made for her by Schiaparelli. It was surprisingly restrained, the black crêpe cleverly designed to make her look taller than she was. The bodice was entwined with François Lesage's delicate embroideries, silver leaves and pink flowers on sinuous, winding branches. Verity did not much care for jewellery but she wore a pendant – ivory, coral and gold on a gold chain – given her by Edward, as he put it, 'to remember Guernica'. It was the first piece of jewellery he had ever given her and she was touched but hesitant about accepting it. When a man gave a girl something as precious and beautiful as this, he was making a claim whether he admitted it or not. Her father was the only man before Edward from whom she had ever accepted clothes or jewellery. In the end she had kissed him on the lips and said she would treasure it. The pleasure it gave him was reflected in his eyes and she was glad she had not rejected it. Neither of her two previous lovers, the American novelist Ben Belasco and her political mentor David Griffiths-Jones, had been the sort who would think of giving her presents.

'I say, Miss Browne, you look perfectly splendid,' said Roddy, sitting himself down on the sofa beside her. 'That's a topping dress. I mean, I know nothing about frocks and that kind of thing but . . .'

'Be a dear and stop burbling,' Isolde Swann said, perching her shapely bottom on the arm of the sofa. 'Miss Browne has no wish to hear your views on fashion, I'm sure.'

'No, of course. Sorry and all that. I'm afraid I'm a bit of an ass. Can't think why you put up with me, Izzy old thing.'

'I love you, that's why,' she said, patting the top of his head in a proprietorial way. 'Don't you agree, Miss Browne, that love makes you – what's the phrase? – *tout comprendre, tout pardonner?*'

Verity hesitated. 'I'm not sure I have ever been in love . . .'

'Oh, I say, I thought you and Lord Edward . . .'

'I do believe, Roddy, you are determined to put your foot in it. I do apologize for this poor goof, Miss Browne.'

'No,' said Verity, flailing about, 'I do love him but I don't know . . . it's all so complicated. You see, I live such an absurd life, my job . . . never in one place for more than a minute. It's really not fair on any man. Oh dear, please let's talk about something else.'

She realized that this was the very first time she had acknowledged her relationship with Edward in public though it would be folly to think the announcement would come as a surprise to anyone who knew them. In fact, she had blushed to the roots of her hair, which was under a hairdryer at the time, when riffling through the pages of *Tatler* she had happened to see a photograph of Edward and herself taken at Brooklands with a coy caption referring to her 'war wound' but assuring readers that she was being tended by 'the most eligible man about town, Lord Edward Corinth, younger brother of the Duke of Mersham'. She prayed Edward would never see it. It was just the sort of gossip he hated.

'But surely the only important job a woman has is to look after her husband and bring up his children?' Roddy said.

With a great effort of will Verity did not shower him with abuse but merely replied, 'I am sure that is true for many women but not for me, I am afraid.'

To her relief he began to talk about the New Year's Eve dance the Castlewoods always held at Swifts Hill.

'You will come, Miss Browne?' He turned to Castlewood. 'Sorry, old boy, that was rather cheek but . . .'

'No, Roddy's right,' Castlewood broke in. 'Ginny was going to ask you. We would so like it if you could come. It is so rare for me to make new friends – when I do I hate to be parted from them.'

He started to talk about his house, which was clearly the great love of his life. Taking Verity over to admire the radiogram, he told her, 'I can put on a record in here and we can listen to it here, in my study or in the dining-room. It's American. I saw it when I was last in New York and I knew I just had to have it for Swifts Hill.'

He slipped a record, black and shiny, out of its brown sleeve, holding it delicately between his palms at the rim. Placing it on the turntable he said in a low voice, 'One of my favourites. Shall we dance?'

It was 'Stormy Weather', a favourite of Verity's too, and for a moment she was inclined to accept his invitation if only to see whether he *would* dance with her. Instead, she laughed to show she knew he was joking and said, 'Was I very rude?'

'To Roddy? Not at all. I thought you were very restrained. I was full of admiration. He's such an idiot but not vicious – at least, so I believe. I can't understand what Isolde sees in him, though. She could have any man she wanted but she chooses . . .'

'He's very good-looking.'

'You think so?'

'In a sporty way,' she added hastily. 'Not my type but, you must admit, they make a beautiful couple.'

'Well, indeed. You must have a long talk with Dominic. He has studied these things and he advocates – what does he call it? – controlled breeding. He thinks that we have to weed out the weaklings and bring forth a new generation of supermen. Have you heard of the German philosopher Nietzsche? Of course you have! He said – and I took the trouble to memorize the passage – "experimental science is the last flower of asceticism. The investigator must discard all his feelings, hopes and fears as a human person and reduce himself to a disembodied observer of events on which he passes no value judgement."'

'You mean you don't have to take into account whether you are doing right or wrong? Surely, that's just what makes us human? Some of us call it conscience.'

'It's for the *greater good*, Miss Browne. Individual morality just confuses the issue. Who cares what you or I think is good or bad?'

At that moment Dominic Montillo came up to them and with his rather braying laugh said, 'Castlewood, did I really hear you talking about Nietzsche to a pretty girl?'

'We were just saying how beautiful Isolde and Roddy are – as a couple, I mean.'

'That's right! And they will have beautiful children. Does that appeal to you – as a Communist – Miss Browne?'

'Playing God and breeding beautiful children?'

'Yes. You don't believe in God so you must believe that man is god. Take a look at Roddy. You see he has a square-shaped head while Isolde's is oval.'

'Is that good?'

'Indeed it is. When you have time, you must let me show you some of the fruits of my research. A round head is a clear sign of degeneracy. Square or oval are strong shapes.'

'And what is mine?' she asked, catching a glimpse of herself in the mirror. 'It looks round to me.'

'No, oval . . . square . . .' For a moment Montillo was at a loss. 'If I may, I will take some measurements sometime?' She had managed to embarrass the good doctor and had no intention of helping him out.

It had occurred to Verity that, at dinner, there would be more women than men which would be awkward but, just as the butler announced that dinner was served, they were joined by the local doctor and another man to whom Verity took an instant and instinctive dislike even before he opened his mouth. He was very thin – mere skin and bone, stubble on his face and very little hair on his head. His teeth were bad and it was difficult to guess his age – not yet thirty, she guessed, but if he weren't so hunched and had more flesh on his bones he might look younger. Whereas the doctor had donned a creased and ancient dinner-jacket, the young man, whose name was Graham Harvey, arrogantly flouted convention and wore grey-flannel trousers secured by a rope belt, an open-neck white cotton shirt and plimsolls, worn through at the toes. It was such a blatant statement of contempt for the conventions of polite society that she expected Sir Simon or Virginia to send him packing but instead they welcomed him warmly as one of the family. Virginia explained that he rented a cottage on the estate and was writing a book.

Verity went into the dining-room on Sir Simon's arm. She felt him clutching her a little too tightly for comfort and hoped he was not going to be a bore. It was another extraordinary room. Her eyes went straight to the ceiling of which the recessed central portion was entirely covered in aluminium leaf on a blue background, with built-in concealed lighting which made the aluminium shimmer. The floor had a marble perimeter sur-rounding a buff-coloured carpet. The fireplace consisted of polished, ribbed aluminium panels surrounding an electric fire from which light – imitation logs illuminated from within by light bulbs – but no heat emanated. The fireplace was surrounded by black marble inlaid with a Greek key pattern. This was repeated on the ebonized doors to the room. On the walls hung three genuine Turner seascapes alongside a circular barometer and an electric clock.

Verity was seated, rather to her embarrassment, next to Sir Simon who naturally sat at the head of the table. To her alarm, Graham Harvey was on her other side. She gulped as she felt her host place a hand, fleetingly, on her knee. She had a feeling this was going to be a meal she would remember. The dining-room chairs were upholstered in pink leather. It looked odd – almost comic – but it certainly set off her Schiaparelli dress and, of course, the designer loved pink.

'Do you like it – the room?'

'Oh, was I staring, Sir Simon? I'm so sorry but I have never seen anything like it.'

'But do you like it?' he repeated.

'You have to give me time to absorb it all but, yes, I do. It's very elegant. May I ask who designed it?'

'Peter Malacrida – a friend of ours. Italian. Have you met him?'

It so happened that she had, in the Ritz in Paris. He was one of Belasco's drinking partners. An Italian playboy who also wrote for various newspapers and had written a couple of successful plays. She had not realized he was also an interior decorator.

'Yes, I met him in Paris – the Marchese Malacrida?'

'That's right. He also designed our house in London.'

Verity remembered how elegantly Malacrida had tried to detach her from Belasco and the difficulty she had had in convincing him that he would be unsuccessful. She was glad he was not here to tell stories.

The sound of a Mozart piano concerto wafted through a panel in the walls. Music, as her host had promised, was laid on. It ought to have been horribly vulgar but somehow it was too eccentric for that. It was not to her taste and it was not 'English' but she was enjoying it as theatre.

To change the subject she asked Sir Simon if he was planning any more expeditions. 'It was so exciting when they almost reached the Pole.'

'I'm too old myself to go on expeditions but my Foundation, which I set up to further scientific and social work, is financing – at least in part – an Anglo-German expedition to the roof of the world.'

'The roof of the world?'

'Tibet! To the sacred city of Lhasa, the Forbidden City. Tibet is the last truly secret place on earth. Not even Sven Hedin, the Swedish explorer, reached Lhasa. Have you read James Hilton's *Lost Horizon*?'

'Shangri-La, whose people had the secret of eternal youth?'

'Yes, an icy dream-like place in the high mountains with answers to questions man has always sought.'

Castlewood was becoming very excited. His eyes shone and his soup was still untouched. She noticed that, at the other end of the table, Montillo was listening intently while nodding and smiling as Virginia told some story about Mah-Jongg.

'What sort of answers?'

'Miss Browne,' he looked suddenly grave, 'it is my belief – our belief – that Tibet is the cradle of our Aryan race.'

'But the Tibetans aren't blond and blue-eyed,' Verity expostulated.

'No, but my friend Bruno Berger has given me a copy of an extraordinary book, *Die Nordische Rasse bei den Indogermanene Aliens*. It proves that our Aryan ancestors went east from the Nordic heartland in northern Europe through Persia and deep into central Asia – to Tibet. Sometime I shall show you photographs of Tibetan noblemen – they do look Aryan . . .'

'My dear, finish your soup. We are all waiting.' Virginia was warning her husband that he was on his hobby horse and that not everyone was listening with sympathy.

As if to prove his antisocial credentials, the young man beside her said, 'That's all tommy rot, Castlewood. It's the sort of mad theory the Nazis like.'

Sir Simon opened his mouth to respond but thought better of it and sank back into his chair.

Verity looked at her neighbour with interest. These were the first words he had spoken at dinner and she wondered exactly who he was. A licensed fool, perhaps, to insult his host without being reprimanded? Having delivered his opinion of Sir Simon's scientific theories, he relapsed into sulky silence. Verity, to cover her embarrassment – although neither man seemed in the least embarrassed, merely belligerent – asked Sir Simon a question about the building of the house. She sighed with relief as her host, in good spirits again, described the trials and tribulations of creating Swifts Hill. He was clearly a dreamer – not woolly and unpractical but a driven, even ruthless dreamer. He espoused projects and ideas that appealed to the romantic in him. He said himself that he liked the word 'impossible' when applied to some idea he had because he could then prove that it was after all possible. Swifts Hill itself might be minimal in design but the building of it was the expression of an idea as fantastic as any medieval castle. To emphasize what he thought was important, he leant right over to Verity and put his hand on hers or on her arm, as though he had to touch her in order to communicate his enthusiasm more directly than through mere words.

Sir Simon's volubility covered the silence of two of his guests. Maud Pitt-Messanger was steeped in profound gloom and said not a word. She was grieving for her father, no doubt, but her depression seemed too severe to be solely derived from her loss. Graham Harvey, too, seemed gloomy but his eyes glittered and Verity felt he was preparing himself for another outburst and, sure enough, he was.

When he had stopped talking about Swifts Hill, Sir Simon asked her about Spain. He knew the country well but had not been there since the outbreak of the civil war. She told him something about what she had seen but was careful not to get into politics. She guessed that her host might well support General Franco and the Rebels and had no wish to get into a slanging match on the subject. However, she found herself describing the destruction of Guernica and the death of her friend, the photographer, Gerda Meyer.

Before her host could make any comment, Graham Harvey, seeming to drag the words unwillingly from somewhere deep inside him, said harshly, 'You think of yourself as a Communist, do you not, Miss Browne?'

'I do because I am,' she answered crossly. 'Would you like me to show you my Party membership card?'

'And yet you sit at the tables of the rich, dressed in what I believe must be a very expensive frock . . .'

Verity was unnerved by this brutal attack and expected Sir Simon to come to her rescue but he seemed unperturbed and merely smiled at her, perhaps hoping for a 'scene'. She had the feeling he wanted to see her angry and, for this reason, she refused to be. She noticed that Maud was watching Harvey intently, though whether with approval or disapproval it was hard to say.

'If my eyes do not deceive me, Mr Harvey, you sit at the same table as I do and, if you think wearing dirty trousers and worn-out gym shoes makes you a member of the proletariat, think again.' She was pleased with her response and thought she had never disliked anyone more than this streak of a man, thin to the point of emaciation, whose unpleasant body odour made her feel nauseous. By this time the whole table was silent, listening to what the young man had to say.

'I have heard Castlewood talking about you,' he said with studied insolence. 'I gather that you are to marry a minor aristocrat. He showed me a photograph of you both in what I believe is called a society magazine. I don't wish to be rude,' he smiled for the first time but it was more of a smirk, 'but just because you found yourself in Guernica and "scooped" – isn't that the word? – your journalistic rivals, that doesn't make you a Communist – not in my eyes. Not though you carried a card given you by Lenin himself.'

It was such a blatant attempt to rile her that Verity's anger was dissipated. She did the best thing possible and broke into laughter which was echoed – with relief – round the table. Sir Simon might be disappointed at being done out of a row but he clearly admired the way she had overcome her difficulty. 'I can't take you seriously, Mr Harvey. Who are you trying to impress?'

'That puts you in your place, Graham,' Sir Simon said with a laugh. 'I agree with Miss Browne. You are a poseur. I don't recall what you have done to further the revolution. Unless . . . he's writing a book Miss Browne – an attack on the Government, I believe. They must be shaking in their boots – assuming he ever finishes it. Are you near to finishing it, Graham?'

Verity was interested to see that her antagonist seemed un-abashed by Sir Simon's teasing which verged on the cruel. He replied with some dignity, 'As a matter of fact, I wrote the final words of the final chapter before coming here tonight. It was why I had no time to change, for which I apologize.'

'Graham! How exciting,' shrilled Virginia. 'When may we read it?'

'Not yet . . . not for a while,' he said coldly. 'I read your book on the civil war, Miss Browne. I thought it . . .' he paused and Verity wondered what insult would follow, 'very interesting. I have not myself been to Spain but I have talked to many who have and they bear out what you say . . . for the most part.' He sank back into silence and – a minute or two later – Verity caught him with his eyes closed and wondered if he were asleep.

After they had finished eating, Virginia caught her husband's eye and rose from her chair. She led the ladies out to 'powder their noses', as she put it coyly, leaving the men to 'put the world to rights over their port'. It was a convention Verity always found absurdly old-fashioned and, normally, rather insulting – as if she might be expected to have nothing to contribute to the post-prandial conversation. She knew, from what Edward had told her, that the conversation was usually unenlightening, very often degenerating into a list of prejudices and bigotries spiced with ugly sexual 'jokes' which according to Freud – so Edward had informed her – reflected the English upper-class male's fear and, possibly, hatred of the female sex.

On this occasion, however, Verity was grateful to leave the dining-room to the men and even flashed Sir Simon a smile as he drew back her chair to facilitate her escape. When they reached the drawing-room, Verity took a cup of coffee and made a beeline for Maud who had flung herself, inelegantly, into an armchair well away from Virginia, Mrs Cardew and Isolde who remained by the coffee tray. She picked up a magazine but Verity could see that, as soon as she decently could, she would slip away to her bedroom. Before she did, Verity was determined to ask the questions she had wanted to put to her ever since she had entered the house. She sat herself down in a chair opposite Maud and stirred coloured coffee sugar into her cup as noisily as she could. Maud pretended not to notice her presence and pressed *The Field* to her face – she was obviously very short-sighted – hoping her persecutor might take the hint and leave her in peace. Unfortunately for Maud, Verity never took hints of this kind.

'I was so sorry about your father, Miss Pitt-Messanger. Have the police any clue as to who might have done such an awful thing?'

Maud shied like a startled horse. Verity had chosen the direct approach over anything subtle, which Maud might have chosen to ignore or misunderstand.

'Oh, Miss Browne, I didn't see you. My father . . . ? I really don't know. I don't think so but they tell me nothing.'

'They have talked to everyone sitting nearby in the Abbey, I suppose? Surely someone must have seen something?'

'Apparently not. There were lots of people milling around, you know.'

'And I suppose someone might have come in from the cloisters?'

'Yes.'

Verity felt she was not getting anywhere. 'You must be very anxious to find out who . . . hated your father enough to want to kill him. Did he have any enemies?'

Maud looked uncertain and then – to Verity's dismay – she began to cry. Verity kicked herself. She had been too brutal. 'I'm so sorry, I did not mean . . . Please, take this.' She proffered a clean handkerchief.

'Many enemies,' Maud answered, surprisingly.

Verity was encouraged. 'So the police have . . . you know . . . leads to follow up?'

Maud turned to her fiercely. 'I really don't see what it has to do with you. My father was a beast of a man. Everyone hated him and I'm glad he's dead. There, I've said it. Now, please leave me alone. The men will be back soon and you can fascinate them instead of persecuting me.'

Verity was abashed and, unwontedly, at a loss for words. She saw Mrs Cardew and Virginia looking at them. She thought bitterly that Edward would have charmed Maud into giving him a complete account of everything that had happened since the murder. Her technique, she appreciated, had got her nowhere. She might as well have hit the poor girl over the head with a rubber truncheon. She had rushed the fence and her horse had refused. 'I am so sorry, Miss Pitt-Messanger, I have been impertinent. I apologize. I just wanted to help.'

'Help! Why should you . . .?' She waved the magazine she held in protest and mopped her nose with the handkerchief. 'Why should someone like you care about me? Is it some game you're playing?'

'How do you mean, "someone like me"? I'm just . . .'

'Don't pretend you can't see how all the men fawn over you and say how clever you are . . . but the looks they give you . . . disgusting. That dress . . . ! Then they look at me. Or rather they don't look at me unless they have to.'

Verity found herself blushing. It always annoyed her that, though she saw herself as a hard-bitten journalist, she could blush so easily at any personal remark.

'You think the men . . . ' she began but Maud butted in.

'It was bad enough with Isolde looking so . . . like a Wagnerian goddess but Graham was right. How can you call yourself a Communist when you wear dresses by . . . is it Schiaparelli? . . . and let these rich men drool over you?'

Verity blushed again but tried to hold back her anger. 'I am sorry if I have offended you in any way, Miss Pitt-Messanger. I was not trying to show off. I just wanted to . . .'

'Get another scoop?' With a snort of disgust, Maud got up from her chair, tossed her magazine on the sofa and strode out of the drawing-room.

Verity looked round nervously to find everyone looking at her. Mrs Cardew said gently, 'Whatever did you say to the poor girl, Miss Browne?'

'I . . . I was trying to be friendly,' she said lamely, 'but I think she thought I was being patronizing. I did not mean to be.'

Virginia laughed. 'Come over here, Crumbles, and stop looking so forlorn. Maud's in a bad way. You see her whole life was her father and though she couldn't make up her mind whether she loved or loathed him – I think both at the same time – she misses him. I imagine it must be a bit like being in chains for years and then, when they are removed, you still feel the weight of them.'

'What sort of man was her father? He was a great scholar, wasn't he?'

'That's what they say,' Mrs Cardew answered. 'He was famous for the work he did in Assyria. He discovered the tomb of some king or other. I don't remember the details.'

'Yes,' broke in Isolde, 'but then it turned out his assistant – what was his name? I remember! Sidney Temperley – anyway, he had actually found the tomb and resented Pitt-Messanger taking all the credit. He came back to England and kicked up a bit of stink.'

Virginia took over the story. 'And then he died – of cholera they said. It was all rather fishy. There were rumours that he had committed suicide but who knows? The worst thing was that Maud convinced herself that she and Temperley had been going to get married. No one can say if she was fantasizing or if there was some truth in it. Anyway, the poor child never forgave her father. Pitt-Messanger's reputation suffered but he managed to find some money somewhere – from Simon among other people – and started digging in Egypt, in the Valley of the Kings.'

'He found something sensational,' Isolde said, 'but I can't remember exactly what.'

'That's right,' Virginia said, combing her Pekinese's fur with her fingers. 'He had this mad idea – at least I assume it was mad – that he had found the grave of . . . I can never remember the names of these people. Wait a minute, I've got his pamphlet here somewhere. I was trying to read it before Maud arrived.' She flicked through the pages until she found what she was looking for. 'Here we are! He says he found the grave of Nebhepetre Mentuhotep, the founder of the Middle Kingdom. 2008 to 1957 BC. It was all so long ago and, what with the time running backwards, I can never make head or tail of it. Anyway, he found a letter. It told of Lutenheb – a beautiful Helen of Troy-type queen – whose beauty caused a war – a civil war, I think. Here, take it up to bed with you.' She gave Verity the pamphlet. 'Tomorrow I'll show you some of the beautiful things he gave us in return for Simon's help in funding his expedition. We've got a gallery above the great hall. A sort of small museum.'

'You knew Pitt-Messanger well, Ginny?' Verity asked.

'Simon did. We met him in Assyria and he was very kind and took us round all the tombs. As I said, Simon got so enthusiastic he offered to finance the dig for a year.'

'That was generous,' Verity said.

'It helped that his work seemed to support Simon's views on breeding. Apparently the ancient Assyrians were like the Spartans and bred a warrior class. I don't remember the details. You must ask Simon. He'll love to tell you.'

'Lord Benyon also got him some funding, I believe,' Verity said meditatively.

'Yes. He could be very good at getting money out of the rich,' Mrs Cardew said, a little spitefully, 'but I still hold that he was horrid to Maud.'

'Poor Maud!' Virginia said. 'That's why I feel we owe it to her to be patient and try and help her find her feet.' She sounded quite sincere and Verity suddenly remembered why she had liked her so much at school.

At that moment they were joined by the men. Montillo went over to Virginia and whispered something in her ear before leaving the room. Sir Simon came straight over to sit by Verity.

'Ginny was telling me about Mr Pitt-Messanger,' she said, thinking she might as well use his enthusiasm for her company to find something out. 'He was a good archaeologist? I know nothing about the subject.'

'Oh, yes, Miss Browne . . . Verity. I must be allowed to call you Verity.' She smiled her permission. 'He was a good archaeologist – almost a great one – but he was dogged by bad luck. As a very young man he had dug with Leonard Wooley at Ur of the Chaldees. He helped discover the tomb of Queen Pu-abi who was buried along with her retinue and her oxen.'

'I have never heard of her!' Verity exclaimed.

'Nor has anyone. She was queen about 2600 BC when writing was in its infancy and she is not mentioned in any of the scrolls. However, they did find many wondrous things – a lyre, I remember him showing me, covered with rolled gold, a small statue of a golden donkey and many other implements made of gold and silver. Yes, and a wooden board for playing some game which might have been similar to chess. Most of it is now in the British Museum.'

'So long ago!' Verity marvelled. 'I can't get my mind round it. But you say he had bad luck?'

'Yes. As is always the case with archaeology, which usually involves some form of grave robbing, he was said to be cursed. He stumbled on an extraordinary killing chamber. Seventy-four skeletons – mostly women – in a pit. Certainly human sacrifices, probably made to celebrate the funeral of some king. It was horrific and the evil was supposed to have attached itself to those who had disturbed the dead.'

'So what happened?'

'I don't know the details but he quarrelled with Wooley and the two men never spoke to each other again. I expect they could both be bloody awkward. Well, I know Pitt-Messanger could be. Then he went off to Nineveh to assist Reginald Campbell Thompson. It was a pretty exciting time – the first proper excavation of the capital of the Assyrian empire.' Verity looked a bit vague. 'You remember Jonah and his whale? He lived in Nineveh and was its chief prophet. Nineveh was one of the greatest cities of the ancient world until the Medes and the Babylonians destroyed it about 600 BC.'

'That was where you met him? I mean, not in 600 BC but when he was excavating Nineveh? '

'That's right – four years ago in Iraq on the banks of the Tigris. You have no idea what an amazing place it is. Mosul stands just across the Tigris from Nineveh and the landscape is quite different from the desert sands round Ur. The plains of Northern Mesopotamia may be the cradle of the human race, you know. It is certainly fertile and temperate enough. Pitt-Messanger had some interesting theories about the development of the human race which made a lot of sense to me. I loved Mosul with its pleasant gardens and shady houses. Even Ginny liked it and it must have seemed like paradise to those ancient peoples. Mosul! I can picture it now – the sun glinting off the minarets and domes of the mosques, the artificial lakes and water gardens . . . It seemed like something out of the *Arabian Nights* after Ur, burning in the desert, whipped by sand storms which cut your flesh and blinded you.'

'And Pitt-Messanger found . . .?'

'Well, for one thing he worked out the chronology of Nineveh, dividing it into five eras. He found a tomb strikingly similar to the Mycenaean tombs in Greece, dating from the Halaf period, about 5000 to 4000 BC.'

'Was that the tomb Sidney Temperley claimed to have discovered?'

'It was a ridiculous storm in a teacup. These discoveries are group finds and often the actual moment when a tomb is exposed is witnessed only by a native.'

'But that's not what Pitt-Messanger thought?'

'You have to remember how arduous these digs are, Verity. People are always getting ill what with the dirt and the rats and mice. Everyone gets cranky. Mind you, Pitt-Messanger held that . . . now how did he put it when I complained of a bad headache? I remember – "pain was a benign secretion of a disorder and an essential part of the healing mechanism." He said that enduring pain was a virtue and that we white northern Europeans were better at it than the black races. In fact, he went so far as to say that illness is due to a lack of moral fibre and that the sick should be put out of their misery. Poor Temperley was often ill so you can imagine how that went down with the Professor!'

'Keep a stiff upper lip and all that. But you said this place was healthier than Ur, with a much more temperate climate?'

'Yes, but it was still a strenuous dig. There's so much that can go wrong. There's never enough money for one thing. The natives steal everything they can lay their hands on. Officials are demanding bribes. And you are so far from home. People will quarrel over a pot of Oxford marmalade, let alone a royal tomb.'

'Did he finish the dig?'

'No. It may not ever be "finished", as you put it. There is so much to find there. Pitt-Messenger's health was failing him. He needed something easier.'

'Ginny was telling me about his work in Egypt.'

'She told you about the beautiful queen he found in what they are now calling the Valley of the Queens?'

'She said she would show me your museum tomorrow.'

'Why not now? Or are you too tired?'

'I'm not too tired.'

'Isolde? Will you come? I know Emily has seen it many times.'

'Yes, I think I'll go to bed if you don't mind, Simon.'

'Where's Maud?' Sir Simon asked.

'She's gone up to her room,' Virginia told him. 'Dominic was worried about her and has gone to see she's all right. He's such a considerate man. Dr Morris went with him.'

'And Graham?' Sir Simon inquired of his wife.

'He said he had to tidy up his book and disappeared out into the night.'

'Typical!' Isolde said. 'He can be so charming' – Verity looked amazed – 'but he delights in being antisocial. He wants us all to know he hates the rich and yet he lives off Simon. He's just a sponger.'

'I say, Izzy!' Roddy exclaimed. 'I think you're being a bit tough on the man. I won't pretend he's my favourite character but he's just . . . He's just who he is. I rather like that.'

Verity, Isolde and Roddy got up to follow their host.

'It's not really a museum, you know,' Sir Simon said, suddenly modest. 'Just a few things I've picked up on my travels.'

When they reached the great hall, above which the museum was located, they found the lights weren't working. 'The fuse often goes,' Simon explained. 'I'll change it in the morning. I've got to have the whole of this side of the house rewired. There's a torch somewhere on a table. Be prepared is my motto. Ah, here we are.'

With the powerful beam shedding its light before them, they

crossed the great hall with its tapestries and ancient armour, circumvented the massive oak dining-table Sir Simon had had made and at which the Castlewoods feasted on high days and holidays, and climbed the narrow staircase up into what was called the minstrels' gallery. Their footsteps echoed on the stone so that Verity had an urge to walk on tiptoe. She tried not to trip over her dress because the stairway was steep and the stone steps uneven. She was relieved when they came at last to the glass showcases. The lights were not working here either but Sir Simon shone his torch on the ancient papyri, the beads and jewellery and a fantastic head-dress once worn by a queen of Babylon. He picked out for them a splendid golden necklace – the prize object in the collection – which shimmered in the torchlight.

Verity said, 'It's beautiful but is it safe? These glass cabinets don't look very strong.'

'No one would steal these things. They are too well known. I mean, if you took this necklace to any dealer they would know its origin and that it had been stolen.'

Verity thought her host was complacent. 'So there's no alarm? I'm surprised the insurance company doesn't make you keep it all in a safe.'

'It's not insured,' Sir Simon said casually. 'As you say, they would not let me display the collection and what is the point of having objects like these if you cannot admire them? In any case, we stole them from a tomb so, if anyone steals them from us, they are doing no more than we did.'

'Admirable philosophy!' Roddy remarked.

Verity said nothing but thought that Sir Simon was criminally lax leaving such ancient and beautiful works of art unprotected.

'Shall I read you the translation of this letter? It's quite fascinating.' Sir Simon pointed his torch at the card in front of the papyrus. '"They have begun to eat men and women here. The entire land is dead with famine. We shall all starve."'

Sobered by this ancient cry of despair, they moved to the last case – which was empty.

'Hello!' Sir Simon said sucking in his breath. 'I do believe . . .'

'Surely there was a knife here . . . a gold dagger,' Roddy said. 'It had a stunning handle, most intricately carved. Assyrian, I think. Where have you put it, old boy?'

'I haven't put it anywhere,' Sir Simon said in a low voice. 'It has been stolen. It must have been.'

'Could Ginny have removed it?' Isolde suggested.

'She would never do such a thing without telling me.'

'But look!' Verity cried. 'Shine your torch over here.' She pulled at the glass and the door swung open. 'I thought so. It's not locked. It hasn't been broken into. Where do you normally keep the keys to the cabinet, Sir Simon?'

'In the safe in my bedroom. Oh God! I had better go and look and see if they are there. Damn and blast! I suppose I should call the police.'

'What time is it?' Verity asked.

'Almost midnight,' Roddy told her, consulting his watch in the torchlight.

'I think we should go back to the drawing-room. You can check your safe, Sir Simon, and we can raise Lampton and ask him to put a fuse in the fuse box.'

Sir Simon did not seem to mind Verity taking charge and Roddy just nodded in agreement.

Ten minutes later Verity, Isolde and Roddy were back in the drawing-room explaining to Virginia what had happened.

'I didn't take the dagger out of the display case,' she said in alarm. 'Who could possibly have removed it? It must be some sort of practical joke.'

At that moment Sir Simon reappeared looking shocked and anxious. He was very pale.

'The keys aren't in the safe. I guess that . . .' Normally so self-assured, he sounded uncertain.

'I showed the Cartwrights round last weekend when you were in London but I didn't need to use the keys.' Virginia sounded defensive.

'I suppose I must have left them out on my dressing-table instead of putting them in the safe.'

'When did you last have them out?' Verity asked.

'I don't know. Let me think . . . two weeks ago. Something like that. I remember! I wanted to show old General Robertson the dagger and . . .' He stopped, suddenly stricken. 'Oh God! I never thought . . .'

'I don't think it makes very much difference if the burglar had the key or not,' Verity said matter-of-factly. 'Anyone could have got into the display cases with a strong screwdriver.'

'Still,' said Roddy, sensibly, 'the fact is that the burglar *did* use the key and that implies that he – or she – saw them in Simon's dressing-room. It makes it unlikely to have been an outsider.'

There was no answer to this and they all looked at each other in dismay.

'I can't suspect any of the servants . . .' Virginia began. 'They are all completely trustworthy and, even if one of them were dishonest, why choose now to burgle the collection?'

'And why take one object – the dagger – rather than the whole lot?' Roddy added.

Verity looked at him with interest. Perhaps he wasn't the fool she had taken him for. 'The burglar might have thought it was the easiest to dispose of,' she suggested, without much conviction.

'Lampton's changing the fuse in the gallery. The police will be here any minute,' Sir Simon said. 'I rang the station as soon as I knew the keys weren't in the safe. The constable gave me Inspector Jebb's telephone number at home. I felt a bit of embarrassed at bothering him. He was in bed, of course. I apologized for waking him and told him it could wait till the morning but he insisted on coming round now. I know he'll think I have been much too careless. By the way, where's Dominic?'

'I told you. He went with Dr Morris to make sure that Maud was all right,' Virginia replied. 'I don't know why he has been so long.'

'Ah, here he is,' Sir Simon said. 'Dominic, have you heard what has happened? Why, what is it, man? You look as though you have seen a ghost. Let me get you some brandy. I need some myself, come to that.'

'Castlewood, you must come at once. We have done all we can but she has lost a lot of blood.'

'Who . . . ?' Virginia asked faintly, dropping the Pekinese off her lap.

'Didn't I say? It's Maud. She has cut her wrists.'

Sir Simon was first out of the room, followed by the others. Verity remained where she was, undecided. She was curious but that was surely a frivolous reason for invading the poor girl's privacy. She told herself that she was only a guest. Maud did not even like her. She had no medical knowledge. She would be in the way. Then her journalist's instinct took over and she hurried after them. In the hall she stopped, wondering which of the staircases to go up. She could hear a babble of voices but the acoustics were strange and she could not make out precisely where the noise was coming from. For a moment she felt like Alice in Wonderland trying to decide which door to go through and unsure of what she might find on the other side.

In the end she chose the staircase nearest to her. She found herself in the Castlewoods' suite of rooms. A door was open and a glance showed her that they had separate bedrooms. This was Virginia's. A dozen or so soft toys lay on the bed and cushions were strewn everywhere, many bearing winsome mottos such as 'Home is where the Heart is'. A large doll sat – obscenely, Verity thought – in an armchair. At first she had the idea that Virginia was pretending she was still a child but then, with a flash of insight, she saw that it was the bedroom of a woman who wanted desperately to be a mother but had been frustrated. Guiltily, she opened the door into Sir Simon's bedroom. It was surprisingly bare. There was no elaborate panelling or old masters on the walls. The bed was low and simple on a cast-iron frame. There was a door into what she supposed must be his dressing-room. Quickly, she walked across and looked in. It was quite small. The first thing she saw was the safe in the wall. He had moved a picture to one side to get at it and now it lay open, inviting further burglary. She was strongly tempted to see what was in it but her curiosity was checked when she heard steps approaching.

Praying it was not Sir Simon or Virginia, she stayed out of sight and whoever it was walked by without stopping. She thought it might have been a man by the heavy tread. She went back to the top of the stairs and listened. The babble of voices guided her down a corridor to a bathroom from which the naked body of Maud Pitt-Messanger was being lifted by Sir Simon and Roddy Maitland. Maud's bedroom was just across the passage and Isolde helped the men to dry her, lay her on a towel in her bed and cover her with blankets.

Dr Morris, or perhaps Montillo, had already bandaged her wrists and she seemed to be sleeping or unconscious. Verity poked her head into the bathroom. The bath was a large one on four sturdy legs. The water, the colour of light burgundy, was still in the bath. The floor was awash where it had spilled as the men had lifted her out. An old-fashioned razor lay on the floor beside the bath. She bent to pick it up. It had an ivory handle carved with the initials E.P.M. She guessed it must have belonged to Maud's father. A tartan wool dressing-gown lay on the floor. She picked it up and, as she did so, a small brown leather diary fell out of the pocket along with a handkerchief. Guiltily, and for no very good reason, she leafed through the diary which she at first thought was empty. Leafing through it again, she saw there was one date – April 27th – against which were inscribed the letters E.P.M.

She decided on the spur of the moment to secrete the diary so she could examine it more carefully. Perhaps she had missed something. She was faced with the problem that her dress had no pockets. She contemplated putting it in her brassiere but that would mean almost undressing. She had an evening bag but that was downstairs. There was nothing for it but to leg it back to her room, hide the diary and then return. There was a good chance that, in the mêlée, her absence would not be noticed. She darted out of the door and bumped into Roddy.

He seemed more embarrassed than she was. 'Oh, I say, sorry and all that. I was just . . . I thought I ought to clean the bath, don't you know.'

It sounded lame to Verity. 'The maid will do that.'

'I know, but the water . . . and the blood. I thought . . . not fit for her to see, if you get me. Is that the razor?'

Verity had put it on the round stool beside the bath. 'Yes, I think it must have been Mr Pitt-Messanger's. It has his initials on the handle.'

As Roddy picked up the razor and examined it, she hid the diary behind her back. 'How is she?' she asked, with an intensity which owed more to her shock than a real concern for Maud.

'The doctor thinks she'll be all right. Thank God he was on the spot but then again, I suppose Dominic would have coped by himself if it had been necessary. It was prescient of them to see the poor woman was suicidal.'

'Anyone could see she was at the end of her tether,' Verity said, squashingly.

Roddy, rather abashed, said, 'Well then, I'll clean up the bath.'

'I'll . . . I'll see if I can help Maud. It's rather silly but I'm not too good with blood. I've seen a lot of it . . . in Spain and it makes me feel sick.' She put her hand to her mouth and muttered, 'Back in a sec.' She took off for her room leaving Roddy looking rather surprised.

Verity cast around for a hiding place and, after a moment's hesitation, slipped the diary into one of her shoes. She glanced at herself in the mirror and grimaced. Why on earth had she stolen it? An instinct? Was she being absurd? There was probably nothing sinister about its single entry but it struck her as odd for Maud to have taken it into the bathroom if she was planning to commit suicide.

When she returned, no one seemed to have missed her. Everyone was crowded round the bed staring at Maud. She was as white as the towel she was lying on but she was alive. Her breathing was light and fast and her eyelids fluttered. She was moaning. Isolde was sitting on the bed holding her hand very gently so as not to disturb the bandages.

Virginia touched Montillo's arm. 'She will have you to thank for saving her life. If you hadn't gone after her to see how she was . . .'

'Morris and I were both worried about her. I thought she might need something to help her sleep but when I knocked on her door, there was no answer. We were just about to go downstairs again – I thought she must already be asleep – when Morris noticed the bathroom door was open. The light was on and there was steam pouring out into the passage. I put my head round the door and saw her.'

'It must have been awful.'

'Yes, but I'm more used to this sort of emergency than other people. In my sanatorium, I have many patients with nervous problems. I have had my eye on her ever since she has been here and it has been quite obvious that she is mentally unstable. I might suggest she spends a few weeks in my sanatorium. She has obviously been traumatized by her father's death and she might benefit from a complete change of scene. For now, I think it would be best if we all went downstairs and left her alone with the doctor. It won't do her any good to have a crowd round her bed. She just needs to sleep and regain her strength.'

Verity knew he meant to be kind but there was something

arrogant about the way he talked of Maud as damaged goods which grated.

Virginia led the way downstairs. When Dr Morris reappeared in the drawing-room he was able to reassure them that Maud was in no danger.

'Thank God we found her in time. It would have taken her an hour or two to bleed to death – longer perhaps. She'll be very weak tomorrow and must stay in bed but she'll be all right. I will visit her about midday.'

'And I'll look in on her before I turn it,' Montillo added.

'Now, Lady Castlewood, I think I will go home,' Dr Morris said, wiping his eyes with his handkerchief. 'I am not as young as I was and to see a young person in Miss Pitt-Messanger's state makes one feel even older. Mr Montillo has been telling me about his sanatorium in the South of France. He has suggested that Miss Pitt-Messanger might benefit from sunshine and sea bathing. I am inclined to agree with him.'

As Dr Morris was being shown out, Inspector Jebb arrived. The two men knew each other well and Morris gave him a brief account of Maud's suicide attempt before getting into his ancient Austin and driving off. It was after one in the morning and, in the end, there was nothing for Jebb to do but examine the glass case from which the dagger had been stolen and take brief statements from Sir Simon Castlewood and his guests. He agreed that questioning the servants was something better done the next day.

'You are absolutely sure it has not merely been lost or mislaid, Sir Simon?' he asked.

'We will search the house from top to bottom tomorrow but I really don't think it could have been.'

'Have you a photograph of the dagger which we can circulate to dealers in this sort of antiquity?'

'Yes, certainly. All the important finds from any archaeological dig are photographed and catalogued.'

'So you can let me have a detailed description of the dagger? Presumably it was very valuable?'

'Very valuable, Inspector. It was unique and therefore, I hope, unsaleable.' Sir Simon was rapidly recovering from the double shock of the theft and Maud's attempted suicide and his tone was almost patronizing. He was, after all, a Justice of the Peace.

4

Despite the glories of her bedroom and Psyche keeping guard over her as she slept, Verity had a restless night. As dawn dispatched the shadows, she lay staring up at the ceiling trying to make sense of what had happened the previous evening. Maud, unable to get over her father's death, had tried to kill herself. It was natural that she should be grieving – her grief exacerbated by the circumstances in which he died – but Verity was sure there was more to it than that. Perhaps there was guilt given that, at least according to Virginia, she hated him for depriving her of life as she wanted to lead it.

On an impulse, she got out of bed and went to the window and looked out over the garden. In the cold light of early morning, the lawn running down to a belt of trees looked silver – cool and calming. She washed her face under Psyche's amused, rather quizzical gaze, then slipped on a shirt, slacks and a jersey. She tiptoed downstairs and made her way to the front door. It was locked and there was no key in the door. Frustrated, she went into the drawing-room. She seemed to remember that the windows had not been secured and she was right. She opened one, sticking out her tongue as she did so at the plaster panel by Gilbert Ledward of a naked man standing on a column looking up at a squadron of aeroplanes. Sir Simon had told her it represented the modern world's debt to classical civilization but it looked to her like a phallic symbol – a typical male fantasy of aggression. It reminded her, uncomfortably, of the horror of modern warfare. She jumped down three or four feet on to the wet grass and her canvas shoes were immediately soaked. For no very good reason, except sheer delight at being free of the house, she started to run. By the time she reached the trees she was sweating, though her feet were cold. She stopped, turned round and looked back at the house. It had a strange beauty despite its aggressive modernity and the great hall lay alongside it like an ocean liner.

A hand came over her mouth to stifle a scream and another pulled her back into the shadow of the trees. She shook herself and dug her heel into her assailant's unseen ankle.

'Little vixen!' a voice said as she was released. She turned to see that her attacker was Graham Harvey. He was stroking his leg and smiling wryly. Verity was furiously angry. 'How dare you jump on me like that! You gave me the most awful shock. Anyway, what are you doing here?'

'I may as well ask what *you* are doing here. My cottage is just a quarter of a mile away and when I can't sleep I like to walk in the garden. What about you? Why have you left your comfortable bourgeois bed to wander in the cool of the morning? Perhaps you couldn't sleep either?'

Verity was still angry but she was also getting cold. 'I would give anything for coffee. My feet are soaking. I had no idea the dew would be so heavy.' He looked at her for a moment and then turned, motioning her to follow him.

The cottage, though small, was comfortable enough. There was a primitive-looking cooker on which a kettle sat. A pile of books lay on the floor. She noticed one was the bestseller no Marxist writer could be without: Stalin's *Measures for Liquidating Trotskyites and other Double-Dealers*. Beneath it, she could see a well-thumbed copy of Lenin's *Socialism and War* and, rather surprisingly, a polemic on the nature of Communism by Trotsky. Harvey told her to take off her shoes and gave her a dirty-looking towel with which to wipe them. There seemed to be no running water because he took the kettle out to the back door and there was the sound of water being poured into it from a can.

'There's a well,' he explained grudgingly. 'The water's sweet but it's not so easy having a bath.'

She recognized that he was trying to be civil so she refrained from making a smart remark indicating that she had noticed as much at dinner the previous evening. She spied a pile of paper beside a small typewriter. 'Is that your book? Tell me about it.'

'You don't have to be polite, you know.'

'I had no intention of being polite. I am still waiting for you to apologize for attacking me. You might have given me a heart attack.' He smiled a little sourly but made no effort to apologize. 'Anyway, I'd like to hear more about it.'

'Well, if you really want to know, it's an attack on the whole rotten thing – the way we live now.'

'I see.'

'No you don't. I'm not sure I do. It's the rage. It seems to blur my vision. I know I should be more effective if I were cool and clinical but I just can't be.'

'That's what I feel about the war in Spain,' she admitted.

'I really did like your book, you know. I liked it because it was so angry. I only came to dinner to meet you.'

'You didn't show it,' she said, gratified but still suspicious.

'When I saw you dolled up in all your finery with all those men leering at you – I don't know, it just made me mad. I wanted to smash that man's face in but, of course, I can't.'

'Whose face? Roddy's?'

'No. He's just an oaf. One of those bad actors who come on stage in the first scene and say, "What ho! Anyone for tennis?"'

She giggled. He had an unexpected gift for mimicry. 'I don't see you as a regular theatre-goer.'

'Why should I be? Even if I had the money I wouldn't want to see rubbish by fairies like Noel Coward. Why isn't anyone writing plays about what is *really* happening in England?'

'Like Shaw?'

'Yes, but he goes in for satire. I want . . . I want anger. I want to make greedy pigs like Castlewood lift their snouts out of the trough for long enough to see what is going on right under their noses. When I was on the Clyde last year I saw things which . . . burned my eyes. Children starving . . . literally starving and living – if you can call it living – in dank basements without light.' He was becoming excited and Verity, who the night before had considered him ugly, now found him disturbing, almost attractive. 'I say – have you come across a fellow called Bill Brandt – a photographer? I met him in Sheffield. He was photographing everything he saw. He gave me this one.'

He threw over a creased photograph of three dirty, thin-faced children peering out of a basement window. 'Stepney. It breaks your heart, doesn't it?'

She looked at it and then at him. 'And this is what your book is about? Is it a novel – *Love on the Dole*?' She was referring to Arthur Greenwood's bestselling account of surviving poverty.

'No, it's a polemic. Or it will be if I ever get to finish it.'

'Last night you said you had finished it.'

'I had to,' he grinned, immediately looking younger. 'I couldn't let those goats think I was a complete failure. I have all these notes but, when I get down to pulling them together, they just won't . . . I don't know.'

'I had the same sort of problem when I was writing my book on Spain. I couldn't make it come out right. There was just too much to say and I didn't know how to put into words what I had seen.'

'But you *did* finish it.'

'I met a wise woman – she's dead now – who gave me some advice. I can't even say exactly what it was but somehow it broke a barrier and I suddenly found myself writing. It was a blessed release, I remember that much.'

'Are you writing another one?'

'I have thought about it but it seems almost too late for books. There's a war coming which will bring everything tumbling down around our ears for better or worse.'

'You are probably right,' Harvey said despondently. 'Franco looks as if he has won the war in Spain. I think I'd like to die on the barricades. To die in Madrid!'

Verity looked at him suspiciously. 'It's not very romantic – dying.'

Graham looked sheepish. 'No, sorry. I was being self-indulgent. Of course,' he said, sounding more cheerful, 'Mikhail Bakunin said that the lust for destruction is a creative lust. Perhaps Armageddon will herald the revolution.'

'I didn't mean it isn't worth you finishing your book. Didn't Sir Simon say it's about politics?'

'It's about the *failure* of politics and politicians. In fact, I've called it *A Study in Failure*.'

'My friend, Edward Corinth, whom you despise so much, thinks Churchill will be our saviour when the war comes.'

Harvey's lip curled. 'Churchill! He's the worst of them.'

'That's what I think, too,' Verity said eagerly. 'He did his best to destroy the General Strike.'

69

'And he succeeded. He's a Fascist. I've got a few pages here of things he has written, his wit and wisdom!' he added ironically. He riffled through a thick wodge of paper until he found what he was looking for. 'Listen to this – his solution to poverty: "The unnatural and increasingly rapid growth of the feeble-minded and insane classes, coupled as it is with a steady restriction among the thrifty, energetic and superior stocks constitutes a national and race danger which it is impossible to exaggerate . . . I feel that the source from which the stream of madness is fed should be cut off and sealed up before another year has passed." That was twenty years ago but listen to this about the Arabs, and from someone who fought in the trenches. "I do not understand the squeamishness about the use of gas. I am strongly in favour of using poison gas against uncivilized tribes." Churchill's what is called a social Darwinist which seems to mean that his class must subjugate every other class and race. It's sickening stuff.'

'But Edward says he stands up to the Fascists.'

'He is on record as having admired both Hitler and Mussolini. He now calls himself a Zionist but he said this of the Jews: "They constitute a worldwide conspiracy for the overthrow of civilization and the reconstitution of society on the basis of arrested development and envious malevolence."'

'He said that?'

'On the record.'

'So you don't share Dominic Montillo's belief in racial improvement?'

'That man is truly sinister. I felt I was dining among wolves last night.'

'I thought you liked Sir Simon but you call him a pig?'

'I owe him for this.' Harvey waved his hand at the cottage. 'He means well but, come the revolution, he'll be one of the first to be strung up.' He smiled grimly and Verity shivered. He might be joking but she did not think so. He was eaten up with hatred and she thought that, under certain circumstances, he would be capable of killing Sir Simon Castlewood himself. 'He heard about my being unable to finish my book because I had nowhere to live and nothing to eat and he lent me this. I am grateful but I don't like being grateful and I don't like him. That stuff he was telling you about at dinner – Tibet and his Aryan heritage . . . that poisonous nonsense. Bruno Berger, who's behind it, is a Nazi – a member of Himmler's SS. Castlewood's getting into something he shouldn't and I'd like to help him see it for what it is but he'd never listen to me. I'm just his fool and jester. He likes having me around to insult him and his friends. It makes him feel good to have a tame Communist at his table. When I said that about you being a traitor to the cause eating his food, I meant me, of course. I'm betraying everything I believe in by taking his crust.'

'Well, why don't you just leave? If it's money . . .'

'It's not just money. I have to stay near . . .' He hesitated.

'Near what? Near whom?'

'It doesn't matter. I will leave soon, but not just yet.'

Verity decided not to probe further. Instead she said, 'Sir Simon is quite taken in by this man Montillo.' She sipped her coffee. It was surprisingly strong and bone-warmingly hot. She stopped shivering.

'As I understand it, Montillo wants perfect physical specimens like Isolde Swann and her jackass of a boyfriend to breed a new race of supermen. And she's agreed to have her baby there.'

'She must be mad!' Verity said, scandalized. 'Is she pregnant?'

'Not that I know of. They're probably both virgins. They are planning to marry next month – from Swifts Hill. Roddy "hasn't a bean", he told me.'

'I can see it all!' she exclaimed. 'They are to be used as a breeding experiment so they must marry and Isolde must give birth under Simon and Montillo's control.'

'You may be right. I expect Montillo will insist on accompanying them on their honeymoon to make sure he knows how to impregnate her.' They both laughed but Harvey added, 'To be fair, Montillo is a good surgeon. A friend of a friend of mine who had a child born with two fingers stuck together went to him and now you wouldn't know the child ever had a deformity.'

'I refuse to be fair,' Verity said firmly. 'Montillo's a Nazi. That's what Hitler is trying to do – breed a super-race. I wouldn't be surprised if he doesn't steal Isolde's baby off her. He has some idea of bringing up children away from their parents. He says it was what the Spartans did.'

'Hang on,' Harvey expostulated, now suddenly the 'reasonable' one. 'I think you are exaggerating. He's an unpleasant man but this is England, not Germany.'

They were silent for a few moments and Verity held out her mug for more coffee. When Harvey had finished pouring it from his battered metal pot, she said meditatively, 'So it was Sir Simon, not Roddy, whose face you wanted to smash in?'

'Yes, but not because of his views on race.'

'Why then?'

'Because he was pawing you, if you must know.' He sounded disgusted with himself.

'Me? What do you care? I thought you hated me.'

'No, damn it. I ought to hate you because you call yourself a Communist and then I watch you kowtowing to these people but . . .' He got up and came over to her. For a second, she was sure he was going to kiss her and she had no idea how she would respond. In fact, all he did was say, 'But I don't.'

Verity's attempt to regain her bedroom without attracting attention proved a failure. The open window had been discovered by Lampton who had raised Sir Simon and he had come down in his dressing-gown to survey the scene of what might be another crime, or at least an attempted crime. He had immediately gone to check that none of his other precious artefacts had been stolen and was relieved to find everything there – except, of course, the dagger. Roddy had a gun and, as Verity arrived, was setting off to search the grounds with Montillo. Isolde stood behind them, looking fetching in her nightwear.

'Gosh! I hope you didn't think . . . I felt like a walk – it was so beautiful this morning and I couldn't find the key to the front door. I hope I haven't . . . I'll go and dress. Won't be long.'

Verity slid up the stairs, leaving them open-mouthed but mercifully silent. Hadn't they ever heard of a guest wanting an early-morning walk, she thought crossly?

It began to rain about ten so there would be no tennis, for which Verity was secretly grateful. She was not very good at games. She had played a little tennis at school but being short had not helped her game and she did not like doing things she was not good at. She recognized it as a weakness but not one she intended to do anything about. If she had been asked to play, she could have claimed she still was not fit enough but that would have been a lie and she despised lying to avoid social embarrassment. Although she had now physically recovered from her wound – just the occasional pain in her shoulder when she least expected it – mentally she was more fragile. The fact was – and she faced it with her customary honesty – she was afraid to return to Spain. Each time she returned she had found it more and more difficult and after Guernica she felt she had had enough.

She had an idea, which she knew to be irrational, that she had escaped death on at least three occasions but, if she tempted fate again, she might not be so lucky. When she was in the front line with the bombs falling and bullets flying, she was all right. The adrenaline kicked in and her obsessive desire to see what there was to be seen and report it to – it had to be said – a largely indifferent world made her forget the danger. The waiting, the apprehension was bad, however. Gerda Meyer, who had died beside her in Guernica, reduced to bloodied pulp by a Luftwaffe pilot, had told her once that danger was a drug and she had to have her 'fix'. She courted danger in the certain knowledge that it would be the death of her. Verity was not like that. Her courage, she had begun to think, was of limited supply and the gauge was showing empty.

Added to that there was something inexpressibly sad in witnessing the death of a good cause. She had no idea how long the Republic would fight but no reasonable person could avoid seeing that Franco and the Rebels had won and that it was only a matter of months before Madrid fell. A guerilla war fought from the mountains could continue for years but the real war was lost. Much more important and something she would never confess – not even to Edward – was that the cause for which the Republic had taken up arms – the defence of a democratically elected government – had been contaminated. The Republicans now took their orders from Moscow and these included 'liquidating' anyone who opposed the Stalinist line. She had begun to believe that the Communists hated other left-wing parties more than they hated the Fascists. She decided to ask her employer, Lord Weaver, if she could report for the *New Gazette* from some other country facing the Nazi threat. There were plenty to choose from. Her German was almost non-existent but that could be remedied. She would take a Berlitz course as soon as she was back in London.

She sighed and looked out of the window. The rain streaked the glass. Virginia was playing Lexico with Mrs Cardew. Isolde was asleep on the sofa with *Vogue* clutched to her bosom. The men had donned Wellington boots and gone out for a walk. Verity decided she would go and check on Maud.

Maud was not asleep. She was lying on her back, gazing forlornly at the ceiling. A battered E. Phillips Oppenheim shocker with a lurid cover lay beside her. Verity picked it up. '*Slane's Long Shots* – any good?'

'I don't know – I don't seem to be able to concentrate on anything.'

'I came to return your diary.'

'My diary?'

'Yes, I found it in the bathroom when you . . . after you were found by Dr Morris and Mr Montillo. I don't know why but I thought you might not want anyone else to see it, so I decided to hang on to it until you were better.'

'Why should I mind if anyone read it? There's nothing in it.'

'No, of course not. Except . . . I swear I only glanced at it but . . . but it is empty except for some initials – E.P.M. Is that your father?'

'His initials, yes.'

'His Christian name was . . .?'

'Edgar . . .' she muttered. 'Not that anyone ever called him that. His people – the few that were close to him . . . who worked with him – they called him the Prof or just E.P.M.' A little colour came into Maud's cheeks. 'What did you think? That I had a lover?'

'No, I mean, why not? Why shouldn't you have a lover? Wasn't Temperley your lover?' Maud blushed scarlet. 'Oh God, I'm sorry. Let's talk about something else . . . or would you rather I go? I can see why you don't like me – I'm about as tactful as a rogue elephant.'

'You heard that story, did you?' Maud said truculently but Verity had an impression she was quite proud of having a reputation as a breaker of hearts.

'Is it true?'

'It's true. In the desert these things can happen. Not much competition there, you see – not many women.'

'You are always putting yourself down. Were you . . .?'

'Lovers? Yes, we were if you must know.'

'You kept it secret from your father but he found out?'

'Guess how he found out?'

'Someone saw you together?'

'No, I got pregnant.'

'Gosh!' Verity's eyes widened. 'So what happened?'

'My father sent me back to England and I had an abortion,' she said bleakly.

'You couldn't have married Temperley and kept the child . . .?'

'No. My father wouldn't hear of it. He got in a rage and said I was a whore and . . . much worse. He was very frightening when he was angry. It's different for you. You do what you want. That's one of the things I envy about you.'

'And I suppose there was no way you could have had the baby . . .?'

'It would have ruined my reputation and my poor bastard – how would he ever have held his head up? He – or worse, she – would never have forgiven me.'

'What about Temperley?'

'He didn't know until it was all over. It affected his health.'

'He died of cholera?'

'That's as good a word to put on a death certificate as anything else.'

Verity was silent. She knew anything she tried to say in the way of condolence would not be welcome.

Maud went on. 'The ancient Egyptians believed that, if you spoke the name of a dead loved one, you would make them live again. I wish it were true. I wish . . . I wish I had something . . . someone to remember him by. Can you guess who carried out the abortion?'

'Not . . . not Montillo? But that was what – twenty years ago?'

'He was a young doctor on the make in those days. He has never been averse to doing the odd abortion,' she said wryly. 'He had – has – a lot of smart clients who don't fancy risking some back-street abortionist.'

'He operated in England?'

'In the South of France. It's easier to pay off the police there and rich women can say they are going for a rest cure on the Riviera rather than having some embarrassing "illness" in London.'

75

'And you have never been in love again? You're clever and . . .'

'What man looks for brains in a woman?' Maud said with a snort of laughter. 'Anyway, as it happens . . . why do you think I am here? Do you think I wanted to meet Montillo again?'

'I thought Virginia . . .'

'She is very kind but I still wouldn't have come except for him.'

'Him?' Verity suddenly had a flash of inspiration. 'You mean Graham Harvey?'

Maud nodded. 'Does that surprise you?'

'No, I think . . .'

'He doesn't like you,' she said smugly.

Verity thought of their dawn talk in his cottage. Was Maud the reason he had said he could not leave – "not yet"? 'I think that behind that sarcastic manner of his lies a kind heart and a keen brain. Or am I being sentimental?'

'No, you're not,' Maud said, 'but I am surprised you can see it.'

'You love each other?'

'Yes.'

'So why did you try to kill yourself? Why don't you get married and live happily ever after? Your father can't stop you now.'

'No, and he would have hated Graham,' she said with obvious pleasure.

'So . . .?'

'Graham won't marry me. He says he's too poor to marry and, in any case, he thinks marriage is bourgeois.'

'But you have plenty of money now.'

'Can't you see? That makes it worse. He could never bear to live off a woman.'

'So it's important his book is a success?'

'Yes.' Maud's eyes brightened. 'Even if he doesn't make a lot of money out of it, publishing it will make him feel . . .'

'Worthy of you?'

'Don't laugh, but yes. He keeps saying he's a failure but I tell him he can't be if I love him. He likes that.'

'Why are you telling me all this? I thought you didn't like me.'

'I don't dislike you. I'm just jealous you live the life you want to lead. I wanted to ask you . . .' She hesitated.

'What?' Verity was curious. What could she do for this unhappy couple?

'If you could help him finish it . . . the book, I mean, and get it published . . .'

She was pleading and Verity had no idea how to respond. If she did what Maud asked, might not Graham – it sounded so arrogant even to think of it and she would never say it – but might he not fall in love with her? And that would destroy his and Maud's happiness. 'I'll willingly help get it published – not that I think he'll need help from me but he doesn't need me to help him write it. He says he's finished it.' Maud could not be allowed to know that Graham had told her he hadn't even started it.

'I don't think he has finished it,' she said sadly. 'I'm not sure he ever will.'

'I can't help Graham with his book,' she said decisively. 'We're . . . we're different . . . we look at things differently.' In fact what she really meant was that they were too similar in their outlook on the world. 'In any case, I have a job to do. I'm a journalist . . . And he would not want me to help him.' She knew she was offering too many excuses.

'Of course,' Maud said meekly. 'I expect you are right. I hope you didn't mind me asking?'

'No, of course not. As I say, once it's finished I'll help all I can.'

They were silent again, thinking about what had been said.

'So you tried to kill yourself because Graham won't marry you?'

'I wasn't really serious about killing myself.' Maud smiled almost naughtily. 'I knew Dominic would save me.'

'You wanted Graham to feel . . .?'

'No, I wasn't blackmailing him . . . I don't know – I just felt very low.'

Verity glanced at the bedside table. 'Are you taking these to pick you up?'

'Benzedrine? Yes, it's quite a new thing. Montillo got them for me.'

'Well, be very careful. I used them in Spain when I was very tired but had to be alert. I took too many and started getting hallucinations.' She laughed. 'My enemies would say most of my reporting is an hallucination but it isn't. It's so cosy, here in

England, what I have seen in Spain must seem unreal – like a nightmare.'

Maud's eyes widened. 'I will be careful. They do make me feel funny sometimes.'

There was a pause and then Verity said, 'Has he been to see you?'

'Graham? No, he probably doesn't know yet.' She sounded like a naughty child – flirtatious and rather desperate.

Verity felt guilty. Why had it not occurred to her to tell Graham about Maud cutting her wrists? 'I'll make sure he knows,' she said. 'Can I ask you a question?'

'Yes.'

'Tell me if I am being impertinent, but did you love your father? Ginny says he wasn't very kind to you.'

'Ginny's a good woman but she talks about things she knows nothing about.'

'He wasn't cruel to you . . . your father?'

'He never thought so! It's not fair to say he was ever unkind to me deliberately – except for that one time. It was just that he lived for his work. He was always searching for that one great find which would give him a place in archaeological history . . . he wanted to be another Schliemann.'

Verity tried to look as if she knew who Schliemann was.

'Don't say you don't know who Schliemann is?' Maud said, quite shocked.

'I think I do . . .'

'He discovered Troy. He dressed his wife in what he said were Helen's jewels. He called his children, poor mites, Agamemnon and Andromache. At least my father didn't call me Sheba!' Maud seemed quite animated and Verity was pleased that she had made her smile.

'I know what you mean,' she said soberly. 'I love my father but it's difficult sometimes.'

'Why?'

'He's a lawyer . . . a barrister. He only represents what he sees as good causes. I admire that. He defends the indefensible . . . Fenians, murderers . . . anybody who no one else will help. He spends his money on supporting the *Daily Worker*, which I write for so I know it doesn't make any money.' She laughed to show she was not complaining. 'I love him but I never see him.'

'And your mother. . .?'

'She died when I was born. I suppose I killed her but I am being melodramatic – forgive me. I like to think it gives me an excuse for not leading a normal life.'

Maud was interested now. 'You mean being a journalist and not settling down with a husband and children?'

'I do. It's not approved of.'

'Not even by . . . by your friend, Lord Edward?'

'He says he doesn't mind and I honestly think he believes it but, of course, he *does* mind.'

'That's why you won't marry him?'

'Yes. I think it would be unfair on him and on me. You see, I love to be free. I can't bear to be chained . . . not even to someone I love.'

Maud looked thoughtful. 'I understand. It was different for me. I could not escape. I did not want to escape . . . not for most of the time anyway. I loved my father. I wanted to help him in his work but in the end, I suppose I thought I had sacrificed myself for . . . for a heap of bones.'

'What about your mother?'

'She died when I was seven, She was what they would call now a hysteric. I think she was just selfish. Oh sorry, I ought not to say such things about my mother but whenever she wanted something and was frustrated she would scream.'

'Literally?'

'Yes, literally. She had migraines. When she got one she would scream like an ill-behaved, dispossessed child. My father would have to massage her neck for hours. She used it as an excuse not to sleep with him.'

'But you . . .'

'Yes, I was born . . . I don't know how because they never shared a room. She never forgave me for the pain I had caused her. It's a terrible thing to say but I think I was glad when she died.'

'And he had his triumphs . . . your father. I read about them in his obituary.'

'He was lucky. There has to be luck in archaeology. You can dig for months . . . years even and find nothing, while someone with half your skill can dig a few thousand yards away and find gold. Actual gold. My father's very first big find was when he was working with Leonard Wooley in Ur of the Chaldees. He found several tombs . . . a royal cemetery. Abraham's city they called it. Among the first things he found was a gold dagger and sheath – maybe five thousand years old. The hilt was decorated with lapis lazuli and studded with gold. The blade was burnished gold in a sheath of solid gold, its front intricately carved in filigree. It was the most beautiful thing I had ever seen. Then he found a gold wig that a king would have worn. It was two thousand years older than Tutenkhamun.'

'It must have been wonderful. When did your father become involved with Sir Simon?'

'He financed the 1933/34 season. He hoped to prove some ridiculous theory he has on race.'

'Did your father believe in it . . . this theory?'

'He went along with it. He needed the money. He would have said anything to get it.'

'So he wasn't a friend of Sir Simon's?'

'My father had no friends,' Maud said bitterly. 'He had disciples and he had enemies . . . a bit like Jesus,' she added, making a choking sound which might have been a laugh.

'And Mr Temperley . . .?'

'Sidney found this tomb at Nineveh . . . but I don't want to talk about it. My father claimed . . . he said he found it. What did it matter? It was my father's dig. No one was going to cheat him of the glory but . . . you can't imagine how important it is to find something newsworthy. Most of the time archaeologists just turn up rubbish – I mean literally rubbish. From ancient rubbish dumps you can piece together how a whole civilization lived, worked and died, but it's not dramatic. It's not beautiful. It is only interesting because it is so old . . . because it survived.'

At that moment there was a knock at the door and, without waiting for an answer, Virginia came in with Dr Morris.

'Oh good,' she said, 'I see you are feeling better, Maud? I hope Verity hasn't been tiring you?'

'No. I *am* feeling better. Miss Browne and I have been talking of fathers. It seems we have more in common than I had at first imagined.'

5

Saturday morning found Edward at rather a loose end. He woke early and, feeling a little queasy, made himself a cup of tea, dosed himself with Lacteol and then Eno's for good measure and went back to bed with the paper. After returning from Chartwell, he had spent a long evening at Brooks drinking and smoking too much and playing backgammon increasingly badly. It was hardly surprising he had woken with a headache. There was nothing in the newspaper and he fell into an uneasy doze. Twenty minutes later he woke with a start and found he had a stiff neck. He tossed away *The Times* in disgust and jumped out of bed. The sun was shining and he did not feel in the least like staying in London for the weekend. He did his stretching exercises and wondered, as he always did when he was flat on his back with his legs in the air, if he was getting old. He tried to work out why he was so restless and came to the conclusion that it was the almost tangible *absence* of Verity that so disturbed him. He imagined her surrounded by tweed-suited hearties enjoying herself and playing fragile, which she did sometimes when she wanted to ingratiate herself with the male sex. It didn't work with him, he told himself, pursing his lips. He knew her too well. She was as tough a nut as ever fell off a tree and cracked open a man's skull. But then, he reminded himself, she could be deliciously vulnerable and he would want to protect her. Was that an act? No, she was complicated and that made her interesting.

Then there was Fenton – he missed having his valet bring him his lapsang souchong in the morning, knowing instinctively when he was awake and shamming sleep. The tea would be exactly the right temperature – not too strong, not too weak –

and, ten minutes later without fail, Fenton would inform him that his bath was drawn. That, too, would be just the right temperature so that he might be tempted to sing 'Stormy Weather', which he did execrably but to his own satisfaction. All through the day there were these little rituals, culminating in a whisky and soda dead on six o'clock which he drank before dressing to go out to the club or to dinner. If he were not in the mood to go out, Fenton would grill him a chop and he would sit in his smoking jacket pretending he was as much an old fogey as his older brother, the Duke of Mersham.

He wondered idly if he could ever bear to live with Verity for any length of time. He loved her. Was it exaggerating to say she obsessed him? But, in many respects, a valet was much to be preferred to a wife – particularly if that wife were as messy as Verity. He stooped and with one finger lifted a pair of her knickers off the floor. He caught a scent of her body and – absurdly – looking round to see if he was being observed, pressed them to his face and breathed deeply. Annoyed with himself and faintly disgusted, he chucked them in a corner. Then it occurred to him that Fenton was due back from Margate the next morning and it wouldn't do to have him clean up after Verity.

Edward knew some men would laugh at him for minding what his valet thought but he and Fenton had a relationship based on mutual respect for each other's feelings. He retrieved the knickers and then went round the flat collecting up further evidence of Verity's residence. He thought, ruefully, that she would never get away with murder. She left too much evidence behind her. He tossed all her stuff into the battered suitcase which, until yesterday, had accompanied her on every journey and then pushed it into a cupboard. Rather to his surprise, Verity, who normally did not care about such things, had looked critically at the case the day before and gone out and bought a smart one into which she had tipped a few necessary garments before catching the train to Swifts Hill with Mrs Cardew.

He paced about smoking, unable to decide what to do. Eventually, he decided he must get out of his rooms or he would suffocate. He went to the telephone in the hall, raised the receiver, hesitated and replaced it on the stand. He returned to the drawing-room and poured himself a gin and tonic though it was still only ten. Glass in hand, he walked indecisively back into the hall and eyed the black Bakelite warily. Finally, he made up his mind and put in a trunk call to Mersham. He had an excuse for bothering his brother and sister-in-law, he told himself. His nephew Frank was due back from New York – might already be back – and he could show avuncular concern without revealing he was simply at a loose end.

The Duke hated the telephone and employed a butler – Edward sometimes thought – solely to answer it for him. So it was with surprise that he heard Gerald's clipped voice shout, 'Yes? Who is it?' The Duke always shouted down the telephone on the grounds that the person he was speaking to was too far away to hear him unless he did. 'Ned, is that you? Amazing thing, these instruments. I hadn't even picked up the what-d'you-call-it and there you are.'

From which incoherent babble Edward was made aware that his brother had been just about to ring him. 'I say, Gerald – what's the news of young Frank?'

'Well, that's exactly what I was telephoning you about. Are you still there?' There was a sound, which might have been the telephone being shaken, and then the Duke's voice again even louder. 'Can you hear me?. You know how I hate these bally things. We are at our wits' end and . . . and . . .'

'Hang on a minute, Gerry. Is Frank ill? Where is he?'

'He's here at Mersham – arrived two days ago. Of course he's not ill. Why should he be ill? He's just been on holiday.'

'So what's the problem?'

'Oh dash it! We don't know what the problem is. He just lies on his bed and stares at the ceiling . . .'

'Is he eating?'

'Not according to his mother. I can't say I have noticed anything.'

'Sounds to me he's in love.'

There was a strangled cry at the other end of the line. 'Whatd'y'mean?'

'I'm sorry, Gerry, but it sounds like a bad case of love. I know the symptoms – uninterested in food, lying about mooning . . . Has he said anything to you about a girl?'

'No. I say, Ned, could you possibly come down for the night and talk to the boy? The thing is, he's going up to Trinity – at least I think he is. But he keeps on saying he's going back to America . . . says he is going to be an American. I ask you!'

Edward smiled to himself, remembering his own early passions which at the time had seemed of world-shattering significance. Could he now even recall the names of the girls? He closed his eyes and visualized a black-haired buxom girl who always smelt slightly of bleach – the daughter of a college servant – who had relieved him of his virginity. Now, what had she been called? Something out of a novel by Walter Scott . . . Ah! he had it: Rebecca. He sighed. Wasn't there something . . . some disturbances called the Rebecca riots? He had written an essay on the subject for his tutor, G.M. Trevelyan. He realized with a start that his brother had ceased wailing at him and was calling for an answer.

'You still there, Ned? Say, you'll come . . .'

Mersham Castle – whenever he saw it after an absence – made his heart beat a little faster. He regarded it as his home. It was where he had spent the happiest days of his childhood. He had explored every cranny and, he was sure, knew it more intimately than his elder brother though nobody could love it more than Gerald. He stopped the Lagonda – as he often did – just beyond the gates, turned off the engine, took off his goggles and flying helmet and drank in the evening air. He lit a cigarette and contemplated the house, trying to pin down its allure. It was seven o'clock and the light was softening. The ancient brick had begun to blur at the edges as though it might one day vanish into thin air. He had never found adequate words to describe it and had therefore given up trying. Epithets such as 'ethereal', 'floating', 'fairy-tale', were used by visitors with wearying regularity but none captured the mystery of Mersham Castle, built over three hundred years ago by the Swedish lady-in-waiting to a virgin queen.

He recalled Duncan's words outside Macbeth's house – 'This castle has a pleasant seat, the air nimbly and sweetly recommends itself unto our gentle senses.' And how had Banquo confirmed his king's commendation? 'This guest of summer, the temple-haunting martlet, does approve.' He thought that, if ever he were to write a novel, he would call it *This Guest of Summer*.

Then he reminded himself that all this had been a forerunner to murder. Duncan had been murdered by his host – an unforgivable sin. Was pleasure always bought at such a cost?

He tossed his cigarette out on to the gravel and restarted the car. To coax and chastise a nephew was surely not such a high price to pay for a night or two in such a place.

'Ned!' The Duchess kissed him on the cheek. 'How good of you to come.' Edward was very fond of his sister in-law and squeezed her hand affectionately.

'Connie! How are you? I gather the boy is causing Gerald heartache?'

'He said you diagnosed love?'

'I did. If you leave us alone after dinner to play a rack or two . . .'

'Of course, and he is smoking too much – in his bedroom. He knows it upsets me when he smokes so he tries to hide it from me but he would never make a very good criminal. His sins find him out. Isn't that *Hamlet*?'

She was trying not to sound worried but Edward knew that Frank mattered more to her than anyone or anything else. He wanted to say that he thought the same about Verity – that she wasn't adept at concealing her tracks – but restrained himself for fear of provoking embarrassing questions.

At dinner the Duke was silent except for barking an occasional remark at Edward with reference to the imbecility of the Government, the iniquity of death duties, the outrageous behaviour of the Duke of Windsor who, according to *The Times*, was planning to meet Hitler in Berlin, but was perhaps most bitter at the local council which was doing its best to prevent him improving the farm workers' cottages.

Frank, who had greeted his uncle with a pleasant display of affection, had relapsed into dreamy silence. Edward eyed him speculatively as he made conversation with Connie on anodyne subjects such as the village fête and the new vicar who was said to be 'high church'.

With dinner at an end, Edward suggested a game of billiards to his nephew before they turned in. He hoped the invitation did not sound too premeditated.

They strolled downstairs to the billiard room, which was cool and restful.

'Mind if I smoke?' Frank said, a silver cigarette lighter in his hand. Edward was chalking his cue.

'Not at all, old chap.' Edward had given up trying to stop him smoking. After all, who was he to preach? He had smoked his first cigarette on his tenth birthday and had been sick as he leant over to blow out the candles on his cake. As far as he knew, it had not done him any harm in the long run. For fifteen minutes there was only the calming click of ivory ball cannonading with ivory ball to break the silence. Edward was content to let his nephew begin the conversation. Frank was playing with the careless confidence of one who could not mind less if he won or lost and consequently won. Edward, who rather fancied himself at billiards and had won the Club tournament three years in a row, could not hit a thing. Missing an easy pot, he threw down his cue in exasperation and went over to the side table to pour himself a brandy. Still not wanting to ask Frank directly if he were in love and, if so, with whom, he asked how he had got on in New York. The boy had been acting as a dogsbody for Lord Benyon.

'Bad business – Benyon being killed like that,' he said. 'Is it wrong to thank God that you remained in New York and did not accompany him to Germany?'

'Yes,' Frank said, showing genuine emotion for the first time, 'that was horrible. No one seems to know how it happened. Could he have been . . . assassinated, do you think? After all, they tried to kill him on the *Queen Mary*.'

Edward was dubious. 'They would have had better opportunities and, anyway, they had no motive to kill him, once it became known that Roosevelt would not help us rearm. In any case, they would not have deliberately destroyed the pride of their air force. The Hindenburg was a flying advertisement for German air superiority.'

'He was very good to me. Taught me a lot. I'll always be grateful to him. I was sorry not to have been in England for his memorial service.'

'Nothing happened in New York, then?'

'How do you mean? I met a lot of good chaps. People introduced me to people – you know how it is.'

'But you weren't tempted to stay on?'

'I'm going up to Cambridge in October, don't you remember?' Frank replied virtuously.

'Yes, of course. I am glad to hear it. You'll have a good time there. You missed the coronation. Your father looked very fine in his robes.'

'Yes, I meant to come back but, I don't know, I kept on putting it off. Missed the boat, you might say.'

There was a silence – rather awkward on Edward's side but apparently not on Frank's. To fill the silence, Edward told him a little about his meeting with Churchill – betraying no confidences – and asked him if he had heard the word 'eugenics'.

To his considerable surprise, Frank seemed excited by his uncle's casual question. He lost his otherworldliness and seemed energized by the word. He dropped his cigarette in an ashtray, put his cue down on the green baize and came to sit beside him in one of the battered brown-leather armchairs ranged about the room which Edward privately thought were more comfortable than any of the overstuffed chairs in the drawing-room.

'How funny you should mention eugenics, Uncle. The fact is I met the most ripping girl in New York called Miss Schuster-Slatt. She has studied the whole question of race regeneration and she made me think, I can tell you. She'll be in Cambridge in the autumn – the fall, they call it – which makes me quite eager to go up, don't y'know.'

'Is she reading for a degree or is she . . . ?'

'She's reading politics and economics, I think.'

'Where did you meet her – Miss Schuster-Slatt?' Edward asked mildly.

'I was taken by this girl to a meeting of . . . now, what was it called?'

'Which girl took you to the meeting?'

'I really can't remember. Some girl . . . what does it matter which girl?' There was an arrogance in his tone which made Edward wince. He knew what it was like to be an English 'lord' in New York. Everything – and that included women – came just that little bit too easily for the good of one's character. 'Now you've put it out of my mind. No, I remember. It was called the League for the Encouragement of Matrimonial Fitness.'

Edward wanted to laugh. Instead he inquired, 'Miss Schuster-Slatt was speaking?'

'She was – on the sterilization of the unfit.'

'And you found nothing . . . ugly about that?'

'No, why should I? Surely it makes perfect sense to strengthen the race by weeding out the weak and the imbecilic.'

Edward recognized that these were Miss Schuster-Slatt's words, not Frank's, but it still made him unhappy to hear him parroting them.

'You're not a fool, Frank,' he said sharply. 'Surely you see what is happening in Germany? That's just the sort of theory the Nazis use to justify the most terrible injustices. Who decides who is imbecilic? It is our duty to defend the weak – not destroy them.'

Frank seemed not a whit disturbed to find that he had awoken in his uncle something very much like anger. It had the effect of making him dig his heels in.

'All right, but don't lose your rag, Uncle. Sadie – Miss Schuster-Slatt – is not advocating murder, for goodness sake. She and her . . . colleagues are only concerned to improve the health of our society.'

'Whenever I hear the word "society", I shudder,' Edward said, realizing that he was in danger of losing his temper but unable to restrain himself. 'Society is made up of individuals who agree to live by certain rules. It's what the Communists and the Fascists have in common. They justify their most horrible policies – institutionalized murder very often – by saying it is for the good of society.'

'But, surely, my uncle died because he believed in our society,' Frank said haughtily. 'Are you saying patriotism is wrong?'

'No, of course not. Don't mention Franklyn's name in the same breath as your Miss Schuster-Slatt, I beg you. He was the best of us. I still say though that even patriotism can be misused. It's a slippery word. But that's beside the point. You know perfectly well what the Nazis are doing to the Jews and to others in "society" of whom they disapprove. You have heard of these camps into which people go without being charged with any crime and from which they never reappear?'

'I am not defending the Nazis. I just said . . .'

Edward unwisely lost control of himself. 'I should bloody well hope not,' he yelled. He got up from his chair, grabbed a cue and paced about the room.

'And do you fancy you love this Schuster-Slatt woman?' he demanded, even more unwisely.

'It is nothing to you if I do, Uncle. Now, I think I will go to bed, if you don't mind.'

As the door closed behind him, Edward snapped the cue across his knee in frustration. He had done exactly what he would have expected the boy's father to do and he would have tut-tutted and said 'How typical.' He should not have shouted at Frank but he loved him and could not bear to see him espouse views that were so abhorrent to him and, he would have hoped, to any civilized man. He told himself that Frank was a schoolboy and Cambridge would educate him, but it was alarming to hear that Miss Schuster-Slatt would be there. He felt suddenly despondent.

On the Sunday morning, they walked across the field to the little church which served the castle and the village to hear matins. The Duke had his own high-backed pew – in which he was wont to slumber – from where Edward was able to study the memorials to his ancestors, most of whom had died in battle from the Crusades to the Crimea. He was still angry and disgusted – with himself as much as with Frank – that his brother's sacrifice had been called into question. Franklyn's body had been brought back from France and buried in the family vault but a plaque on the wall noted that he had given his life for his country in the first weeks of September 1914. He had at least been spared those long dark years of trench warfare which had destroyed the minds and bodies of hundreds of thousands of young Englishmen.

Edward closed his eyes and pictured – as he had a thousand times before – his brother, revolver in hand, running across a green field. He had led his men against grey-cloaked figures kneeling behind a machine gun. He would have recognized it to be his duty – no question – but did he know he was running towards his own death and the death of most of the gallant fellows who followed him? Steel helmets had not yet been issued to British officers and the bullet which had plucked off his cap, with it plucked away his life. For Edward, and for all those left alive at the Armistice, this was the defining moment: England's little professional army utterly destroyed, vanished into thin air. Now, a new war threatened. The war which politicians had promised would never come because what they called the Great War was the conflict to end all conflicts. As Edward looked down the pew at Frank's profile, he wondered how he had dared be short with him the previous night. It looked as though he and his generation would be called upon to deal with the mess his uncle's generation had made of the world.

At lunch, he made every effort to be cheerful and suggested his nephew might like to stay with him in London for a few days. There was, of course, Mersham House in Hill Street but the Duke seldom used it unless he was attending the House of Lords for some debate about which he had strong feelings. Edward had put Frank up for his club and thought he might like to meet some of the younger members he did not already know. He was pleased that the boy seemed uninterested in 'doing the season' – a ritual he had endured under protest finding it demeaning – a marriage market in which deals were made with women hunting men down like frightened foxes. Frank had received a host of invitations to balls from mothers who judged that the next Duke of Mersham might make a suitable husband for their girl but he had accepted very few of them and actually gone to even fewer. It was as though his brief taste of danger, when he had run away to Spain to join the International Brigade, had made him awkward with boys of his own age and impatient with girls whose knowledge of the world was restricted to what their mothers gleaned from *Debrett*. And yet, Edward thought, his nephew must have his fun before the lights were turned off and the world was once again plunged into darkness.

Frank accepted his uncle's invitation and it was silently agreed between them to forget their little tiff over Miss Schuster-Slatt. In the broad light of day, she did not seem a serious threat. Edward had enough confidence in his nephew's good sense to believe that if she were what he thought she might be, Frank would soon be bored with her. Anything else he might say could make Frank attach himself to her more firmly rather than give her up. Before he left for London, he was able to have a few words with his brother in private and reassure him that Frank was suffering pangs of puppy love which should be ignored.

Edward was never quite sure how the row had started. They were sitting in the drawing-room in Albany later that evening. He had been waxing enthusiastic about Winston Churchill but become aware that Verity was not chirrupping comments – in fact had been completely silent.

'What is it, V? You look as though you've sucked on a lemon. I suppose you are going to tell me that you still hold the view that Churchill is an "enemy of the people" – isn't that how you described him? Forgive me for saying so, but that's utter nonsense and, if you met the man, you would know it.'

It was quite the wrong thing to say. Verity puffed herself up like an angry toad and let him have it.

'He *is* an enemy of the people and I have no intention of forgiving you for allowing yourself to be mesmerized by him. And I certainly have no intention of meeting him.'

She went on to give him a summary of Graham Harvey's views on Churchill's shortcomings and Harvey would have been proud of the way she had memorized his arguments. When she had finished, they looked at each other with dislike, each wondering how they could possibly have thought they were in love with someone so pig-headed.

'That's not you speaking, is it?' Edward said at last, his nose looking more hawk-like than usual.

'What do you mean? Of course it's me speaking.'

'But all those quotations carefully taken out of context . . . All those "views" lumped together from thirty years of politics. I bet if someone had collected your more idiotic "statements of fact",' he went on icily, 'it would make as much sense as . . . Comrade Stalin's.'

Verity had never seen Edward so angry and it was borne in upon her that Churchill had become very important to him. He was usually so wary of politicians and cynical about their motives but she saw that, for some reason, he had let his defences drop and taken this man, whom all good democrats detested, to his bosom. And, quite simply, she would not have it.

'It is true that while I was at Swifts Hill, I met a man called Graham Harvey who is writing a book about Churchill and he gave me some interesting facts and figures – but the views are mine. He merely gave me evidence to back up my instinctive dislike of the man.'

'Well,' said Edward with a great effort, 'let's agree to differ, shall we? Tell me what you found out about Pitt-Messanger's death.'

Coldly, Verity related the events of the weekend including what Maud had told her of her affair with Sidney Temperley, the abortion carried out by Dominic Montillo and Maud's suicide attempt. She mentioned finding the diary in the bathroom, empty except for Pitt-Messanger's initials against April 27th.

'I checked to see if it was her father's birthday but he was born in October and Maud in June so it must be another date important to her.'

Edward listened in silence and, when she had finished, said, '"And most of all would I flee from the cruel madness of love, the honey of poison-flowers and all the measureless ill."'

'You are quoting poetry again! I have told you before it irritates me.'

'Sorry, it's Tennyson's *Maud*. It just popped out. I wish there was some way of meeting Simon Castlewood. I have grave doubts about this Foundation of his. This doctor fellow – Montillo – is, I believe, a charlatan and maybe worse. We agree on that at least, I imagine.'

'Certainly, and there is no problem about you meeting Castlewood. I was asked to invite you to a cricket match next weekend. He makes up a team every year, apparently, to play the village side. I said I was sure you would come but that I would send a telegram to confirm.'

'Very good! Do we know who else will be playing?'

'Edmund Cardew, Roddy Maitland for sure. I don't know who else.'

Edward clicked his fingers. 'I wonder if I could bring young Frank with me. He might benefit from a change of scene and he loves cricket. He was in the eleven, you know.'

'Why does he need a change of scene? I thought he was going up to Cambridge in a couple of months.'

'He is but he has fallen in love with a Miss Schuster-Slatt – an American girl with views about racial purity similar to Montillo's. Maybe they even know each other. Let's get everyone together and stir the pot. Who knows what hornets we will set flying around our heads! I tell you what, before we go I'll have a word with Chief Inspector Pride. If I catch him in a good mood, he may bring me up to date with his investigations into Pitt-Messanger's death. The fact that there has been silence from that quarter makes me suspect that the investigation has stalled.'

'Hornets sting, don't they?' Verity said, the gloom lifting slightly. 'We had better be careful. By the way, why are you suddenly so interested in Swifts Hill? Is it because you want to find out who killed Pitt-Messanger or is it something else?'

'I'm not madly interested in who killed the old boy. From all I hear, he had it coming to him. He seems to have ruined a few lives – not least his daughter's. I am concerned about what devilry Montillo and Castlewood may be up to with their Frankenstein ideas about developing a "pure" race – whatever pure means. You agree they ought to be stopped?'

'Devilry may be too strong a word for it but I certainly hate "eugenics". It doesn't sound like science to me, just witch doctor stuff, but I may be wrong. My only worry is that Virginia invited me to Swifts Hill as a friend. If I end up making trouble for her husband, she will have every right to feel betrayed.'

'I hope it won't come to that but, if it does, I'll take all the blame.' He grinned at her but she did not return his smile.

It was just three days ago, Edward thought wryly, that they had been in bed together, feeling part of one another and contemplating a life together. Now a coldness had sprung up between them like a stalactite. Drip, drip – an icicle coming between them. But he would never give in to her on this one matter – his admiration and faith in Winston Churchill. He believed he had found his cause and he intended to stick to it – whatever the price he had to pay.

6

Technically, the cricket pitch was part of Swifts Hill but, when Sir Simon bought the estate and began work on the house, it had been given to the village for the recreation of residents and his tenants. It was, Edward thought as he came off the pitch, an archetypal scene. The sun shone, the grass was very green and the white flannels very white. The pavilion – a small wooden structure with a wooden platform in front of it – stood to his right. There was a scoreboard on which a thin, earnest youth hung numbers painted in white on tin panels. The village had declared at a hundred and twenty-nine and the knowledgeable among the spectators took the view that this was a winning score. It was four o'clock and time for tea.

Tea was very important to the players. It was rumoured that one of the best bowlers in the village team had been lured away to play for a neighbouring hamlet with the promise of better teas but there was certainly nothing to complain about today. Trestle tables were groaning under cakes and ale. Fenton was helping the ladies dispense cucumber sandwiches, potted meat sandwiches and strawberries and cream. There was strong 'sergeant-major' tea, lemonade and ginger beer to drink, and scrumpy for the unwary. The village captain, Herbert Jenks – in civilian life the village butcher – as a matter of course tempted the Castlewood players, dry from their exertions, to slake their thirst with a pint or two of this dangerously unassuming local cider. Sir Simon had forcibly to remove a pint of it from Frank, just as he was about to sink it in one brain-numbing swig.

Virginia bustled about achieving very little of a practical nature but, Edward observed, raising everyone's morale and bridging any awkward conversational gaps between the 'gentlemen' and 'players'. She was obviously popular with the tenants and villagers. She had a word for each of them, never at a loss for a child's name and seemingly up to date with the state of old mother Barker's rheumatics, Police Constable Peake's painful feet and the 'brittle bones' which made the life of the retired school-mistress, Miss Tabitha Summerly, an agony. Virginia's Pekinese, Halma, had chummed up with Mrs Cardew's Lulu and together they chased cricket balls and had to be hauled off the pitch in disgrace. Sir Simon had taken Mah-Jongg from his cage and attached a long piece of string to his collar which enabled him to run up and down scaring the ladies and entrancing the children who fed the lemur sandwiches and ice-cream.

Edward had not bowled well and was feeling annoyed with himself. He took a cup of tea and a sandwich gratefully from Fenton and looked round for Verity. She was sitting on the grass by herself looking cool in white. He had been trying to have a quiet word with her ever since he had reached Swifts Hill but had been frustrated. He had driven her down from London in the Lagonda that morning but they had given a lift to Edmund and Maggie Cardew so he had not been able to talk to her about anything private. As soon as they arrived, Verity was swallowed up by the house party – particularly the male members. Edward assumed it was not deliberate but he felt he was being spurned in favour of her new admirers, notably Roddy Maitland, Edmund Cardew and, most obviously, Sir Simon. Frank was occupied with Miss Schuster-Slatt whom he had driven down in his brand-new convertible Hudson Terraplane – a black and yellow monster with bright red leather seats. It was a present from his parents and Edward did not approve. At Cambridge, only the richest and showiest of men had their own cars which had to be garaged in the town.

All this admiration did not make Verity popular with the ladies, Edward observed. Only Mrs Cardew, who treated her like a favourite daughter-in-law, seemed to appreciate her. Verity, who had never had a mother, always blossomed when she found a motherly woman to fuss over her. As he now approached her, he was forestalled by Graham Harvey who sat himself beside her and launched into something which sounded like a tirade from where Edward was standing. Verity gazed at him, seem-ingly entranced. Inevitably, he and Edward had disliked each other on sight and had hardly exchanged a word. She said

95

something and Edward fumed as he watched Harvey put his hand on her arm and make some sharp comment which, he thought sourly, she would never have taken from him without protest but which she accepted from Harvey with studied meekness. With his 'lean and hungry' look and his deplorable views on Winston Churchill, it was the last straw when he turned out, rather improbably Edward thought, to play cricket.

Annoyed and frustrated, unwilling to play gooseberry, Edward took his sandwiches and tea over to where Maggie Cardew was sitting on her own.

'May I?' He gestured with the sandwiches to the vacant chair.

'Of course, Lord Edward. Please do.'

'Miss Pitt-Messanger looks happier,' he observed. The news of Maud's suicide attempt was common knowledge so he knew Maggie would understand what he meant.

'Oh, yes. I wonder why she did it. So awful, don't you think, to try and harm yourself? You would have to be so miserable to try. I know I would never dare.'

He wondered if she was giving him a coded message that her disfigurement did not make her unhappy enough to consider ending it all. Chewing on their sandwiches, they watched Maud in companionable silence. The scars on her wrists were healing but she still wore bandages which she made no effort to conceal. She had dressed with some attempt to look her best in a short-sleeved summer frock which, though hardly fashionable, made her look younger than she was. She wore a wide straw hat round whose brim she, or perhaps Virginia, had woven wild flowers which gave her an appealing aura of innocence.

Edward turned back to Maggie. It was odd, he thought, how quickly one forgot her disfigurement and she was certainly restful after Verity.

'What could be more English?' he said vacuously. 'What more innocent way can there be of enjoying a beautiful summer day than a village cricket match?'

'Oh, do you think so?' she said, sounding surprised.

'You don't then?'

'Well, I don't know about the village team but, when you think about it, there is so much going on among our own friends. I'm not sure "innocence" is the word I would use.'

'I don't quite follow you.'

'Well, take you for example. You are cross with Miss Browne because all the men swarm round her and she seems quite willing to let them. And you are cross with your nephew for liking that American woman with the odd views on sex which she insists on sharing with everyone. Then Isolde is cross with Roddy for having a crush on Miss Browne and he dislikes Mr Harvey who seems to have some sort of hold over her, while you, of course, cannot even bear to exchange a word with the man . . .'

'Please stop, Miss Cardew!' Edward laughed. 'Am I such an ogre?'

'Disappointed love is a dangerous condition. Oh, I am sorry! How rude of me. But you must admit, your Miss Browne has made herself universally unpopular with us women.'

'You think Roddy is stuck on Verity?'

'It's pretty obvious, I should have thought. I have just seen Isolde take Roddy behind the pavilion – for a kiss, I assumed – but she reappeared a few moments ago wiping her eyes. Even Ginny is annoyed – at Simon. She knows well enough what he's like with women but normally he has the decency to hide his infatuations from her.'

'Simon Castlewood has a roving eye?'

'You could put it that way. I think – and I am sure Miss Schuster-Slatt would agree – that he is a typical predatory male determined to spread his genes to every female who will let him. What is it they say? A woman requires a commitment before she makes love to a man. A man requires only an opportunity. Oh, now I have shocked you.'

'Not shocked me, but you have alarmed me. What a good detective you would make! And to think, when I first met you, I thought butter would not melt in your mouth. Now I am quite afraid of you.'

'I hope not, Lord Edward. I find you intelligent and attractive and I think Miss Browne is being rather foolish giving you the run-around but then we women so often don't appreciate what is under our noses. Look, Mr Harvey has gone off to "pad up". Isn't that the expression? She is alone now. Should you not go and sit with her?'

'I would rather sit with you,' he said politely.

'I don't believe you but it is nice of you to say so.'

'No, it's true,' he said, and found that it was. 'In any case, that good-looking young German is talking to her now.'

'Adam von Trott.'

'Is that his name?'

'He's the one you ought to be afraid of. Now, if you'll forgive me, I'll go and help Ginny. It was so good of you to take pity on me.'

'What do you mean, Miss Cardew? I will be most upset if you think I came to sit with you because I was sorry for you. You don't need anyone's pity.'

'No, I don't and, when Dominic has repaired my face, I'll need it even less.'

'Montillo?'

'You know he is a most experienced plastic surgeon? He says it should not be at all difficult to make me presentable again. I am so excited.'

She did not sound excited and Edward was intrigued. What an extraordinary girl this was. She was more intelligent than any of them but her tongue was sharp and might make her enemies.

'If I sit with you much longer, people will begin to talk,' she said, rising. He, too, rose to his feet.

'Let them talk. I would be flattered if anyone thought you were taking an interest in me.'

She smiled and moved away.

The young German had been captured by Miss Schuster-Slatt, who wanted his views on German marriage and was not to be denied, so Edward took the opportunity of a few moments alone with Verity. He plonked himself down beside her.

'At last! I've been waiting to have a word with you alone. Don't you want to know what I found out from Pride about Pitt-Messanger's murder?'

'Yes, of course. Tell me all.'

It was the right thing to say but he could tell that she wasn't really concentrating. He went ahead with his report anyway. 'Basically, they are no further on. They have interviewed everyone who was sitting in the immediate vicinity of the Pitt-Messangers but no one knows anything or saw anything.'

'So someone must have been hiding in the cloisters?'

'It seems the only possibility, although they still think Maud saw something which she doesn't want to tell them or doesn't *know* she saw.'

'You mean some trivial thing which she doesn't realize is significant?'

'That's right.'

'And Sidney Temperley . . .?'

'I was coming to him. Pride has done quite a lot of research into Pitt-Messanger's past and, though he had lots of enemies, they are either dead or accounted for. Temperley died, as we know, of cholera. There's no suggestion that there was anything fishy about it. There were rumours at the time that Pitt-Messanger had in some way "done him in" but there was nothing to them. Several people on the dig went down with cholera at much the same time – dirty water, I suppose – though only Temperley died. Apparently he wasn't a fit man. The climate didn't agree with him.'

'But there was a quarrel?'

'Yes. Temperley claimed he had found this extraordinary tomb but Pitt-Messanger insisted he kept quiet and that he, as leader of the excavation, took the credit.'

'And then Temperley wanted to marry Maud. That must have made things worse between them. You told Pride about that?'

'Not about her abortion. We agreed that was confidential. Still, I am a bit worried about it. It might be relevant and Pride won't like it if he finds out we have not told him everything we know.'

'I don't care. Maud told me about it in a very private moment. I ought not to have told you and I certainly forbid you to tell the police. Can't you just see Pride bullying the poor girl to give him all the grisly details?'

'I suppose so,' Edward said with some reluctance.

They watched the cricket, which had resumed now that tea was over. Sir Simon and Graham Harvey were opening the batting.

'Why was the old man so against Temperley? Was he just jealous?'

'Pride thinks he didn't like the idea of the two people who were most essential to him getting together, which makes sense. Pitt-Messanger was always thinking people were conspiring against him and no doubt he thought this was another conspiracy, all the more deadly for being close to him. Pride also said Temperley had no money – no way of supporting a wife.'

'What a selfish old swine. I'm glad he was killed!' Verity exclaimed. 'He had money. He could have financed their marriage. He owed his daughter that for all the unpaid work she had put in on his digs.'

'Well,' Edward said reasonably, 'he needed all the money he could raise for his work. However, the fact is Temperley had a reason to kill him but, of course, he didn't.'

'No. He died – conveniently for Pitt-Messanger – and Maud's life was ruined. Is there anyone else . . . a relation of Temperley's who might have sought to avenge him?'

'Don't let's be dramatic, V.'

'There's Maud's brother – the one who ran off to sea. How old would he be now?'

'I should have told you. Pride confirmed what Mrs Cardew told us: the boy's name was Edwin and he was seven years older than Maud. Pride discovered he was born with a harelip and a cleft palate. Now here's the interesting thing. He went for an operation to a brilliant young surgeon, a friend of Pitt-Messanger's . . .'

'Montillo?'

'Correct.'

'Did it work – the operation?'

'Possibly – possibly not, but the boy was never seen again.'

'Good Lord! How old was he?'

'Fourteen or fifteen.'

'And Maud . . .?'

'She was told he had run off to sea.'

'She believed it?'

'I don't know, V. She might have done. She was only seven when he disappeared. It is one of the things I want to ask her before Pride gets to her. He frightens her and I know she will clam up if he tries to bully her.'

'Golly!' Verity said excitedly. 'So Montillo may have murdered Maud's brother.'

'Hang on, V! That's jumping the gun. Montillo may have a perfectly reasonable . . .'

'Why hasn't Pride asked him . . . Montillo, I mean? Isn't this what the police call a breakthrough?'

'He's going to. He has asked him to come to the Yard for a chat.'

'Who told him about Edwin's cleft palate?'

'Pride dug up – not literally, of course – a family friend who remembered the deformity because Pitt-Messanger had been so upset about it.'

'Wouldn't you be upset?'

'Of course, but Pitt-Messanger apparently took it as a slur on his genes. He thought his children ought to be perfect specimens . . .'

'That's disgusting! I'm not surprised everyone hated him.'

'Look, V, if Montillo had something to hide and Pitt-Messanger was blackmailing him – well, he had a motive for murder.'

'Was Montillo at Benyon's memorial service? I don't remember hearing he was a friend of his.'

'No, he wasn't at the Abbey. It was the first thing Pride checked.'

'But he may have slipped into the cloister and pounced . . .'

'He might have, but why do it that way? It's pretty far-fetched.'

'Should we speak to Maud about this?'

'Pride asked me to keep it under my hat for the moment. When he has interviewed Montillo, then we can speak to Maud, though I have to admit, I am tempted to drop a hint . . . ask her a casual question and see what she says.'

'Where is Montillo, by the way?'

'He's not here – at least not until this evening. Sir Simon tells me he doesn't play cricket. He's gone to London for the day – to see Pride for one thing – but he is coming back tonight.'

'Gosh! Pride has done well,' Verity said grudgingly. She did not like him and he certainly did not like her but she gave credit where it was due. She contemplated what Edward had told her. 'Pitt-Messanger was killed by a dagger from one of those Hittite tombs, wasn't he?' she said at last.

'Yes, and that certainly suggests an archaeologist was involved but they haven't been able to trace where the dagger came from – certainly not from a public collection. The expert from the British Museum had never seen it before.'

'Were there any other archaeologists in the Abbey?'

'Not that Pride has been able to discover.'

'Did anyone have any idea that Pitt-Messanger would sit where he did?'

'No. As you know, where we were sitting in the nave there were no reserved seats. It was first come, first served.'

'Or a surgeon.'

'What do you mean, V?'

'Well, the killing was done by someone who knew how to use a knife.'

'That's a thought, certainly.'

They meditated on this for a moment and then Verity said, 'So Pride has no idea what became of Edwin?'

'Assuming he isn't dead, he may be in Australia for all we know. It is possible Montillo can throw some light on his whereabouts.'

'He's not going to admit he killed him, or even that he died on the operating table.'

'We must wait and see.'

For a moment they were, once again, a team happily exchanging information and theories. Edward saw Sadie Schuster-Slatt and Frank sitting some way off. She appeared to be lecturing him and he was listening intently. 'What do you think of that Schuster-Slatt woman?' he asked Verity.

'Oh, she's not too bad.'

'I think she's perfectly awful and a bad influence on my nephew.'

'I shouldn't get yourself all worked up. It's not as though she is going to marry Frank.'

'You don't know. She might.'

'Well, so what if she does. I expect his aristocratic genes would benefit from some new, hardy American ones. Sadie certainly thinks so. She was telling me how inbred the English aristocracy is.'

Verity smiled to show she was joking but Edward did not like her tone.

'How can you say that? The woman's a monster – vulgar, loud-mouthed . . . What did she say to me when we were introduced? "You guys are just too much! Dooks and lords and all that shit. Who in hell needs that stuff."'

'What's wrong with that? She talks a lot of sense. I like her and so does Simon for that matter.'

Edward was shaken. Sadie . . . Simon . . . Verity was way ahead of him and he wasn't sure he wanted to follow. He took a deep breath. 'Well, never mind that. Do you want to continue with this investigation or should we just forget it? As you say, Pride seems to be doing all right without our help and anyway, you don't seem very interested. I suppose with all your new friends . . .'

'Please don't use that tone of voice with me, Edward. It's not my fault if Frank is in love with an American. I thought you liked Americans.'

'You know I like Americans. I just don't like . . . I don't know what's wrong with you, V. Anything I say is wrong and you bite my head off. And while we are having a row, I might as well say, I don't like that man Harvey. It's not fair on Maud for one thing. You said she was sweet on him and now she sees him fawning over you and ignoring her. He's a . . .'

'Please, Edward. Don't make a fool of yourself,' Verity said frostily. 'What you say is quite unfair.'

'If only you'd listen to reason for once!'

'I never listen to reason. Reason is just what someone else thinks I ought to be doing or saying.'

In fact, she did feel a bit guilty and that made her cross. She had not told Edward about having had a dawn coffee in his cottage. She told herself that she and Harvey had politics in common – nothing more – but in her heart she knew he was getting too fond of her company for other reasons. She had told Edward what Maud had said to her – how they were lovers – but she could not help wondering if this was Maud's fantasy. She was trying to pluck up courage to ask him.

'Don't let's row, V,' Edward pleaded.

'I'm not having a row,' she insisted. 'Watch out! Maggie Cardew is looking at us. I've decided I don't like her and she certainly doesn't like me. I think she's after you.'

'And I think you are wrong. She's a highly intelligent girl who sees things the way they are – that's all.'

'Meaning I don't?' She looked at him, chin out, eyes blazing.

'Anyway, what do you care if she's "after me", as you put it?' Edward said, getting up.

He was bewildered. What was eating her? He never thought he would say it but he was getting fed up with her moods. She was so changeable . . . unpredictable. It had been what he had loved about her but now . . . 'Oh, well caught, sir!' Edward clapped loudly. Harvey was out. He had been unexpectedly caught at long leg by Police Constable Peake. He walked back to the pavilion waving his bat, acknowledging the plaudits of the crowd. Edward continued to clap as Roddy Maitland went out to the crease in his place. As Roddy passed Harvey, he patted him on the back and seemed to be congratulating him. Edward grunted in disgust. He couldn't think why everyone thought Harvey had done well. Ten was not a great score as he – Edward – was determined to prove. He felt a hand on his and saw it was Verity's. She was trying to apologize.

'I'm sorry if . . . if I have been a bit cool but I really do hate this thing you have got for Churchill. I wish you'd talk to Graham about it.'

Abruptly, he removed his hand from hers. 'I have no wish to speak to that man about Churchill or about anything else, thank you. I'll plough my own furrow and I'm sad if it's one you don't like.'

'You're being a baby . . .' was Verity's parting shot as he strode off.

He pretended not to hear. He felt rather a cad but he was damned if he . . . He let his sulk take him over. There was some pleasure in being unhappy. Irritated and angry – with himself as much as with Verity – he was not best pleased to be accosted by Maud Pitt-Messanger. He needed to speak to her but this wasn't the right moment.

Seeing his black look, she retreated. 'I am so sorry to bother you,' she stuttered.

He tried to smile. 'You are not bothering me. I wanted to talk to you anyway.'

'About my father's death?'

'Yes.'

'I do have something to tell you,' she said slowly. She looked round to see that they were not overheard. 'I think you already suspect . . .'

'That you killed your father?' Edward blurted out.

'So you did know! It's rather a relief, really . . . that someone else knows.'

He took her arm. 'You've not told anyone else?'

'Graham knows, of course.'

'Graham! And what did he tell you to do?'

'He said I should keep quiet because no one can ever prove anything and that anyway my father deserved it . . . which he did,' she added defiantly.

'But it was a very wicked thing to do,' Edward said gently, still holding her arm.

'I know. I am wicked. That's why I tried to kill myself. I love Graham but . . . but I don't think I can live with the burden of it.'

'You've told me now.'

'Yes, I've told you and it is easier but I know I must still be punished. He told me I should be.'

'Who? Graham?'

'No, he thinks I was justified but what can ever justify killing one's father?'

Edward knew he ought to feel nothing but revulsion and horror but actually he felt profound sadness and compassion for this distracted woman who had rebelled against a lifetime of misery.

'So who else have you told? Hold on a moment. That's Castlewood out. They're calling for me to go and put my pads on.'

'Don't leave me, Lord Edward,' she said pathetically, holding on to him. 'I'm so frightened.'

'I won't be very long, I promise you. I'll be out quickly and then I'll meet you down by the river. We can talk there undisturbed.' He looked into her eyes and saw the despair in them. 'Come on, Maud. Don't give up. There is a way out of all this. You were provoked. First your father would not let you marry Temperley and then Graham . . .'

'Oh, no,' her eyes widened. 'That's not why I killed him. I killed him because . . .'

'Coming!' Edward shouted in response to an urgent call from the pavilion. 'Maud, I want to hear all about it. I promise you, we can sort all this out. I am glad you have told me. I didn't see who else could have killed your father but . . . Yes, coming!' he cried in answer to another shout. 'I'll be back in just a few minutes. Wait for me down by the river. We'll talk it all over then. Be brave.'

'I'm not brave,' she whispered, but Edward had already gone.

The ladies sitting around the ground had, for the most part, no interest in the cricket match itself and concentrated their attention on the males, so dashing in their crisp white flannels, and in particular on Lord Edward Corinth and his nephew. Frank, as the heir to a dukedom, would have attracted attention even if he had not been so good-looking. It was known that Lord Edward was accompanied by Verity Browne. Some of the more literate ladies explained to their friends, who attempted nothing more demanding than *The Lady* or *Woman's Realm*, that she was a journalist – a foreign correspondent, no less – and that she had been wounded in Spain. They also whispered that she was a 'free thinker', whatever that meant, and believed in Free Love, which did not bear thinking about. They found her pretty but she was too small and too thin to be beautiful. They could not explain why the men flocked round her. She did not wear the sort of clothes they expected from studying the pictorial papers. She was simply dressed in a white skirt and blouse with a white jacket thrown over her shoulders. She had a splendid hat, though – straw, topped with two peacock feathers. She wore no make-up and no jewellery except for a pendant on a gold chain round her neck. It seemed hardly surprising that she and Lord Edward did not spend much time with one another as she appeared more interested in the young German aristocrat. According to the vicar's wife, who was a source of reliable information on the Swifts Hill house party, he was a friend of Sir Simon's called Adam von Trott.

Much more interesting to these ladies was that Frank Corinth, who was certainly a lord and possibly a viscount – opinions differed on this – had chosen to escort not a nice English girl but a vulgar American with a loud rasping voice and views on everything.

'You're just so cute,' she told Frank, as he hand-fed her a strawberry. 'I do believe I'll have to rewrite my paper on the degeneracy of the English upper classes.' She turned to Verity who had come up to them after her 'words' with Edward. 'I carried out this survey six months ago when I was in Oxford, Miss Browne, and my conclusions are fascinating. I sent out over a thousand questionnaires on the subject of what constitutes fitness for marriage. I received the most extraordinary replies.'

'Was this on your own initiative?' Verity inquired.

'On my own initiative? Oh, I see what you mean. No, I am working with my friend Mr Alfred Kinsey. Do you know his work at all?'

'I am afraid I have never heard of him. Is he at Oxford?'

'No, no. He's American. A very great man. You have never come across his *Origins of Higher Categories in Cynips*?'

'I am afraid not. What's a cynip when it's at home?'

'A gall wasp.'

Verity was still in the dark. 'He's an entomologist?'

'He's a sexologist. He's studying the evolution of the sex organs.'
Frank blushed and Verity smiled. 'It sounds rather . . . obscure.'

'Not at all. He studied 160,000 specimens of gall wasp. I
intend to make the same rigorous study of the human.' She was
getting excited and that meant noisy. Frank glanced round,
hoping no one was listening. 'Most people think that what they
do sexually is what everyone does – or should do. I've discovered totally different patterns – uncharted variations.'

'You think you can study sex scientifically?' Verity said, now
rather intrigued.

'Yes. I am appalled at people's ignorance – particularly *young*
people's. Did you know that a year ago in Chicago, George
Gallup carried out a poll and found that twelve per cent of
upper-middle-class women had venereal disease and most had
no idea how they had got it? You see, human beings are animals
and their so-called perversions are rooted in primate behaviour
and in that sense "natural". For instance . . .'

Fortunately, Verity thought, Miss Schuster-Slatt was interrupted by a call from Sir Simon for Frank to get ready to bat. He
was to follow his uncle. Wickets were falling too quickly if the
Castlewood team was ever to reach fifty, let alone a hundred and
thirty. Frank loped off to the pavilion – glad to escape further
revelations of 'natural' perversions, Verity thought – and she was
left alone with Miss Schuster-Slatt. They watched Roddy slide a
ball between the slips and call for Edmund Cardew to try a
single. She clapped dutifully as Roddy sprinted across the crease
as the wicketkeeper whipped off the bails. The umpire was
appealed to but shook his head. He was safe.

'He's playing a dangerous game,' Miss Schuster-Slatt said. 'I
mean, I know nothing about cricket but wasn't he almost –
what's the word? Frank told me . . . yes, I've got it – stumped.'
She was triumphant.

'So who do you blame for all this sexual ignorance, Miss
Schuster-Slatt?' Verity could not resist asking.

'Please call me Sadie. I guess we should be allies, Verity. May
I call you Verity?'

'Of course,' Verity said faintly. Sadie was rather overwhelming.

'I blame the Church,' she said emphatically. 'Christianity has created a web of taboos and prohibitions which have done much to destroy human happiness. What we need is less religion and more sex education.'

'Another six!' Verity clapped enthusiastically. 'Mr Maitland's doing well, isn't he?'

'Is he?' Miss Schuster-Slatt said, surprised.

Roddy was in fine fettle, sending the balls tossed at him by the village blacksmith this way and that but mainly into the stream which flowed to one side of the ground providing a natural boundary. The village boys enjoyed nothing more than to run barefoot and screaming into the water to retrieve balls. The blacksmith was becoming more and more angry at Roddy's contemptuous dismissal of his best efforts and his colour was so high that his captain was relieved the doctor was close at hand to administer first aid in the event of his having a seizure.

Miss Schuster-Slatt went off to watch Frank put on his pads. Verity smiled as she heard her ask him to explain cricket to her. If Christianity was a web of rules and arcane rituals, what did that make cricket? At that moment, there was a cry of pain from the crease. The blacksmith's fury had finally erupted and he had sent down a bouncer which Roddy had taken on the forehead. The peak of his cap had protected him from the worst of the blow but he staggered about in considerable pain, cursing like a costermonger. Dr Morris came on to administer first aid and urged him to retire hurt. Roddy would not hear of it and gazed venomously at his tormentor. If the man wanted to play dirty, then he would get what he deserved. The game resumed, everyone feeling less somnolent than before. Unquestionably something had happened. The mood had changed. This was war.

Once it was clear that Roddy would live to fight another day, Verity wandered off to rest beneath an oak tree. She liked seeing Roddy banging the ball about but even that was beginning to pall for her. She took off her hat and dropped gratefully into a deck-chair. She gazed out at the sunlit pitch. It was absurdly hot for England. Unfortunately, Roddy had been put off his stroke by the blow to his head and lifted the blacksmith's next ball high but not hard enough towards the cars parked under the trees where it fell into the safe hands of Harold, the Swifts Hill gardener's boy. Roddy was magnanimous, congratulated Harold on his catch and returned to the pavilion to much applause and an ecstatic Isolde, who greeted his return as though he were Achilles come back from the wars. Throwing her arms about his neck, she kissed him with a fervour that made Edward feel rather a prude. She was certainly making it plain to anyone who was interested that Roddy was her man. Still, he could not imagine Verity making quite such a show of her feelings in public – not for him, anyway. Especially not for him, he muttered to himself.

Verity watched Edward stride on to the pitch and ask for middle-and-leg from the vicar, who was umpiring. She could hear his cut-glass, rather nasal voice quite clearly. She felt she hardly knew him when he was engaged in these male rituals. This was a class activity of which she instinctively disapproved, despite the evident pleasure the event was giving to villagers and gentry alike. She was surprised – and perhaps a little disappointed – that Graham Harvey seemed happy to play and, what was more, play for the Castlewood eleven, not the village. She sighed. Could there ever be a social revolution in a country as conservative as this? Perhaps, she thought guiltily, it might need a war to shake things up.

She watched Edward dig a mark at the crease, beating his bat on the grass as though he was killing some unfortunate beetle. Satisfied at last with the damage he had done, he took time to look about him at the spread of fielders before nodding to the bowler to signify that he was ready for anything the man could throw at him. Verity put her hand up to shield her eyes. The sun was beginning to sink towards the horizon. With the sun behind him, Edward was almost a silhouette. She wondered if she were being self-indulgent, permitting herself to fall in love with a man like him whose background, political views and attitude to life were so different from her own. Perhaps they were doing each other no favours. He could make her crosser than anyone she had ever met. Maybe the compromises they had to make to remain together were damaging them both.

She admitted to herself that she was becoming seriously disturbed by his – in her view – uncritical devotion to Winston Churchill. It seemed to highlight how very differently they viewed the world. She also knew she had had an influence on him and that he had lost many of the prejudices of his class and sex, but were these superficial changes? She knew he had a respect for her and for her ability to do a difficult job well, but could they ever be happy together? He was a product of his class and, when she had first met him, he had tried to patronize her. She had often had to shock him into seeing that when he called her 'my dear' or said things such as 'don't you worry about that', he was not being considerate but was belittling her. Although he would never use such language to her – or indeed to any woman – now, could a leopard change its spots?

Edward was what he was – more intelligent than most and certainly better educated – but he was still a man and an aristocrat. Miss Schuster-Slatt might be vulgar and rather absurd but wasn't there something in what she said? If sexual relations could be subjected to scientific analysis, would not much of what she instinctively disapproved or distrusted about the relationship between the sexes – such as the institution of marriage – be shown to be artificial and without justification? Miss Schuster-Slatt had put most of the blame on outdated religious practices and, as a Communist, Verity agreed with her. Human relations ought to be conducted on simple, uncomplicated lines. She was a capitalist in this respect at least: sex ought to be regulated by the laws of supply and demand, need and the satisfaction of need. She groaned aloud. Why did everything have to be so complicated? She wanted Edward but she hated the idea of being tied down. Might it not be better after all if they parted? It would be painful but better a clean break than a wounded romance limping into an uncertain future.

She must have closed her eyes because she was startled into wakefulness by a hand resting lightly on her shoulder. Towering over her, standing almost to attention, the young German, Adam von Trott, was asking her – in his perfect English – if she would like some lemonade. She accepted the glass he offered and, taking this as some sort of permission, he knelt beside her. An English boy would have talked of the cricket or the weather but never of anything serious. Von Trott, however, at once began asking her about Spain and, in particular, about the razing of Guernica. She responded immediately to his seriousness about politics, flattered that he had sought her out. Virginia had told her something of his past and she had been intrigued. He had been a Balliol Rhodes Scholar, one of the first Germans to come to Oxford after the scholarships had been suspended during the war. He had been a prominent member of the Oxford Labour Club and was in every sense an outstanding figure. He was tall, romantic-looking, with a ringing laugh and – as Verity now had cause to appreciate – great personal charm. As a foreigner and a German to boot, he was a remarkable figure to his contemporaries. It helped that his father was an aristocrat and had been one of the Kaiser's ministers. His mother was a descendant of John Jay, the first Chief Justice of the United States. His home was a castle – Imshausen in the Trottenwald in Hesse.

They were soon talking earnestly – agreeing and completing one another's sentences – as though they had known each other in some other life. They both hated war, believing it to be a terrible wickedness perpetrated upon the innocent by evil men. He was fiercely patriotic but hated the Nazis. When they finally stopped talking, they found themselves gazing into each other's eyes. Verity saw his romantic passion and feared that, before long, he might be faced with an impossible decision as to where his loyalties lay.

'Are you . . . playing?' she said at last, indicating the cricket pitch with a wave of her hand. Her voice shook a little but his was quite firm.

'I cannot play this game but Sir Simon said I should learn how to play it if I wished to understand the English.'

'So you are batting . . .?'

'Last of all – number eleven. Sir Simon tells me that the game will be over before I am made to bat. I hope so. I do not want to make a fool of myself.'

'You won't do that,' Verity said and, without knowing why, blushed. She peered at the green sward. The batsmen, the bowler beginning his run and the crouching wicketkeeper were blurred and it occurred to her that she might need spectacles. It was one of the annoying things about cricket that the action took place so far away.

Edward was settling in at the wicket when he was unlucky enough to run out his solid, if rather dull, partner. Edmund Cardew had been at the wicket for almost an hour but had scored only five runs. Edward – on the last ball of the over – slipped what he thought might be a single past the wicketkeeper and shouted at his partner to run. Cardew had, unfortunately, turned his back on him, believing the over had ended and, when Edward called to him, was very slow off the mark. The man in the slips made a grab at the ball and managed to sling it at the wicketkeeper before Cardew could reach the crease. The bails were off and he had to walk back to the pavilion, where he was greeted by sparse if sympathetic applause. It looked like a piece of arrant selfishness on Edward's part and he knew it. He apologized effusively as Cardew set off for the pavilion but Cardew was unable to hide his fury.

'Hard luck, old chap,' Frank said, as he hurried on to the pitch hoping for better luck.

'I say, Uncle!' he said when Edward came to meet him. 'That was a dashed silly thing to do.'

'I know! I don't know what I was thinking of. Will Cardew ever forgive me, do you think?'

'I very much doubt it.'

'We'll take it slowly, eh, Frank?'

Until the end of the over, Edward played with all the flair of a dead man, blocking the ball even when he might have hit it. As they met in mid-wicket while they waited for the new bowler to take the ball and rearrange his fielders, Frank said, 'Don't overdo it, Uncle. We don't want to turn the pitch into a graveyard. The natives will get restless if we don't score. There's probably only a couple more hours of light – three at the most – and we've got a long way to go.'

At that moment, they were distracted by a shout from the pavilion and saw Sir Simon waving what looked like a dog's lead in the air. Mah-Jongg had somehow slipped his collar and was on the loose. The village boys paddling in the stream scented a hunt and soon spotted the animal running towards trees on the other side of the pitch. Hallooing, they ran after him and managed to drive the lemur on to the pitch where Edward, Frank and most of the fielders joined the chase. Since Mah-Jongg was not a sprinter, they soon caught up with him. Surrounded, he stopped and stared at the ring of faces, mewing in protest. His bushy tail waved angrily and his wicked-looking face dared anyone to come near him. One of the boys, braver or more foolish than the rest, threw himself on the lemur and caught him. He immediately let out a fearful howl and dropped him again. Mah-Jongg had bitten him to the bone and was once again at liberty. Chaos reigned as the chase resumed and it was a full ten minutes before the lemur was recaptured – by Roddy wearing cricket gloves. Meanwhile, the wounded boy was taken off to the cottage hospital to be disinfected and patched up.

Play resumed with the scoreboard showing fifty-five for the loss of four wickets. Frank, aware that there was very little time if they were to reach a hundred and thirty and win the game, started knocking the ball about and, after a couple of fours, hit a full toss with a resounding thwack. At first he thought it would be caught at the boundary but to his great satisfaction it went well over and dropped into the stream. The boys splashing about in the water looking for the ball were shouting and waving their arms excitedly. Frank waited modestly for the applause and was a little surprised when it died out rather suddenly.

'Well done, old chap,' said Edward, leaving his crease to congratulate his nephew.

'What's all that shouting about?' Frank said, puzzled. Edward looked round and saw a small crowd gathering at the water's edge.

'I say, something's up all right,' Frank said and suddenly. 'I hope I didn't knock someone out.'

Everyone was walking or trotting over to the boundary to see what the matter was. As Edward and Frank approached, they saw what looked at first like a heap of clothes in the water. Dr Morris was directing the efforts of two young men to carry the dripping bundle on to the grass. It was so heavy that it slipped out of their hands back into the water.

'Good Lord!' Edward exclaimed. 'Isn't that . . .?'

Verity had removed her shoes and stockings and waded into the water, which hardly came above her ankles. She saw Edward and said, 'It's Maud. She's . . . I think she's dead.'

There was a hush at her words and the crowd parted to let Edward through. Why this happened Verity did not know. When she thought about it later, she had to acknowledge that Edward had an air of authority which people instinctively respected. Maud was on her back and her dress had ballooned about her. Her straw hat with its circlet of flowers floated limply beside her. Her sodden clothes made it awkward to manoeuvre her with dignity but, with Verity holding her head and Miss Schuster-Slatt – who was also in the water – holding her dress round her legs, Maud was half-carried, half-dragged on to the bank.

113

'Is she drowned? Can she be revived?' Edward asked the doctor, who had had his hand on her pulse.

'How could she have drowned?' Verity demanded. 'The stream is so shallow here and she is on her back. I don't understand it.'

Edward, still in his cricket pads, knelt clumsily beside her and suddenly exclaimed, 'Look here, doctor!'

He was pointing to her side from which a pink dribble was staining the grass. Very gently, they turned her on her front and saw the hilt of a dagger.

'She has been stabbed,' Verity said unnecessarily.

The police constable, who had been fielding at the boundary, made a great effort to pull himself together. 'Get back, everyone. Please give us some room here.'

Sir Simon appeared. 'What's happening? I was in the pavilion . . . Oh God! Is that Maud? Has she committed suicide?'

'No, indeed, sir,' the police constable said. 'She has been murdered. Do you see the knife?'

'Good heavens! That dagger . . . it's the one from the collection . . . I'm sure of it.' He leant forward to examine the hilt more closely but the constable barred his way. 'Don't touch, sir. Might I ask you to send someone up to the house to telephone the police station? I will remain here until Inspector Jebb arrives.'

'Yes . . . yes . . . of course,' Sir Simon said, retreating, understandably dazed by the disaster which had overtaken them. 'I'll go myself . . . straight away. Murder at Swifts Hill – I cannot believe it! Where's Ginny? Where's my wife?'

'She went back to the house,' Isolde said. 'I'll go and tell her what has happened and ring the police.'

Edward and Verity stood up and, with Dr Morris, stared down at the dead woman.

'A very great tragedy,' the doctor said. 'To be honest, Lord Edward, I would not have been surprised if the poor lass had killed herself. Some suicide attempts are little more than cries for help but I thought, when she cut her wrists, she knew what she was doing. But this . . . Who could have done such a thing? And why?'

'That's what we must find out,' Verity said grimly.

Edward made a little grimace. 'We let her down . . . I let her down. You were right, Verity. I said Pitt-Messanger's murder wasn't our business but of course it was our business. She was so frightened . . .'

'Frightened?' Verity said in surprise. 'Why do you say that?'

'She told me so.' He sighed. 'I suppose there is no more harm that I can do her.'

'You've done her harm?'

'She confessed to me, just before I went in to bat, that – as I suspected – she had killed her father.'

'What!' exclaimed the doctor. 'She murdered her own father? For God's sake, why?'

'I thought it was because he had made her life a misery and prevented her marrying the man she loved.'

'Sidney Temperley?'

'Yes, V, and then he told her she could not marry Graham Harvey – not if she wanted his blessing and his money. I thought that might have tipped her over the edge.'

'That's why she killed him?'

'Isn't that reason enough, V? But, no. In fact . . . Damn it! She was about to tell me why when I had to go and get ready for my . . .'

'You put *cricket* before finding out why she murdered her father!' Verity looked at him as though he was mad.

'I said I would see her in a few minutes down by the river . . . as soon as I was out.' Edward said miserably. 'She said she was frightened but I thought she was frightened about what would happen to her now she had confessed.'

'She was frightened of her murderer,' the doctor said.

'And you abandoned her to him.' The scorn in Verity's voice made Edward wince.

'You cannot blame me more than I blame myself.'

'Well,' said Dr Morris after a long pause, 'that's all water under the bridge.' And then wished he had not said it.

Verity felt an immediate, if unreasonable, stab of jealousy. Why had Maud confided in Edward, whom she had only just met, rather than in her? She would not have left her in her moment of need to hit a cricket ball about. She knew she was being unfair but she was bitter. Her vanity had been hurt. She thought she had convinced Maud that she was her friend but, when she needed someone, she went to Edward . . . because he was a man. She told herself not to be idiotic. What did her *amour propre* matter at a time like this?

'But how did the murderer know she had not already told me?' she asked.

'I suppose, if she had, you would have told the police and then, of course, the murderer would have known the game was up. There would have been no point in killing her.'

'Hold on a minute. What are we saying here? Maud's killer saw her talking earnestly to you but he – or she – cannot possibly have known what she was saying.'

'I think he asked her. She told him the truth and so he killed her,' Edward said bluntly.

Verity looked puzzled. 'She would have told him that you now knew she killed her father, so why did he stab her?'

'Because,' Dr Morris said, 'the murderer wasn't concerned about that. What he cared about was that she had not told Lord Edward – and must never be allowed to tell anyone – *why* she had killed her father.'

'That's right,' Edward agreed. 'She said she hadn't killed her father because he had stopped her marrying the man she loved but for some other reason. Once we know what that was, we'll know who murdered her.' He rubbed his forehead, as he always did when he was under pressure. 'I think it must have something to do with her brother and his disappearance.'

'Are you sure she had told no one but you that she murdered her father?'

'Wait a moment, V. I remember now! She said she had told Graham Harvey and he had told her that she was justified in doing what she did.'

'And?'

'And she told me someone else had said she would have to be punished. I'm sure that was what she said.'

'And that someone else was the murderer?'

'I suppose so,' Edward said sombrely.

'While everyone was chasing Mah-Jongg . . .' Verity said, thinking aloud.

'. . . Maud was murdered. It couldn't have been at any other time otherwise the boys would have seen something,' Edward finished. 'Curse that animal. In Madagascar, where Mah-Jongg comes from, *lemures* are spirits of the dead. I wonder who released this particular spirit.' He sighed and murmured to himself, '"Too much of water, hast thou, poor Ophelia, and therefore I forbid my tears . . ."'

7

Inspector Jebb looked gloomily at the scene of the crime. Lord Edward Corinth had explained why the murdered woman was walking near the stream. These amateur sleuths! Any competent policeman – himself for instance – would have asked her a few direct questions and cleared up the matter of her father's death once and for all and, in doing so, prevented her murder. He grunted. Cricket! For the sake of cricket the woman had lost her life. To be fair, Corinth had looked very shame-faced and that girl of his had given him hell, but still . . .

He had told Corinth that the only person who could be blamed for Maud's death was her murderer but, in fact, he did blame him for deserting her at such a moment. Jebb stroked his chin and considered. Was he being harsh? He had a prejudice against the aristocracy but he had to admit that Lord Edward seemed to be less arrogant and more sensible than most of his breed. He snorted derisively. He must put the man out of his mind and concentrate on solving the murder.

The corpse had been photographed and removed in an ambulance. His men were already searching the stream and the banks. He needed to find exactly where Maud Pitt-Messanger had been killed. There was grass and mud on the back of her shoes and clothes which showed she had been dragged some distance although Dr Morris was almost certain the body had been put in the water immediately after the stabbing because the blood was still liquid and there was no sign of rigor mortis. The stream was so shallow that the body could not have drifted more than a few feet. The murderer would have been in a hurry and might have left something which could help identify him, but the water had washed away much that might have been helpful to the investigation. The crowd which had gathered on the bank when the body was found and the efforts to remove it from the stream had literally muddied the ground.

The savagery of the stabbing meant the killer had to be a man – or an exceptionally strong woman – and surely no ordinary woman could have dragged the body into the stream. The village boys, still in a state of high excitement, were able to say that the body had definitely not been there when they had gone off to chase the lemur. Jebb was familiar with Mah-Jongg. He had seen the nasty little creature in its cage when he had been called to the house to investigate the theft of the dagger. What was Lady Castlewood thinking of, keeping such a thing as a pet?

What about the timing? The boys had recovered a ball Corinth had knocked over the boundary into the water just before he had run out Cardew. It seemed fairly obvious to Jebb that the killer had seen Maud walking alone by the stream. The only people near enough to notice anything untoward were the boys. So the murderer released the lemur to cause a distraction, counting on Maud to remain where she was. She was probably too wrapped up in herself to hear the hullabaloo or, if she had heard it, to join the chase. The objection to this theory was that the murderer would have been hard pushed to release the lemur, rush back to the other side of the ground and kill Maud before Mah-Jongg was recaptured, And wouldn't he have been seen hurrying *away* from the chase as everyone else hurried to join it? Mrs Cardew, who had remained in her deck-chair throughout the incident, had seen no one running or even walking towards the stream. Furthermore, the murderer could not have counted on the lemur biting the boy and it taking so long to recapture the animal.

Perhaps he had not been responsible for the lemur's escape. Perhaps he had simply taken the opportunity fate had provided to kill the woman who threatened him. If what Lord Edward had said was correct and Maud was waiting to tell him something important, maybe her killer had not had the chance to *plan* anything. Or perhaps there was an accomplice who created the distraction to give the killer time. Jebb kicked at a molehill. Was this case going to be a mountain or a molehill? He couldn't be sure.

Could Maud have been paddling in the stream when she was attacked? It was a hot day – but, no, she had her shoes on and there was the grass and mud on her clothes. Then there was the fact that the body had been *laid* in the water, not thrown in. There was an element of . . . he would not say ritual, but at least deliberation. The killer must be a cool customer. Given that he could have had very little time and must surely have feared being noticed by someone returning from the lemur hunt, it was odd that he had taken the trouble to drag the body into the stream and lay her out as though she were resting on her bed. Corinth had mentioned Ophelia and he had nodded knowingly but, when he got home, he would have to send his wife to the library to check in Shakespeare exactly how the girl had died. He remembered seeing a reproduction in a magazine of a painting of a girl on her back in a river with flowers in her hair. He had an idea that it was Ophelia but it might have been The Lady of Shalott. He shook himself – what did it matter? This was real life – or rather real death – not fantasy. He scratched his head.

The only other time he had investigated the killing of a woman, she had been walking alone after dark on her way to meet her lover. The murderer had, unsurprisingly, turned out to be the husband. *This* murder had peculiar features – most notably being carried out in full view of twenty-two cricketers, two umpires and several dozen spectators – but it ought not to be too difficult to establish who had done the deed. He hunched his shoulders and pursed his lips. It *ought* to be easy but he had an intuition that it might not be quite as easy as it should be. For one thing, there was the difficulty of the murder having taken place at Swifts Hill. It was awkward to start accusing a powerful man like Sir Simon Castlewood of harbouring a murderer among his guests. He knew Sir Simon reasonably well and respected him. He was a Justice of the Peace, a friend of the Chief Constable and a generous contributor to the Police Benevolent Fund.

He sighed and turned to walk up to the house. One thing was certain. The interviews must take place as quickly as possible, before those present had time to forget what they had seen or concoct their own version of events. Of course, he must interview all the village team and their supporters but the village eleven was fielding when the murder took place and visible to all. Anyway, which of them was likely to know Maud Pitt-Messanger, let alone have a motive to kill her with a knife stolen from Sir Simon's museum? He needed a complete list of those who had been *watching* the cricket. Perhaps one of them had taken the opportunity of carrying out this savage killing while all eyes were on Lord Edward Corinth and his good-looking nephew. It was ridiculous how there was still this fascination with the aristocracy.

He chewed his moustache and harrumphed. It was his opportunity to prove himself and he was determined to solve this crime before the Chief Constable insisted on bringing in Scotland Yard. All eyes would be on him. There would be a lot of interest in the press because, apart from Sir Simon, other well-known figures were involved. He gathered that Lord Edward and Verity Browne were celebrities of a sort. Well, he would not be put down by any of these London folk, he assured himself. There was one obvious suspect – the doctor fellow with the foreign-sounding name, Dominic Montillo. He would interview him first. He had been in London but had returned to Swifts Hill shortly after the body was found. What if he had been lingering in the bushes, stabbed the woman and then calmly got back into his car and arrived at the house when he said he did? The road was only a field away from the stream at the point where the body was found. He suspected all foreigners on principle. There was that German – Adam von Trott. He was both a foreigner and an aristocrat – probably a Nazi spy. He checked himself. He must not jump to conclusions. He knew himself to be a capable detective and a good judge of character. He had a job to do and he would do it.

He walked up to the house and met a worried-looking Sir Simon on the steps. On cue, he said, 'Would you like me to telephone the Chief Constable, Inspector? This is a terrible business. I imagine you will want to call in Scotland Yard . . .'

'I don't think that will be necessary but thank you all the same, Sir Simon,' Jebb said firmly. 'I will, of course, be making a report to Chief Inspector Pride. If Miss Pitt-Messanger's confession to Lord Edward was true – and there is no reason to think it was not – then that case is closed. The Chief Inspector can wind up his investigation into the Professor's death. What would be helpful, sir, is if I could use a room in the house to interview everyone who was watching or taking part in the cricket match.'

Sir Simon looked dubious but nodded his assent.

'Sergeant,' Jebb spoke sharply, 'start making a list of everyone who was in the house and the grounds today. You have the names and addresses of the boys who found the body? Very good. Let's get down to work. I am afraid the scorer must write "game abandoned", eh, Sir Simon?'

After the corpse had been removed in the ambulance, Verity walked back to the house with von Trott. She was so obviously deep in thought, the young man asked her what was 'biting' her. 'That is the expression, is it not? I am always trying to improve my colloquial English.'

'That is what we say,' Verity agreed with a wry smile. 'What's biting me is that I came down to Swifts Hill to solve Professor Pitt-Messanger's murder. Instead of solving anything, I allowed his daughter to be killed more or less in front of me. To cap it all, I failed to see what was staring me in the face: that it was Maud who had killed her father. At least Edward got that bit right.'

'Of course you didn't consider it,' he said. 'People don't kill their fathers. I think it's much more likely she convinced herself she had killed him. From what you say, there were hundreds of people in Westminster Abbey when the old man was killed. How can you possibly know if one of his deadly enemies was not lying in wait for him?'

'The police have interviewed everyone . . .'

'Leave it to the police. It's not your responsibility, Verity. You are a journalist not a detective. Am I right?'

Verity grimaced. He was right, of course. She was being put in her place. In her own defence she said, 'They're not so different. I am a journalist. I search for the truth. We – Lord Edward and I – have stumbled across one or two violent deaths and investigated them.'

His brow clearing, Adam said, 'Of course, I remember hearing about it. "Partners in crime" – is that what you call yourselves?'

'No, Adam,' and he flushed with pleasure that she used his first name so naturally, 'that is *not* what we call ourselves.'

'You are more than partners?' he inquired mildly.

She hesitated and he saw the look in her eye with which Edward was well acquainted. 'I am sorry,' he said quickly. 'I do not wish to be . . . Love has its own rules. *L'amour ne se commande pas*. I understand. As they say in my country, "*Von Herz zu Herz geht ein weg*" – there's a path that leads from heart to heart.'

'You do *not* understand and "nosy" is the idiom you are looking for,' Verity said sharply but with a smile. 'Anyway, I am going to investigate this murder even if you think it's not my business.'

'May I help?' he asked shyly.

She glanced at him in surprise. 'You may,' she said graciously.

Edward saw her walking back to the house in earnest conversation with the young German. He knew a certain amount about von Trott and what he knew made him disposed to like him – but what if he and Verity . . .? He was wise enough to know that the worst thing he could do would be to look as if he cared whom she chose to flirt with.

Back at the house, still in his whites and with a heavy heart, he went to the public telephone which Sir Simon had installed so bizarrely but so usefully in the hall and put in a trunk call to Scotland Yard. He knew Inspector Jebb would report to Chief Inspector Pride that, just before she had been killed, Maud Pitt-Messanger had confessed to having murdered her father but he wanted to make his own confession, if only to ease his conscience. He had not only failed to prevent another murder – that was bad enough – but might actually have precipitated it, when he could so easily have prevented it. He would never forgive himself.

Pride listened to what Edward had to say and told him he had been right to let him know immediately what had happened and that he would telephone Jebb without mentioning who had apprised him of Miss Pitt-Messanger's killing. He made no judgement and offered no absolution.

'Jebb's a good man but he'll need help sooner or later. If he turns me down now, as he probably will, I'll tell him he's a fool if he doesn't take you into his confidence.'

Edward was pleased and surprised. 'Good of you, Chief Inspector. By the way,' he added casually, 'are you allowed to tell me what you discovered when you interviewed Montillo?'

'I don't see why not,' Pride said after a pause. 'Precisely nothing, is the answer. He denied ever being asked to operate on

Pitt-Messanger's son. He said he had never even heard about a son and suggested it might be a figment of Maud's tortured imagination. Maud, he told me, is – I should say was – a highly strung woman, unstable at the best of times, and her father's death had preyed on her mind. He said her attempted suicide showed this and we should not believe a word she said.'

'Preyed on her mind? He wasn't hinting that he *knew* she had killed her father?'

'No. We were assuming he was murdered by person or persons unknown, as they say.'

'But if, when he and Dr Morris found Maud after her suicide attempt, Montillo had managed to talk to her without the doctor being present, she might have told him what she told me. She implied that she had confessed to Graham Harvey and one other person, who could have been Montillo. What occurs to me, Chief Inspector, is that Montillo may have hurried back to Swifts Hill and shut her mouth for good. He may have thought that being with you at Scotland Yard gave him a perfect alibi.'

'Your three minutes are up,' the operator interrupted.

'Not a theory I want to discuss on the telephone, Lord Edward,' Pride reprimanded him and put down the receiver.

It was almost eleven and they were all tired. Jebb had interviewed everyone at Swifts Hill. He would talk to the villagers and tenants in the morning. As Pride had forecast, Jebb turned down his offer of immediate assistance but agreed they should meet at the end of the week to discuss the progress of the investigation. Jebb rather hoped that by then he would have made an arrest.

While Jebb was carrying out his interviews, Virginia did her best to act normally but, inevitably, the conversation would return to the murder. There was an air of suppressed excitement among her guests which she knew was 'bad form'. They should all have been deeply upset but the truth was that none of them counted themselves a friend of Maud's. Virginia alone genuinely mourned her and, as Maud had been killed while her guest – 'under her protection', as she put it – she felt guilty and shocked at the disaster that had come upon them. Her plan had been to keep a close eye on Maud until she got over her grief for her father. Instead, she had attempted suicide and had then been killed – probably by someone who ate at her table. Virginia wondered if the dead girl had any friends she ought to get in touch with. She knew she had no living relatives. It was all too sad.

The following morning – Sunday – they all, with the exception of Verity and Graham Harvey – went to church and prayed for Maud's soul. After lunch, Jebb reinterviewed everyone, finally announcing that any of the guests who wished to leave Swifts Hill could do so provided, of course, they left addresses and telephone numbers where they could be contacted.

Verity and von Trott returned to London with Edward in the Lagonda. They discussed the murder for most of the journey and Edward was disconcerted that Adam took it for granted he was to help Verity in her unofficial investigation. He did not say anything but could not help feeling that, while two was company, three was a crowd. When he dropped them off together in the King's Road, he asked Verity if she wanted him to help her move into her new flat. She had told him that she was moving her things from the Hassels' to Cranmer Court on the Wednesday. Verity looked embarrassed and said he wasn't to bother as Adam had offered to help. Edward was hurt and suspicious – as it turned out, quite justifiably.

Verity had so few possessions that the move took less than an hour. Adrian Hassel ferried her clothes and books and tactfully left her and Adam to sort them out. Adam then accompanied her to Peter Jones where they bought a collection of kettles, pots, pans and other necessaries, ordered some chairs and a sofa, a couple of rugs and – rather extravagantly – a radiogram, even though she had as yet no records to play on it. They were finished by lunchtime and, feeling suddenly hungry, Adam suggested they go to the Blue Cockatoo in Cheyne Walk.

Like naughty schoolchildren playing truant, they feasted on 'bangers and mash' washed down with beer which Adam said was truly disgusting. Hetty, the Blue Cockatoo's famously rude waitress, treated them gently and, as they left, made them sign her autograph book. 'I don't know if you're famous now, dears, but I sense you will be soon. Look, they're all in my book. Sir

William Orpen who does those paintings, Mark Hambourg who plays the violin, Douglas Byng the scientist and then there's Ellen Wilkinson and the Houston Sisters and all that lot.'

As they wandered back to Cranmer Court, slightly the worse for wear, Verity grabbed Adam's hand and asked shyly, 'Do you think she's right – Hetty, I mean? Will we be famous, do you think?'

'You're famous already, Verity,' he replied, 'but I never will be.'

'You don't think you will be Chancellor or President – when the Nazis are gone, of course?'

'I'll be dead by then,' he said coolly.

'Please don't say that,' Verity begged him. 'I wish we lived in some other century. This must be the worst.'

'We cannot change the century we live in. What matters is what we do with our time here on earth.'

'But, Adam, why did you say you will die?'

'I don't know,' he answered, not looking at her. 'I just know it will happen. It is my *Sonderweg* – my special path. I have no choice. *Ich habe genug*. It is enough.'

When they got back to the flat, Adam said he ought to go but Verity begged him to stay. 'I feel so sad. I don't know why.'

'It must be the beer,' he laughed.

'Don't tease. I've just remembered, I have got a bottle of Rioja under the bed. We must drink to my new life in my new flat.'

'But there aren't any chairs,' he protested.

'We could sit on the floor.'

'On the bare boards? No, I'm too old. But you have at least got one piece of furniture.'

'You mean the bed?' she said seriously, looking up at him. 'My father gave it to me. It came from Heals.'

'I didn't mean . . .'

'I was rather hoping you did,' she said awkwardly. 'It's a very good bed.'

Without another word, he leant over and kissed her and she kissed him back. He was so tall and she was so small that it was not easy. With a lop-sided smile, she suggested they try out the bed for comfort. She wanted this handsome, self-doomed German to make love to her. God alone knew if it was lust or love. She simply did not care. She knew she was betraying

Edward and deserved to burn in hell – if it actually existed – but none of it seemed to matter a jot. Guilt and all the rest of it would follow as day follows night but, after so much death, she wanted only to feel his body on hers, his skin against her skin and his sweat mingle with her own.

The following morning she went to the *New Gazette* and was given a message to go at once to Lord Weaver's office. She had telephoned her story to the office from Swifts Hill. She had told Sir Simon she would have to do it. He was too well known not to make Maud's death of interest to the general public and there were already reporters from other newspapers, local and national, in the village cobbling together accounts of what had happened. She argued, speciously perhaps, that it was better for the Castlewoods if she wrote an accurate, if necessarily incomplete, account for the *New Gazette* than allow rumour and scandal to damage the reputation of Sir Simon and his guests. The ancient dagger, the stream, the cricket match – it was a colourful story and Verity was pleased with it. She hoped as she knocked on his door that her friend and mentor, the proprietor of the paper, wanted to congratulate her on her scoop.

In fact, to her chagrin, he did not seem to be aware that she had written anything and assumed she had been on sick-leave. Weaver had other things on his mind and launched straightaway into an analysis of the political situation in Europe and how Spain was no longer important.

'I'm not interested in Spain,' he said bluntly, 'and nor are my readers.'

Verity felt an overwhelming sense of relief. She had dreaded he would order her back there and she could never admit to him that the prospect of returning to that war-torn country now frightened and depressed her. 'That war is over and, as our star foreign correspondent,' he smiled wolfishly to show he was doing his best to make her feel good, 'it is time you moved on. You are quite recovered, aren't you?'

At once her shoulder began to ache but she said firmly that she was quite recovered.

'Good. You don't speak German, do you?'

'I'm taking lessons from a friend,' she said, thinking of the afternoon spent in the arms of Adam von Trott. She had made him promise to make love to her in German and, laughing, he had agreed. She was his *Liebling*, his little *Blumenkohl*, his *Säugling* and other nonsense, and she loved it.

'Excellent, because I want you to go first to Vienna and then to Prague, depending on how the situation develops.'

'Not Berlin?' she asked, disappointed.

'No, we have a very good man there, Mike Petersen, but Bill Harrison – who was in Vienna – has had a heart attack and is on his way home to recuperate. In any case, Vienna is where it will happen.'

'I am sorry. I had no idea Bill was ill. But why do you say it's Vienna where it will happen? What will happen?'

'Hitler will do what he has promised, for once, and incorporate Austria into the German Reich. My sources say it's just a question of when, not if.'

'And Prague?'

'Czechoslovakia will be next,' Weaver said grimly, lighting a cigar. 'We have never had anyone in Prague. It just seemed too far away to matter to our readers but I have a hunch all that's going to change.'

'So you think there might be war after all?' The *New Gazette*'s official line, proclaimed every day at its masthead, was: There will be no war.

'I'm still hopeful it can be avoided. When I met Herr Hitler last month, he gave me his word . . .' Weaver looked troubled. It had seemed such a coup to meet the German Chancellor and receive his promise in person that he had no intention of making any further territorial demands in Europe. Even in the short time which had elapsed since the meeting, he had begun to doubt Hitler's good faith. Lloyd George, who had accompanied Weaver to Berlin and knew something about German aggression, had said to him only the other day – and Weaver had printed his comment in the paper – 'I have never doubted the fundamental greatness of Hitler as a man. I only wish we had a man of his supreme quality at the head of affairs in our country today. Mussolini is temperamentally an aggressor. I have never thought that Herr Hitler was, and I do not believe it now.' He hoped his old friend was right but he was beginning to doubt it.

'So when do I start?' Verity asked eagerly.

'Soon, but before you go, I have a little job for you. Entertaining, I hope, and certainly instructive. I want you to go down to the South of France and interview the Duke of Windsor. He has let me know that he is intending to visit Hitler himself to discuss . . .' Weaver picked up a letter from his desk and scanned it, 'housing and working conditions of the poor in Germany and Britain.'

Verity was aghast. 'Why me? I don't know anything about him and I despise what I do know. Joe, I'm a Communist. He won't see me even if . . .'

'Housing conditions, workers' rights and so on . . .' Weaver repeated. 'I thought you would be interested.' He was playing with her. 'He is going on to the States immediately afterwards. I thought you might give him the names of some of your friends among the union leaders whom he could see. He is determined to be a man of the people.'

'That's nonsense, and you know it. What are you trying to do to me? Make me a laughing stock?'

'I really can't see what you are making such a fuss about. Most journalists would give their eye teeth for such a chance.'

'I'm grateful . . . of course I am,' Verity spluttered, 'but he'll never see me. Why should he?'

'Because I have asked him to and . . .'

'And?'

'And you will be accompanied by Edward . . .' He held up his hand to stop her interrupting. 'As you know, Edward is a friend of Wallis. He did her a favour and she is very good about returning favours.' He was referring to Edward's success in retrieving some love letters the Duke had sent Mrs Simpson and which had been stolen by one of his former mistresses.

'I see,' Verity said coldly. 'And Edward has agreed to this?'

'He has,' Weaver said firmly. 'He can't write the story but you can. It's another scoop! You ought to be overjoyed.'

'I get it! The Duke will talk to Edward and he will repeat it all to me and I can pretend . . .'

'Got it at last! Now, are you going to do what I say or is our relationship going to end here?'

Verity was very fond of her employer and he had been very good to her but she knew he was not a man to cross. He would never forgive her if she refused this assignment and, if he wanted to, could not only fire her but prevent her being employed by any of his rivals.

'Sorry, Joe,' she capitulated, 'I'm an idiot. It's good of you to give me this. I promise I'll come up with the goods.'

After two more days of intensive interviews, Jebb was forced to admit to himself that he was no further forward. He shut himself away in his office at the police station, told his sergeant that he did not want to be disturbed and filled the fountain pen he had been given to celebrate twenty years with the force. He took a blank sheet of paper out of his desk drawer, shifted in his seat, sucked at his pen and sighed noisily. What did he know? He knew – or thought he knew – that Maud had been killed when everyone was distracted chasing after Mah-Jongg. Several people had seen her walking alone by the stream, not watching the cricket but brooding. One or two – including Sir Simon, Lady Castlewood and Isolde Swann – had tried to talk to her but she had asked to be left alone. She had not been seen alive after the incident with the lemur. That would seem to let out those who had been actively involved in the chase or on the cricket pitch.

No one had admitted to having seen who had released the lemur – 'that bloody mongoose', as Jebb insisted on thinking of the animal – but he had an idea that Mrs Cardew knew more than she was telling. Mah-Jongg – what a silly name! He gathered it was some kind of parlour game – a favourite of Lady Castlewood's. Anyway, it had been left with water and food in the pavilion, tied up to a chair on a long leash. Someone had helped Mah-Jongg slip his collar – he couldn't have done it on his own – and that person might well have been wearing gloves because it would have rash of anyone, other than the Castlewoods, to go near the animal.

Jebb had arranged for all the batting gloves and wicket-keepers' gloves in the pavilion to be sent up to London for Chief Inspector Pride's people to look at. Nothing had been found to indicate that they had been in contact with anything more sinister than a cricket ball – except for the pair Roddy had worn to catch the lemur. Not that this had dismayed Jebb. He knew, if there had been 'lemur' on any of the gloves, it would prove nothing. Most of the kit in the pavilion was used by anyone in either team who needed it. None of the village eleven had their own gloves and neither did most of the Castlewood eleven.

Jebb had not yet sullied his sheet of paper with a single word. Now he wrote down: 'Suspects' and drew a line under the word. He thought for another two minutes and then added alongside, 'Murder Weapon'. He looked thoughtfully at what he had written. He had been called to Swifts Hill on the Friday night of the previous weekend when Sir Simon had reported the dagger missing. He was glad now that he had insisted on going up to the house immediately, even though it had meant getting out of bed. True, he had not discovered anything of any importance – there were no fingerprints on the glass cabinet except for Sir Simon's and a maid's – a girl called Hannah Warren – who had dusted the cabinet the previous day. She said that she always dusted the cabinets before Sir Simon had guests as he often took some of them to view the antiquities. Hannah seemed a sensible girl and he had no reason to disbelieve her.

'It was so beautiful and so . . . evil. I think it had killed people before,' she had said, surprising Jebb with her powers of imagination.

That seemed to narrow the list of suspects considerably. Maud Pitt-Messanger's murderer had to be someone who knew about the dagger, had access to it and had not been chasing the lemur when it was likely the murder was committed. This let out that journalist woman, Miss Browne, who might have had access to the dagger but did not know of its existence until Sir Simon had told her it was missing. She seemed very thick with Lord Edward Corinth for whom Chief Inspector Pride appeared to have some respect. This was odd because Jebb knew Pride disliked the aristocracy almost as much as he disliked politicians and journalists. It also let out Edward and his nephew, who had been on the cricket pitch chasing the lemur when the murder took place.

Roddy Maitland had chased the lemur although he could have stolen the dagger. His fiancée, Isolde Swann, did not pass either test. No one could swear to having seen her chasing the lemur and she certainly had access to the dagger. She was the only woman at Swifts Hill who was strong enough to kill Maud and drag her body into the stream. Dr Morris had said that the strength needed to stab Maud suggested that the killer was a man or a very strong woman. Jebb put her in the column headed 'Suspects', misspelling her name as he did so.

He consulted his notes. The morning after the dagger disappeared he had interviewed all the servants and failed to find one with any motive to steal it. Most of them had been in the Castlewoods' employ for many years and all had good references. If a servant had wanted to steal anything, he or she would hardly have stolen one of Sir Simon's antiquities because they all knew that they had been photographed and catalogued and no servant could have easily disposed of such an object. There were many other things in the house which could more readily be turned into cash, if that was what was wanted.

Of the guests in the house from the Thursday when Hannah dusted the display case and saw the dagger, to the Friday evening when Sir Simon discovered that it was missing, there was only the doctor fellow, Dominic Montillo, and the Communist writer chap Graham Harvey to consider. It was difficult to see Mrs Cardew as a serious suspect. No, he put his money on either Montillo or Harvey. Montillo could well have returned to Swifts Hill on the day of the cricket match in time to leap out of the bushes and stab Maud. On the other hand, would he have had the dagger with him? And he could not have arranged the lemur's escape.

As for Harvey, Lord Edward had some idea that he might have been Maud's lover but the idea of a lovers' quarrel didn't ring true. Harvey had admitted that Maud had told him she had killed her father. He said he thought her overwrought imagination had given her delusions. She was not sleeping. She was depressed and taking Benzedrine. According to Dr Morris, that might well have given her hallucinations. Harvey said he had told Maud not to repeat her 'confession' to anyone. He said he had hoped someone would soon be arrested for the old man's murder and then Maud would understand she had been imagining she had killed him. However, Jebb solemnly added Harvey's name under the heading 'Suspects' and that of Dominic Montillo.

What about motive? Jebb started another column and headed it 'Motive'. Neither Isolde Swann nor Montillo had a motive unless, as Pride suggested when they had spoken on the telephone, Montillo had wanted to silence her before she said something which might damage him or his reputation. Perhaps, as Lord Edward seemed to believe, Maud had said something to Montillo when he and Dr Morris found her after her suicide attempt – something so damaging that he had to stop her talking. Harvey, too, might have a motive but he hadn't uncovered it yet.

Who else? Mrs Cardew's two children, of course, the girl – what was her name? He scratched his head with his fountain pen and that did the trick. Margaret! They called her Maggie – with the horrible burn scar – and her brother, the MP, Edmund – Teddy. Jebb did not like politicians and would be happy to suspect any one of them of murder but neither Cardew nor his sister could have stolen the dagger . . . They weren't in the house when it disappeared. And, anyway, he could not find that they had the shadow of a motive. Wait a minute though! They had been at the Abbey when the Professor was murdered. Had they seen Maud stab her father and were they blackmailing her? But then why kill her? What if someone else had stolen the dagger for them . . .? He made a note and then scrubbed it out. It was too far-fetched. In any case, Maggie Cardew was such a nice girl and she wasn't strong enough to commit the murder. The brother then – he *was* a suspect so Jebb added his name to the list.

Hang on though – going back to the women – there was that secretary of Sir Simon's – what was her name? Miss Berners – Sylvia Berners – a Jew and a foreign Jew at that. He had nothing against Jews, he told himself. What they were doing in Germany was quite wrong but still . . . She had a flat at the back of the house. It had been very generous of Sir Simon, she had said, but it suited him too as he did not keep normal office hours and liked to have his secretary on call twenty-four hours a day. Jebb wondered idly if she were Sir Simon's mistress but dismissed the idea. He might be a womanizer but he would hardly sleep with a woman under his own roof and under his wife's nose. Miss Berners had seemed very nervous, he thought, when he interviewed her but that might be because – as a Jew – she had learned not to welcome police interest in her. She, too, had no alibi – she said she was alone in her flat, reading and listening to the wireless. As for motive . . . Jebb sighed. Something might materialize but then again, would she have the physical strength to kill Maud and lay her in the stream? He did not think so.

He drew a caricature of a hook-nosed Jew. She was a refugee from Germany, Sir Simon had told him. In Jebb's view, there were altogether too many of these refugees and they should go back where they belonged. He had agreed with something he had read at breakfast the other morning in the *Daily Mail*: 'The influx of foreign Jews is overwhelming the country.' Jews and Communists! They made all the trouble in the world in his opinion. Talking of Communists, perhaps Harvey had crept into the house, stolen the dagger and used it to kill Maud. Perhaps he was in league with the Communist journalist, Verity Browne. Certainly, Harvey had not been in evidence when the lemur escaped from the pavilion.

He felt he ought to be able to see who had done the deed but, for the life of him, he could not. Maybe the way forward was to look more closely at Maud Pitt-Messanger and who had a previous connection with her. He would also have to reread Chief Inspector Pride's report on her father's killing. It had been good of Pride to send it him. There must be something he was missing.

He looked again at his notes of the interviews he had carried out after the dagger had gone missing. He had been very stern with Sir Simon, and said, 'Did you not think to have your exhibits better protected? A burglar could have taken the whole collection in a matter of minutes. There was no alarm . . .'

'I have been intending to have new, secure cabinets made but I am afraid I never got round to it. But you see, Inspector,' Sir Simon had said in mitigation, 'these are well-known pieces to archaeologists. They have been much studied and photographed. No burglar would have been able to take them into Sotheby's or Sonerschein's – or anywhere respectable – and offer them for sale.'

'They could have smuggled them over to the Continent and sold them there,' Jebb had suggested.

'Possibly, in Amsterdam . . .' Sir Simon had agreed. 'But, after all, the dagger wasn't stolen, was it? Just borrowed.'

'No sign of the keys to the cabinet, I suppose?'

'No sign at all, I'm afraid, Inspector.'

Perhaps he would have another word with Lord Edward

Corinth. He had been helpful when he had interviewed him – not at all superior. He believed Maud had killed her father and that her confession had not been a drug-induced delusion. He thought the murderer must have seen her talking earnestly to him and acted quickly to shut her mouth. The urgent call he had received from the pavilion to pad up was premature. He could have heard Maud out and still been ready to go out and bat. So who had called him? He said he wasn't sure and he wanted to be sure before he said anything which might incriminate an innocent person.

Jebb looked gloomily at his sheet of paper. He had thought he was going to be able to solve this case in just a few hours but now he was beginning to think it might take longer. All his suspects had wanted to leave Swifts Hill and get on with their lives and he could not stop them. Even Sir Simon – he was going to the South of France 'on business', whatever that meant, and Jebb really could not ask him to cancel his trip. And the German lad . . . He had gone off to London with the Browne woman . . . Well, damn it, let them all go. He needed time to think. The Chief Constable had given him ten days and then he was to accept Chief Inspector Pride's offer of assistance. It would be a blow to his self-esteem but he was beginning to think he might welcome a little help. He tore up his sheet of paper and threw it in the wastepaper basket.

8

Edward collected Verity from her flat – he wasn't allowed in –
at ten to catch the Golden Arrow from Victoria Station at
eleven. At Dover, they boarded the *Canterbury* and an hour
later were in Calais. Neither had felt much like eating even
though the Channel had been oily smooth. Edward had bought
a two-pound bar of Cadbury's motoring chocolate and they
nibbled on this. In Paris – which was uncomfortably full of
visitors to the great Paris Exhibition – they split up, Edward to
call in on the Embassy where some papers were waiting for
him and Verity to visit a friend – a journalist called Alan
Moorehead who worked at the *New Gazette*'s Paris office and
whom she had met in Spain.

As he waited for her at the Gare de Lyon just before six,
Edward could not help thinking ruefully of how, when he had
last travelled on the Blue Train, he had fantasized about having
Verity beside him – how they would enjoy a day, or even a night,
in Paris – perhaps dining at the Ritz or Maxim's, or maybe
somewhere more intimate. How they would relish the hustle
and bustle at the Gare de Lyon, the officious blue-and-gold-uni-
formed officials, the excitement of that moment early in the
evening when the great train steams off on its long journey
towards the sun. Verity, who he was always amused to find
loved luxury, would indulge herself and surrender to the
ministrations of an obsequious steward. He had imagined them
flirting over the excellent meals and how they would spurn
advances from other passengers, content with their own
company. Then bed in the comfortable miniature cabins, soothed
by the beat of the wheels against the shining metal track. To
make love on a train! Could there be anything more romantic!

Instead she was cool and perfectly friendly but repelled any gesture of intimacy. It seemed, for no apparent reason, that they were no longer lovers. Edward was bewildered and hurt. Had he done something to offend her? Had he got too close or was it that damn Communist, Graham Harvey, and his hatred of Churchill that had soured their relationship? He had made an effort to talk to Harvey at the cricket match, aware that he had established some influence over Verity which he suspected of being malign. Harvey had been surly and monosyllabic and Edward had to accept defeat. However, he thought he understood the man's appeal. He was an outsider – hostile to conventional morality and seemingly uninterested in what people thought of him. In addition, he was utterly certain in his faith in Communism. Edward knew the type and considered them most dangerous because, as fanatics, they were not open to argument.

Verity's belief in Harvey's austere creed had been undermined in Spain, he knew, and he wondered if, perhaps unconsciously, she was looking for someone to rebuild the foundations of her belief. What she had seen in Spain had shocked her – not just the atrocities carried out by the Fascists but those, equally cruel, which were the work of her friends and allies. And, what was worse, these brutalities had been directed very often not at the enemy but at political allies who had failed to toe the Stalinist line. In particular, she now had evidence that many so-called Trotskyists had been murdered or made to endure show trials in which the guilty verdicts and death sentences had been passed before the trial started. Some of the victims had been known to her. And yet she had invested everything in the Communist cause. Was she now to become an apostate? It did not bear thinking about. At all costs she must remain true.

In Harvey, Edward reckoned, she had found a man who would – like a Jesuit in Elizabethan England – gladly go to the stake for his faith. His certainty massaged away her uncertainties. He was ugly, humourless, driven by his contempt for the society in which he had to live. Verity would like – at least sometimes – to be as he was but she loved life too much and was too intelligent to sacrifice her common sense at the altar of blind fanaticism for long. It was that which prevented Edward from despairing. For the moment Harvey was her Father

Confessor and her conscience. She wanted to be a martyr to the cause. Edward told himself he must wait until her crisis of faith had been resolved.

And the situation was complicated by the German – in many respects Harvey's antithesis but, in his way, just as attractive. Edward had no idea if Verity had slept with Adam – he rather thought she had – and did not really care. He just knew that she worshipped him. He was her ideal, as Churchill was Edward's. He was a heroic figure – a reincarnation of a medieval Teutonic Knight – a patriot but an enemy of Fascism. Edward saw much to admire in the young man but was afraid that the time would come when he would be fatally compromised by having to choose between his country and his hatred of Fascism. Adam was not a Communist but an aristocrat with strong views on how men should behave to one another. Edward could empathize. He had no difficulty in imagining his own position if a Fascist party had come to power in England as, for a brief moment, had seemed possible. He would have opposed it with all his might but, in his own eyes at least, remained a patriot. These were dangerous times when everyone had to make a stand for what they believed in.

The combination of Harvey and Adam von Trott was a heady brew and he feared Verity had found his innate dislike of extremism in all its forms unpalatable. On that first occasion he had taken the Blue Train to the South of France, he had been on his way to Spain in a rather panicky attempt to protect her from unspecified danger. This trip, in the so-called 'millionaire's train', should have been sheer pleasure followed by an easy few days in the sun, a fascinating dinner with the Duke and Duchess of Windsor and then home again to domestic bliss. As it turned out, Verity was not in the mood to enjoy luxury. She was not sullen or irritable but cool and professional, which was worse. He could have dealt with her anger – he often had before – but this unforgiving *friendliness*, as though he was an acquaintance whom she tolerated rather than liked, was difficult to accept. He attempted to tease her but that merely produced surprised stares or blank incomprehension. He tried to engage her in serious conversation on matters he knew to be important to her – the Munich exhibition of so-called degenerate art, by which the Nazis seemed to mean all modern art; the war in China where the Japanese were behaving with extraordinary cruelty to Chinese civilians; and, on a lighter note, Amelia Earhart's mysterious disappearance on the last leg of her round-the-world flight from California. Only when he mentioned, unwisely, Churchill's disappointment at not being offered a position in Neville Chamberlain's new cabinet did he receive more than a formal response.

'Mr Churchill!' She spat out the name. 'Well, you know my opinions of him. If he were in the cabinet, we would probably have declared war on Russia by now.' She stopped and took a breath. 'But I won't discuss him with you because you will only go on about how he will save the world.'

Edward could have wept with frustration.

It was a relief to reach Cannes. Lord Weaver had offered them the use of his villa on Cap Martin and, in other circumstances, it would have been the perfect place to relax, make love and soak up the sun. Now, it was unthinkable and they stayed at the Carlton in such splendour that Verity was visibly uneasy. Edward wished now he had never agreed to Joe's request to accompany her.

'She'll need looking after,' he had said, 'you know, chaperon-ing. You'll have to stop her making a fool of herself and talking Communist clap-trap to the Duke.'

Both men had smiled guiltily, knowing how Verity would hate being talked about in this way. Edward had welcomed the chance of being alone with her for three days. Surely, in three days he could woo her back? Now, he knew he was wrong. If it had been a normal quarrel they might have made up their differences in bed but it wasn't that sort of disagreement. Edward was feeling a little guilty because he had a particular reason for meeting the Duke of Windsor of which Verity knew nothing. Churchill had asked him to pass on a letter to the Duke in which he strongly advised him not to tour Germany and meet the Nazi leaders. Churchill pointed out that such a trip would be a tremendous public relations coup for Goering and Hitler and make the King very angry. Churchill, who had supported the Duke when he wanted to remain king while marrying Mrs Simpson, was still regarded by the Duke as a friend and ally although he and Wallis had been disappointed that he had not attended their wedding in Tours. Despite the Duke's regard for Churchill, Edward thought it most unlikely that he would take any notice of his advice but it was his clear duty to make the effort to give it him. The Duke was too pig-headed and politically naive to see the use to which he was being put by the Nazis.

The Duke and Duchess, who had married only a couple of months earlier and might therefore be presumed to be enjoying their honeymoon, were living at the Villa La Cröe in Antibes, owned by one of Lord Weaver's friends and rivals, Sir Pomeroy Burton. It was a pleasant, shady house with green shutters and delightful gardens. Edward and Verity presented themselves at the villa about six o'clock the next day and were led by the butler on to the terrace where the Duke and Duchess were having cocktails with two or three friends. Edward noted with amusement that Verity made what might almost have been a curtsey and, in happier times, he would have stored away the memory to rib her about it later. His mind was on the tricky question of what he should call the Duchess. He knew the Duke liked her to be addressed as Her Royal Highness even though, at the abdication, this title had been expressly denied her. In the end, to please the Duke, he did use her royal title and was glad he had done so when he saw him smile. For a few moments, he was busy with Wallis who patted his arm and wanted to know all about Verity. It was quite a shock when he suddenly saw that the distinguished-looking man at the other end of the terrace was Simon Castlewood. He was sitting beside a pretty, snub-nosed, bright-eyed girl dressed with just too much care to be English.

Sir Simon seemed equally surprised to see Verity and Edward, and possibly a little embarrassed, though he tried not to show it. Clearly, the Duke had not bothered to inform him who else had been invited to dinner. The Duchess was charming to Verity in her cool way and took her to sit beside her in a bamboo armchair. The Duke was on his feet mixing a cocktail – something he liked to do himself – and greeted Edward courteously, inquiring after the journey and what the weather had been like in England. There was, of course, no mention of their previous meeting. This had been frosty though Edward had done them a considerable service in retrieving letters the Duke had written Wallis which, had they been published, would have embarrassed them. No one likes to be in someone else's debt, as Edward knew to his cost. That was all forgotten now and it was clear that he was to be treated like any other casual acquaintance.

The other guests were Serge Voronoff – a strange-looking man who, the Duchess explained, was famous for 'monkey glands' – and the Duke's most loyal friend and supporter Major Edward 'Fruity' Metcalfe. He was less a guest and more a member of the Duke's entourage. Edward knew him quite well and they shook hands warmly. Metcalfe seemed to greet him with something like relief. As soon as he could, Metcalfe took him off into a corner and explained that all was not well at La Cröe. Since the King had abdicated, he had become increasingly irritable and complained constantly of slights and insults from the English community in Cannes and Monte Carlo as well as from the many prominent visitors to the South of France. 'He's so touchy!' Metcalfe confessed. 'When he heard the *Cutty Sark* had been seen in Cannes harbour a week or two ago and the Duke of Westminster had not asked to see him, he wouldn't eat or sleep for forty-eight hours and, of course, he blames me.'

'Why does he blame you?'

'Because I'm here,' Metcalfe replied simply.

'And the Duchess?'

'She's very good with him but the truth is, he's beginning to bore her.'

'Do they go to the casino?'

'Occasionally, but David always imagines he is being stared at and, of course, he is. What would be worse,' he said with a grin, 'is if he weren't. He's not quite the figure he was. Last time he ventured out to the casino in Cannes, he was actually jostled by people wanting to get past him to the *chemin de fer*. The trouble is that there are so many ex-kings here.' He counted on his fingers, 'The ex-king of Portugal, the ex-king of Spain, the ex-king of Yugoslavia, the ex-king of Egypt . . .'

'Do they socialize – the ex-kings?' Edward asked, grinning.

'They all belong to the Cercle Nautique. It's the grandest club on the coast.'

At that moment the Duke, seeing them gossiping, came to interrupt.

'What are you two finding so amusing?' he inquired sourly.

'Lord Edward was just asking me about my white dinner-jacket. I said they were all the rage here but doubted they would catch on in England,' Metcalfe said smoothly.

'Hmm,' the Duke said. 'As long as you weren't conspiring. He'll report everything back to Winston, don'ty'know?'

'He will be delighted to hear you are well and happy, sir,' Edward replied with as much sincerity as he could manage.

They went in to eat about nine and the food was very good – melon with tomato ice, eggs with crab sauce, chicken with avocado pear salad and an elaborate fruit pudding, and Edward started to enjoy himself. He was very much aware that this was an occasion he would always remember and probably bore his friends with for years to come. The Duke dominated the conversation. He seemed to take to Verity and questioned her closely on social conditions in the cities, a subject on which she could talk for hours. He obviously felt he still had a part to play in England and had not yet thrown off the habits and concerns of kingship. He was lively and well informed and discussed the welfare of the Welsh coal-miners with real passion, saying he wanted to see them clean, healthy and contented. He asked Verity to tell him about the Jarrow March, on which she had reported, and complained that Baldwin had refused to let him meet the marchers. Edward, while appreciating that the Duke was interested in the social conditions of his former subjects, was faintly repulsed by his tone of voice. It was as though he wanted the miners to be clean and healthy in the same way that he might want his dogs or horses to be fit and well.

Edward talked to the Duchess and soon recalled how charming she could be. She wanted to know all about her friends – some of whom were also Edward's – and the London 'season'. 'I don't want to spend my life in exile,' she told him. He had very little opportunity to talk to Sir Simon's pretty friend but gathered she was an actress and French. She seemed charmed that Edward could speak to her in her own language, confessing that she found the 'English tongue' difficult but the men *charmants*.

After dinner, they all rose together and strolled out on to the terrace for coffee and liqueurs. There was no hint from the Duchess that the ladies should leave the gentlemen to talk amongst themselves. It was almost as if she did not like to leave the Duke alone with his guests in case he said something he ought not. When the Duke beckoned to Edward to follow him, he caught the quick glance of warning she shot him. He walked after the Duke into a small conservatory where, standing, they lit cigars and Edward gave him Churchill's letter. The Duke made no attempt to read it but slipped it in his pocket.

'I know what it says but you can tell them I won't do it. I won't give up my tour of Germany. It is incumbent on me to go,' he said pompously, his voice sounding rather shrill. 'Someone in authority must go and do what they can to prevent this unnecessary war. I like the Germans and I like what Herr Hitler has done for his country. We are natural allies – Germany and England – Aryan races with more in common than we have with the southern races. We should combine to fight off the threat of Communism.'

Edward hoped he did not know, or had forgotten, that one of his guests was a Communist. There was something about his use of phrases such as 'southern races' that made Edward feel he must have been talking to Sir Simon and he risked saying, 'May I ask you, sir, what you think of Castlewood's views on purifying the race?'

The Duke took the cigar out of his mouth and plucked at his bow tie, a mannerism he had when he was nervous. He looked at Edward as if trying to decide whether he could talk frankly or not. Edward's expression remained blandly interested.

'I think he is right,' he said simply. 'In fact I have agreed to be patron of his Foundation. It is one of the things I shall be discussing with Herr Hitler – one of the ways in which our two nations can cooperate. Herr Hitler has had remarkable success, you know, in freeing his country from the tyranny of the Jewish bankers whose rapacity brought Germany to its knees.'

Edward was dumbfounded. He had guessed when he saw Sir Simon that he was there for a purpose but he never imagined Sir Simon devious enough to involve the Duke in the Foundation. And what he had said about Jewish bankers! Edward wondered who had taught him to spout such nonsense – Ribbentrop, perhaps. He was a close friend of the Duchess – some even said her lover. The Duke must have seen something in his eyes and, realizing he had been indiscreet, added hastily, 'Just an idea, you know. I had rather you kept it to yourself.'

Edward was able to avoid making any promises as they were interrupted by a call from the Duchess, who seemed to sense the

Duke was in danger of an indiscretion. The two men walked back on to the terrace, both relieved nothing more needed to be said. It was a lovely, starlit night and the flag bearing the Prince of Wales' feathers hung motionless from a pole in the garden. Seeing Edward glance towards it, the Duke said, 'When I became king, they had to take it down as there was no Prince of Wales. So I didn't see why I shouldn't have it here.' Edward thought it was precisely because the Duke could not see why it was in poor taste to fly it here in exile that he had lost his crown.

At midnight, they thanked their hosts and made ready to depart. The Duke inquired when they were returning to London. Edward said the next day and he noticed the Duke's left eye twitch as though in pain. He had been in high spirits throughout the evening, obviously happy to be with his 'Wally' whose hand he grasped at every opportunity, but he was homesick. He did not like foreigners other than Americans and Germans. His last words to Edward were surprisingly warm, 'Do come again. We like visitors from England. Never enough . . . never enough . . .'

'What was he doing there?' Verity asked, as soon as the car had driven away and they were standing in the hotel foyer.

'Sir Simon? He asked the same thing of me. I said you had come to interview the Duke and I had come along for the ride. How did you get on, by the way?'

'I got enough to write my article but I need to think about it. What he said was all right – I mean he seemed genuinely concerned about unemployment, the need to tear down the slums and replace them with good quality housing, but there was something about the way he said it . . . I don't quite know, but it was as if he was talking about an inferior race. Maybe I am being unfair. He could certainly quote the facts and figures.'

'So what was your general impression of the "royal couple",' Edward inquired with studied sarcasm. Her response surprised him.

'I felt sorry for them. Of course, he will live a wasted life now, with nothing to do but drink and idle away his time, but that's the nature of royalty. If he had been an ordinary man, he might have done something useful with his life. He cares about the poor which is more than . . .' Her brow furrowed. 'The whole stupid arrangement ought to be swept away – and it will be

143

soon. Royalty can hardly survive the war when it comes. Ordinary men and women will vote them out and we'll have a republic.'

Edward wasn't so sure but merely asked, 'You think he would have made a good king?'

'I don't see why not. As I say, he cares about the working classes. He said he hoped he could bring a little glamour into blighted lives and I don't say he is wrong.'

'So you'll write a sympathetic article about them?'

'I haven't thought what I shall say yet, but I think they have been hard done by. I shall describe what I saw.'

'Did you find out who Voronoff was? I didn't really speak to him,' he said, changing the subject.

'Yes. What an odd-looking man! He works at the Beauty Institute. He injects monkey glands into elderly women and they become young and beautiful. Some nonsense like that.'

'Ugh!' Edward shuddered. 'What you women suffer to please us men.' He winced, knowing his joke would not amuse.

Verity scowled but restrained herself from snapping his head off. Instead she said, 'Does Jebb know Sir Simon is here?'

'He gave him permission for a brief "business trip" but I doubt he knew he was visiting the Duke and Duchess. I certainly didn't. She's a looker,' he could not resist adding, rather unwisely.

'Who?' Verity said coldly. 'The Duchess?'

'No, silly! Sir Simon's girl. I saw you talking to her. I bet Ginny doesn't know he's escorting . . . what is she – a film actress? One can appreciate what he sees in her, of course.'

'Can one?' Verity's tone had gone from cold to icy. 'As a matter of fact, her name is Natalie Sarrault and she is making a film at the Victorine studios in Nice.'

'And is she his mistress?'

'Perhaps, I didn't ask her. But I don't see what it is do with us, as long as Ginny doesn't mind.'

'Or doesn't know. You don't mind seeing your friend betrayed?' he added brutally.

Verity blushed but refused to be drawn. 'I liked her. In fact, she has invited me to go and watch her filming tomorrow before we return to London. I thought it might be interesting. I think there'll be time if I start early enough.'

Edward digested this. 'Am I invited?'

'Not specially, but I suppose if you want to come . . .'

'No, I think I'll check up on Montillo's Beauty Institute. Sir Simon was telling me all about it. Apparently, it's only a few miles out of town. I asked him if I could look round it and he was suspiciously keen that I should do. He said he couldn't take me there himself as he has a business meeting with the Duke – which I think involves playing golf at Cagnes – but he would telephone and they would be expecting me. By the way, I very much fear he may induce the Duke to become a patron of his Foundation. It is just the sort of bloody silly thing the Duke would do. He wants to be seen to be doing "good works" and have it reported in the English newspapers.'

'It may be all above board . . .'

'I don't think so, V.'

There was nothing more to be said so they wished each other goodnight and went off to their separate bedrooms. Edward would have given a lot to have been able to take her in his arms but that was impossible. Would they never again be at one with each other? Was this stiff politeness all that was left? It seemed so. It took him some time to get to sleep and he awoke with a headache.

Verity had never been to a film studio but she had a vague idea that it would be glamorous. She imagined she would see beautiful women and handsome men being ordered about by tyrannical directors like the Austrian-born Eric von Stroheim. A photograph she had seen of von Stroheim dressed in leather boots and riding breeches had made a considerable impression on her as dictators like Benito Mussolini had adopted the same style of dress.

The Victorine studios on the eastern outskirts of Nice were very different from what she had imagined. They consisted of several large hangars which reminded her more of Croydon Aerodrome than anything else. When she nonchalantly announced to the uniformed security guard at the gate that she had an appointment with Natalie Sarrault, she had half-expected him to bow and scrape before escorting her to some palatial dressing-room. In the event, he was singularly unimpressed and

145

made her repeat the name before admitting he knew whom she was talking about. Then, in a bored gesture, he directed her across a swathe of tarmac to an ugly office building. There, an elderly woman, who seemed to be some sort of secretary, took her through a warren of passages to one of the hangars she had noticed earlier.

Here there was some activity. A simple wooden set representing a bedroom was raised on a platform. Several large and unwieldy-looking cameras were standing idle while a man, who she assumed must be the film's director, was brushing Natalie's hair. This was a very different Natalie to the beautifully dressed, shimmering girl with whom she had dined the night before. She was dressed in a flimsy cotton frock, rather dirty and torn near her breasts. She caught sight of Verity and gave her a little wave. Verity responded before perching herself on a broken-backed chair and making herself as inconspicuous as possible.

At first, she was interested and looked about her, planning in her mind an informed, light-hearted article on the French film industry. There were three or four men sitting on upturned crates playing cards, each with a cigarette in his mouth, who she thought might be cameramen. She was now inclined to think that the man brushing Natalie's hair was not the director but to do with make-up as, having finished her hair, he began to dab at her cheeks with a powder puff. After twenty minutes nothing had happened and she began to get bored. Her chair was uncomfortable and she thought she might go for a walk. At that moment, the director did appear with a lanky youth who, Verity assumed, must be Natalie's 'lover'. At the director's urging, the youth took Natalie in his arms and said something. Verity could not quite hear what it was but the director obviously thought he could say it better. For the next half an hour this scene was repeated until Verity, glancing at her watch, realized she would soon have to return to the hotel if she was to pack and catch the train.

Unexpectedly, a break was called and Natalie, seeming a little shy, made her way over to Verity. She spoke rapidly and, although Verity's French was good, she had to concentrate to understand what she was saying.

'That silly boy!'

'Who?'

'Henri. He can act but he is so scared of Jean, he is paralysed.'

'Jean?'

'Oh, I am sorry. I forget you do not know these people. That is Jean Marceau. He is very good but he does not know how to treat people to get the best out of them.'

'What's the film about?'

'It's about a young man devoured by jealousy. Every day when he leaves for work he believes his wife goes off to have an affair. It kills him in the end.'

'And you play his wife?'

'Yes. I am sorry to have kept you waiting. It takes so long. We have to make the film in two languages.'

'Two languages at the same time?'

'Yes, in French for our country and in German for UFA.'

'UFA?'

'They are a big German film company. Have you got time to eat? The canteen is just next door. It is not good food, you understand, but we can talk there.'

When they were seated at a trestle table with two bowls of cold soup in front of them, Natalie asked, 'Is it true you are a Communist?'

'Yes, it's true. Who told you? I mean, it's not a secret but . . .'

'Simon told me.'

'Ah!'

'Yes, I am his mistress – *une femme de trente ans*, as we say. Does that shock you?'

'No, but his wife is a friend of mine.'

'He does not love me,' she said with a shrug. 'And I do not love him but it is amusing. We like each other and I am saving up to be married.'

'To be married?'

'To Henri, the young man in the picture.'

'Simon pays you?'

'Now you *are* shocked! He does not pay me but there are *cadeaux*. It is capitalism, is it not? He wants to be entertained and to have sex and I enjoy going out to smart places and meeting important people. It is fair, I think.'

'You have known him for a long time?'

'Since three years he has been coming here.'

'Not on holiday?'

'No. He says his wife does not like the sun.'

'Then why does he come?'

'Because of *l'institut* – the Institute of Beauty, of course. You know about it?'

'I have heard of it. In fact my friend who you met last night, Lord Edward . . .' Verity tried to sound casual and failed. 'He is there now . . . to look around.'

'He is very good-looking.' Natalie looked sly. 'Simon says he is rich. A rich, English milord,' she repeated dreamily.

'Yes, well. Tell me more about Simon Castlewood. Have you met his friend, Mr Montillo? He's a doctor.'

'Of course! He is often here.' She seemed to take offence, perhaps because Verity had not confided in her about her English lord. 'Why all these questions, Miss Browne?' Suddenly alarmed, she said, 'His wife . . . she does not want evidence for a divorce?'

'No, no,' Verity said hurriedly. 'Nothing like that. It is just . . . This Institute . . . who goes there?'

'It is very popular. All the rich ladies of a certain age go there to stay beautiful.' She giggled. 'You have heard of monkey gland injections? That was why Monsieur Voronoff was there last night. The Duchess . . . you understand? But that is – what do you say? – "old hat". There is something new now . . . very secret. There are experiments . . . He can take away your wrinkles *comme ça*.' In a brief but highly graphic gesture, Natalie ran a finger beneath her eyes as though it were a knife. 'But you are a newspaper reporter, are you not? Simon . . . he says I must tell no one. You promise you will not betray me?'

She looked upset and scared. Verity reassured her. 'I am a war correspondent, you understand. I do not report on beauty for my newspaper. I promise I will say nothing.'

Natalie relaxed. 'A war correspondent! Then you must be very busy. There is so much war and there will be more. But why are you here? There is no war on the Côte d'Azur.'

'Not yet,' Verity agreed, 'but I fear there will be soon . . . in a year or two.'

'The Boches!' Natalie almost spat the word. 'They spoil everything.'

'But no one seems to care down here. The hotels are full. All the rich and famous are still coming to Cannes and Monte Carlo.'

148

'That is so,' she agreed.

Verity thought for a moment. 'Natalie, are you sure there is nothing odd going on at the Institute? I mean, apart from the new operation, or whatever it is, to remove wrinkles?'

Natalie looked worried. 'Maybe, I do not know but . . . perhaps at the hospital . . . There is a private clinic . . . it belongs to the Institute. Very sick people go there . . . to die, I think. They lie in chairs in the sun and wait to die. I have seen them.'

'I see . . . a sanatorium for the terminally ill?'

'And they look after people who have deformities. I think I have heard Simon say people who have been burned . . . who have scars or who are born with seven fingers . . . that sort of thing.'

'That sounds very good.'

'Yes, but . . .'

'But what, Natalie?'

'I do not know but sometimes the operations . . . I used to know a nurse who worked there for a little and she left because she did not like the operations.'

'What sort of operations?' Verity demanded.

Natalie looked frightened. 'I know nothing. Please forget what I have said. It is nothing.'

'Can I speak to the nurse . . . your friend?'

'No, she died.'

'She died?'

'In a car accident. It was very sad.' Natalie wiped her eyes.

'Are you crying?'

'No, the bright lights when I am filming . . . they hurt the eyes. Jean says I am to marry a rich man before I go blind.'

'And will you?' Verity inquired.

'No, I will marry Henri and stop making films and have babies.'

Verity wondered what Natalie would make of her decision to do exactly the opposite.

The Institute of Beauty was a long low building of white stone with a superb view of the Golfe de St Tropez. Edward had hired a car from the hotel and was glad that he had left immediately after breakfast as the road proved slow – narrow and twisting

149

but certainly picturesque. It seemed odd to site the Institute here rather than in Cannes or Nice because it was hard to reach, even by train. There was only a light railway from Hyères. Furthermore, the *mistral* which blew down from the Esterels would, he thought, make it unbearable for winter visitors.

However, all was explained when he arrived. He found the place without too much difficulty although the Institute clearly did not feel the need to advertise itself. There was a simple brass plate at the entrance with the name in three languages. This was a retreat – a secret place for rich women to get away from their husbands and lovers and rejuvenate themselves in private. Out of sight of prying eyes, they could be waxed, manicured, caked in mud, exfoliated and injected with excretions from exotic plants and unfortunate animals sacrificed in the cause of female vanity. The receptionist asked him to wait but confirmed that he was expected. He took a brochure – which featured a photograph of a wise but youthful-looking Dominic Montillo – and began to read. It laid out in detail the many treatments available. He was particularly interested in the courses of injections for which great claims were made. These seemed to involve introducing into the bloodstream a nightmare concoction of liquids derived from exotic animals including baboons and turtles as well as pigs, cats and even goats. His stomach revolted and he was glad to turn to the plant-based treatments which used a wide variety of oils and unguents from all over the world.

A door opened as he was reading a cheery little paragraph on varicose veins, and an efficient-looking woman in her late thirties came forward and grasped his hand.

'I see you have been studying our brochure, Lord Edward. I hope you found it interesting?'

She introduced herself as Monique Guillet, the Institute's chief administrator. He was sure she was French but her English was faultless and must have been learnt in England. In her crisp, starched uniform one would have taken her for the matron at some smart London hospital. She had obviously been briefed by Sir Simon to give him a guided tour and she was determined he would see everything. Rather to his embarrassment, he was urged to look into every hot room, cold room and water massage room as well as the sauna, the 'dip' pools, the indoor and outdoor pools, and the solarium. Everwhere he went, he met ladies in white gowns with towels round their heads, usually accompanied by a 'nurse' – or at least a member of staff dressed as a nurse – who ignored him. He dreaded running into someone he knew although most of the women were unrecognizable in their 'half-cooked' state, as he described it later to Verity.

There were a few areas into which, to his relief but Mme Guillet's regret, he was not permitted to venture. He had no wish to be caught peering at women naked except for an olive oil dressing or disturb those being scraped and kneaded in the massage rooms. It was all so transparently 'above board' that the hairs on the back of his neck bristled. Edward chided himself for his cynicism. He must not jump to conclusions just because he knew Montillo and did not like him. What was it to him if these women were being relieved of their money with amazing rapidity? There was nothing illegal in that if they or their husbands thought it money well spent.

Mme Guillet seemed not in the least surprised that Edward should be so interested in the Institute. Perhaps she thought that – as a friend of Sir Simon's – he was being asked to invest in the business or perhaps she was simply not interested in what was not her affair. At the end of the tour when they were sitting in her cool office at the back of the building, Edward congratulated her. 'It is all very impressive and spotlessly clean. I am most impressed. By the way, are your staff medically qualified or is that not necessary?'

'They are all qualified for the work they do – massages and beauty treatments – but they are not *medically* qualified.' Edward thought he detected a hint of *froideur* in her voice.

'I see that of course, but I gather you also offer courses of rejuvenation treatments which involve injections and so on. Are these overseen by a doctor?'

'Yes, Mr Montillo, or an associate doctor, would be present when any injection is given.'

'But he spends a lot of time in England?'

'There are two doctors in Nice and one in Cannes who visit the Institute on a regular basis.'

'But Mr Montillo is the head of the Institute?' Edward smiled, trying to look genial but failing.

'That is correct.' She seemed about to say something else but in the end kept her lips firmly closed.

'Some of these courses use monkey glands . . .' He was looking at the brochure, 'beeswax, civet – that's cat, isn't it? They must be tested and approved by some medical authority, surely?'

'I am afraid, if you have medical questions, you must address them to Mr Montillo. I am not qualified to answer them but every treatment we give is proven to be safe and effective.'

'Oh, so you are not a nurse? I thought in that uniform . . .'

'I am not a nurse and do not pretend to be medically trained. I wear this uniform because cleanliness is a priority here, as you have observed. It would not do for me, or any of the staff, to wear their ordinary clothes in the Institute.'

'No, of course. May I ask – your English is so good, Mme Guillet – have you lived in England?'

'I have. The Institute is international. Our clientele come from all over Europe and America. Most of the staff speak at least one other language. I also speak German and Italian.'

'I see. Well, I must not take up any more of your valuable time. You have been very kind. I am most grateful to you for showing me round. It is all – as I say – most impressive.'

She allowed a smile to unfreeze her face. 'I am glad to be of help, Lord Edward. I will show you out.'

As he was shaking her hand at the main entrance, Edward said casually, 'I think Sir Simon mentioned that Mr Montillo also ran a laboratory near here?'

'There is a laboratory attached to a small private hospital – we call it the Clinic – a few miles away in the hills above St Tropez. It is where Mr Montillo carries out complicated medical procedures and where some of the beauty preparations we use are made. You know, of course, that he is a respected plastic surgeon. He has done much to pioneer treatment for physical deformities. His work in the field is, I understand, very much admired.'

'Would he carry out surgery to improve a person's appearance?' he asked innocently.

'Cosmetic surgery?'

'That's right. You see, I have a friend who has a bad burn scar which has spoilt her looks. Would he be able to help her, do you think?'

152

'I could not possibly say, Lord Edward, but Mr Montillo is a very remarkable man. If anyone can help your friend, I am sure he can.'

Mme Guillet sounded a little too enthusiastic, he thought, but it was understandable that she should want to speak well of her employer. She might suspect that anything she said would get back to him. She was obviously relieved when Edward said, 'Next time I come, I must ask Mr Montillo to show me round the Clinic. Not today though as I am returning to London.'

She gave him a look which he could not quite interpret. It was not that she appeared apprehensive but she was certainly not quite at her ease and she closed the door after him with almost tangible relief.

9

As they recrossed the Channel, which this time was choppy and uncomfortable, Verity seemed more than usually agitated. Edward asked her what the matter was and she confessed that she was unhappy at having to conceal from Virginia that her husband had a mistress in Cannes. She had nothing against Natalie herself – in fact, she liked her – but she had naively thought Sir Simon was happily married to her friend. Mrs Cardew had hinted that he had an 'eye for the girls' and she should have known when he put his hand on her knee at dinner that he was not to be trusted, but it still came as a shock. She herself did not believe in marriage but she expected those who did to abide by the rules.

'I agree,' Edward said, glad to find something they could agree on. 'And what's more he and Montillo have this Beauty Institute which I think is a cover for something else.'

'But you looked round it and saw nothing except a gaggle of women with more money than sense being pampered.'

'Yes, but I did not go to the Clinic. I'm beginning to think I ought to have stayed another night in Cannes and paid it a visit.'

'We promised Jebb we would be back in England today.'

'I'm not worried about Jebb. Any detective work we can do in France will benefit him. Still, you are right. I did want to get back.'

'To report to Joe – or is it Churchill?' Verity said sourly. 'What were you talking to the Duke of Windsor about in the conservatory?'

'Ah well . . .' Edward wondered if he could tell her the truth

'Don't tell me if it's embarrassing. I know you were running an errand for that man but don't feel you have to tell me about it.'

154

He bit his lip. 'Churchill did give me a letter to deliver to the Duke. It was advice on how to comport himself – who to talk to and who not to.'

'Like Hitler, you mean?'

'Yes, well . . .' Edward surrendered. 'It would be a public relations disaster if he went to see him in Berlin. The King and the Government would wash their hands of him. He would never be allowed back into England.'

'Go and see Hitler? He wouldn't be that silly, would he?'

'He might.'

Verity thought about it as she looked over the waves towards the white cliffs. She was a good sailor but it would be a relief to be back on dry land.

Suddenly she said, 'By the way, while we are talking of secrets I suppose I had better tell you that I am going to Vienna with Adam . . . Joe wants me to report from there and then Prague . . . but,' she added bitterly, 'I expect he has already told you.'

'He didn't tell me about Adam,' Edward said calmly.

'No, that's our idea. He's going to show me around. You can see what a help he'll be. He knows everyone and my German isn't very good yet.'

'Are you going as . . .' the wind whipped across his face as though trying to blow the words away over the white cliffs, 'his lover?'

'Yes, I'm afraid so.' Verity turned to face him. 'You see, we think the same way. I shouldn't have . . . You and I don't belong together . . . I'm sorry.'

'I'm sorry too. I thought we did belong together.'

'I told you, I need to be free.'

'To sleep with anyone you fancy,' he said, allowing bitterness to salt his words for the first time.

'Edward . . . I don't just fancy him. I love and admire him.'

'But you have only known him a few days.' He heard the pleading in his voice and hated himself.

'What does that matter?' she said defiantly. 'Please, I don't want to discuss it. I just thought I should tell you . . . so that there were no . . . misunderstandings.'

'I understand.' He hesitated and then contradicted himself. 'No I don't. I thought we loved each other.'

'We do, but it has to be as loving friends. Can we still be friends?'

'I can,' Edward said with an effort, 'if you can, though I . . . '
He paused again. What was the point of bleating about his love
for her? Why was it that, however badly she treated him, he still
loved her? He grinned wryly. She saw his grin and seemed
relieved. Perhaps she had been expecting a 'scene'.

'After all, we have a murder to solve – two murders – and not
much time.'

He knew she was trying to tell him that she still wanted to be
partners and he smiled again, more warmly.

She said, 'I may not have time to finish it . . . If it takes longer
. . .' She looked at him appealingly. 'You must finish it. Please,
Edward, don't look at me like that. I *have* to go to Vienna. It's . . .
It's my destiny.'

'I know,' he said simply.

She took his cold hand in hers. 'You must solve it . . . for me
. . . for us.' She smiled and for a moment they were 'together'
again.

'Shall we go over it all again?' he asked.

'When we get off this bloody boat.'

At the breakfast table the next day Edward found, alongside his
kippers, a pile of letters. He quickly set aside what were
obviously bills and turned to the three remaining envelopes. The
first was from Mrs Cardew. She said that, on returning from
Swifts Hill, she had immediately come down with pneumonia.
'At this time of year! Too ridiculous,' she wrote in a shaky hand.
'I am recovering but I'm as weak as a kitten, so forgive my writing! I not only bore myself but poor Maggie who is looking after
me. What did I do to deserve such good children?'

She went on to say that she had been thinking about the
cricket match and the discovery of Maud in the river. 'Of course,
I did not go chasing after Mah-Jongg. I stayed where I was and
from my deck-chair I could see everything. I have been thinking
hard and I believe I may have seen something odd. I suppose I
ought to tell the police but I am not certain enough – if you know
what I mean. The last thing I want to do is to cast suspicion on
someone perfectly innocent, so I thought of you. If you could ask
a few tactful questions . . . It's probably nothing and I will quite
understand if you don't want to have anything more to do with

that horrible tragedy. That poor unhappy girl . . . I can't believe she deserved to die except in so far as we all must account for our sins eventually. I don't want to be morbid but I think my reckoning is not so far away now and, the odd thing is, I really don't mind. I have had a good life and I don't wish to be a burden to my children. Oh dear! I have just read this over and it sounds maudlin but I won't tear it up. I have the feeling that you might understand . . .'

Edward picked up the second letter, addressed in a recognizably German hand. There was a small crest on the back of the envelope and he knew it had to be from Adam von Trott. He was unsure if he wished to receive letters from the man who had seduced his girl, but as soon as the phrase 'his girl' had formed itself in his mind he became aware how absurd it was. Verity was not his girl but still . . . Curious, he slit open the envelope with his silver paperknife.

'My dear Lord Edward,' he read. 'Verity – Miss Browne – tells me you fence. I wonder if you would do me the honour of a bout or two at the London Fencing Club. The truth is there is something I would like to discuss with you. Without meaning to, I believe I may have behaved improperly and I would like the opportunity of explaining myself. If that is acceptable to you, may I suggest twelve o'clock on Wednesday? I may be reached at the above address.'

There was something a little awkward, almost peremptory, about the young man's letter but Edward excused it knowing that he would certainly not be able to write a letter in German half as fluently. He was reluctant to discuss Verity with von Trott, which seemed to be the purpose of the proposed meeting. On the other hand, he would like to get a better idea of how his mind worked. He felt it incumbent on himself to be friendly to a 'good' German who must be in a most unenviable position politically.

He picked up the third envelope and examined it narrowly. Again, the hand was foreign. The number 7 was written in the Continental way but looking at the postmark he saw it came from Swifts Hill. When he slid the letter out, he saw that it was written on Swifts Hill writing paper but was from neither of the Castlewoods. Just for a moment, he had wondered if Sir Simon had written him to keep quiet about the young lady in the South of France and was glad that he had been wrong. His respect for Sir Simon had not survived the discovery that he was unfaithful to his wife and though he was sure it was not his place to enlighten Virginia – if she needed enlightening – he had no particular wish to see him again, with or without his wife. He did not make the mistake of imagining his morals were much better and he knew that in the 'smart set' having affairs, keeping a mistress, or whatever you liked to call it, was taken for granted, but it still shocked him which he knew was stupid and illogical.

'Dear Lord Edward,' the letter began, 'forgive me for writing to you as a complete stranger but I do not know who else to turn to. I am a refugee and refugees do not like to have anything more to do with policemen than they can help. I have certain loyalties too, which makes my position most difficult. From everything I hear about you, I am convinced you are a man of honour and will help me if you can. I shall be in London on Wednesday morning and I wish to call upon you about nine. If that is not possible, please do not write to me here at Swifts Hill but leave a message with your porter. I will quite understand. I have to tell you that Sir Simon does not know I have begged this interview with you and I would be glad if you could keep it to yourself. I am sorry to sound so secretive but you will understand why when I see you.'

After he had finished his kippers, he went into the hall to telephone Verity and remind her that they were meeting for lunch at Derry and Toms. There was no answer. Holding the receiver gave him an idea and he dialled Mrs Cardew's number. If it were convenient, he would call in and see her on his way to Kensington. Maggie answered and seemed touched and pleased that he had responded so quickly to her mother's letter.

'She's not well and the doctor isn't much use. He just tells her to stay in bed and keep warm. She seems to have something on her mind and I know it would ease her to talk to you.'

Maggie squeezed his hand when she let him into the flat and Edward thought what an attractive girl she was. He was quite used to her burn mark by now and hardly noticed it. She led him into her mother's bedroom which was very warm. The old woman had made an effort for him, he saw. She had put on a little rouge. Her hair was brushed and she was wearing a lacy dressing-gown. But all her efforts could not disguise the fact that she was very ill and Edward thought she really ought to be in hospital. She was breathing with difficulty and her voice was husky. Her Pekinese lay on her bed, also breathing heavily and looking depressed.

'I am so sorry to see you like this, Mrs Cardew. I was so hoping that the air at Swifts Hill might have . . .'

'You are very kind, dear Lord Edward,' she panted, 'but I am as well as can be expected. My doctor wants me to go to hospital but I have refused. I want to die in my own bed. If I go into hospital, they will push me around, poke instruments into me and in the end I will die just the same.'

'Mother, please don't talk about dying. You're going to get better. The doctor said there was no reason why you should not get over this.'

'It is all in God's hands, my dear. Now, will you be a good child and leave me with Lord Edward for five minutes. There is something I want to say to him in private. Go for a walk round the garden or go to the shops. You need some fresh air.'

'But Mother . . .'

'I mean it,' she said firmly. 'If I want anything, Blackie will get it for me.'

When Maggie had left, Mrs Cardew said, 'I am so worried about that child. Her disfigurement has prevented her from having the social life enjoyed by other girls of her age.'

'I think she is very attractive,' Edward rejoined. As he said it, he realized he meant it.

'It's very good of you to say so, Lord Edward, but even if you told her so, she would not believe it. That's why I want to live until Dominic Montillo has operated.'

'She told me she was going to have the operation when we were at Swifts Hill. I am glad. Her scar doesn't worry me but I can see it is a nuisance for her.'

'More than that, she lacks confidence. To be frank with you, Lord Edward, she is in danger of becoming an old maid. She has a sharp tongue and she uses it to push away men who get too close. You understand? She's always thinking she will be rejected and *she* wants to be the one who ends the relationship. She hates to be pitied . . . Well, you can guess . . .'

Mrs Cardew stopped, short of breath after her speech.

'I quite understand. I hope it works out for her. I was in France a few days ago and I visited the Beauty Institute. I thought it very impressive. They told me Montillo does cosmetic surgery at his private hospital a few miles away but I didn't have time to go there.'

'Yes, it would be wonderful if he could help my girl. He intends to take skin from her thigh, I believe, and . . . I don't know the medical terms but it's a miracle what they can do nowdays, isn't it?'

'It is. And he will do the operation himself?'

'Yes, of course.'

'May I ask how Maggie got burnt?'

'A childhood accident. She was six and she was playing in the kitchen. She was very fond of Mrs Adkins, our cook, and she doted on Maggie. However, I should not have allowed it. Kitchens aren't for children. When Mrs Adkins was looking the other way, Maggie pulled a frying pan off the stove and splashed herself with very hot oil. I have always blamed myself and, of course, Mrs Adkins, was distraught. She died not long after, still grieving. It was a great tragedy. Maggie was such a pretty girl.'

'She is still,' Edward repeated. 'Well, I am so pleased you have told me. Perhaps I may be able to help . . . chauffeur her about, that sort of thing.'

'You are very kind but Edmund will look after her.'

'Of course.' There was a silence and Edward broke it by saying, 'But you said in your letter that you wanted to tell me something about the day poor Maud was found dead?'

'Yes. Pass me that glass of water, will you, Lord Edward? I get so very dry talking. Such a nuisance as it's what I enjoy most.' She drank and, when Edward had taken the glass from her, she seemed stronger. 'It's probably nothing at all. Certainly it is nothing to bother the police with, but I know from what Ginny told me that you have a reputation for finding out what really happened when . . . on occasions like this. Is there any truth in the rumour that is going around – that Maud killed her father?'

'She said as much to me,' he said simply, 'but she was in a depressed state and taking drugs and sleeping pills. She may have imagined it.'

'But you don't think she did imagine it?'

160

'No. To be honest, I don't know who else could have killed him.'

'That poor, tortured woman! I can't find it in my heart to condemn her. I pray she has found peace at last. God is merciful.'

'I hope so too. I do feel guilty about Maud, Mrs Cardew. You see, I was there in the Abbey when her father was found murdered and because I was also there when she died . . . I feel I have to help clear it up, if I can. Find out who did such a wicked thing. She said she was going to tell me something about her father. I fear she was killed to keep her from telling me . . .'

'It's terribly sad.' Mrs Cardew shook her head. 'The old man was a monster. I was glad when I heard he was dead. That was wrong of me, I know, but it's the honest truth. I thought, now at last Maud can live her own life, but it wasn't to be.'

'She could never get over what she had done to her father – it's the primal curse, parricide – even if he deserved to die.' He looked at the old lady and wondered what she knew and what she guessed. 'So what did you see?' he asked, trying to bring her to the point.

'Well, as you know, I was watching the cricket from a deck-chair next to the pavilion. In fact, I wasn't watching the cricket. I have always found it insufferably boring. I was watching everything else. Anyway, I saw the lemur slip out of the pavilion. Lulu, my dog, saw him too and barked. She tried to chase him but she's so slow she couldn't catch her own shadow and Mah-Jongg ran off. I called out and then other people saw him. I was still sitting there when everyone joined the chase. I remember Roddy Maitland pretending he was hunting and shouting view-halloo! About two minutes later, when the chase had gone off towards the trees, Miss Berners – you know? Sir Simon's secretary – came out of the pavilion. She's a Jewish refugee. The Castlewoods have done so much to help refugees, Lord Edward.'

'So you think Miss Berners let Mah-Jongg off the leash?'

'I think she must have. The pavilion was empty except for her.'

'And did she see you . . . when she came out of the pavilion, I mean?'

'Yes.'

'Did you speak?'

'No, she just smiled at me and walked away.'

'What kind of smile?'

'How do you mean?'

'Well, was it a smile of triumph?'

'Oh, no. Just a smile of acknowledgement.'

'She wasn't asking you to keep quiet about what you had seen?'

'In a smile? No, Lord Edward. It was just a smile. I'm sorry, I realize now I ought to have asked her what she was doing.'

'Where did she go to then?'

'She walked off towards the stream.'

'You are sure?'

'Yes, but I don't know if she reached it. I was distracted by the chase. Mah-Jongg had gone in a circle and was running towards me. It was very funny – all the little boys and the men pretending to be little boys.'

'So, sorry to go on about it, but was everyone chasing Mah-Jongg except you?'

'I think so. Of course Ginny was up at the house but Isolde was there with Roddy and Simon . . . oh, and Teddy. Or was he? You know, I can't be sure. Then you and your nephew joined in and some of the villagers. It was quite a mêlée. I'm not a very good witness, am I?'

'You are a very good witness. The main thing is you were in one place for a considerable time. And Miss Berners – did you see her later?'

'No. She keeps herself to herself. She's very discreet. She doesn't like mingling with Simon's guests, which I think is quite right.'

'Do you like her?'

'I don't know her. She seems a perfectly nice, well-behaved young woman and suitably grateful for what the Castlewoods have done for her.'

Edward hesitated. 'So you did not see anything else? How about when Maud was found dead in the stream? You were still in your deck-chair?'

'Still in my chair, I'm afraid.'

'That was ten minutes after you saw Miss Berners come out of the pavilion?'

'I would say nearer fifteen. But you were there, Lord Edward.'

'I was at the crease and rather bound up with the match until we got involved in the chase.'

'Of course. How good-looking your nephew is! I hope he hasn't been ensnared by that terrible American girl.'

'No, I don't think so. You think she's terrible?'

'Don't you?'

'Well, yes, I do rather. So you saw nothing suspicious?'

'I'm afraid not.'

After Edward had said goodbye to Mrs Cardew, he went to see if he could find Maggie. He discovered her in the courtyard, sitting on a bench.

'She's dying, you know,' she said, as he sat down beside her. 'I really don't know what to do. Dominic – Mr Montillo, I mean – has had a cancellation and he says he can do my skin graft later this week but with my mother so ill, I don't think I should leave her for any length of time.'

'How long would it take – the operation?'

'Only a day but he would want to me to stay for at least a week so he can dress it and keep an eye on me. Apparently, there's a chance the new skin may not take. He's been very honest about the risks.'

'But you wouldn't be any worse off if it fails?'

'He says not. I know you don't like him but he's very experienced.'

'I don't know what to make of him, Miss Cardew.'

'Please call me Maggie.'

'To be frank, I'm not entirely happy with the hospital or whatever it is he runs down there in the South of France.'

'What do you mean?'

'I don't want to slander him.'

'You have to tell me now. After all, if you know something and you let me go there without telling me . . .'

'There's a rumour that he carries out abortions there,' Edward said flatly. 'It may not be true but . . .'

'That doesn't shock me. I think our law is medieval. Poor girls are left to the not-so-tender mercies of back street abortionists. They suffer at the hands of dirty, untrained, struck-off doctors or worse . . . I think under certain circumstances abortions ought to be allowed and carried out in hospitals.'

Edward was shocked but tried not to show it. 'I have always thought life to be sacred.'

'I'm not advocating murdering babies but if it's early enough ... Well, let's forget it, but what you say isn't enough to put me off.'

'There is one other thing. Can I ask you not to repeat this to anyone because it is slander, unless I can prove it?'

'Of course.'

'Eugenics. I expect you've heard Sir Simon and Montillo talking about it. Do you know what it involves?'

'It's the science of improving the health of the race, isn't it?'

'It's not a true science, in my view. It means the poor and the weak are prevented from breeding.'

'How?'

'Various ways. Castration is the most brutal but this whole notion of race is suspect. We are all mongrels with blood from a hundred invasions and intermarriages from time immemorial. The Aryan race that Hitler keeps going on about is a fantasy. It doesn't exist. It never has and even if it had there would be nothing special about it. It's just an excuse for singling out the Jews and anyone else they don't like the look of and eliminating them.'

'Surely you exaggerate.'

'I wish I did. Take, for instance, this absurd expedition Sir Simon is planning to Tibet. You heard him talk about it?'

'Yes. I thought it sounded very exciting.'

'The purpose, as he explains it, is pure lunacy – to measure the heads and other physical features of the Tibetan nobility to see if they are Aryans. You must see that it's ridiculous.'

'But not dangerous.'

'Of course it's dangerous! People like Sir Simon are encouraging a fake science that pretends to differentiate between people. Some are to be designated *Übermenschen* and others can be treated as subhuman.'

'I think you are mistaken. Sir Simon would never subscribe to such ... theories.'

'I don't say he would but others will.'

'Like Mr Montillo?'

'Yes.'

'Roddy and Isolde seem to live at Swifts Hill,' Maggie said suddenly, changing the subject.

164

'They do seem to be there a lot. They're not well off, I gather, and no doubt Swifts Hill is better than being stuck in some stuffy London flat.'

'I think there's more to it than that. Roddy hasn't got a proper job and I think he's hoping Sir Simon will take pity on him and offer him something.'

'But Sir Simon's not there a great deal, is he?'

'No, but dear Ginny has a lot of influence over him so it does them no harm to be nice to her.'

'Now, surely, you are being a bit cynical?' Edward suggested.

'I suppose you think I'm a bitter old maid.'

'I think nothing of the sort. I think you are a very attractive woman with a sharp tongue.'

'Does that frighten you?'

'It might if I hadn't known Verity for so long.' He laughed to show he was joking.

'She seems to have fallen for that German boy. I did warn you he was dangerous.'

'Yes, I remember,' he said curtly.

'He is very good-looking.'

He glanced at her. 'You're teasing me.'

'Maybe. So what do you think? I'm offered this chance to have an operation. Dominic won't charge me for it and, whatever you say about him, he's a brilliant surgeon. But if I go away and my mother dies . . .'

'She'll want you to grab your chance. Ask her. She's not a selfish person and she loves you.'

'You're right. I will.'

'And can I take you out to dinner?'

'Before or after?'

'Your operation? Either. To me you are beautiful with or without your scar.'

10

Verity was feeling wretched. She knew perfectly well that she was behaving badly towards Edward but there was absolutely nothing she could do about it. She could not stop thinking of Adam. She longed to be with him and she no longer thought of going back to Spain or her friends there. If this wasn't love, it was something worse.

In the meantime she went in to the *Daily Worker* to deliver an article on the idle rich of the Côte d'Azur. She had asked Morris Block, the editor, if he would like a few hundred words on the Duke of Windsor but he told her it was their policy – as she ought to know – never to mention the royal family, even to attack it. 'It's an irrelevance, Miss Browne, and will be swept away with the class system when the time is right. We would do it too much honour to mention it.'

There was a sneer in his voice which annoyed her. Why was it that neither the editor of the *Daily Worker* nor the editor of the *New Gazette* liked her? Neither could deny that she had delivered more than her fair share of scoops. If it weren't for the fact that her father financed the *Daily Worker* and Joe Weaver backed her at the *New Gazette*, she suspected that she would have been out on her ear long ago. It puzzled her that so many of the people she worked with did not appreciate her talents. She had an idea that her colleagues at the *New Gazette* thought she was Weaver's mistress. If that was what they wanted to believe, there was no point in trying to correct the impression. Denials of that sort, she knew, cost nothing and were worth nothing. However, she was inclined to think it was simple jealousy, or merely a general dislike of women in any sort of authority, which ensured that most of the men she worked with would wear a smile to her face but abuse her behind her back. She wondered if there would ever be a woman prime minister.

While she was in the office, she spoke to an elderly man called Fred Wells who had always seemed to like her in a fatherly way. She had respect for him and maybe that showed. He was the nearest thing the *Daily Worker* had to an archivist and librarian and she asked him on a whim if he had anything on Montillo. He did not but, when she mentioned Simon Castlewood, his face lit up. A few minutes later, he put on her desk a large brown file full of press cuttings. More importantly, it contained a useful brief biography. Fred explained that he kept a file on most people of any standing in case something blew up and copy was needed in a hurry.

'Not just Party members and supporters?' she asked, surprised.

'No, of course not. Enemies of the Party too. We have to know the enemy. You must have learned that, lass.' Verity allowed him liberties she would never have allowed Edward which included being treated as a little girl and referred to as 'lass' rather than 'comrade'.

Thanks, Fred. I'll just run through the file and give it back to you before I leave the office.'

'That's my girl, but remember, nothing is to be taken out of the building or I'll have your guts for garters.'

'No, no, Fred. I'll make a few notes. That's all.'

Half an hour later she returned the file to Fred and thanked him.

'It was useful?'

'Very useful. I am most grateful.'

'Well, don't get too involved with that lot,' he warned her. 'They may be charming on the outside but they'll cut you to pieces soon as look at you.'

'Oh, don't worry about me. I stayed with them – the Castle-woods. Lady Castlewood and I were at school together.'

Fred shook his head in disbelief. 'Fraternizing with the enemy! No wonder Mr Block says you're not to be trusted. He says you're bourgeois through and through and in the end you'll lie on the softest bed.'

Verity was at a loss for words. She had suffered so much for the cause and risked death often enough in Spain, only to be told that she was an enemy of the people. She would have burst into tears except that she had long ago vowed never to cry at mere words, however hurtful and particularly when they reflected on her competence. It was just what men expected you to do – dissolve into floods of tears so they could patronize you.

Fred had not meant to be unkind but, seeing her face, realized he had been indiscreet. 'But we all think you are a star,' he added. 'Your stories are the only ones anyone reads and that makes people jealous. Don't take any notice of them. You're the sort of person who will always arouse strong feelings. You go on and do what you think is right and don't worry about what they think. Let Morris grind his teeth. He needs you more than you need him.'

'Thank you, Fred,' she replied with as much dignity as she could muster. 'I shall certainly do that.'

As she walked down Cayton Street into City Road, she thought about what she had learned. Castlewood was a puzzling fellow. His father had been an out and out crook who had made a fortune during the war supplying the army with sub-standard equipment at outrageous prices. The *Daily Worker* had not existed then but Fred, or someone else in the office, had put together a brief account of his exploitation of the workers and the Government's need to find uniforms, helmets and other vital equipment at whatever cost. It made unpleasant reading. His son had taken a different line. He supported numerous charities, including a major London orphanage, and was top of anyone's list of philanthropists to be approached when a new charity was being set up. He had also sponsored scientific expeditions to the Poles, as Verity already knew, and other exciting ventures including Amelia Earhart's – it now appeared, ill-fated – attempt to fly round the world. In addition, he had set up an organization to help Jews leave Germany and come to Britain.

It was an impressive record but, set against that, he was known to have links with the Nazis and to have dined at the German Embassy in London on several occasions. The Anglo-German Fellowship had sprung out of the discredited Anglo-German Association which had been openly anti-Semitic. Sir Simon, Lord Londonderry and General Sir Ian Hamilton were just a few of the great and the good who were active

168

members. He espoused ideas on eugenics which were beginning to look less and less reputable and seemed to support the Nazis' policies of racial purity. He was a womanizer – notes on several of his mistresses were helpfully included – and his Foundation – an organization through which his money was funnelled to his various charities – seemed to have so many clients that even Fred Wells admitted to being unable to list them all.

Verity could have added one: Dominic Montillo's Institute of Beauty. Adam had offered to help her investigation and she thought she might ask him if he could find anyone in the German Embassy who had access to a file on Montillo or Sir Simon and would be prepared to let him look at it. It might be possible to pin down Sir Simon's specific contacts in the Nazi Party in London and Berlin. But where was this leading? It was Edward and Winston Churchill who wanted to discover whether the Castlewood Foundation was funding some unpleasant experiments at the behest of the Nazis. Her priority was to discover who murdered Maud. She wondered if she could find out more about Professor Pitt-Messanger. From all accounts he had been an awkward man given to quarrels and disputes. Perhaps Edward could ask Chief Inspector Pride if he had found out anything interesting.

She sighed. It was still glorious weather and the thought of leaving London for Vienna and then perhaps Prague – even though Adam would be with her – suddenly seemed less appealing. In Vienna, she would be living among people who not only tolerated the Nazis but, according to Adam, would shortly welcome becoming part of a greater German Reich. As a foreign correspondent and a known Communist, she might be attacked or even murdered. She wondered if she should, after all, tell Joe Weaver that she could not go.

It was strangely comforting – though it ought to have been embarrassing – to be meeting Edward for lunch. There *had* to be something special about their relationship if she was able to lunch with him so soon after informing him that she was going off with another man. But then, she had to admit, Edward wasn't any ordinary man. Edward had suggested, to cheer themselves up, they eat at the café on the roof of Derry and Toms, the Kensington department store. It had only just been completed and was the work of Ralph Hancock, the landscape artist whom Edward had met once or twice at Mersham where he had supervised some improvements to the Knot Garden.

A hundred feet above street level with fine views over west London, the roof garden extended for a remarkable one and a half acres and consisted of three distinct gardens – the Spanish, Tudor and English Woodland complete with a stream upon which ducks floated, serenely unaware of the bizarre nature of their habitat. Edward was already there when she arrived. His good manners could be relied upon, she thought, smiling. He would never allow a lady to wait alone for even five minutes. He rose to greet her and Verity was again aware that, whatever his disappointment or even justified resentment, he never let it show. They walked peacefully around the garden, talking about nothing very much, and Verity felt calm and content – as she almost always was in his company.

At last, sipping ginger beer – 'I've not had ginger beer since I was a boy. I had quite forgotten how good it is on a hot day' – and nibbling potted meat sandwiches, they got down to business.

'I've talked to both Pride and Jebb on the telephone and neither seems very much further forward. Apparently, I would guess against Jebb's wishes, Pride has been put in charge of both investigations since they are so obviously linked.'

'What about the use of two ancient daggers as murder weapons? There are no clues from them?' Verity asked.

'You would think there ought to be, but it appears not.'

'No fingerprints, of course?'

'No. If there were any on the one which was used to kill Maud, they would have been washed away in the stream. And Maud was wearing gloves in the Abbey, as were all the women.'

'Maud? You are certain she killed her father?'

'Ninety-nine per cent certain. She told Graham Harvey she had – not just me. She may have been confused but I don't think she was hallucinating. Although there was a moment when I suspected Edmund Cardew. It's odd that he was present on both occasions.'

'So were we.'

'Quite. Anyway, although his mother knew Pitt-Messanger, Cardew himself had no obvious connection with them when the

170

Professor was killed. They had never met. He had no possible motive for killing the old boy.'

'What about Maud?'

'I don't know, V. Maybe. By the way, I have just had a rather interesting talk with Mrs Cardew.' He went on to explain how she had seen Miss Berners leave the cricket pavilion shortly after the lemur escaped and that he had received a letter from Miss Berners.

'So are you going to see Miss Berners tomorrow?'

'Yes. She says she will be with me about nine. Do you want to be there?' He did not add that he hoped she would *not* be there as Miss Berners might not welcome her presence. Fortunately, Verity was sensible enough to know that.

'No, she won't want to see me. I'd probably mess things up. I'll go to the *New Gazette* and rifle around in the files there. There may be something on the Castlewood Foundation.' She told him what she had found in the *Daily Worker* file. 'Don't forget,' she added stiffly, 'I am only interested in the Castlewood Foundation so far as it relates to the murders. I count Ginny as a friend and I would hate to think I had been spying on her and her husband.'

'Even if it made a good story for either of the rags you work for?' he teased her.

'Well, I suppose . . .' She looked doubtful.

'Anyway,' Edward said hurriedly, 'I want to know what unforgivable crime Pitt-Messanger committed that turned his daughter into a parricide.'

'What about this man Temperley? There's bound to be stuff on the scandal at the *New Gazette*. I'll get on to that. What's your next move?'

'I think there are still questions to be asked at Swifts Hill. I might see if Ginny can give me lunch.' He hesitated. 'How long have you got before you go to Vienna?'

'I don't know exactly . . . not more than ten days. I ought to be there already.'

'Well then, we'd best get cracking. We might need to make another lightning visit to the South of France before you abandon me for good.'

Verity bit back a retort. She did not want to give him an excuse to say anything about Adam or about loving her and the

171

dangerous moment passed. For his part, Edward decided not to tell her that he was meeting Adam. It was up to him to explain the invitation if she ever got to hear about it. If she did, Verity might see conspiracy and betrayal but Edward had no doubt that Adam was an honourable man who would rigidly adhere to the behaviour expected of a German aristocrat of the old school.

It was prompt on nine when Fenton answered the door to Miss Berners. Edward, who was just finishing his breakfast, got the feeling she might have been having a cup of tea at the ABC in Piccadilly or walking in the park until she considered she could reasonably knock on his door.

'Please do come in, Miss Berners. Will you have breakfast? Fenton can run you up eggs and bacon or a kipper.'

'No thank you, Lord Edward. I have had breakfast.'

'A cup of tea or coffee then?'

'Coffee, please, if it is no trouble.'

'And a cigarette?' He held out his cigarette case and she took one. Edward lit it for her and she sank back in her chair. 'You needed that,' he remarked, seeing her take a second lungful of smoke.

'I did, yes. You see, Lord Edward, it is difficult for me to be here.'

'You had to start very early?'

'Not that. I mean I did start early but that signifies nothing. I do not sleep much, you understand. No, I mean it is difficult to go behind my employer's back.'

'It is easier than going to the police?'

'Yes, that is right. The police . . . even in England we Jews do not go to the police. They come to us.'

Edward looked at her attentively. He thought she might be thirty but it was difficult to be certain. She was thin – almost gaunt – her high cheekbones giving her face a handsome if severe expression like some bird of prey. Her nose was prominent, her black eyes large in her pale face. Her black hair was cut short and hidden beneath a small black hat. Altogether, she appeared to be typical of the 'repressed spinster', so often the butt of cruel jokes.

'I don't quite know why I chose to confide in you, Lord Edward,' she said frankly, 'but when you were at Swifts Hill I heard it said you investigated crimes and . . . and you were an honourable man.'

It was a surprising statement and he was absurdly pleased. 'Take your time, Miss Berners. If there is anything I can do . . .'

'First of all, I must tell you that I am *Mrs* Berners, not Miss.'

'Indeed, and your husband . . .?'

'He is still in Germany.' Her coffee cup rattled the saucer as she replaced it.

'He stayed behind because of his work?' Edward hazarded.

'He's an engineer. They took him away. I didn't know where.'

'Who took him away?'

'The authorities. They said he was required for special work.'

'You don't know who he works for?' he said gently.

'Thanks to Sir Simon, I do now. When he disappeared, all they would say was that he was doing secret work . . . for the fatherland and I was not to look for him. They said he might be able to write to me but I could not write back.'

'And did you get a letter?'

'One letter only . . . after one month – when I had given up hope. He said he was safe and well and that I was not to worry about him.'

'That must have been a relief.'

'He is a Jew . . . I am a Jew. His letter means nothing. Of course I must worry,' she said vehemently.

'The letter was in your husband's writing . . . You recognized his hand?'

'I did but he may have been forced to write it. I think it is unlikely he could write what he wanted.'

'Of course you are right. Is he a very good engineer? They will not hurt him if they need him.'

'He is a fine engineer . . . turbine engines. I do not know what a turbine engine is exactly, but it is important.'

'That's good,' Edward said, trying to get her to look on the bright side.

'I think I shall never see him again,' she said flatly.

After a long minute of silence, during which both of them thought about the horror of a world in which a man could be removed from his wife and made a slave without there being any redress, Edward said, 'So how did you come to England?'

'I knew my life was worth *this* if I stayed in Germany.' She clicked her fingers. 'They were rounding up Jews – we had no rights . . . no future.'

'You had no children?'

'No, it was my great regret but now I am glad.'

'What work did you do?'

'I translated into French and English . . . books, plays . . .'

'So where did you go?'

'I went first to France . . . to Paris and then to Cannes, where I had friends.'

'There was no difficulty about a passport?'

She looked at him with amazement. 'Of course it was difficult. I had to sell everything and pay the money over to . . . to the man who issued passports. I had to pretend it was for work and that I would return. I had a publisher friend in Paris for whom I had translated the novels of Hesse and Mann.'

'And what happened when you got to Paris?'

'My friend helped me to find work translating French into German. I had to go to Cannes to help with a film script they wanted translating. There I met a met a friend of Sir Simon's – a film actress – and she introduced me to him and he said he would help me.'

'Was that Natalie Sarrault, by any chance?'

'Yes, do you know her?'

'I have met her. Sir Simon has many friends in France and Germany, I know. You said he has been able to find out . . . ?'

'He has. He was very kind. It took time but he has learnt that Heinrich is working in the Ruhr in a factory owned by IG Farben. You know them?'

'Of course. They own factories across Europe. Can he get your husband released?'

'He is trying but it is not easy. My husband is an expert in his field and they will not let him go if they still need him. There are no troublesome trade unions any longer at IG Farben. And he is a Jew. He is not important,' she said bitterly.

'But surely Farben is a respectable company . . .?'

'You think so? They finance the Nazi Party.'

'I did not know . . . Are you sure?'

'I am sure. With Sir Simon's help, I have done research. Georg von Schnitzler – he runs the company, you understand? – he is one of Hitler's closest allies.'

'But if Sir Simon cannot do anything, how can I help?'

'You have friends in the Foreign Office . . .'

Edward sighed. 'I will do my best but I am not hopeful. My influence is very limited, I am afraid, Mrs Berners.'

'But that is not why I have come to you, Lord Edward,' she said, suddenly eager. 'Sir Simon . . . I owe him so much. He has been most kind but . . .'

'But what . . . ?'

'You know I am his personal secretary?'

'Yes.'

'So I see all his private papers.'

'And you have seen something which worries you?'

'What should I do if . . .? Is it wrong of me to say what I have seen in my confidential position?' She literally wrung her hands.

'Anything you tell me I will keep secret unless or until you give me permission to repeat it or until I discover the same information from other sources.'

'You promise? Your word as an English gentleman, Lord Edward?'

'You have my word on it.'

She seemed satisfied.

'The Castlewood Foundation has a board of governors and Sir Simon is the chairman. One of his closest friends is an American, John Dulles, who is also on the board of IG Farben and Standard Oil of New Jersey.'

'I fear many American businesses have links with the Nazis.'

'I must tell him,' she said suddenly resolute, 'I cannot work for him if he helps the Nazis. They are doing terrible things to my people . . .'

'Yes, you must tell him how you feel. Perhaps he will have some explanation . . .'

'And there is more,' she said slowly. 'When I was in Cannes I heard . . .'

'About the Institute of Beauty? I have been round it. There is nothing wrong with it that I could see.'

'You have already suspected . . .?'

'I have found nothing.'

'Natalie told me in confidence – which I am now breaking because I feel I must – that the horrible man you met at Swifts Hill, Mr Montillo . . . he runs a laboratory and a hospital and they do . . . experiments.'

'What sort of experiments?'

'Natalie would not say exactly but she cried when she told me. She said they took babies away from their mothers and . . .'

'And did what . . .?' A chill struck Edward and he wished he did not have to hear what this woman was about to tell him.

'They make experiments to see why races are different and why the Jews and races from the south . . . from Africa are inferior to the Aryans.'

'Experiments on babies . . .?' His voice was icy cold.

'Natalie would not tell me very much but she said, when she slept, she had nightmares.'

After a minute Edward said. 'You were right to tell me. I shall go back to France and see what I can find out. Perhaps there is some . . . some explanation . . .'

But what explanation could there possibly be, he thought, if what this woman was telling him was true, and what reason had she to lie? She owed Simon Castlewood her life and perhaps her husband's life. She had struggled with her conscience and decided to confide in him. He wished she had not. He did not want to know, but now that he did, he had to know it all. It might be the evidence Churchill needed to get the Castlewood Foundation closed down.

As she was getting up to go, he tried to reassure her, 'You did right to tell me, Mrs Berners.'

She took his hand and looked into his eyes. 'Lisel. That is my name. Call me Lisel. No one else does in England. You will go on . . . finding out about the Foundation?'

'I shall. If it is, as you suspect, corrupt, Sir Simon must some-how be shamed into seeing the error of its ways.'

'And if he does not?'

'Then the Foundation must be smashed. I will smash it.' Edward spoke in a low voice but she did not for a moment doubt his resolve. 'If you think of anything else, Lisel, which might help me, I hope you will let me know. And if . . . if you have to leave Swifts Hill, please let me know where you are. We may be able to help one another.'

He suddenly remembered that he wanted to ask her about Maud's murder. It seemed almost trivial now.

'Before you go, there is one question I must ask you about the day Miss Pitt-Messanger was murdered.'

She looked at him and a tiny smile curved about the corners of her mouth. 'You think I killed the poor woman?'

'No, but someone did. Did you see anything strange that day?'

'It was all strange. That cricket. It is a game without proper rules, I think.'

'Stop playing with me, Lisel. You know what I mean. Someone saw you come out of the pavilion just after Mah-Jongg was released.'

'The old woman? I thought she had seen me. Yes, I did release him. I wanted him to escape his chains. It is cruel to keep him – a wild animal as a pet.'

'He was quickly recaptured,' Edward said drily.

'Yes, as I knew he would be but, at least for a short time, he was free. My husband is a captive. Maybe he will never be free – not even for a moment.'

'So, you did not release him to create a distraction? You see, while everyone was chasing Mah-Jongg, it seems likely Maud Pitt-Messanger was murdered.'

She looked dismayed. 'It was my fault she was murdered?'

'I am not saying that, but did you see anyone down by the stream after you left the pavilion?'

'I saw Mr Montillo and I saw Sir Simon. They were talking together.'

'You could not have seen Montillo – he was in London that afternoon.'

'I saw him, I tell you.'

'Did they see you?'

'I don't think so. They were talking too much.'

'Did you see anything else . . . anyone acting suspiciously?'

'I saw Mr Cardew but he was not doing anything suspicious. He was just walking.'

'Did he meet Montillo and Sir Simon?'

'Maybe. I did not see. I went up to the house.'

'Did you see anyone there . . . Lady Castlewood, for instance?'

'No, only the butler, Mr Lampton.'

'Did you speak?'

'No. I do not think he likes me. I think he says "bloody foreigner" behind my back.'

Edward smiled. It was a joke but he knew that, for many people in England it was not a joke – Jewish refugees were just 'bloody foreigners'.

11

The blades clashed and sang. The sweat rolled down Edward's face behind his mask but Adam von Trott, seemingly tireless, lunged and lunged again until Edward cried, '*Kamerad.*' He lifted the mask from his face, took a towel from the chair and wiped himself.

'That was humbling,' he admitted wryly. 'I thought I was fit but you are fitter. Where did you learn to fence?'

'At the University of Göttingen. I was elected a member of the Göttingen Saxons, the best student corps. I fought several duels.'

'I thought duels were illegal in the new Germany?'

'They are but we still fought them. The scar on the cheek was as much a mark of honour as it was in the old Prussia.'

'No wonder you can make mincemeat of me. Mind you, you are still a young man. I am having to accept middle age. How old are you, if you don't mind me asking?'

'I was twenty-eight last week.'

'Did you celebrate your birthday?'

'Verity helped me celebrate it,' he replied flatly.

Edward laughed. 'So we are fighting over a girl! How romantic. Please. Adam, neither of us owns Verity. She will do what she likes whether we approve or not.'

'She loves me,' he said belligerently.

'*Kam der neue Gott gegangen, hingegeben war ich stumm,*' Edward quoted.

'You speak German?' Adam said, surprised.

'I'm learning. Know thine enemy.'

'*Touché*! When a new god approaches, I surrender without a word,' he translated. 'That sounds defeatist to me.'

'Realistic, I would say.'

179

'Am I right in saying that Hofmannsthal goes on, "*halb mich wissend und halb im Taumel, betrug' ich ihn endlich und lieb' ihn noch recht*!" Unable to stop myself, I basely deceive him though loving him still.'

'That's too dramatic,' Edward shrugged his shoulders.

'*Die Grenzen meiner Sprache bedeuten die Grenzen meiner Welt*. The limits of my language mean the limits of my world.'

'Who said that?'

'The philosopher, Ludwig Wittgenstein. Have you heard of him?'

'I heard him lecture once at Cambridge. I hardly understood a word even though he was speaking English.'

Adam laughed. 'He's a great man – Viennese, you know, not German – and a friend of my family.'

After they had showered, they sank into armchairs, Edward feeling limp and lethargic after his exertions.

'What is it that makes you tick, Adam?' he inquired.

'What makes me tick?' He looked puzzled.

'What drives you – what is most important to you?'

'Oh, I understand! Patriotism of course.'

'My country right or wrong?'

'I suppose so. I hate the Nazis and I will never rest until they are expelled from government – from my country – but that makes me love my country more. If you see your pet lion being torn to shreds by jackals, you hate the predators but not the lion.'

'Tell me, Adam, is it true you are joining the Foreign Office when you get back to Berlin?'

'I cannot without joining the Party.'

'Which you won't do?'

'Never, but it is my duty to rid my country of these vermin from the inside. I could never go into exile.'

'So what *will* you do?'

'I have been offered a job at IG Farben by a friend of my family, Ministerialrat Dr Buhl.'

'But IG Farben is controlled by the Nazis!'

'I know. It is very difficult. I probably won't take the job but I must do something to help my country.'

'So, if there's a war, you would never go to England or America?'

'I am a patriot, Lord Edward. Surely you can understand that. Would you leave England and fight against your country even if you hated the government in power?'

'No,' he agreed, without having to think about it. 'I would not.' He paused and then asked, 'The Jews – how is it possible to treat them as if they were not human?'

'We don't all treat the Jews that way,' he said gruffly, obviously uncomfortable. 'As a child, I lived for some time with an old Jew and loved him dearly. Do you know the expression *Schutzjuden*?'

'Protected Jews? Who are they?'

'Ever since the Middle Ages, we nobles have protected the Jews on our estates and we will continue to do so.'

Edward thought it would be unkind to press him further. He must know it was impossible for him and his aristocratic friends to protect the Jews. However, he thought he might as well mention Lisel Berners' husband and see if Adam could use his influence to bring him to England.

'When you were at Swifts Hill, did you meet Simon Castlewood's secretary, Miss Berners – a Jew?'

'No, I don't think so. Why?'

He explained the situation and Adam said he would see what he could do.

'Why did you want to see me?' Edward asked, when it seemed they had nothing more to say to one another.

Adam roused himself. 'I had two reasons for inviting you to fence. No, three – I heard you were a good fencer and they were right.'

'I had a good tutor – Fred Cavens. Do you know him?'

'Of course, one of the best.'

'And your two other reasons . . .?'

'First of all, I felt instinctively that I could trust you. We are two of a kind with the same background. We play the game by the same rules, shall I say. I wanted to be sure that you understood me and that – what is the expression? – I was not being a cad.'

'By taking my girl?' Edward smiled ruefully. 'I told you before that we both have to accept that Verity is not some ordinary girl but her own unique self. God – or whoever in the Communist Party fills in for God – made only one of her. As I said, no one owns her. She is a free spirit.'

'I believe she still loves you,' Adam said naively.

'But she loves you more.'

Adam thought about this. 'She loves me differently. Perhaps it will be as Gaunt said in *Richard II* – our "rash fierce blaze of riot cannot last". We played it at Oxford. I was the fascist Duke of Northumberland.'

'Maybe.' Edward was suddenly bored with this boy. It was in bad taste to discuss Verity in this way and he knew she would not forgive either of them if she ever found out. 'What was your other reason for wanting to see me?'

'It is nothing but Verity said you were investigating that poor woman's murder – Miss Pitt-Messanger.'

'Yes.'

'Two things really. I know that both Castlewood and the surgeon, Montillo, have many friends among the Nazis.'

'So I have been told,' Edward said drily.

'You knew that?'

'I did but Verity was going to ask you to find out more about them – their links with the Nazis. Something bad is going on and Montillo is at the heart of it. I am thinking of going back to Cannes to do some sleuthing.'

'Sleuthing?'

'Make some inquiries. What else?'

'It's probably not significant but you should know I saw Lady Castlewood walking down towards the stream a few minutes before Miss Pitt-Messanger's body was found.'

'She, at least, could not have murdered Maud,' Edward said briskly. 'She isn't strong enough.'

'Maybe so, but that's not it. She had been talking to the maid – the pretty one, you know, who is such a great favourite with Sir Simon? I went up to the house to fetch a book – cricket can be rather dull to a foreigner,' he said with a grin. 'I saw the maid in tears and Lady Castlewood stalking off towards the stream. Naturally, I did what any man would do who finds a pretty girl in tears – I put my arm round her and asked what the matter was.'

'And what did she say?'

'She said, "Not you too," and pushed me away and ran into the house.'

'"Not you too"? Someone had been bothering her?'

'Adding two and two together, I would say Lady Castlewood might have been scolding her for some indiscretion . . .'

'With Sir Simon?'

'I think so. I thought it might be important but I expect you will say it is tittle-tattle – a word I learnt at Oxford.'

'Yes, but a detective must listen to tittle-tattle. Why didn't you tell Verity?'

'It's not something to tell a woman . . . You think I am old-fashioned that I do not like to talk about sex with a lady?' Edward raised his eyebrows but said nothing. 'It is not polite and Lady Castlewood is her friend,' Adam ended, on the defensive.

Soon after, the two men parted and Edward walked back to Albany feeling a little soiled. Adam was an honourable man, he was sure of that, but he was thrashing around in a net which was daily drawing tighter about him, restricting his movements and reducing his options. He was a patriot who hated the Nazis. He wanted to remain in Germany and work for his country without being contaminated by those around him. How could a good German square the circle? Edward was grateful he was spared such a problem. On the spur of the moment, he decided he would accept the job Sir Robert Vansittart had offered him to run the department in the Foreign Office which assessed foreign intelligence. It was his duty.

It would never have occurred to either Adam or Edward to ask the other to keep their conversation at the London Fencing Club a secret from Verity but it was equally certain that neither man would mention it to her. She was not the sort of woman any man with an ounce of common sense would try to manoeuvre or second guess. On the other hand, it was uncomfortable for Adam, who abhorred lying even by omission, to be asked by her, as they lay in bed watching the new day through the curtainless windows, to use his friends in the German Embassy to investigate Sir Simon's links with senior Nazis.

He got out of bed, ignoring Verity's protests that it was only seven thirty, and began to dress. When he was in London, he used a flat lent him by a friend, presently in Hamburg on business, but recently he had been living with Verity in Cranmer Court. It was as though, after helping her move in, he had forgotten to move out. It was still hardly furnished with only the radiogram from Peter Jones, the bed, a table, a couple of chairs and a telephone – which she had insisted on installing immediately she bought the flat as a necessary tool of her trade. There was a public telephone in the main entrance hall, which was sufficient for many of the residents, but Verity could not picture with any pleasure the porters listening in on her private conversations.

They only had one record – 'Stormy Weather' – which they played incessantly. Adam found himself humming it now as he looked out over the river while he pulled on his trousers. Battersea Power Station smoked in the distance and the sun reflected off roofs, glistening after a recent shower.

'Yes,' he said, sounding perhaps a little too prepared, 'I believe Sir Simon has links with several of our beloved leaders and also with IG Farben. I am going to ask my friend, Fritz Schieff, whose flat I am using . . .' he glanced round at Verity stretched naked on the rumpled sheets and corrected himself to 'whose flat I was expecting to use.'

'It's a lovely flat,' she said drowsily. 'Come back to bed, Adam. We can go there this afternoon if you want.'

'I have written to Fritz,' he said firmly, ignoring the interruption, 'to see if he can find out anything about Sir Simon's links with IG Farben. As you know, Fritz is in Hamburg which is where the company has its headquarters.'

Verity sat up, pulling the sheet over her breasts. 'You have already written to Fritz? What made you think of doing that?'

Adam stared ferociously at the power station and said, as casually as he could, 'It was something Lord Edward said.'

Thoroughly awake now, Verity looked at Adam's back silhouetted against the window and bit her lip. Was her new lover in cahoots with Edward? Was there some conspiracy of which she was the subject? She hoped not. Edward had an unnerving way of undermining her relationships by remaining on good terms with his rivals. But, she checked herself – that sounded smug and arrogant. Did she really think of the two men in her life as rivals? It was absurd. She loved Edward and respected him. He was – and she had no idea how it happened – her closest friend and occasional lover. But Adam was something else; her true love. His body, as she saw it against the light, milk white – almost luminous – straight-backed, slim-waisted, made her want to crush him in her arms. But what of his mind? She knew him to be honourable, intelligent and a committed anti-Fascist but what did he really think about her? Was she just 'entertainment' or was this 'true love' for him too? She feared his only true love was his country, which he simultaneously despaired of and valued above all else.

As if in answer to her unspoken question he came back to the bed and sat upon it. He leaned over her, put his arms on her shoulders and looked into her eyes. 'Marry me,' he said.

'You don't mean that,' she gasped. It was a shock. She had never expected such a declaration and it knocked the breath out of her as though she had received a blow to the stomach. She had said the first thing that came into her mind and it wasn't the right thing to say. He had got up again and his back view told her he was hurt. She tried to explain what she had meant – it wasn't that she did not love him but rather that they were trapped in the nexus of two worlds which had, in this explosive moment in history, come into each other's orbit. 'I am a Communist and you are a German aristocrat.'

'Yes,' he said bitterly. 'For a Communist, you seem to have a way with the aristocracy.' He regretted it the moment he had spoken. 'I'm sorry! I didn't mean it. I just . . . I was jealous of . . .'

'Forget it,' Verity responded but his words had wounded her to the heart. What did it say about her if her lover could accuse her, of all people, of being a hypocrite?

She hardly heard Adam as he went on, 'I'm not a Nazi, Verity. I'm a patriot. I will fight for my country if it comes to war with England. Though I will do it with a heavy heart, I shall fight.'

'Well then,' she said gently, 'we shall be on opposite sides. If I married you and we went to live in Germany, I could not possibly stop doing everything I could, however feeble, to oppose the Nazis and we should both end up in a concentration camp. I could never allow that.'

'Well then? Have we any future together?' He turned to look at her and she saw the pain in his eyes.

'We must seize the day. Come with me to Vienna – just for a few weeks – and help me establish myself. I know it is selfish of me but I will need you and not just as a lover. In any case, you promised to teach me German. I can't get by on endearments, you know, *Liebchen*.'

'*Leben muss man und lieben; es endet Leben und Liebe. Schnittet ihr Parzen doch nur die beiden Fäden zugleich.* One must live and love; life and love must end. If only, Destiny, you'd cut both these threads at once. Goethe.'

'You love poetry, don't you?' She got out of bed and went over to him at the window. 'Come back to bed. Touch me here. Can you feel how much I need you?' She stood on tiptoe, put her arms around his neck and kissed him on the lips.

With a reluctance which quickly turned to eager passion, he returned her kiss. He shook off his trousers and carried her over to the bed. 'I love you!' he cried as he thrust himself into her as if this were their last moment together. Later, he lay with his head on her breast and she stroked his hair and stubbled cheek, murmuring endearments. He shivered and she pulled the sheet over them as their sweat cooled. He lit a cigarette for her and then one for himself. A black cloud passed over the sun and darkened the window. Rain began to spatter against the panes.

'I am so scared,' she whispered in his ear.

'You are as brave as a lion,' he said, raising his head a little and looking at her with surprise.

'No, no. I am scared most of the time.'

'Scared of what?'

'Of everything – of what awaits me in Vienna, of the coming war, of losing you . . .'

'You are not going to lose me.'

'Not today, not tomorrow, not next week, but I will lose you. We both know that.'

'I don't know that,' he contradicted her, 'but, if you are right, we must – as you say – *carpe diem*. By the way, I am lunching at the Embassy tomorrow with a friend of mine. What would they say if they knew I had been sleeping with the enemy?'

'Maybe they do know?' Verity said, eyes wide in alarm. 'Are you sure you are not being watched?'

'The Gestapo is not yet active in England,' he said soothingly. But Verity was not soothed and held him tightly as if, once he left her arms, she would never see him again.

Edward put in a trunk call to the police station at Tunbridge Wells and asked to speak to Inspector Jebb. He was put through with very little delay and before he could say a word Jebb said, 'Is that really you, Lord Edward? I shall have to start believing in telepathy. I was about to telephone you and ask whether you would mind coming down and having a word.'

'You aren't going to arrest me, I hope, Inspector?'

'Indeed not, your lordship. The fact of the matter is Chief Inspector Pride was with me yesterday and suggested I might talk to you. I have to confess that we have come to something of standstill, a cul-de-sac, if you follow me.'

'When would you like to see me, Inspector? I am yours to command.'

'That's very good of you. Would tomorrow be too early for you?'

'Will Chief Inspector Pride be there?'

'Regretfully, the Chief Inspector has to be in court tomorrow.'

'What has he done?' Edward inquired, possessed by an urge to be jocular.

'No, my lord, you misunderstand me. He is giving evidence in the case of Mr Harold Mottram. You may have read about it in the newspapers.'

'The Indo-China fraud case?'

'That's correct. Far be it for me to prejudge a case but Chief Inspector Pride is very satisfied he will get a conviction.'

'Well, that is very good news. I shall be with you at – what shall we say – ten thirty?'

As soon as he had put down the receiver he picked it up again and asked the operator to put him through to Swifts Hill. The butler, Lampton, answered and told him that Sir Simon was away but Lady Castlewood was at home.

When Virginia came to the phone, Edward was concerned to find she was not her normal buoyant self. Her voice trembled as if she had been crying.

'Is that you, Lord Edward?'

When he told her that he was coming down to see Inspector Jebb and asked if there was any possibility of a bed for the night she was positively effusive.

'That would be wonderful. I very much need advice and I thought of you but, to tell the truth, I was frightened to ask you. Isn't that absurd? You would be doing us all such a favour if you would come.'

He wondered to whom the 'all' referred but she supplied the answer before he had to ask the question.

'Lampton told you my husband is abroad but Roddy and Isolde are here.'

Jebb said, 'I keep on thinking I'm just about to crack it when I come across some insuperable objection.'

He and Chief Inspector Pride were seated with Edward at a small table in the room used for interviews. Mottram had changed his plea to guilty and Pride had been told that he need not take the stand after all. The police station was small and badly in need of expansion and improvement. What had once been a sparsely populated area was now experiencing a rapid growth in population. Tonbridge and Tunbridge Wells were thriving and what Jebb disparagingly called 'stockbroker houses' were springing up everywhere, destroying a countryside which had not changed over many centuries.

'You know these people. You have inside information,' Pride said. 'I told Jebb you would help if you could, Lord Edward. I was right, wasn't I?'

Edward looked at him speculatively. He had never particularly liked the man but he knew him to be a good police officer. 'I am flattered that you should think so, Chief Inspector. Can you bring me up to date with the two investigations and then I can add any crumbs of information I happen to have picked up.'

'Certainly. As far as my investigation into Professor Pitt-Messanger's murder in the Abbey is concerned, I have decided to accept the confession Maud Pitt-Messanger made to you. I have failed to find any other credible suspect. We know the old man had his enemies but none of them were in the Abbey as far as we have been able to discover. In any case, most of them are academics – men as old as he was and therefore hardly likely to commit murder, however much they might dislike him.'

'You've traced no one related to Sidney Temperley then?'

'The man who claimed to have discovered that tomb . . .?' Jebb interjected.

'And who was more or less engaged to Maud Pitt-Messanger,' Edward added.

'Nothing,' Pride said ruefully. 'It was the obvious lead but, as far as I have been able to find out, there are no living relatives and no close friends. No one, in other words, who might have wanted to avenge his death.'

'But something is worrying you?' Edward prompted.

'Yes . . . if the girl hated her father so much for taking away her one chance of a husband and a normal life, why wait so long before doing away with him? She would have had hundreds of opportunities to kill him in the privacy of their own home. Why choose to do it in the most public place imaginable?'

'Because at home, if her father had died unexpectedly for no obvious reason, she would have been the obvious suspect. But in a public place . . .' Jebb said.

'Correct,' Edward agreed, 'but there is more to it than that. I believe she must have found out something which sparked off this moment of madness.'

'Something like what?' Pride asked doubtfully.

'Well, I'm only guessing, but it may have been about that brother of hers who disappeared when she was only a child.'

'Didn't he run away to sea?' Jebb inquired.

'He may have done,' Pride said heavily. 'I discovered that he had a harelip and a cleft palate. Miss Pitt-Messanger believed – according to what she told Miss Browne – that Mr Montillo operated on him. Montillo, when I asked him about it, denied it, saying he did not even know of his existence.'

'Huh!' Edward expostulated.

'You don't believe him and I'm not sure I do,' Pride said. 'You think someone told Maud what had really happened to the boy. She blamed her father for whatever it was and stabbed him. It certainly explains the dagger. It could have been one in the Professor's own collection.'

'Or the boy came back unrecognized and stabbed his father,' Jebb suggested.

They thought about this and finally Pride said, 'Have you any ideas, Lord Edward?'

'I do, as a matter of fact, but it's only an idea. Let me do a bit of digging and I will report back.'

'So who murdered Maud Pitt-Messanger?' Jebb sighed. 'It must have been someone staying at Swifts Hill because they had to have easy access to the dagger. The murderer chose it quite deliberately when he or she – but probably he given the strength required to drag the body into the water – stabbed her. He chose to use the dagger rather than a less showy weapon like a kitchen knife or . . .'

'Or a cricket bat,' Edward put in. Pride laughed.

'No, I am serious, Chief Inspector,' Edward continued. 'We take it for granted that Maud was stabbed – like her father – but it would have been easier to knock her on the back of the head with a heavy implement. Then unconscious – if not dead – she could be dragged into the water and drowned.'

'But she wasn't drowned.'

'No, Jebb. So, if you think it was a man who killed Miss Pitt-Messanger and someone with easy access to the dagger, that surely doesn't leave many suspects.'

'No, my lord. Sir Simon himself and Mr Montillo, who may have returned from London earlier than he said . . .'

'Miss Berners is adamant she saw him talking to Sir Simon.' Edward had given the two policemen an edited account of his meeting with her.

'Yes,' Pride said. 'We'll have to ask both gentlemen if they did meet earlier than we had thought – without of course saying who saw them together,' he added, seeing Edward's face.

'Mr Maitland, Mr Cardew, the young German, von Trott, and – begging your pardon, my lord – yourself and your nephew . . .' Jebb continued.

'Quite right, Inspector,' Edward concurred. 'And don't forget that I was also in the Abbey when her father was killed.'

Jebb smiled uneasily but pressed on with his list. 'Dr Morris – but we can rule him out, I think. Mr Harvey . . .'

Pride raised an eyebrow. 'The Communist gentleman who lives on the estate?'

'That's him, Chief Inspector,' Edward said, a little too eagerly. 'I don't like the look of him and Miss Pitt-Messanger had confided in him. He might have known more than was good for him.'

'Miss Browne seems to have seen a good deal of him at Swifts Hill,' Jebb said, not looking at Edward.

Edward frowned. 'They're both Communists, if that's what you mean, but I don't see what else they could have in common.'

'Miss Browne visited Mr Harvey in his cottage very early on the day after the dagger was stolen,' Jebb said mildly.

'She did what? She never told me . . .' Edward said in surprise. 'I mean, she told me she had talked to him but not . . .'

'Not *when* she talked to him? She probably did not think it relevant,' Pride said, trying unsuccessfully to be tactful.

'Mr Harvey told me they discussed Mr Churchill. Apparently Mr Harvey does not care for the gentleman.'

Edward was silent. He would not humiliate himself by asking Jebb for any further details of the conversation. He would get that out of Verity himself as soon as the opportunity arose.

Jebb said carefully, 'We have to consider the possibility that Miss Browne took the dagger out of the case while she was being shown it and then passed it to Mr Harvey. She must have had some reason for meeting Mr Harvey when she did. Mr Harvey says it was accidental but we only have his word for that. She says she went for a walk because she could not sleep.' Jebb was consulting his notes. 'Harvey was also out walking and they met and went back to his cottage for coffee. Miss Browne was wet and chilled.' He finished reading.

Edward said nothing but looked like thunder.

'Mind you,' said Pride, 'reading your notes of your interview with Sir Simon, Jebb, it doesn't look as though Miss Browne would have had an opportunity to remove the dagger before Sir Simon pointed out that it was missing.'

'True,' Jebb acknowledged quickly, 'and she would not have known about the dagger before Sir Simon took her to see the collection.'

The two policemen looked at each other but carefully avoided Edward's eye. Edward, head bowed, said nothing. With relief, Jebb went on consulting his list. 'That's the eight men on Sir Simon's team. The other two were Sir Simon's tenants who were press-ganged to play for him. Neither are serious suspects as they are unlikely to have known about the dagger and hadn't met Miss Pitt-Messanger.'

Edward roused himself. 'Right, that's eight and Dominic Montillo. One of us killed Maud and I think I know who it was but I don't know why. Will you give me twenty-four hours, Jebb? No, give me a week – I may have to go down to the South of France to get my facts straight, you understand.'

Jebb looked at him curiously. 'Very good, my lord. I would be most grateful for anything that you can come up with. It may be that one of these gentlemen will talk more freely to you than they will to me.'

'The South of France?' Pride said, stroking his chin. 'You think the two murders are connected to Mr Montillo's beauty clinic?'

'It was remiss of me not to look at his laboratory and hospital. The Beauty Institute was all above board but, the more I hear of his other place, the less I like it. Miss Cardew is to have an operation there to remove her scar, which gives me an excuse to visit.'

'You think it is safe for her?'

'I don't think Montillo will harm her, if that's what you mean. He is, by all accounts, a first-class cosmetic surgeon.'

'You know her brother is an investor in the Beauty Institute?' Jebb said.

'No, I didn't. Did he tell you?'

'Yes, but there's no secret about it. I believe Sir Simon arranged it. Cardew needs money and he wanted to help him.'

'Thank you, Jebb. I think I understand everything now.' Edward looked at his watch. 'I must go. I am expected at Swifts Hill for lunch and I need to talk to Graham Harvey and to Isolde Swann and Roddy Maitland.'

At lunch, Virginia was nervous and almost irritable with Roddy, which was so unlike her that Isolde looked at Edward in consternation and he raised his eyebrows to show that he too was alarmed. As soon as lunch was cleared away, Virginia whisked Edward up to her boudoir and to his embarrassment broke into sobs.

'Hey there, Ginny. What's the matter? If there's anything you want to tell me . . .'

'It's Simon . . . it's so humiliating.'

'He's in the South of France?'

'Yes, at a board meeting or something. Dominic and Teddy Cardew are with him.'

'There's no problem with the Institute?'

'No. Why, should there be?' She had stopped crying and was looking at him in alarm.

'No, I was just . . .'

'It's nothing like that. It's . . . it's his women.'

Edward squirmed in his chair and wished he was anywhere else. 'His women?' he repeated weakly.

'Don't pretend you don't know about them,' she said sharply. 'He makes very little effort to hide his . . . his sordid little affairs from me, so I'm sure you know about them.'

'Well, I'd guessed . . .'

'I don't care what he does, provided he doesn't do it in front of me.'

'And he has?'

'It's so bloody. I discovered he was having an affair . . . no, not even that. Just a . . . what do you call it? A "roll in the hay" with one of the maids here . . . under my very nose. We had a fight and I told him I would throw him and his floozie out. He told me to calm down and that I was not to take it out on Hannah . . .'

'Hannah?'

'Yes, Hannah Preston. I ought to have known better than to employ a pretty maid. Anyway, he said she couldn't be sacked and that I was not to ask why but he had not . . . made love to her. I told him I did not believe him and he shrugged his shoulders and left.'

'You'd like me to talk to Hannah and find out if Simon was telling the truth and there is nothing "going on"?'

'Would you?'

'And is this the only thing that's worrying you?'

'No, it's not the only thing. I'm worried how much time he spends at the German Embassy. This mad expedition to Tibet . . . and there's this business with Isolde and Roddy.'

'What business?'

'He . . . Dominic seems to have some . . . some designs on their baby. You know . . . he wants to breed a super race and he thinks Isolde and Roddy are the perfect couple. It's all madness. I honestly think Simon is going mad and Dominic . . . I used so to like him but now I think he's driving Simon to do something . . . something silly. Tell me I am imagining it all?'

'I can't tell you that, Ginny. I think Simon has got himself into some sort of trouble with Montillo but, with luck, it's not too late. Look, let me speak to Hannah and then to Isolde and Roddy. Now, wipe your eyes. It's not as bad as all that.'

He only hoped he was right.

Hannah Preston was a very pretty girl of about twenty with a delightful smile and sparkling eyes. She was still in her uniform – mob cap, belted apron over blue-striped shirt and blue skirt. It was Hannah with whom Verity had noticed Roddy flirting at tea on her first visit to Swifts Hill. She was no longer smiling, her eyes were dull and her brow furrowed. Edward was being as gentle with her as possible and had chosen to talk to her in the servants' sitting-room which was little more than an alcove off the kitchen. He thought she would be more at ease here than in the drawing-room on the other side of the green baize door.

It was odd, he thought – thinking of Mersham as much as Swifts Hill – that even the most benevolent employer would not think of carpeting the stairs in the servants' quarters. The lighting was bad and was not helped by the ubiquitous brown paint on the walls. He knew Hannah shared a room with another maid in the attic which he guessed was hot in summer and cold in winter.

'Hannah,' he said when they were seated, 'I want you to remember that I am not a policeman and I'm certainly not your employer. Anything you say to me I promise to keep to myself, unless you give me leave to do otherwise.'

She nodded but did not look reassured.

'From what Lady Castlewood tells me, I know the family think very highly of you and that you work very hard.'

'No one has a right to say otherwise.' She had a husky voice which at any other time would have carried a hint of laughter.

'No, indeed. What time does your day start?'

'I get up at five and we – me and the other servants – have breakfast here in the kitchen at five thirty. Then I do the fires and clean the grates, polish the brass, clear up in the drawing-room and Sir Simon's study. After that I take early tea to guests who want it . . .'

'When do you stop in the evening?'

'After dinner.'

'So, when there are guests, you may be up till eleven o'clock?'

'Not usually so late but Mr Lampton likes me to help clear the dining-room after dinner and Cook needs me in the kitchen to help with the washing-up.'

'Those are very long hours, Hannah.'

'I'm not complaining, my lord. Sir Simon and Lady Castlewood are very considerate. We have a break after tea is served in the drawing-room and when Sir Simon and Lady Castlewood are by themselves there is much less to do.'

'And when they are in London . . .'

'Then we have to clean the house and do all the jobs we don't have time for when the house is full.'

Edward was beginning to feel distinctly uncomfortable. He knew perfectly well that what he took for granted when he was staying in a country house – hot water, food at any time and someone always on hand to press his clothes or clean his shoes – was only possible because of the silent and often invisible work of the servants. It was easy to forget what that might entail.

'So you don't have much time for any social life?'

'I am sorry, my lord?'

'I mean going out and having fun.'

'No, sir. I have a half day off every Wednesday and a full day off every second week. And a week's holiday . . . I'm not complaining.'

'I know that, Hannah, and I wasn't trying to trick you. I just wanted to get an idea of how you spend your days. I suppose you want to be head housemaid one day or would you have to move to a larger establishment?'

'I have never thought of it, my lord. I am quite happy here.'

Quite understandably, Edward thought, if she had any aspirations she wasn't going to share them with him.

'Forgive me if I am being impertinent but I had heard that . . . that you and Mr Lampton . . .'

Hannah coloured and looked mutinous.

'Nothing to do with me, of course,' he continued hurriedly. 'It's not idle curiosity. The truth is – how shall I put it – I wondered if . . . and I promise we are speaking in complete confidence . . . I wondered if . . . a pretty girl like you . . . sometimes had to fend off unwelcome attentions from . . .' He took the plunge, hoping she would not burst into tears or slap his face, '. . . people staying in the house. I mean, I understand that Mr Maitland thought you . . .'

'Not Mr Maitland, my lord.' Her voice was so low he could hardly hear her. 'Has Lady Castlewood been saying anything to you?' She looked up and her eyes were blazing but also glistening with tears.

'She doesn't blame you . . .'

'She says it's my fault . . .' she burst out, seemingly unaware of the tears which were rolling freely down her cheeks, 'but it's not. I'm a good girl but if Mr Lampton ever got to hear of it . . .'

'He wouldn't want any more to do with you . . .?'

'He's a Methodist, my lord – very strict.'

'But Lady Castlewood knows . . .'

'She said I would be turned out without a reference if she ever caught Sir Simon with me. I didn't encourage him. I don't even like him – not that way, anyhow.'

'He tried to kiss you?'

'He will . . . *fondle* me any time he catches me alone. I hate it, but if I make a fuss it'll be me who gets the blame. You don't know what it's like, my lord. If you are thrown out without a reference, you end up starving or on the streets. No one will employ you without a reference – particularly if you are thought to be . . . to be *wanton*.'

It was an old-fashioned word but Edward thought it quite explicit.

'I can assure you, Hannah, that it won't happen but if you are in any trouble, you should telephone me at the number on this card.'

She looked at Edward's visiting card uncomprehendingly but put it in the pocket of her apron.

'You won't say anything to Sir Simon . . .?' she asked, suddenly alarmed. 'He won't like it. I'll have to leave . . .'

'Please, Hannah, look at me. I promise you can trust me. I won't mention your name and I will never let on what you have told me but I can and will stop Sir Simon . . . interfering with you. If you do have any more problems, be brave and find somewhere you can telephone me. If I am not there, you can leave a message with my valet, Mr Fenton. You have met him, haven't you? Just say Hannah called and I will know who it was.'

'You are very kind, sir. I don't know why . . .'

'I wanted to understand why you stole the dagger.'

The thrust was deadly and, for a moment, he thought she was going to faint.

'How did you know?' she said in a low voice.

'I didn't know for sure but I couldn't see who else it could be.

You were cleaning the glass and you looked at this beautiful thing and thought – what? – that you could defend yourself with it?'

'I thought – if I had it – I could say I would only give it back if he stopped . . . stopped bothering me.'

'But he could have simply called you a thief and the police would have taken you away.'

'I wasn't thinking clearly,' she said, her voice trembling. 'It was on the spur of the moment, you understand. I saw the keys on the dressing-table. I suppose I thought he wouldn't dare to denounce me because, if he did, I would say why I had taken it – the dagger, I mean. But, of course, no one would have believed me. I'm only a maid and Sir Simon is a magistrate. Oh God, will I go to prison?'

'Not if you tell me what happened. How did the dagger end up killing Miss Pitt-Messanger?'

'I wish I knew,' she wailed. 'I was . . . I didn't know what to do when I heard.'

'When you took the dagger – when was that by the way?'

'When I was dusting the cabinet on the Thursday before Sir Simon discovered it was gone.'

'What did you do with it? You couldn't keep it in your room?'

'No, Mary would have seen it – the girl I share with.'

'You hid it somewhere?'

'In the cricket pavilion, my lord – under a broken bit of floor. I couldn't hide it in the house. I knew the house would be searched. I wished I had never taken the thing.' She was sobbing now.

'So when did you last see it?'

'When I hid it, my lord.'

'Which was when?'

'That Thursday afternoon. As soon as I had taken the thing, I wished I hadn't. I knew I had to keep it hidden but it was so big.'

'Why didn't you just put it back?'

'It was difficult, my lord. I thought someone would see me. And anyway,' she added defiantly, 'since I *had* taken it I thought I might as well use it . . . not against anyone – but like I said – to keep Sir Simon . . .'

'At bay?' Edward suggested.

Hannah managed a tiny smile. 'You could say that, my lord.'

'Right!' Edward lay back in his chair which creaked alarmingly. 'Someone either saw you hide it in the pavilion or found it by accident later. If only we knew who that could be.'

'I don't know, my lord. I've been racking my brains but I just don't know. Will I have to go to prison, my lord?'

'No, I think I can assure you that you won't go to prison. I will tell Sir Simon – and the police if need be – that you borrowed the dagger to protect yourself and, when it was taken from where you had hidden it, you were too frightened to confess what you had done. Sir Simon will not, I am sure, want you to explain in court your reasons for taking the dagger,' he said grimly. 'One last thing – the keys . . . what did you do with them?'

'I was going to put them back on the master's dressing-table but I thought I'd be caught so I threw them in the moat. In a clump of nettles . . .'

When Edward left, Hannah seemed much happier. He had offered to ask Lampton if she could have the rest of the day off but she would not hear of it.

'I'd be better working, thank you, my lord,' she said firmly. 'I need to have something to keep me busy.'

He had no doubt of the truth of her story and he was beginning to have an idea who might have taken and used the dagger, but how to prove it? That was the question.

12

Adam now realized he had made a mistake. He had gone to the German Embassy to talk to a friend of his about the Castlewood Foundation. When he arrived in Carlton Gardens he was told his friend was no longer able to see him and instead he was to see a Major Stille who was described as Head of Security. Adam said that rather than waste the Major's time he would come back another day but, as he turned to leave, he saw his way was barred by two men in grey suits, neither of whom would meet his eye.

'So, Herr von Trott,' said Stille, waving him into a chair, 'what can I do for you?'

Stille had greeted him with arm outstretched and a 'Heil Hitler'. If it was a test, Adam failed it because he merely nodded his head in response.

'There's nothing you can do for me, thank you, Major. I would not dream of wasting the time of a busy official of the Reich.'

Stille ignored what might have been construed as sarcasm. 'You want to know about Sir Simon Castlewood and the Castlewood Foundation? Is that not correct?'

'I have recently stayed at Sir Simon's house – played cricket there in fact – and I was interested how far his activities went.'

'His activities?' Stille pretended to be puzzled.

'I wanted to establish that he was a friend of the Reich,' Adam said, trying to sound virtuous.

'Indeed? Well, Herr von Trott, a very great honour is to be accorded you. You shall hear from the Reichsführer himself how much we value the "activities" of Sir Simon Castlewood.'

'Himmler is in England?' Adam was surprised.

'You must call Herr Himmler Reichsführer if you wish to have a future in Germany,' Major Stille reproved him. 'No, he is in Berlin and it is there you will go tonight. A special aeroplane will pick you up from Croydon in two hours.'

'In two hours! But that is absurd. I would have to pack . . .'

'There is a car waiting for you. One of my men will take you back to your flat and then on to the aerodrome.'

'I . . . I . . .' Adam spluttered.

'You are worried about your rendezvous with the Communist – what is her name? – Verity Browne.' Stille knew precisely who Verity was and hated her with particular venom for having made a fool of him several years earlier. 'She is an enemy of the state and not worth a moment's thought. However,' he said grudgingly, 'if you *must*, send her a note. Tell her . . .' he grinned wolfishly, 'that you have had a more important invitation. In fact, I have been meaning to have a word in your ear. It is not good that you should consort with people such as her. As an aristocrat from a family which has done the state service, it is not right that you endanger yourself and your friends by mixing with . . . with scum like her.' He used the word '*Abschaum*'. 'Our enemies are your enemies, Herr von Trott. You must remember that.'

Moments later, Adam was bundled into an embassy car, its window blinds pulled down to prevent him from seeing or being seen.

So this is what it feels like to be arrested, he thought. This is what it feels like to be taken from the street and removed to some hellish camp. Powerless! That was the word. Squeezed between the two soberly suited men who had barred his way earlier, he was being taken . . . to Berlin? Or was that just a lie so that he would come quietly? Perhaps he would be disposed of and no one would ever know what happened to him. He tried to shake off his terrors.

At Croydon, the car drove over to the far side of the aerodrome and he had a brief glimpse of a plane decorated with swastikas before he was pushed up the steps. He was hardly seated before the propellers were turning and he felt the wheels trundle over the grass. A moment or two later, they were in the air. He had no passport – no papers of any sort – just a few clothes and a toothbrush in a small bag at his feet.

It was the first time he had been in an aeroplane and he thought that, if he lived to fly again as an ordinary passenger, he would never sit easily in his seat remembering this first journey into fear. He had no book to read. His two companions were silent and would not answer his questions so he was left alone with his thoughts. He would not think about what was to come. Whatever horror lay in store for him, it would come quickly enough. He preferred to think about Verity and wonder if she would be worried about him. In his flat – under the basilisk gaze of his leather-coated companions – he had written her a brief note saying something had come up which meant he might not be around for a day or two. He dared not say more because he knew his note would never reach her if he was indiscreet. He insisted on giving it himself to the porter to post who looked at him curiously and would have said something but was not given time.

He meditated too on what Verity had said about their relation-ship – how it could never come to anything because they were on two sides of an impenetrable barrier – he a German patriot and she an English Communist and an enemy of the Reich. Would he not be wise to give her up – for her sake as much as his? His path was hard enough without deliberately making it harder. There were plenty of German girls of his own class from whom he could choose a mate. He had had such girls before. But there was something about Verity – something that hooked and held him. She was beautiful – at least he found her so and, to judge from the reactions of the other men at Swifts Hill, he was not alone. But there were plenty more beautiful. It was her sharpness, her strength of will, her individuality, her profound sense of her own worth that fascinated him. But then again, while all of this was true, he still could not put his finger on what made her so attrac-tive to him. After thinking about it, the best he could come up with was that she was dangerous. Not always, of course; she could sheathe her claws and when she lay asleep in his arms she seemed so vulnerable. Sometimes she would whimper and even cry out, which spoke of bad dreams. He had never asked her about her dreams and never would but it made him want to protect her. It must be what Corinth saw in her, he supposed. He dozed, was woken, given hot soup and then dozed again.

They landed in Berlin and Adam, tired, dishevelled, dis-orientated and cold, was taken to the magnificent baroque palace – Prinz-Albrecht Strasse 8 – the headquarters of the SS. He was allowed to wash and tidy himself up and then – after this mad rush across Europe – was left to stew in a waiting room for hour after hour. At first he was indignant, then resigned and finally despairing. He told himself the whole procedure was designed to emphasize the Reichsfürer's absolute authority and to lower his morale. If this was the idea, it certainly worked.

When he was finally taken into Himmler's poky little office, he had no idea how much time had passed since he had made his ill-considered visit to the Embassy in London. Himmler nodded at him to sit down in front of him. Adam had never seen him before and was immediately struck by his ordinariness. This pasty-faced, bespectacled clerk was the second most powerful man in Germany but everything about him seemed designed to play down his power. He needed no huge desk or uniformed guards to proclaim his position. And yet for the first time Adam felt cold fear turn his bowels to water. He wondered if he could ask to go to the lavatory as if he were a schoolboy hauled up in front of the headmaster. He knew he could not.

Himmler continued to write and Adam's cold fear turned to sweaty panic. He wondered what form his interrogation would take. Would he be asked why he had not joined the Party? Would he be shouted at or even hit? Just as he felt he must scream, Himmler spoke. His voice was low and reedy and Adam found himself leaning forward to hear him, but there was a latent passion in his speech that was more sinister than any overt rage. He asked after Adam's parents and then inquired about his studies. He appeared to know everything about him and, which was almost risible, he seemed to be a snob. Adam remembered hearing that Himmler had some fantasy that he was the reincarnation of Henry the Fowler – a famous German king – and the fact that Adam's father and grandfather had served the Kaiser seemed to impress him.

He did at last ask why Adam had not joined the Party and the SS, which he described as the Aryan aristocracy of the new Germany. 'That little word "von" means nothing now,' he opined. 'The best from all classes, that is the nobility of the Reich. You should be proud to be an *SS Mann*. The SS are heirs to the Teutonic knights, dedicated to *Elitebewusstsein* – elite consciousness.'

Adam ducked and dived, trying to avoid signing his own death warrant by expatiating on his hatred for all things Nazi while not committing himself to joining the Party. Himmler did not press him unduly but went on to discuss the Castlewood Foundation which he hoped would finance, at least in part, the expedition to Tibet.

'The *Welteislehre* is the true scientific theory – not that Jew Einstein's,' Himmler said, banging his fist on the table to make his point. 'The supernatural ancestors of the Aryans were frozen high in the mountains and released from their icy tombs by the thunderbolts of the gods. This is the vision we share with Sir Simon Castlewood and I am very glad you have become his friend. We must find the Master Race. It is our destiny.'

So that was it, Adam thought. Himmler wanted him to persuade Sir Simon to confirm the funding for this ridiculous expedition. He breathed a little easier. If he was useful to the Reichsführer he was safe but, if Castlewood decided in the end not to go ahead, then he would be blamed. He guessed that deep below him prisoners – enemies of the Reich – were being tortured in blood-spattered cells. He shivered.

Himmler hammered home his message. 'Sir Simon can get us permission from the British Government to travel through India to Lhasa. One day we will not need permission,' he said thoughtfully, 'but, for the moment, we must make these arrangements with the British. You must see that everything goes – how do the English say it – "swimmingly".'

Himmler smiled and Adam thought it the most evil expression he had ever seen. It suddenly occurred to him that he might as well ask a favour of the grinning mask in front of him.

'There is one thing which might help, Reichsführer. Sir Simon has a Jewish secretary – a Mrs Berners. Her husband – Heinrich Berners – was conscripted to work for IG Farben. He's a turbine engineer. Sir Simon would, I know, be grateful if he were permitted to join his wife in England.'

'This sentimentality about the Jews,' Himmler said, his grin fading. 'It must cease. They are not worth a second thought.'

'However . . .' Adam persisted.

'It will be attended to but I shall expect to see Sir Simon's gratitude expressed in a concrete way. You understand?'

'I understand, Reichsführer. Thank you.'

He now knew what he had only suspected – that the Reich was ruled by madmen who would bring chaos and destruction to the Germany he loved. At that moment, he pledged his life to opposing the regime at whatever cost.

Edward looked at Virginia and she looked at him.

'He's gone? Gone where?'

'I don't know,' Virginia said. 'Why? You surely don't suspect Graham Harvey of murdering Maud.'

'Not that, no,' Edward agreed.

'What then?'

'It's just possible, Ginny, that he may try to do something to Simon or . . .'

'But why?' She was pale and agitated. Her Pekinese looked up at her, puzzled and disconsolate. 'Graham owes Simon everything. He wouldn't hurt him . . . would he?'

'I really don't know. He might. You know Maud and he were lovers?'

'I didn't know that,' Virginia said slowly. 'Are you sure? They never gave any hint of it . . . at least when they were with me. But are you saying that Graham blames Simon for what happened to Maud? That's preposterous.'

'It may be a bit more complicated than that. I think Maud knew something about the Institute of Beauty and the Clinic and was on the point of talking . . .'

'And that was why she was murdered? But *who* murdered her? Not Simon – he wouldn't hurt a fly.'

'Look, Ginny, I have spoken to Isolde and Roddy and they told me things about the Institute . . . I think I have no option but to go to Cannes and find Harvey before he does anything silly.'

'But you can't be sure he's there. He could be anywhere. He may be in London trying to find a publisher for his book.'

'Tell me what he said to you before he left.'

'He thanked me and said he wouldn't need the cottage any more. He had finished his book and was planning to enlist in the International Brigade and go to Spain. He said he had had enough of theory and wanted to do something . . . for the cause.'

'Well, I know for a fact that he hadn't finished his book. He told Verity.'

'He may have wanted to go to Spain all the same.'

'Maybe, Ginny, but Verity says he knew that battle was lost

204

and it was futile to try to fight against the inevitable. Anyway, if he was going to Spain, he would have to get there via the South of France.'

Virginia was suddenly angry. 'I think this is all nonsense. I don't understand why you have decided Graham is so dangerous. Simon used to say he was just a crackpot. A theoretician – not a man of action. I think he liked the fact that Graham was so ineffectual while he was a man of action. It made him feel superior.'

'Would you mind if I had a look round his cottage?'

'No, but what on earth do you expect to find?'

Half an hour later Edward was back clasping a crumpled sheet of writing-paper.

'I found this letter in the wastepaper basket by his desk,' he said, handing it to Ginny. 'I can't think why he didn't destroy it properly. It's from his Party chief.'

'Party chief?'

'Yes, all Communist Party members are given a senior CP figure to whom they are answerable and whose orders have to be obeyed without question. Verity says they have to be organized to defeat Fascism.'

Virginia was reading the letter, her brow creased in puzzlement. 'It says he must expose the Castlewood Foundation as a Fascist front. But that's absurd!'

'I am afraid not,' Edward said unhappily. 'Sir Simon has close relations with the Nazi Party in Germany and has met Himmler on several occasions. This Tibet expedition is Himmler's idea.'

Virginia had gone very pale and her Pekinese whined at her feet, unhappy at being ignored. She spoke slowly, as though trying to come to terms with something she already knew but had refused to recognize. 'Simon has these mad ideas about race, I grant you, but he would never do anything to damage this country. He is patriotic above everything. That's why he likes to fund these exploring expeditions . . . to see the Union Jack raised at the North Pole or wherever.'

'I don't doubt his patriotism,' Edward said gently, 'but I fear he is being manipulated.'

'By Dominic?'

'By him, and through him, by Himmler. Montillo thinks of himself as a scientist. His interest in eugenics is not some idle whim but an obsession. I have been reading some of his research papers. He's a dangerous man.'

'I don't believe it. He helps people. Look at what he's doing for Maggie. She's on her way to the Clinic now.'

'He's a fine surgeon and he has done some good work but, to be blunt, he makes my blood run cold. He believes in killing the disabled and what he calls the racially impure in order to foster "racial purity". You know Simon has agreed to pay for Isolde's wedding?'

'Of course! He discussed it with me. I thought it was very generous. Roddy doesn't have a sou, you know.'

'And in exchange,' Edward went on remorselessly, 'Isolde has said he can have her baby when he's six – if it's a boy – and bring the child up in a special boarding school in Germany. It's a new idea he has – or rather an old one. The ancient Spartans bred a special warrior class which was raised without parental contact in an all-male community.'

'Like an English public school,' Virginia said, brightening.

'Much more extreme than that. Himmler has already started special "schools" like this. After the age of eight they never see their parents again. They join the SS which becomes the only family they recognize. He wants to breed supermen – Teutonic knights whose sole loyalty is to the Führer and to him as the Führer's deputy.'

'But they can't expect an English boy . . .'

'It would be a tremendous coup for Himmler to have an English Aryan among the elect.'

'But Isolde . . . Roddy . . . they would never agree . . .'

'They didn't understand what was being asked of them until I explained the implications of the agreement,' Edward said. 'Like you, they thought their son – if they have a son – would just be going to a German military school. They were happy to agree to that.'

'But that's quite mad!'

'Of course it is, Ginny,' he said in exasperation, 'but don't you understand? The Nazis are mad – or Himmler certainly is.'

'If what you say is true, you must stop Simon getting involved. He's not bad, you know. Just . . . foolish . . . a dreamer.'

'I understand, Ginny,' he said more gently. 'I'll do what I can.'

'What about Isolde and Roddy?'

'They are going back to London, Ginny. It's for the best. I am giving them a lift.'

'We meant well,' Ginny said pathetically, as Edward walked towards the Lagonda.

13

Harry Bragg was in a state of high excitement. 'It's brand new – a Lockheed Electra modified specially for the guv'nor. I'm only just getting the hang of her but she's a real goer.'

Bragg was Lord Weaver's personal pilot and he got sick of idle days and sometimes weeks, waiting for his employer to choose him over his chauffeur and Rolls-Royce to ferry him about the country. This trip to the South of France was more like it. The previous day he had tightened every nut and oiled every part that moved and now – as dawn broke – he greeted his passengers with a whoop of delight as they strode across the grass towards him. He shook Edward's hand warmly and tried to shake Verity's but she kissed him instead. He blushed happily. Since his disfigurement in the war he had been shy of girls and always expected them to avert their eyes when they saw him. He rather hoped Edward was the man to liven things up. Edward had wanted to pilot himself but Weaver had insisted that he would only lend his aeroplane if Bragg was at the controls.

'My dear boy,' he had said, 'you have hardly flown since you were in Africa and these new planes – so Bragg tells me – are much more sophisticated than the kites you flew held together with glue, string and prayer.'

Edward had lost the argument and now, as he looked at the machine, he was glad he had.

'I can't wait to see how fast this bird'll go,' Bragg said. 'The guv'nor won't let me stretch her but you won't mind taking a risk or two. I wanted him to buy a Focke but he wouldn't hear of it.'

'Because it's German?' Verity inquired.

'They make the best,' he said simply. 'I wish it weren't so, but it is. When the war comes, we'll be lucky to beat the new Luftwaffe. Whatever you say about this Hitler fella – he values his flyers. Wish we had someone like that. They say Churchill makes a stink about the state of our air force in Parliament but no one seems to take any notice.'

'Well, it doesn't affect you,' Edward said tactlessly.

'What you mean, Corinth? Are you telling me my flying days are over?'

'No, of course not,' he corrected himself hurriedly. 'I just meant the new generation . . .'

'There aren't enough of them,' Bragg said emphatically. 'And not enough machines for them to practise on for that matter.'

Despite the seriousness of their mission – a mission that demanded speed and justified rejecting the train for the air – there was a holiday atmosphere about their jaunt. Verity had flown very little but loved it and begged Harry to teach her to fly when she was back in England.

'Glad to but the guv'nor said you were going to Austria.'

Edward scowled and Verity felt her stomach knot. It was true. There would be no time for flying lessons – not this year at any rate. She immediately thought of Adam and wondered where he was and what he was doing. He had sent her a note to say that he had been called away on urgent business but that he would be back in time to accompany her to her new billet. She could only guess at what the business was which had taken him away from her but she trusted him absolutely.

She glanced at Edward and saw the expression on his face. 'Cheer up!' she said, taking him by the arm and shaking him. 'Don't look like a dying cow. The world's not going to end quite yet. I'll be all right, though why you should care . . . It's kismet, or whatever you call it. If you're going to sulk every time I go away on an assignment, it's going to be impossible.'

She seemed to have conveniently forgotten that, on this occasion, she was going with her lover and it was not unreasonable of Edward to be jealous. He had convinced himself that, if he was to have a chance of winning her back, he must not 'make scenes' and become – dreaded word – a 'bore', but it was not easy. He wondered if, after all, he ought to put up more of a fight – tell her he loved her and that she was not to take lovers – other than himself. He grinned to himself. Who was he trying to fool?

They reached Cannes at five that evening with only one stop on the way to refuel and eat a hot meal. Bragg was cock-a-hoop that the flight had gone so smoothly and professed himself delighted at the way the Electra had behaved. He had achieved a top speed of 300 mph, and a tail wind during the first part of their journey across France had got him talking about 'breaking records'. Edward and Verity said their goodbyes to Harry as he was returning to England but would come back to collect them if required.

A car was waiting for them – a black *Traction Avant* Citroën, which amused Edward as he associated it with the French police – and they drove into Cannes where they had reserved a suite at the Carlton. Edward felt comforted to see the great hotel with its twin cupolas, supposedly modelled on the breasts of La Belle Otéro, one of Edward VII's mistresses. However, once again the luxury put Verity in a bad temper and she inquired why they could not have stayed at some modest hotel instead of 'this plutocratic monstrosity'. If Edward had any idea that Verity might sleep with him – for old times' sake – he was unceremoniously disabused of it. He had a fleeting glimpse of a huge double bed in a room large enough to house a family of six, before he was directed to a second smaller bedroom next to the sitting-room.

The suite overlooked La Croisette – Cannes' palm tree-lined promenade jutting out into the sea – along which holiday-makers and locals strolled, determined to forget international tensions and the posturing of politicians. Beyond, Edward could see the Iles de Lérins. In the evening light, the sea was blue velvet, studded with the lights of the yachts which bobbed lazily on the water. Verity joined him at the window and he suggested a stroll among the crowd of pleasure seekers ambling up and down below them.

'*Quel paradis*! Isn't this what heaven should be?'

'I don't believe in heaven, remember?' she retorted, and then felt she had been boorish. 'But you're right, it is beautiful.'

They abandoned any idea of unpacking and were soon on La Croisette breathing in the scent of oranges and unidentifiable herbs wafted to them on the breeze. Edward, daringly, took Verity's arm and she did not shrug him off. By mutual consent, they put off any discussion of strategy and returned refreshed, half an hour later, to bath and dress for dinner.

The Carlton's dining-room was elegant and redolent of a more gracious age. Verity suddenly found she was hungry and studied the menu with interest. Edward ordered Veuve Clicquot *rosé* to drink as they mulled over the bill of fare.

'Let's make this special, shall we, V?' he pleaded. 'Put aside your principles for a few hours for my sake and enjoy this place. You can't know how long it will be before it's blown to smithereens. We may not have many more nights like this – just you and me at peace in such a beautiful place.'

His appeal did not go unanswered and her face softened. 'Sorry for being a prig. You know me – I love luxury and hate myself for it. Very painful but I won't take it out on you, I promise.'

Her smile had its usual effect of making him go weak at the knees. It seemed criminal to him that they couldn't end the evening in bed together but he knew he risked ruining everything if he tried to persuade her. With suitable gravity, they gave themselves up to the pursuit of culinary delight. They finally agreed on *fonds d'artichaut* with *sauce hollandaise, filets de sole Véronique* and, to end, *pêches pochées au Muscat de Frantignan avec crème anglaise.* Edward went into a huddle with the sommelier and chose a white burgundy – the Corton Charlemagne 1928 from Louis Latour. It was everything he had expected – true nectar, cold and delectable after the dusty, uncomfortable flight. At last, over brandy and cigars – Verity insisting on a Havana all to herself – they could no longer delay planning a strategy.

'The trouble is, I don't seem to be able to think straight. Was that second bottle of burgundy a mistake?' Verity asked him dreamily. She wondered if, after all, she would allow him to take her to bed. She so longed to be taken care of and to lie in the arms of this man she loved and trusted. Chastened by a realization of her own lack of moral fibre, she reminded herself that she was in love with Adam. How was he managing, she wondered? She hoped he wasn't involving himself in some rash opposition to those who would be Austria's new rulers. But of course he would. *She* would be, if she were with him. Personal safety had to take second place when set against the creeping evil of Fascism. Adam was convinced that Hitler was about to order his tanks into Vienna and he had told her he wanted to put some steel into the spines of those who would oppose the takeover of their country. She shivered.

'What are you thinking about, V?' Edward inquired gently.

'Oh, nothing.'

'Was it Adam? I expect you wish he were here.'

'No, I am happy here with you . . .' She put a hand out to touch his. 'On a job, so to speak. I'll say it again, if you like. I do love you. But . . .'

'You love him more?''

'Differently. I'm faithful to you in my fashion, as the song has it. I'm sorry if it's not enough. Please don't look like that. I was just hoping he was not in danger.'

'Why should he be?'

'He couldn't say much in his note but I think he may have had to go to Vienna. Things seem to be coming to a head there and I know he was involved in setting up some sort of opposition network.'

'That will be dangerous and almost certainly futile.'

'Yes, he knows that but he doesn't want history to say that there were no Germans who stood up to Hitler. Anyway, he seems to think that, because of his family, they wouldn't dare touch him but I'm sure he's wrong. They don't care who they have to kill to get what they want. I can't bear the idea of him being sent to some awful camp and . . .'

'He can look after himself,' Edward said comfortably, irritated that Adam should spoil this perfect moment.

Verity made a little moue. 'Oh well, let's get down to business. I favour the direct approach. We simply drive up to the Clinic, ask to see Maggie and find out how she's faring. She should have had her operation by now and be recuperating. I wonder if Edmund is with her?'

'I think our first task ought to be to locate Graham Harvey – if indeed he's here. I have a horrid feeling he may be up to something,' Edward countered.

'You're sure you're not just making it up – that he's got it in for Simon – because he's a Communist and doesn't care to be patronized?'

'It's more than that. There's a definite grudge there but I'm still not sure what it is – but I mean to ask him,' he said grimly. 'In a strange way, I have come rather to like him, or, at least, admire him. He's got some sort of integrity. His principles aren't quite mine but I respect them.'

Verity was surprised and rather pleased. It was what made Edward so interesting – she could never quite forecast his views on anything or anyone. 'If he's holed up in Cannes, he won't be at a smart hotel like this. He hasn't a penny to his name.'

'I know and he won't be able to afford to stay here long wherever he is. This isn't a cheap town. I've no idea how to track him down but I have a feeling he will make his presence known somehow.'

'He's not a killer, you know,' she said defiantly.

'I don't say he is but he may be provoked into doing something stupid.'

'Why don't I go and see Natalie and find out what she knows? If Graham is after Simon, she may have seen him hanging about.'

'It's a long shot,' Edward said gloomily. 'Does Harvey know about Natalie?'

'I think he does,' Verity said, laying down her cigar which was now beginning to make her feel sick. 'He said something to me about Simon's mistresses although he didn't mention Natalie by name. Damn it – now we are here, I'm beginning to think it's all a wild goose chase. We can't even be sure he's in Cannes. He might be in London. He might be anywhere.'

The next morning, over strong black coffee, orange juice and croissants that melted in the mouth, they decided to separate – Verity to take a taxi along the coast to Nice to find Natalie Sarrault, Edward to visit Maggie Cardew in the Clinic. They agreed to meet back at the hotel for a late lunch and reconsider their plan of action in the light of what they had discovered.

Virginia had given Edward the address of the Clinic. She had – rather surprisingly, Edward thought – never visited either the Institute or the Clinic, explaining that she disliked the Riviera and disapproved of sunbathing. 'My mother always said it was bad for the skin – dried it up. In any case – as she put it – "the peasants are brown because they have to work outside, poor dears, but ladies are able to keep their skin soft and white, with the help of a nightly application of Nivea Creme".'

Edward thought there was probably more to it than that. Virginia must know that her husband had his mistresses – she

213

probably knew about Natalie – but, as long as he kept them out of sight and preferably in another country, she could ignore them. She certainly wasn't going to compete with them in what was, for her, an alien environment.

He borrowed a car from the hotel and, with the aid of a map, found his way to the small town of Beauville. There was hardly anyone about but he asked directions from a man walking his dog who knew exactly what he was looking for. Probably, Edward thought, the Clinic was Beauville's main employer. Half a mile beyond the town he saw a gate and turned into a gravelled driveway. A wooden noticeboard informed him in three languages that this was the Clinic. Director: Dominic Montillo. A string of impressive-looking letters followed his name. A uniformed guard emerged from a small hut where he had been sheltering from the sun and directed him to the visitors' car park.

Edward drew up in front of the building which – like the Institute – was long, low and white and set in pleasant gardens. He switched off the engine and studied it closely. There was nothing in the slightest degree suspicious about it and he was relieved that he had a bona fide reason for his visit. He did not fancy airing his suspicions that the Clinic was not exactly what it seemed without some evidence.

He put on the wide-brimmed straw hat which he had purchased on a whim the previous evening and pulled at his collar. It was damnably hot and his tie was strangling him. He climbed the white steps, noticing what he thought was a jacaranda among the bougainvillea in the gardens to his left. A hose sprayed a patch of grass to his right. Everything was neat and tidy. The inside was blessedly cool. No one was at the desk but a woman appeared before he had time to ring the bell. He made the little speech he had prepared – that he had been in the neighbourhood and had remembered that his friend, Miss Cardew, was a patient in the Clinic. He added that he was a friend of Mr Montillo's.

The woman heard him out with a fixed smile which revealed gleaming white teeth. Edward found himself wondering whether they were a gift from the Clinic's talented director but told himself not to indulge in cheap cynicism. No, Mr Montillo was not expected at the Clinic today. Yes, Miss Cardew was

214

recovering from her operation. She would see whether she was well enough to receive visitors. Five minutes later, Edward was ushered into a cool room, painted white with two or three paintings of exotic flowers on the walls. Maggie was sitting up in bed with several books lying on the table beside her next to a bowl of fruit and a photograph of her mother. He suddenly realized that he had never thought to bring a gift and began at once to apologize.

'Edward! How very kind of you to come and see me.' She was finding it difficult to speak because her face was swathed in bandages but she seemed genuinely pleased to see him.

'Please – don't try to talk. You must be very uncomfortable.'

'I'm not too bad. This looks much worse than it is. Dominic says most of the bandages can come off the day after tomorrow and then . . . and then we will be able to see how my face looks.'

'He thinks the operation has been a success?'

'He says so. He says it went well but he won't know for another few days yet whether the new skin he grafted on will be rejected.'

'So when will you be able to go home?'

'At the end of next week, I hope. It's all taking a bit longer than I expected. It turned out to be a bigger job than he thought. But, tell me, what are you doing here? I mean, I am so pleased to see you. To tell the truth, I get very bored.'

'But you have visitors?'

'A few. My brother . . . but of course he gets bored too. Can I confess something to you? It's been rather preying on my mind.'

'Of course!'

'I'm worried that Teddy spends too much time at the gaming tables. You see, he has never had quite enough money and, I am sorry to say, when he first came here five years ago, he had beginner's luck and made a large sum of money at the tables.'

'You are sorry to say?'

'Yes, because he has been back several times and on each occasion lost money. He is always hoping for another big win but I think he may ruin himself before it happens.'

'But I thought he had money from his firm – the stockbrokers . . . Thalberg and May, isn't it?'

'Yes, but he has been working there less and less – he has to be in the House of Commons so much. Although he hasn't said so, I think the other partners in the firm have asked him to leave and politics is such an expensive profession.'

'I see. Well, I really don't know what I can do. I can't think he will welcome interference from me.'

'Perhaps you could go to the casino tonight and see if he is there?'

'Which one? There are several.'

'I think he favours the one on La Croisette in Cannes. I can't remember what it's called.'

'I will call in, of course, and I'll come and tell you if there is any need to worry. I'm sure there isn't.'

'Thank you. You are very kind. I don't know anyone else I could ask.'

'He's not got any other sources of income?'

'He invested in the Institute. Sir Simon persuaded Dominic to give him a share.'

'Yes, Virginia told me.' Edward looked grave.

'Why? Do you think there is anything wrong?'

'I've told you what I think . . . what I suspect.'

'But you have no evidence.'

'No. Not yet. I'm sorry, Maggie, I ought not to have mentioned it. Please forgive me.'

'No, you ought not,' she said, her anger muffled by the bandages. 'What you are implying is slander. I'm tired now. I think it would be best if you went.'

Edward left, glad to be outside in the sunlight after the shadowy cool of the Clinic. He had wanted to ask Maggie if she could do some detective work for him but that was clearly out of the question. He was relieved he had not said anything and been snubbed for his pains. After all, she owed so much to Montillo. She would see it – rightly – as a gross betrayal if she helped gather evidence against him. Still, the fact remained, short of a police investigation – which the French police would never initiate unless they had to – only someone inside the Clinic would be able to find evidence of anything illegal going on there. A casual visitor could never gain access to the records. There must be records – Montillo was too well organized not to keep detailed files on the operations he carried out. Without a shred of evidence to back up his hunch, Edward was more certain than ever that something bad was happening in this clean, cool building and he would not rest until he had found what it was.

Verity decided it was better not to telephone Natalie as she might refuse to see her and might warn Simon that something was up. She went first to her apartment but, if there was anyone in, they were not answering the bell. She told the taxi driver to take her to the film studio where, using all her charm, she persuaded the guard at the gates to ring through to Miss Sarrault's dressing-room. A woman answered and said Natalie was on set. Was she expected? No, but Miss Sarrault was a friend and had told her to stop by if she were passing. Could she wait until Natalie was free to see her?

She waited for the best part of an hour in Natalie's dressing-room. When, at last, she did appear she seemed tired and depressed. She greeted Verity with a kiss but was clearly suspicious. She asked if she had come alone and Verity mentiond Edward. Natalie became a little more cheerful and talked about 'Milord Corinth' and inquired if it were true – what Simon had told her – that his father was a duke. Verity – had she chanced to see her face in the mirror – might have seen the corners of her mouth go down and a scowl cross her face. The French are such snobs, she thought scornfully, but she supposed the English were just as bad.

Disappointingly, Natalie had not heard of, or seen, anyone resembling Graham Harvey but she was expecting Simon who had been delayed in Paris.

'He comes on the night train. He said he will come to the apartment to wash and rest and then collect me at the studio for lunch. But why do you want to know? Could you not have talked to him in England?'

'He may be in some danger,' Verity explained disingenuously.

'From this man – what do you say his name is? – Graham Harvey? Why would he want to hurt Simon? He's a good man.'

'I don't know for sure. Perhaps this is a false alarm but if you see or hear anything suspicious . . . someone hanging about the apartment or here at the studio for instance, telephone us. We are staying at the Carlton.'

'I would like to meet Lord Edward Corinth properly. He seemed a charming man.' Natalie's smile was almost a smirk.

'Yes, well' – Verity tried to suppress her irritation – 'perhaps we can all meet. He has gone to see a friend who is a patient at the Clinic. Mr Montillo has operated to remove a scar on her face.'

'He is a very clever man.' Natalie was suddenly suspicious again. 'But I do not understand what you want to talk to Simon about. Is there anything wrong?'

'No, I hope not.' Verity hesitated. 'I think Sir Simon has some bad friends – Nazis, criminals. The Castlewood Foundation – has he told you about that?'

'Yes, a little. It's a charity.'

'Indeed, but it gives support to some unworthy causes – experiments to improve the race. You know what I mean?'

Nathalie looked pale and bit her lip. 'I don't know what you are talking about. I think you should go now. I tell you, Simon is a good man.'

'You will ask him to telephone us?'

'I will tell him you have been looking for him.' She gave a Gallic shrug of her shoulders. 'He may not wish to talk to you. I cannot tell.'

And with that Verity had to be satisfied.

There was a message waiting for her back at the hotel. It was from Simon Castlewood. He was sorry to have missed her but he was having dinner that evening at the villa of friends of his, Audrey and Freddy Lewisohn. Would Lord Edward and she care to join them? About six and they should bring their swimming costumes.

At first, Edward saw this as a distraction and was reluctant to go but Verity argued that they had nothing to lose and anyway, she rather liked the idea of gaining a glimpse of the Riviera's much advertised sybaritism.

'It'll be fun to watch the rich doing what they do best: making fools of themselves. Oh God! I'm already beginning to hate the Riviera. The stink of capitalism bathed in honey! How are these people able to idle away their lives while most people are sweating away at dirty jobs and earning a pittance. And all these ex-kings – they ought to be starving in a gutter or dead. The doorman at the hotel told me that in the last three months he had been tipped by the ex-kings of Spain, Portugal, Yugoslavia and Egypt.'

'Not to mention the ex-king of England,' Edward added.

'I wonder if they know there's a war coming?'

The villa was everything a Riviera villa ought to be and the scale and luxury of it put Verity into a worse temper than ever although, perversely, she enjoyed having her prejudices reinforced. Edward had his fingers crossed that she would not say something rude and get them thrown out. The villa – white with red shutters – rambled across the sun-scorched hill. Inside it was cool – stone and marble but with huge fireplaces, at this time of year ablaze with flowers rather than burning logs. The biggest and bluest swimming pool either of them had ever seen lay in front of the house, designed so that, from the vantage point of a long chair beside it, the water seemed to merge with the Mediterranean in reality several miles away and far below them. The sun was already low in the sky – orange and pink like some exotic flower, preparing for its nightly dip into blue velvet water.

They were warmly welcomed by the Lewisohns and their guests, who seemed delighted to see new faces and hear gossip from London. They were offered cocktails on a silver tray by two young men dressed like ship's stewards in white jackets, black trousers and white gloves. It was quite unreal. The Lewisohns wanted to hear that England was cold and dowdy but neither they nor their guests wanted to know about the political crisis that was brewing. As Mrs Gabriel – a glamorous widow in beach pyjamas with a pale consumptive daughter – said, 'There's always time for a little drinkie before the storm breaks.' However, she did admit to Verity, after several cocktails, that she had been shocked when someone had shouted 'sale Juif' at her on La Croisette the previous day. Edward found one friend, or at least acquaintance – the beautiful and sophisticated Daisy Fellowes. She had what Vogue called La Présence. She was a friend of the Windsors and remarked darkly that the Duke was spending far too much time in the casinos that proliferated along the coast. She showed Edward a local newspaper, published in English for the tourists, whose front page was headlined 'International Friendliness Established Through Tourism.' He laughed hollowly.

There was a slide into the pool and, since no one seemed interested in dressing for dinner, Verity and Edward were persuaded to don their swimming costumes and slip into the milky warm water. He thought her exquisite in her tight-fitting bathing suit and rubber helmet – her figure boyish but essentially feminine.

Verity caught his glance and snapped, 'What are you looking at?'

'Nothing. You have to admit,' he said as he swam lazily over to the far side, 'this is heaven.'

She lay on her back in the water, gazing up at a sky so blue it was almost black.

'What are you thinking?' he asked.

'Just that, when the sun has ceased to shine and the bombs are laying waste to London, I shall always remember this moment.'

'Come on! Don't be so gloomy. It may not happen,' Edward ventured.

'You know it will,' she replied and, turning on her stomach, she swam back to the steps.

She signalled to Natalie for a cigarette and the two of them sat on the edge of the pool, their feet in the water. 'Is it my imagination,' she asked in a whisper, 'or is Simon avoiding us?'

'No, I don't think so,' Natalie replied thoughtfully. 'He's just waiting for the right moment to hear what you have to say.'

'What will you do when war comes?' Verity asked.

'You think it must?'

'Yes, I do.'

Natalie sighed. 'Simon has promised to take me to England.'

'Will you go?'

'I think not. I shall take what comes here. This is where I belong. And, you know, for an actress there will always be . . .'

'Protectors? Men?'

'Yes, of course.'

'Nazis even?'

'I don't expect you to approve, but yes. I know some Germans. They are not all . . .'

220

Verity stubbed out her cigarette in an onyx ashtray shaped like a dolphin. 'I'm afraid they are, Natalie . . . or almost all of them,' she corrected herself, remembering Adam.

She got up and went over to Edward who was towelling himself. 'Natalie says Simon is waiting for the right moment to talk to us.'

'I'm not looking forward to it, V. I have a weak hand. I must bluff and I never was that good at poker.'

In the end, the moment came when Edward least expected it. It was slightly embarrassing because it wasn't clear whether they were invited to stay for dinner. The other guests started to drift away to dress and the Lewishohns went too, saying nothing one way or the other.

Verity was talking to Daisy Fellowes and Edward found himself standing next to Sir Simon. 'I think we had better go,' he said. 'You will want to go and dress and we must not hold you up.'

'Must you?' he replied lazily.

Edward wondered if he was being insolent and the thought prompted him to say, 'Before we go, can I give you a word of warning?'

'A word of warning?' Sir Simon raised his eyebrows.

'Yes. You see the Foreign Office has evidence that the Castlewood Foundation has close links with the Nazi Party and that Himmler himself is taking an interest in your activities.'

'Such nonsense!' he responded with studied indifference.

'It's not nonsense. For one thing, you must give up this mad expedition you are planning to Tibet. It is just a front for the Nazis to pursue their perverted and ridiculous idea of – what do you call it? – racial hygiene. You explained it to me at Swifts Hill. I thought then that it was obscene but I put you down for an innocent dupe of clever villains. The more I have learnt about the Foundation the less I believe that.'

'I am glad to hear it, Lord Edward. I am no one's dupe.'

'I believe you are funding operations at the Clinic carried out by Dominic Montillo which are similar to those being done by German doctors in their asylums and prison camps.'

Sir Simon seemed genuinely shocked. 'That's outrageous! Have you any proof? No, I thought not. I ought to sue you for slander and I will not hesitate to do so if you repeat these baseless allegations. The Castlewood Foundation is a reputable medical charity whose work is applauded on both sides of the Atlantic. I would be angry if your accusations were not so absurd.'

'So you deny that any operations of this kind are being carried out at the Clinic which, I understand, you own?'

'As it happens I do have an investment in Dominic's Beauty Institute – though I don't know what that has to do with you – but I do not own it. If I did, I would be proud to admit it. What operations are you accusing Dominic of carrying out? May I remind you that he is a much-admired surgeon and the work he does repairing ruined faces and physical deformities is outstanding. His patients worship him. He has just operated on Maggie Cardew and the repairs to her will transform her life for the better.' Edward could think of nothing to say. 'And furthermore, though he would not like me to say it, Dominic is doing it for nothing – as a favour to me and to her brother and because he is a good man.'

Edward braced himself for one last attack. 'So you categorically deny that any operations are carried out at the Clinic which would be illegal in England?'

'Such as . . .?' Sir Simon responded coldly.

'Abortions, castrations, experiments on mentally or physically handicapped patients without their permission?'

'These are wild allegations, Lord Edward. I can't understand what has got into you. Now, I think you had better go.'

'The Foreign Office is concerned about your activities. If it hears that you have involved the Duke of Windsor . . .' Edward knew he was making himself ridiculous but decided he might as well finish what he had planned to say.

'The Foreign Office! I don't believe it, Lord Edward. I invited you to Swifts Hill as a gentleman and a friend of my friends. If you ever repeat any of these slurs against me and the Foundation, I repeat, I will not hesitate to sue.'

'Very well. I have tried to warn you but I see it is pointless. One last question, Sir Simon. Have you seen anything of Graham Harvey here in Cannes?'

'Of Graham?' His surprise was genuine. 'What on earth would Graham be doing in Cannes?'

'Trying to kill you, I believe. You should keep a lookout for

222

him. He has been collecting evidence against the Foundation and I am very much afraid that he may take the law into his own hands.'

'Graham . . . attack me? After all I have done for him? Now, I really think you are mad, Lord Edward. Please go before I call the police.'

'Damn, damn, damn!' Edward said as they drove back to the hotel. 'I have been an utter fool. I have shown all my cards and my opponent has laughed at them. I spoke before I had the evidence. That was fatal.'

'No,' said Verity kindly. 'You gave him a warning for which he should be grateful. If he takes no heed of it, he only has himself to blame.'

'Look here,' Edward said after a minute or two. 'I have just had a thought. What if Harvey is after Edmund Cardew and not Sir Simon?'

'Why should he be after Cardew?'

'Because I think Cardew killed Maud.'

Verity opened her mouth to protest but he cut in. 'No, wait a minute – listen to this.'

14

Verity had never been to a casino before. It was capitalism at its worst in her view and her face displayed her disapproval as she and Edward stood, rather self-consciously, in the bar talking to George Forrester – the English bartender who knew everything that went on. The casino on La Croisette was one of the most famous in France. Built to impress, it was decorated in the Empire style with heavy curtains, mirrors, massive chandeliers and gilt chairs scattered about. There were private rooms for the very rich and privileged but from eleven in the morning tables of roulette and *chemin de fer* were always available for play in the magnificent main room. It did not really become crowded until after dinner – the casino boasted a first-class restaurant – and by eleven there was hardly room to breathe.

There was a preponderance of men. The women, although by no means disreputable, were not, Edward thought, what his sister-in-law, the Duchess, would consider ladies. Some of them, Verity was fascinated to see, wore special rings on their fingers in which they could lodge their cigarettes when they played a card or laid a chip on the green baize. Everyone smoked. The sweet scent of Turkish and Egyptian cigarettes and the heavier masculine aroma of Havana cigars lay over the gaming tables like a miasma. There were very few Americans but many Belgians – enriched by their ruthless exploitation of the mineral wealth of the Congo – and some English industrialists who had made fortunes during the war.

'No, my lord, I have not seen Mr Cardew though he comes in most nights when he's in Cannes. He was here yesterday and the evening before.' Forrester looked at the clock above the bar. 'It's probably a bit early for him but I saw the Duke of Windsor come

224

in. Why not try your luck at the tables while you are waiting? The young lady may bring you good fortune.'

Edward decided he would try to avoid bumping into the Duke. He had no business with him and there might be embarrassment. However, he thought he might as well risk a few francs. 'After all,' he said to Verity, 'we don't want to look like private detectives. If you come to a casino, it's expected that you gamble.'

They were directed to the discreet *caisse*, where Edward exchanged fifty pounds for a pile of coloured gambling chips.

Reluctantly, Verity followed him to the *chemin de fer* table. There was an empty chair and she sat down, unaware that she was signalling that she wanted to play. The croupier slipped two cards out of the wooden 'shoe' and she turned to Edward to ask what she should do with them. 'Look at them,' he told her. Gingerly, she picked them up. 'You need nine,' he whispered, 'and you've got it!'

Twenty minutes later, having said *banco* whenever Edward told her to, she rose from the table three hundred pounds richer than when she sat down.

'You have it. I don't want them,' she said, pushing the chips at Edward.

'I'll keep them for you. Now, the roulette table . . .?'

The green baize, the soft glow of the lights, the intent eyes watching the silver ball as it circled and circled before settling in a tiny slot on the wheel mesmerized her. There was something fascinating about the whole experience but she insisted she did not want to play.

'Look at that old woman with the talons,' she whispered.

Edward looked and saw a bejewelled harridan who could have been eighty staring vacantly at the roulette wheel.

'I hate this,' Verity said suddenly. 'It's . . . it's wicked.'

'Let's slip away,' Edward agreed. 'I can't see Cardew but I can see . . . damn!'

It was the Duke of Windsor and, to Edward's surprise, when he saw him, the Duke came straight over with a group of friends, some of whom Edward had met before.

'My dear,' he said, addressing Verity, 'you look ravishing. May I ask, that pendant – did Lord Edward give it you? Wallis would love it.'

Verity blushed and nodded. It crossed her mind that the Duke might be hinting that she should take it off there and then and give it to him to give her.

'I think I am going to be lucky tonight, Fruity.' He turned to his close friend Fruity Metcalfe. 'May I ask a favour, Miss Browne . . . ?' Verity was surprised he remembered her name. 'Will you stand by me at the table and put your hand on my shoulder? I know it is asking a lot but . . .'

She was hardly able to nod her head. Here she was, a paid-up member of the Communist Party, helping the Duke of Windsor win at cards. It was absurd and grotesque but she did not want to make a scene.

The Duke seemed to have a great number of chips of various colours and sizes. 'Where shall I put them – on the red or the black? Even or uneven?' he asked, looking up at Verity.

'Red,' she found herself saying. The croupier swept the ball into its orbit and the thirty seconds during which it spun – creating, momentarily, a silver aurora – seemed to Verity to last an eternity. At last, the ball dropped into a slot bearing a red number.

'Shall I leave it there?' he said, pointing to the pile of chips, apparently entranced by his winnings.

Verity nodded approval and again the wheel spun and again the Duke won.

Edward and Fruity Metcalfe were standing discreetly behind her, Edward praying that she would not do anything silly like overturn the tables and declare herself outraged. As the Duke's luck – or rather Verity's – continued, a small crowd gathered about them. Finally, the Duke declared that he would stop while he was ahead and rose from his chair. He thrust several large denomination chips into the hole where tips for the croupiers were collected and, for a brief moment, Edward wondered if he might make the appalling mistake of trying to give Verity some of his winnings. He must, however, have seen something in her face because, gracefully, he kissed her hand and told her how much he had enjoyed her company.

As Edward turned away from the table, he saw Edmund Cardew and, a second later, Graham Harvey. Harvey, sweating badly in a dinner-jacket two sizes too big for him, stumbled across the room towards them. He had his hand in his jacket pocket. Cardew, who had not seen Harvey, walked towards

226

Edward with a smile on his face. As though in a dream Edward saw Harvey draw a black snub-nosed gun from his pocket.

'No!' he cried, taking two steps towards Harvey and putting out his hand as though expecting him to hand over the gun.

There was a bang and then a shocked scream from a woman standing nearby. Edward felt as though he had received a terrific punch in the chest and he fell to the floor.

As soon as he had fired, Harvey dropped the gun and was immediately overpowered by those around him. He looked at Edward in amazement. 'You?' was all he said before he was taken away.

It had all happened so fast. The Duke had been standing behind Edward and – momentarily unaware of why he had fallen – started to go to his aid. Metcalfe, grasping the danger the Duke was in, tried to hustle him away. As the initial shock passed, the Duke seemed to understand what had happened.

Twisting free of Metcalfe's grasp, he shouted, 'For God's sake, he tried to kill me,' and then, seeing the blood staining Edward's impeccably starched dickey, cried out in a shrill voice – almost a scream, 'I am not leaving until they get a doctor. This man saved my life.' Metcalfe once again took his arm and, still protesting, the Duke was led away.

Verity fell to her knees beside Edward, holding his head, shocked into silence.

Edward was still just conscious. 'V, I . . . I think I have been shot.' To his surprise, his voice was little more than a whisper.

Verity had not actually seen Harvey fire – her view was obstructed by the Duke and his friends – but she had heard the shot. At first, she thought the Duke had been assassinated but, seeing Edward lying on the floor, she understood immediately what had happened. She felt more frightened than at any time since she had left Spain. It was her worst nightmare – Edward would die and she would be truly alone. It was a moment of absolute clarity when she recognized that he was the only person in the world she really loved and trusted. Even her father, whom she adored, could not be more to her than this man dying in front of her.

'Edward! For God's sake – are you . . .?'

'V, it's you, isn't it? My eyes aren't working properly . . . That idiot Harvey took a shot at me . . . I . . . I don't think he meant to.

Hold me, V. I don't seem able to get my breath. I wonder if I'm dying?' He sounded more puzzled than frightened.

Fruity Metcalfe returned from seeing the Duke to his car and knelt down beside Verity. His foolish face was a mask of concern as he took off his jacket, rolled it into a bundle and put it beneath Edward's head. 'I say, old fellow, are you all right? No, I mean of course you aren't. Lie still. An ambulance is on its way. Just don't move. Bravest thing I ever saw, the way you shielded the guv'nor. A genuine hero, what!'

'Where is he?' Edward managed to mutter.

'The Duke? Don't you worry, old chap. He's quite safe and, in any case, they've caught the man.'

'No, I mean . . .' He wanted to ask where Cardew was but could not get the words out. He tried again. 'V, will you . . .?'

Rather stupidly, Edward thought afterwards, he passed out before he could explain to Verity who Harvey's intended victim was, because, of course, despite appearances, he had not been trying to kill the Duke of Windsor. Just before he lost consciousness, Edward saw everything clearly. He realized he knew why Maud Pitt-Messanger had been stabbed to death and why Graham Harvey wanted to kill Edmund Cardew. He wanted desperately to tell someone – in case he forgot or in case he died – but there was no time. He was feeling very cold and he wanted . . . he wanted to see Verity. He could no longer feel her hand. He knew she was there with him but there was something wrong . . . some reason why he could not see her. As he tried to remember what that might be, his eyes closed.

Monsieur l'Inspecteur dragged his fingers through his thinning grey hair and said disbelievingly, 'You are telling me that Graham Harvey was not trying to murder Le Duc but this other man – Edmund Cardew?'

'That is correct, Inspector Carbourd. Is Harvey saying that he was trying to assassinate the Duke?'

'He is saying nothing at all, milord. He has not uttered one word since he was arrested. He will not even speak to the lawyer appointed to represent him.'

To the Inspector's great relief, this English aristocrat spoke fluent French. It was a considerable surprise as, in his experience, the majority of English visitors to Cannes spoke very little French, preferring to talk loudly in English. He had several times been called to the casino, and even to the Carlton Hotel, to deal with English 'lords', some of whom, after investigation, proved to have appropriated their titles, not inherited them. Genuine or not, they were, with very few exceptions, arrogant, stupid and contemptuous of his authority. This one, however, seemed to be the exception which proved the rule. His French was very good, he was courteous – almost apologetic – and yet he was causing more trouble than any of the others by complicating a simple story. As the newspapers had it – and not just the local papers, even *Le Figaro* – Lord Edward Corinth, the brother of the Duke of Mersham no less, had placed himself between the Duke of Windsor and an assassin's bullet. The Duke, *Le Figaro* pointed out, had turned for refuge to France after having been forced by the cold and hypocritical English to forfeit his throne because he had the misfortune to fall in love with a divorced American. That he should now be the victim of such an outrage was an insult to French honour. Fortunately, the would-be assassin had been apprehended but that was almost beside the point.

The French had shaken their heads when the Abdication scandal had broken – not at the King's folly but at the fuss his subjects were making. To them, he was romantic and wronged and now this attempt on his life! No Frenchman was involved, thank goodness, or the whole weight of the Sûreté Nationale would have fallen on the Inspector's shoulders. No, it was simply an English Communist, already known to the English police, and thankfully, he was now behind bars. France was plagued by anarchists and Communists, many of whom had come from Spain when the war went in Franco's favour. Only three years ago, on a state visit to France, King Alexander of Yugoslavia had been assassinated in Marseilles with the French Foreign Minister Louis Barthou. The killer was a Macedonian in the pay of the Ustase, the Croatian Fascist organization, but to attempt to kill the ex-king of England at the casino in Cannes . . .! That was outrageous.

And now this English lord was telling him that the intended victim was not the Duke – was not even himself – but some other Englishman of whom the Inspector had never even heard. Furthermore, he was demanding to be given access to the prisoner and refusing to lay any charges against him.

'But it is not up to you,' the Inspector said angrily. 'This is a criminal matter. It was attempted murder and there is no shortage of witnesses. The doctor says the bullet missed your lung by just so much.' He squeezed his fingers together. 'You should not be alive. It is a miracle. Even without your testimony, this madman will be convicted but I must warn you, my lord, should you refuse to go into the witness box you may be held to have committed contempt of court. But, forgive me! The doctor said I must not tire you. I shall come again tomorrow. Please think about what I have said.'

The Inspector very much hoped that Lord Edward would be reasonable. He had an idea he would be a difficult man to coerce. Even in his weakened state, he was obstinate. And the man had powerful friends. The Inspector had received several telephone calls from the British Embassy – which was otherwise keeping a very low profile – informing him that Lord Edward was a personal friend of the British Foreign Secretary, Mr Anthony Eden, and must be treated with respect. On the other hand, this was the most public case he had ever been involved with and the press – not just the French and British press but American and European journalists – dogged his every footstep and were this minute camped outside the hospital awaiting a statement. Lord Edward's request to interview Harvey would be very difficult to arrange without anyone knowing about it and, in any case, it was quite out of the question for legal reasons. Harvey's lawyers would allege a conspiracy and the case might be jeopardized. Could he safely ignore Lord Edward's claim that the man had been trying to kill someone else? It sounded like nonsense but could he be sure?

The following day, the patient was no less unreasonable and absolutely refused to cooperate.

'I am very sorry, Lord Edward,' the Inspector said, 'but what you ask is quite impossible. You must see that. Now, if you would like a lawyer to question him on your behalf, that might be arranged.'

Edward thought for a moment. 'I do understand, Inspector, that it is difficult for me to have a private interview with Mr Harvey but what if a friend of mine, Miss Verity Browne, were to see him on my behalf? Would that be possible? You have met Miss Browne?'

The Inspector shuddered. He had indeed met Miss Browne and so had the doctors and nurses, and she had made all their lives a misery. She seemed convinced that they were not doing enough to save the life of her friend. He assumed she was the Englishman's mistress but why he should love this *moineau* ... this sparrow of a girl when, presumably, he could take his pick ... and, what was worse, she was a Communist and a journalist! And what was worst of all, she claimed to be a friend of the accused man. He had tried to question her about this and would have to do so again. If it were a conspiracy, he could make neither head nor tail of it. He shuddered again. The English were mad.

'And you know, Inspector,' Edward continued mildly, 'she is a responsible journalist but – as she would be acting as my representative – she would, I know, give you her word not to make anything she learnt public without your express permission.'

The Inspector played for time. 'Is she, as she claims, milord, a friend of the accused?'

'We are both friends of Mr Harvey,' Edward said firmly. 'I know it sounds confusing, Inspector, but it is really quite simple. I will be able to be more explicit after Miss Browne has had an opportunity to talk to him.' He had an idea. 'What if you were present during the interview? Surely that would make it all right? You speak enough English to understand what is being said?'

The Inspector nodded his head but said nothing. He was in two minds. He wanted to get at the truth even if it proved to be more complicated than the obvious conclusion which he and the world at large had drawn – that a Communist had attempted to assassinate royalty. He fondled his bushy moustache, and to Edward's amusement, his hand then went straight to his head as though comparing the luxuriance of his upper lip with his balding pate.

'Well,' he said reluctantly, 'I suppose it might be possible but do you really think Mr Harvey would talk to Miss Browne in my presence?'

'I cannot say but surely it is worth a try? Will you ask Miss Browne to come and see me this afternoon?'

'You wish to discuss this idea with her?'

'I do. I think you will find her at the casino where she is interviewing the staff.'

'You comprehend, Lord Edward? Not one word of this must get out. If anything appears in any newspaper about Miss Browne having special access to the prisoner, I shall have her deported. You must make her understand that I am serious about this.'

Edward took this as consent and smiled his agreement.

'Graham – it's me. It's taken ages to get to see you and I am afraid the Inspector insists on being here while we talk so don't say anything you don't want him to hear. They think the two of us make up a Communist conspiracy!'

Verity tried to speak lightly but it wasn't easy. She was shocked at his appearance. She had not expected him to look well but he was deathly pale and seemed to have aged ten years. He looked up as she came into the cell but said nothing, lowering his head almost immediately.

'Edward wants you to know that he's no longer at death's door and that he doesn't blame you for shooting him because he knows who it was you were really trying to kill.'

It all came out in rather a rush and, for a second, Harvey glanced at her with what seemed like surprise. He remained silent but Verity was encouraged.

'Are they treating you all right? They say you won't see a lawyer. Would you like me to get someone over from England? I think my father would come if I asked him.'

'What are you doing here?' he shouted suddenly. 'No one can help me. I don't want anyone to help me. I just want to die.'

The Inspector made to get up and go to Verity's aid but she waved him away.

'Come on, Graham. Please don't say that. There are lots of people who want you to live. Me, for instance. And Simon. He sent me a telegram to say he will be here tomorrow and I was to get you whoever or whatever you wanted.'

'I don't want any help from that man,' he grunted ungratefully. 'Tell him to stay away, will you?'

'But you will talk to me?'

'What is there to say?'

232

'I just want people to know the truth. You weren't trying to assassinate the Duke of Windsor, were you? You weren't even trying to kill Edward Corinth. I think you wanted to frighten someone else – Edmund Cardew. Am I right?'

Harvey covered his face with his hands. Then looking up, he asked, 'How is he?'

'The Duke?'

'No, not the Duke. What do I care about him? I didn't even know it was him. I don't look at the picture papers and I never read anything about royalty on principle. No, I meant how is Lord Edward? I . . . I didn't mean to . . . damn it, I like the man!'

'He's not dead, Graham, and he's not going to die – at least not yet anyway. I told you. He's tougher than he appears.'

Harvey grimaced. He looked worn out. 'Tell him, I'm sorry,' he mumbled.

Verity leaned forward on her hard upright chair. 'Would it be easier if I tell you what we – Edward and I – think happened and you can tell me if we are right?'

'If you must, but what does it all matter?'

'Of course it matters,' Verity said vehemently. 'I think it all goes back to Maud Pitt-Messanger. She told you and – just before she was murdered – she also told Edward that she had killed her father herself.'

'I didn't believe her.'

'Unlikely though it seems, Edward came to the conclusion that she was telling the truth. She was the only one who could have done it. It was premeditated. Only Maud would have brought an ancient Assyrian dagger to the Abbey – a dagger from her father's private collection, I imagine. No one could possibly have known where Pitt-Messanger would sit and, as far as the police can discover, no one else at Lord Benyon's memorial service had a motive to kill him.'

'What was the motive?' the Inspector asked in English. 'Lord Edward told me about this murder in Westminster Abbey. *Très bizarre!*'

'Well, at first Lord Edward and I thought it must be because Maud had been prevented by her father from marrying the man she loved. Her and Sidney Temperley's lives were ruined by him and the poor man died soon after. We don't know whether he

233

caught cholera by accident or if there was any truth in the rumours at the time that Pitt-Messanger was in some way responsible. Did he substitute infected water for the bottled water they all drank on the dig? We will never know.'

'Maud thought it was an accident. She did not blame her father for Temperley's death.' Harvey spoke slowly and in a low voice.

'And then he wouldn't let her marry you.'

'He couldn't have stopped us.'

'But you had no money.'

Harvey shook his head in frustration. 'I told her I wouldn't marry her until I could support her. When my book was finished . . .'

'But it never would be, would it?' Verity asked cruelly. He shook his head in despair again. 'But that wasn't why she killed him, was it?' she continued.

'No, she killed him because of Edwin,' Harvey agreed.

'Who is Edwin?' inquired the Inspector, puzzled.

It was Harvey who answered him. 'Maud had an elder brother who disappeared when he was a child. They said he had run away to sea but he hadn't. He was born with a harelip and a cleft palate. His father was disgusted by him.'

'I do not understand,' the Inspector said. 'How "disgusted"?'

'He believed in Charles Darwin and his more absurd disciples,' Verity explained. 'He believed that the race should get "purer" and . . .'

Harvey broke in bitterly. 'He imagined that his children would be clever like him and physically beautiful. His son was disfigured and he believed mentally subnormal. He thought such people should be "eliminated" – not allowed to breed – not allowed to live.'

The Inspector was horrified. 'But not his own son! That's impossible.'

'Pitt-Messanger was a cruel man,' Harvey answered. 'But there was hope. This brilliant young surgeon, Dominic Montillo, said he could repair Edwin's face and mouth with a small operation. Pitt-Messanger told him to do whatever he wanted – experiment on the poor lad. What happened I don't know. I asked Montillo but he said Maud had imagined the whole thing and he never even knew the boy.'

'Whatever happened, Edwin died and, instead of being properly buried, his body was . . . was used by Montillo for . . .'

'For experiments,' Harvey finished Verity's sentence.

'No, it's not possible!' exclaimed the Inspector. He thought for a moment. 'But how did Miss Pitt-Messanger discover this? Perhaps it *was* all in her imagination.'

Harvey said flatly, 'That was my fault. Maud and I fell in love. At least, I suppose that was what it was. We were both lonely people. We found each other just by accident at some political rally.' A slight smile curved his lips. 'Maud fancied she was a Communist. It seemed to stand for everything her father hated – equality, serving each other, looking after the weak. Anyway, when she plucked up courage and told her father she was going to marry me, he was furious. No, not furious, scornful. She said he laughed at her. He told her no one would want to marry a freak like her – so ugly. It was then that he told her how much he despised both his children. He told her that Edwin hadn't run away to sea but had been disposed of like the rubbish he was. Maud told me she decided quite coldly, then and there, to kill him. She could forgive him for ruining *her* life but not for what he had done to Edwin.'

'But why kill him in Westminster Abbey of all places?' the Inspector asked.

'It seemed the right place to her,' Harvey said.

'Because it was "holy"?' Verity asked suspiciously.

'No, no,' Harvey said impatiently. 'Because Darwin's disciple, Francis Galton, arranged for him, the arch-unbeliever, to be buried there. Next time you visit the Abbey, spend a minute or two contemplating Darwin's monument at the east end of the nave. He has a long beard and looks like God. It was a terrible joke, which always made Pitt-Messanger laugh, that this atheist – who had done more than anyone since Newton to undermine the Christian religion – should be buried in England's holiest shrine. So it was only justice that another of his disciples, whose "religion" had led him to destroy both his children, should lie near him.'

They were all silent for a moment or two while they digested this. Then Verity said, 'So when I met Maud at Swifts Hill . . .'

'She had gone there to kill Montillo – to complete her work, as it were. But I dissuaded her – or I thought I had. I told her there was a better way. I suggested she made public all she knew

235

about Edwin's death and ruin the reputation of Montillo's bloody Institute.'

'But she tried to kill herself?' Verity put in.

'You have to remember she was hardly sane. You cannot kill your father and remain sane. She had this mad idea – she told me afterwards – of cutting her wrists just badly enough to attract attention. Montillo would patch her up and then she would stab him or make some sort of a fuss . . . As I say, she wasn't in her right mind. I was worried she would do something . . . I don't know . . . something awful. I was intending to creep into the house to see her when I bumped into you that morning. I didn't know she had cut her wrists because I left the house immediately after that horrible dinner the night before and you didn't think to tell me.'

'I'm so sorry. I suppose I thought you knew. Anyway, I didn't know then that you cared for Maud.'

'She was convinced she would be punished for killing her father. I think it was only her love for me that kept her going, and I let her down.'

'So Montillo found her with her wrists cut and bandaged them up. But she didn't attack him or anything?' Verity asked.

'She couldn't – not in front of Dr Morris. However, she did have words with him later that evening. She told him she knew what he had done to her brother and it was that which had made her kill her father. She said she was going to expose the Institute for what it was – a place where criminal operations took place. She signed her death warrant when she told him.'

'I have just remembered something which has been puzzling me. When was Edwin's birthday?'

'April 27th. I know because it was a sacred day for her.'

'How stupid of me! I found her diary the night she tried to commit suicide. It was empty except for the letters EPM against that date. I asked her about it later and she said they were her father's initials, which, of course, I already knew. I never thought of Edwin.'

'But if she had no evidence – just this strange story about her brother – ' the Inspector said, 'surely, Montillo could have dismissed it as the ravings of a mad woman?'

'She told him, which was true, that I had my suspicions of the Clinic and was planning to go and do some detective work in the South of France.'

'And did you find what you were looking for?' the Inspector inquired.

'Yes, I have all the evidence I need. I made friends with a nurse who was troubled by what she had seen in the Clinic. She stole some record books and gave them to me . . . oh, what does it matter now?'

'It *does* matter,' Verity said firmly. 'It explains why you were in Cannes – not to kill the Duke of Windsor but to expose that . . . that horrible place. Where is the nurse? We will need her to give evidence.'

'She died in a car accident – if it was an accident,' Harvey said gloomily.

'So why did you travel to Cannes this time? To kill Mr Montillo?' the Inspector asked.

'I am happy to kill him, Inspector, if I ever get the chance, but he has powerful friends. No, I came to kill Edmund Cardew. It was he who killed Maud at Montillo's urging.'

The Inspector looked thoroughly bewildered. 'Please, I do not understand. Who is this Edmund Cardew?'

Edward listened intently to everything Verity had to tell him. When she had quite finished, he sighed and then wished he hadn't because it was so painful.

Verity saw him wince and asked, 'These flowers are glorious. Who are they from? I haven't even brought you grapes.'

'They are from the Duke of Windsor. And he wrote a very nice note. He is planning to come and visit me after the operation to retrieve the bullet.'

'How very kind of him,' she said sarcastically. 'Perhaps he'll give you a medal.'

'I don't think he has that power but don't sneer. It's nicely meant.'

'I should think so, after you acted as a pincushion on his behalf,' she said hotly.

'No I didn't.'

'I know you didn't but he doesn't know that.' She smiled. 'So, what has the doctor had to say? He thinks you'll live?'

'Don't joke. Remember how sweet I was to you when you got shot. I have been very lucky, apparently, though I have to say I don't *feel* particularly lucky. The bullet just missed my lung. It didn't touch my spine. If it had, the doctor told me – rather too cheerfully I thought – I might have been paralysed. So, as I say, I have to count myself lucky – lucky to be alive and lucky not to be seriously wounded.'

'And the bullet comes out tomorrow?'

'Yes, they think I am strong enough to withstand the probing.'

'Yuk! You know I can't stand blood.'

'You don't have to worry. It'll be my blood and you won't have to see it.' He paused and then said lightly. 'How long can you stay?'

'Another week or even more if I need to. This is a very big story for the *New Gazette*. Joe says . . . well, you can guess what he says.'

'Your lover gunned down in front of you at the Cannes casino . . .? I can certainly guess the way Weaver wants to play it,' he replied drily. Verity said nothing because there was nothing to say. 'But I'm not your lover, am I?' he demanded almost angrily.

'Please don't, Edward. I love you . . . you know I love you.' She spoke fiercely, as though the words were forced out of her. 'Don't make me feel guiltier than I feel already. It just happens that at this particular moment I'm *in* love – which is different – with Adam. I'm sorry, Edward, I really am, but I can't lie to you just because you're ill.'

Edward sighed again and winced again – this time because her honesty hurt him more than his wound.

'So what about Cardew?' she said to change the subject.

'They'll find him. He can't escape. The French police are very efficient.'

'And he killed Maud? You are sure of it? You're sure Harvey is right?'

'Yes, V. I'm sure. When Maud told me she was in danger, she meant, of course, from Montillo. What she did not know was that Montillo had told Cardew how dangerous she was to the reputation of the Institute. Cardew had gambled away the little money he had earned in the City. As an MP, he earned virtually nothing and he had to support his mother and his sister. Montillo gave him a chance to invest in the Institute. It may have been a genuine act of friendship but Cardew clearly stood to lose everything – his investment, his career and the respect of the men he called his friends if the Clinic was exposed as a place where . . .'

'It really was a place where experiments on people were carried out? I can hardly believe it.'

'I'm afraid so. Inspector Carbourd has retrieved the record books Harvey stole from the Clinic and they make it clear – in revolting detail – that Montillo had some contract with German scientists to carry out experimental work of a disgusting nature.'

'And this was profitable?'

'Very, but I don't think that was Montillo's main reason for taking on the work. He genuinely believed these experiments were for the good of the human race.'

'Is he mad, do you think?'

'Montillo? Yes, I suppose so, although I think a jury would find him guilty of murder.'

'But will they ever catch him?'

'That I don't know, V. Someone tipped him the wink and he had time to get out before the police came for him. I guess he's in Germany by now and the Nazis will not give him up easily.'

Verity rubbed her cheek meditatively. 'So Montillo told Cardew he had to get rid of Maud or he would be dragged under with the Institute. I hear he was head over heels in debt and he would have lost his seat in the Commons if he had gone bankrupt. But I still don't understand why Montillo didn't kill Maud himself?'

'I expect he thought he wouldn't get away with it. No one knew of any connection between Cardew and Maud but it was widely known that Maud was Montillo's patient. He thought about getting her to the Clinic – to "convalesce" after she cut her wrists. He could have got rid of her there but, in the end, there wasn't time. She had to be disposed of immediately.'

'And the dagger?'

'Montillo happened to see Hannah hide it in the pavilion, I think. He might have suborned her to steal it for him but I don't think so. She struck me as an honest girl. It was a perfect weapon. There was no way Cardew could know where it had been hidden, let alone steal it. The dagger made it look as though the murderer had to have had access to Sir Simon's museum which Cardew didn't have.'

'And during the cricket match he had every opportunity to take it out of its hiding place.'

'Yes, V. Montillo went off to London to establish the perfect alibi but, annoyingly for him, came back to Swifts Hill too early. He was seen talking to Sir Simon before Cardew had done the deed.'

'Was Sir Simon involved in Maud's murder?'

'I don't know but I'm inclined to think not. He may be a fool but he would never have countenanced murder at his beloved Swifts Hill. I saw his face when he heard that Maud has been killed. He could not have faked the horror he showed then.'

'I wonder if Montillo knew, or guessed, that Maud had told Harvey what she suspected?'

'I am sure he did and he would have been planning to get rid of him as well but he never got the chance.'

'So there were *two* daggers. Maud used one from her father's private collection and she was killed by the dagger in Sir Simon's museum.'

'Yes, V. Ancient evil bringing death through the millennia.'

A nurse came in and asked Verity to leave. She kissed Edward and said, 'Can you forgive me for not being the woman you deserve?'

'You're the woman I want,' he countered.

'And can you forgive me for that?'

'There's no question of forgiveness,' he said ruefully. 'It's a fact of life. You mustn't worry about me. Connie will be here tomorrow.' His sister-in-law, the Duchess, was the woman, after Verity, whom he loved most. 'She'll look after me.'

Verity thought this remark was probably aimed at her but said nothing. Edward knew that she was not good at 'looking after' people. She recognized she was selfish but that was the way she was and it was futile to pretend she was something different.

'And Maggie Cardew will want looking after,' she said seriously.

'Indeed. I understand that her mother is dying.'

'Such a shame. She's such a nice woman. By the way, how is Maggie's face?'

'She seemed optimistic that the operation had been a success.'

'So maybe something good will come out of this awful business after all.'

'Maybe. Now go. You have people to interview and stories to write.'

'Bye, then. I'll come in tomorrow. Keep your pecker up.'

'It's up,' he said.

Verity blushed and, giving him a wave, left the room. She did have a story to write. Inspector Carbourd would have to approve it before she could file it but he was not averse to publicity and she thought she would not have too much trouble with him.

15

The copper beech which shaded the lawn and hung over the river had turned a glorious red before shedding its leaves in the October winds. Mersham Castle was beautiful but melancholy, as though it knew what was to come and feared it. Edward, who loved the place more deeply than words could express, found his mood matched by the changing seasons. Although his health had improved and his wound healed, his spirits were at a low ebb. The Duchess was worried about him but the distractions she offered were rejected. One cold and wet Thursday in late October, she sat on his bed while he ate his breakfast and, with some trepidation, informed him that Maggie Cardew had expressed a wish to see him.

'I have her letter here if you would like to read it. She says she is writing to me rather than you because she has already sent you two letters which you have ignored. Is that true, Ned?'

Edward wrinkled his face and pushed away his eggs and bacon. 'I'm afraid it is, Connie. The truth is I don't know what to say to her. Her brother is in prison waiting to be hanged and I was responsible. What can I say to her that would not add insult to injury?'

'I think you owe it to her.'

'Do I? *Do* I, Connie?' he demanded fiercely. 'I think I have paid my dues.'

'It's up to you, of course, but the poor girl is all alone since her mother died and though Lord Weaver has been very kind to her, she has no real friend.'

'I'll think about it,' he said grumpily. 'I say, Connie, I've been meaning to . . . to tell you how grateful I am to you for taking me in and nursing me and so on. You've been an absolute brick and I truly think Gerald is the luckiest man alive.'

The Duchess smiled and got up from his bed to hide her pleasure. In her most secret imaginings, she had sometimes fantasized about what it might be like to be married to the younger brother. Of course, Gerald was a dear and, in a certain light, he was almost handsome and it was something to be a duchess but . . . but he was dull and, whatever else Ned was, it wasn't dull! She wrapped her silk dressing-gown round her more closely and asked, 'You'll be here for Christmas, won't you? Frank's coming.'

'With that awful American girl?'

'Oh, she's not that bad,' the Duchess said gaily. 'As a matter of fact, I think things may have cooled between them. She took him to some meeting about eugenics and Frank made a bit of an ass of himself – so he says – and rather laid into some women who were spouting nonsense about breeding. He'll tell you the details but there's a certain *froideur* there.'

'Ah! I knew the boy had sense.'

'Is Fenton all right – staying here for so long, I mean?'

'He's loving it. He seems to have "formed an attachment" – his words – with Mary. Have you noticed?'

'Mary? My Mary? What a sly boots! No, I haven't noticed. I must be going blind in my old age.'

She considered for a moment. Mary Harris was her personal maid and it would be inconvenient, to say the least, if she married and left her service. She ticked herself off for being selfish. Why shouldn't the girl be married? She was pretty enough. Connie remembered the time, when Frank was back from Eton for the holidays, she had caught him kissing Mary in the buttery and had had to threaten him with his father.

'So, that's settled – you'll stay at Mersham for Christmas?'

'I would like that very much. Then I shall return to London and resume my normal life,' Edward said pleasantly. 'I'm still hoping for that Foreign Office job I was telling you about.'

'Have you written to Vansittart?'

'No, should I?'

'I just wondered. They may have appointed someone else by now to run that department of industrial espionage or whatever it's called. Surely they couldn't hold it open for you indefinitely?'

'Sh! That's top secret!' he said with exaggerated emphasis. 'I ought not to have told you anything about it. Anyway, the Foreign Office is much too grand to indulge in espionage.'

'I hope not. It would be so like us to play by the rules of a game no one else is playing.'

Edward laughed. 'Connie, my dear, you make me feel better. I wish I had married you instead of letting Gerald have you. You're much too good for him.'

This was so close to what she had been thinking that she hurriedly turned her face to the window. 'What nonsense you talk, Ned. Gerald is a dear and you're a ne'er-do-well who people try to kill. Why would I want you?'

'Of course, I was only joking,' he said, disappointingly.

In revenge, she asked, 'Have you heard anything from Verity?'

His face fell and she wished she had not brought it up.

'I had a postcard. She and Adam are in Vienna. She's says her German is getting quite good. She thought she might come back to London for a few days at Christmas.'

'Well, tell her she would be very welcome here.' Connie spoke with as much enthusiasm as she could manage.

'Do you mean that?' Edward's eyes brightened.

'Of course.'

'Then, I'll write and tell her. I don't think she has anywhere else to go. Her father's still in New York and her friends, the Hassels, are spending Christmas in Paris. Adrian says he is sure this will be the last Christmas of peacetime and he wants to enjoy it in his favourite city.'

Connie nodded. 'It will be good to see her.'

In fact, she found it hard to forgive Verity for treating her brother-in-law with such – in her view – callous disregard. She wanted to slap the girl. To make Ned unhappy was a mortal sin in her religion. In the beginning, she had not wanted him to marry Verity – the Duke could not stand her – but, when she saw how much in love he was, she had decided to do all she could to get them up the aisle. She could not understand what Verity was up to. She genuinely cared for Edward – of that Connie was certain – but she would not commit herself to him. She had some foolish objection to the whole idea of marriage. The Duke was deeply shocked by the immorality of the modern woman, among whose ranks he included Verity. And now, Connie gathered, she was living in sin, as people called it – indeed as *she* called it – with a young German aristocrat. She shrugged her shoulders. Perhaps she was getting old but . . .

'Now leave me, Connie. I shall bathe and then go for my constitutional. The doctor said I must walk for an hour every day when it's not too cold. I feel stale and out of condition. It's going to be a hell of a job getting fit again but I'm determined to do it.'

'And Maggie Cardew?'

'Look, Connie, if she wants to come, that's all right with me but it may end in tears.'

Edward was as nervous as he had been before sitting his finals but, when Maggie came into the drawing-room, he was immediately calm. He got up from the chair, in which he had been pretending to read *The Times*, and took her by the hand. Then, as she smiled at him, he kissed her.

'You would never know, would you?' she said, touching her cheek.

'What? Oh, the scar! It's amazing. Do you know, I had quite forgotten about it. But, yes, now you mention it . . .' He looked at her. 'It is perfect. Montillo may have a lot to answer for but no one can deny that he is a very clever surgeon. You've heard nothing from him, I suppose?'

'I think he is in Germany but he may have changed his name. I haven't tried to get in touch.' She hesitated. 'You really believe he is a monster?'

'I do,' he said gravely. 'He is absolutely determined to pursue his ideas of racial purity and he believes the individual must be sacrificed for the greater good. It's what Verity and I can never agree on. She believes that Communism is the one true faith and, if people have to go to the wall in order to create the perfect socialist society, then so be it. From all I have seen in Spain and elsewhere, I am absolutely certain that any philosophy which is prepared to sacrifice even one person for the greater good is a tyranny.'

'Forgive me! I didn't mean to get on my high horse. I was so sorry to hear about your mother. I wanted to write to you but it was during that awful trial and I didn't know what to say. To

245

think, when we met that day at Cranmer Court, I was to bring such trouble down upon you all. I almost wish we had never met.'

'I am sorry you feel that, Edward, because I don't. You didn't bring trouble on us. Teddy brought about his own downfall. Let's be honest about it.'

'You told me you thought he was spending too much time at the casino but did you know he had serious financial problems?'

'I knew he gambled but not that he was so heavily in debt. I really believe that, when Simon Castlewood and Montillo encouraged him to invest in the Institute, they were trying to help. They all thought they were going to make a fortune.'

'What's happened to it now? Do you know? The Clinic was closed down, of course.'

'The Institute was sold to a French businessman and is still making women beautiful, as far as I know. I don't think many people made the connection between the Institute and the Clinic. Anyway, the rich – and the French rich in particular – are not very scrupulous. They don't become rich by being tender-hearted. Or am I being cynical?'

'No, I'm sure you are right.' He took her hand. 'Maggie, it's so good to see you. I mean it. I just couldn't believe you would want to see *me*. How is Edmund?'

'Surprisingly well. No, not well exactly – but at peace. He's very calm. Sometimes I wish he was a little less calm, to tell the truth. I'm glad for him but his calmness can be a little unnerving. Poor Maud! What a miserable life she led – to be bullied by her father to give up the love of her life and then to be murdered when she had found someone else to love.'

'But she killed her father,' Edward said slowly. 'She knew she had done a very evil thing – whatever the provocation. Tell me, there is one thing which has never been properly explained. Why did Edmund lay her body in the stream? Was he trying to wash away the evidence?'

'I asked him that. He said she had committed a mortal sin when she murdered her father and he merely helped her make atonement. He laid her in the water so it could wash her clean of sin. I think he convinced himself that he was sacrificing her, not murdering her.'

246

'You think he is mad then?'

'I don't know. He seems quite rational but what's happening inside here,' she tapped her forehead, 'it's impossible to say.'

'I'm sorry. It must be very painful for you.'

'No, I think about it all the time and it does me good to talk about it. One thing to be thankful for is that at least Maud did not live to see Graham Harvey try to kill you.'

'He didn't try to kill me, as you know. He didn't even try to kill the Duke!'

'Has the Duke visited you on your sickbed?' she inquired ironically.

'No. He sent me a nice note and he was planning to visit me in hospital but when he found he *hadn't* been the object of an assassination attempt, Fruity Metcalfe says he was quite put out. Insulted, don't y'know. He felt he had been made a fool of. I did try to tell him that the bullet wasn't aimed at him the moment it happened but I couldn't get the words out. No, I don't expect to hear from him again.'

'Why did Harvey take his own life?'

'He left a letter for me. He thought he had failed in everything. He hadn't been able to protect the woman he loved, and he hadn't even been able to avenge her. I got in the way. He couldn't write the book he had researched for so long and – unlike Verity – he hadn't gone to Spain to fight for his beliefs. He said he had had enough of failure and did not want to live in a world dominated by Nazi Germany. So he hanged himself. It's a wretched business. I often think that if Verity or I had been able to talk to him, we might have stopped him.'

'And Verity?' Maggie was smiling and Edward smiled back.

'She's given me my marching orders,' he said, trying not to sound bitter. 'She's madly in love with Adam von Trott and is enjoying Vienna. She likes to be in the front line and, in her view, Vienna is the front line. She believes – and I do, too – that Hitler will walk into Austria in the next month or two and we will not do a thing to stop him. And that will encourage him to walk through the rest of Europe.'

'Is she safe there?'

'Not very but she's not interested in being safe. She wants to report history as it's being made. She says she is uneasy with the title of foreign correspondent. She says she is a reporter – nothing more.'

'But you've not seen her?'

'She may be coming home for Christmas,' he said without much hope.

'And will you . . . ?'

'Oh, no,' he said quickly. 'That's all over. But what about you?'

'Nothing. If I go to a party, I know everyone is looking at me and saying, "There's the sister of the murderer." It's worse than when I had a real scar!' She laughed but without humour.

'We all bear scars. But could we see each other in London? I will soon be well enough to come up for the day and it's time I got back to a normal routine.'

'Are you sure? You are not just being kind? I'd hate you to be sorry for me.'

'I'm not sorry for you, as I told you – it seems so long ago – at that awful cricket match at Swifts Hill. I would like to take you out to dinner and perhaps we could go on to a nightclub. Aren't we allowed any pleasure? I don't think it will be long before we are plunged into darkness so we should take what pleasure we can while we can.'

She looked embarrassed. 'I wanted to ask you . . . The Castlewoods throw a party on New Year's Eve. They've done it every year since they built Swifts Hill. They have invited me and . . . I wondered if you would come with me.' Her words were hurried and it had obviously been difficult for her to ask.

'Of course,' Edward said at once. 'It would be an honour. Will they mind me coming, though? The last time I saw Simon Castlewood in France we didn't part on friendly terms.'

'Ginny particularly wanted me to ask you – and Verity if she were in the country. She's grateful to you for stopping Simon and his Foundation from going too far. I mean, it did go too far, of course . . . You've forgiven me for refusing to help you gather evidence against Dominic? I couldn't do it after all he had done for me.'

'No, of course you couldn't. In any case, the evidence Harvey gathered and von Trott's testimony on how involved Himmler was with the Foundation were enough for the powers-that-be to close it down. Harvey was successful in that at least, though he did not live to see it. Sir Simon was fortunate not to have been prosecuted. I think in the end they thought he was just a

248

crackpot, not an out-and-out villain. Montillo's a different matter, of course, but he'll never be brought to justice.'

'At least Miss – I mean Mrs – Berners got her husband out. That was a miracle.'

'A miracle worked by von Trott. He truly is a remarkable man. I just hope he'll survive. He's walking such a tightrope. Himmler must hold him responsible for the Castlewood Foundation folding and with it the expedition to Tibet.'

'Oh no. That's going ahead. I read it in *The Times*.'

'The Nazis must have funded it themselves, then. But I'm seriously worried that Himmler will think – not without reason – that Adam made a fool of him and he's not a man to forgive that.'

'And now Adam's with a Communist journalist,' Maggie added. 'I can understand why you are worried about them. When Verity comes home at Christmas, you must make her see the danger she's in.'

'She knows very well the danger she's in but that won't stop her. She's steel all the way through,' Edward said grimly.

'Well, that's settled then. We'll go the ball, like Cinderella. Every time I receive an invitation, I think I should accept because there may never be another one. You really believe there will be war?'

'It's inevitable. It's just a case of when. Our beloved Prime Minister gives ground to Hitler time after time in a vain attempt to appease him but you can't appease a ravening wolf. His hunger is never satisfied. If Hitler told his followers he had had enough and he would be making no more territorial demands, he wouldn't last six months. He has to feed his flock with blood or they will tear him apart.'

Maggie shivered.

'I'm sorry. I didn't mean to frighten you.'

'I'm not frightened.'

'And you really aren't bitter about my part in Edmund's . . .'

'No, it would be quite unjust. It wasn't you who stabbed Maud to death.'

'If only I had listened to her properly before I went in to bat that day, your brother would have had no reason to kill her. I would have known what she knew.'

'We cannot live on "ifs".'

'What if your brother . . . if Edmund hears that we are seeing each other? Won't he be . . .?'

'Teddy went a long way to ruining my life so I don't see how he can complain if I have a little happiness. But I have decided not to tell him.'

'Well then,' Edward said, 'that's settled. I feel happier now than I have for a long time. There's the gong for lunch. You will stay, won't you? Connie is longing to meet you. It was she who said we should . . . '

'I would like that very much,' Maggie said rising. 'And then I want you to show me around the castle – if you have the time,' she added gravely.

As it turned out, Verity did not make it back to England for Christmas, accepting instead an invitation from Adam's parents to spend the holiday at the family *schloss* in Solz. Edward was almost fully recovered and his convalescence had been helped by the close friendship which had developed between him and Maggie. They had not become lovers but somehow it did not seem to matter to him. He preferred this easy-going marriage of minds to the 'big-dipper' relationship he had with Verity. He had heard nothing from her for almost three months – not even a Christmas card though that hardly surprised him as she did not believe in Christmas which she had once likened to eating marshmallow drowned in Golden Syrup.

The only cloud over his growing friendship with Maggie was Edmund Cardew. She visited him in Wormwood Scrubs on a regular basis but she had still not told him she was seeing Edward. She said it would do no good and might bring on the melancholia to which he seemed – understandably – prone. His final appeal was being considered by the Home Secretary, Samuel Hoare, but there seemed little chance of a reprieve. Maggie said that, perversely, he was more cheerful now that the waiting was almost over but was this just a façade? He had told her he wasn't sure he could survive long in prison without hope of ever being released and that hanging might, after all, be preferable. She reported that he was very thin and haggard.

The strain on Maggie was beginning to tell and Edward was worried about her. Sometimes she was depressed and lethargic while at other times bright-eyed and determinedly gay, which was almost worse. He asked her whether she really wanted to go to the Castlewoods' New Year's Eve party and she was angry with him.

'Of course we must go,' she said. 'I want to show them that we're all right.'

He nodded but remained uneasy right up to the moment when they arrived at Swifts Hill and were announced by Lampton. He, at least, seemed genuinely pleased to see them. Maggie was looking better than Edward had ever seen her in a new Balmain ball gown, shimmering white silk which clung to her body until it reached her ankles where it flowed outwards. As she danced, no longer self-conscious about her damaged face, he felt proud to have her in his arms. He could not but be aware that all eyes were on them.

Shortly before midnight he found himself sitting with Isolde Swann watching Roddy dance with Maggie. She whispered in his ear that she was pregnant and he congratulated her. He was glad to find her happy and relieved that she was to have the child in the Middlesex Hospital, not in the South of France. Sir Simon touched Edward on the shoulder and asked if he could have a word. Curious but a little apprehensive that he was to be thrown out of the house, Edward followed him into his study. Edward relaxed when he was offered a whisky and a cigar. Sir Simon was obviously not going to berate him.

'Forgive me for tearing you away from the party,' he said. 'Maggie is lovely, isn't she? I'm so pleased to see that you have become such friends. She needs friends with her brother in so much peril.' Edward said nothing, waiting to hear what Sir Simon really wanted to tell him. 'I wanted to explain . . . to convince you that I was quite unaware of what Montillo was doing at the Clinic. When you warned me, I couldn't believe what you were telling me. I thought I was funding serious research into heredity that would help babies born with diseases and defects inherited from parents or grandparents. I want you to believe that I was ignorant of his . . . experiments. I was absolutely horrified when I was told what the police had found down there. I know I ought to have known. I can't even pretend that I wasn't warned. Natalie said she thought something was wrong but I did not believe her either. I have been a fool but I . . .'

'You are right, Sir Simon, you ought to have known,' Edward said coldly, unwilling to make it easy for him.

'I have withdrawn all funding of medical research.' He hesitated and added, 'You know the police found evidence that Dominic was taking money from Himmler himself to . . . to carry out his beastly experiments? Of course you do.'

'Yes, I do.'

'Well, I wanted to say how grateful I am that you and Miss Browne exposed what was going on under my nose without my knowledge. You do believe me, don't you?' He rose from his chair and paced about the room.

Edward did not know if he believed him or not but decided he would give him the benefit of the doubt. 'I'll take your word for it.'

'And I want to recompense Maggie for the money her brother lost in the Institute. Do you think she will take it?'

'I really cannot say. You must ask her yourself.' Edward's voice was ice cold.

They returned to the great hall, ablaze with lights and decorated from the floor to its magnificent roof. Edward parted from his host with relief. As the minutes ticked away and 1937 with all its horrors limped into history, he held Maggie in his arms. When the new year was welcomed with shouts and hurrahs, he kissed her and she kissed him back. Inevitably, he asked himself what 1938 would bring. He had no answers. He tried to banish his fears but they kept crowding in on him. He had just heard from a friend in the Foreign Office that Nanking had been destroyed by the Japanese and the Chinese inhabitants tortured, raped and slaughtered with unparalleled cruelty. It made him sick to the stomach to think of it and he was glad when Maggie asked if he would mind taking her back to London. As they were collecting their cloaks, Sir Simon appeared and asked to have a final dance with Maggie. She could not refuse but Edward watched with a sense of foreboding as he whisked her back on to the dance floor. They had barely completed a circle of the floor before he heard a shriek and Maggie ran towards him. Behind her he saw Sir Simon standing with his hand to his cheek.

'Softly, softly!' he murmured soothingly as she sobbed in his arms. 'Did you slap him?'

'I did,' she said, looking up into his face, her arms still about his neck. 'Was that wrong?'

'It was the right thing to do,' he told her firmly. 'His arrogance . . . his need to play God has brought misery on many people – not just you and your brother. He must face his own conscience but at least we have put an end to his wickedness and your slap may bring him to his senses. Now we shall go. I don't imagine we shall ever come back to Swifts Hill and the thought lightens my heart.'

'And mine too,' she agreed. 'He tried to "buy" me. Did you know he was going to try?'

'I confess I did but I thought it was not for me to tell him you weren't for sale. Was I right?'

'You were right, Edward. Thank you.'

He kissed her once again and then they got into the Lagonda and Fenton drove them back to London.

At ten o'clock on Monday February 21st – the date was one Edward would never forget – he walked across the park to the Foreign Office to discuss his future with Sir Robert Vansittart. There had been several earlier appointments all of which Vansittart had had to break. It was wet and cold and the rain made light of his umbrella, making him regret he had not taken the Lagonda. The international situation was becoming ever more serious and the word 'crisis' loomed out at him from newspaper placards. It seemed only a matter of weeks, or even days, before there would be the ultimatum which would lead to war. It was no surprise to Edward that, when he arrived at the Foreign Office, he found it alive in a way it had not been when he had last stood on the great staircase under the magnificent chandelier. Secretaries were almost running down the corridors and normally sedate men in pinstripe suits were adjusting their ties and mopping their brows. Edward prepared himself to hear that Vansittart was too busy to see him and indeed it was forty minutes before he was told the great man was ready for him.

Vansittart was a man of considerable physical presence. He was tall and ruggedly handsome, perfectly dressed and apparently not the least infected by the excitement bordering on panic Edward sensed in his minions.

'Dear boy,' he said, rising from behind his huge desk and clasping Edward's hand. 'You must forgive me for being elusive but it's been one thing after another. But first let me congratulate you on your recovery. You really ought not to be shot at, at your time of life. I suppose we must regard the Duke of Windsor's life as worth saving? Now, I never said that,' he added, putting a finger to his lips.

Edward opened his mouth to explain that, far from saving the Duke's life, he had simply been trying to disarm a man who was taking revenge for the killing of his lover but it was all too complicated.

'As always,' Vansittart continued, 'you showed resolution and pluck and, if I may say so, more important than either – discretion.' Edward groaned inwardly. It always came down to this – nothing must get out. The status quo had to be preserved and reputations salvaged. 'You ought to have a medal or something.'

'I don't want a medal, thank you, sir,' Edward said with some asperity. 'I merely wondered if you might have some employment for me. I would like to contribute something to our preparations for war.'

'Oh, as for that,' Vansittart said breezily, 'there will be no war.'

'What do you mean, Sir Robert? I thought that if Hitler were to walk into Austria . . .'

'There will be no war because – and I speak in complete confidence – the Prime Minister has taken over the running of our foreign policy himself. He and Lord Halifax will avoid war whatever the cost.'

Edward was about to say something when Vansittart's principal private secretary, Mr Sanderson, entered without knocking.

'What is it, man? Can't you see I am in conference? I thought I said I was not to be disturbed.'

'The Foreign Secretary has asked whether you can spare him a moment,' Sanderson said unperturbed.

Vansittart looked annoyed. He obviously did not like being summoned peremptorily in front of a visitor, even by Mr Eden. Edward saw him wrestle with himself but, of course, he could not do otherwise but obey.

'I'll not be a moment, Lord Edward but I suppose I must see what's up. It's most unlike him to . . .'

Edward murmured that he quite understood and Vansittart got up from his chair and strode out of the room.

Alone in Vansittart's office, Edward was tempted – like a small boy – to run round behind the desk and imagine *he* was His Majesty's Permanent Under-Secretary for Foreign Affairs but he told himself this was not the time to play the fool. He was aware that the job Vansittart might have offered him six months earlier was no longer available. But might there not be something else? He wanted to do his bit. He had got his foot in the door in this great department of state and he had a strong desire to be a part of it. To know more than his fellows, to be at the heart of great events . . . The prospect stirred his blood. He got up to look at the pictures. The portrait of Lord Palmerston was particularly fine and he wondered what that old pirate would have said to Hitler. He certainly would not have had any truck with appeasement.

The minutes passed and still Vansittart did not return. Edward gazed out over the park. He had heard that plans had been made to dig trenches where civilians could take cover in the event of an air raid. He felt the impermanence of everything. He wondered how Verity was and felt his insides twist uncomfortably. Just as he thought he might slip away – it seemed Vansittart was not going to return in the near future – he heard his footsteps.

He was not himself – that was certain. He went straight to a cupboard near his desk, poured a whisky and squirted soda water from a siphon into the glass. Edward was still at the window and it was quite evident that Vansittart had forgotten all about him. He coughed gently.

'Lord Edward,' Vansittart said in surprise. 'Pray let me apologize. The fact is I have had some extraordinary news and – will you have one of these?' He indicated the whisky and Edward nodded. 'The fact is – and I don't see why you shouldn't be the first to hear it – Anthony has resigned.'

'Resigned! Mr Eden is no longer Foreign Secretary?'

'Correct. He will make an announcement in the Commons this afternoon. Not a word until then – on your honour.'

'Of course, but why has he resigned?'

'He says he cannot stay now the Prime Minister has effectively take over the conduct of foreign affairs himself. The PM has been negotiating with Signor Grandi, the Italian ambassador, behind Anthony's back. Apparently, we will recognize Italy's annexation of Abyssinia in return for the withdrawal of Italian troops from Spain, Furthermore, Signor Mussolini is to act as an "honest broker" between the Prime Minister and Hitler. In short, we shall give the dictators what they want in exchange for a promise that they will leave us alone.'

'But that's shameful! What about our treaty obligations to France . . . to the rest of Europe?'

'They count for nothing,' Vansittart said, draining his whisky and pouring himself another one.

'And you . . .?' Edward asked, caught up in the drama and speaking more freely than he had any right to do. 'You remain to serve the next Foreign Secretary . . . Lord Halifax, I presume.' The sarcasm was unintended but that was the way it came out and it seemed to sting Vansittart. Edward wondered afterwards if he had been in some way responsible for Sir Robert's decision to resign but the man had principles and would inevitably have decided he could not stay to put into effect policies which he regarded as against the interests of his country.

'I, too, Lord Edward, shall resign. Have no doubt about that. I fear I will be unable to help you as I had planned. You will have to apply to my successor but that is the way of the world. I wish you luck.'

Edward put down his empty glass. 'Sir Robert, you are a great man and I shall always remember with gratitude your kindness to me. I salute you and admire you. I shall not take up any more of your time.'

Vansittart nodded and Edward saw, as they shook hands, that he was too moved to speak. Peace had been bought at the expense of principle and most people would just be grateful that for one day . . . one week . . . one year more the bombs were not to shower down on them. One day soon, the price would have to be paid with interest. One did not have to be Foreign Secretary to know that. As Edward left the building, he saw Anthony Eden – straight-backed and dapper in his perfectly pressed suit – get into his official car to drive the few yards to Downing Street. It was the end of an era and Edward shivered as he imagined what was to follow.

Fenton looked far from his normal calm self when he opened the door on Edward's return to Albany. 'My lord, I am glad you are back. Miss Cardew is here.'

'Yes, I invited her to lunch. To tell the truth, I had almost forgotten in the excitement. You see . . .'

'My lord, forgive me for interrupting but Miss Cardew is in your bathroom and she won't come out.'

'What on earth do you mean? In my bathroom . . .?'

'She asked whether she could powder her nose and, of course, I said she could. She knows where the visitors' lavatory is so I had no need to show her. When I re-entered the drawing-room, I realized she had chosen to use your bathroom.'

'Well, I don't mind. What's the problem?'

'The problem is that she has been in there for twenty-five minutes. I knocked on the door a few minutes ago and there was no answer. And then, just before you came in, I listened at the door and I thought I heard her moaning. I was just about to break down the door. She has bolted it on the inside.'

It was not like Fenton to take alarm without good cause so Edward hurried through his bedroom and knocked on the bathroom door.

'Maggie! Are you all right?' he called. There was no answer but he thought he heard something which might be a groan. 'Hold my coat, will you, Fenton. I'm going to put my shoulder to the door.'

The bolt gave way without difficulty and the door flew open. Maggie was standing as if in a dream, staring in the shaving mirror. She had Edward's razor in her hand and was just about to make another cut in her cheek which was already striated with bloodied furrows. She had literally harrowed her skin and turned her face to pulp. Edward wrestled the razor from her and, with Fenton's help, half carried her into his bedroom and laid her on the bed.

While Fenton went off to ring for an ambulance, Edward knelt beside her and tried to soothe her. He did not dare touch her face in case, in his ignorance, he made things worse. 'Maggie! Maggie! What made you do this?' Moaning but not crying, she tried to turn her head away. 'Maggie, can you hear me? An ambulance is on its way but I must know why you did this to yourself. Was it my fault? I thought we were happy together.'

'Teddy – he cut his wrists,' she muttered.

'Oh my God. I am so sorry. Is he . . .?'

'He had taken one of my hairpins and I don't know how . . . used it as a knife.'

'But he's alive?'

'Yes. I went to see him in the prison hospital.'

'Well, then – why do this to yourself? Tell me!'

'He . . . he had been told I was . . . I was seeing you.' She swallowed her words but Edward understood what she was saying.

'But I thought you had told him we were . . . we were friends.'

'I did not dare because I knew he would say I was betraying him. He called me a whore . . . he said . . . he said I was more beautiful *with* my scar. He said I was as ugly as sin and no man could love me. He said there was a scar on my soul. He said . . .'

'Oh, my poor girl. How terrible! But you are beautiful. I think you are beautiful.'

'I came to talk to you but you weren't here and . . . and I looked in the mirror and saw that he was right. I am ugly. I deserve to be ugly. All I could do was let my wickedness out. The Harrowing of Hell.'

Edward buried his head in the sheet. The suffering of this woman would know no end. He suddenly thought of Verity finding the razor in Maud Pitt-Messanger's bathroom at Swifts Hill on the night she slit her wrists. Yes! The Harrowing of Hell just about described it – the desire to be released from the inferno and to find redemption in blood.

The ambulance arrived and a temporary bandage was wrapped round Maggie's cheek. Edward went with her to hospital and she seemed to find some comfort in the pressure of his hand in hers. He thought she might be repulsed by him but what she had done to herself seemed to have brought her some sort of peace. It was as if, having paid the price, she no longer had any guilt.

Four hours later, quite exhausted, he returned to his rooms. Fenton brought him whisky and asked after Maggie. He told him that her life was not in danger but that she would be very much scarred.

'I am sorry to hear that, my lord. I blame myself for not having broken down the door much earlier but when I showed Miss Cardew into the drawing-room she seemed quite her normal self.'

'Don't blame yourself, Fenton. I think it was only when she saw herself in the mirror that her grief and guilt broke through. Rationally, she knew she was doing nothing wrong in being friends with me. I was not her brother's enemy but, unfortunately, I proved to be his nemesis. Seeing herself without the scar she had lived with for so many years, her reason broke down and she was overwhelmed with guilt. I am no Freud but I believe what she did is not dissimilar from holy men whipping the skin off their backs to punish themselves for being human.'

To Fenton, he sounded bitter and deeply depressed. The telephone rang, much to his relief, and he went off to answer it.

'It's the Duchess, my lord. She asks for a word with you.'

'Oh God! I suppose I must,' Edward said, levering himself out of his chair. Much as he loved Connie, he really did not want to speak to anyone just now.

'Ned, I'm sorry to bother you but I felt I had to tell you.'

'Tell me what?'

'It's Frank. He has gone to America with Miss Schuster-Slatt.'

'But he's at Cambridge,' Edward said stupidly. 'It's still term time, isn't it?'

'Yes, and I think this will get him sent down.'

'But why has he gone to America? I don't understand. Did he tell you?'

'He wrote to me. He said he wanted me to understand. He loves America. He wants to be an American and he is going to work with someone called . . .' Edward heard paper rustling. 'Mr Kinsey. Have you ever heard of him? Frank says he's some sort of scientist.'

Edward heard her voice shake. Connie was trying to be brave but she was very near the edge.

'The stupid boy! I thought he had finished with that Schuster-Slatt woman. I thought . . . I hoped she had scared him off. Blast and damnation! They're not planning to get married or anything?'

'He doesn't say so. Ned, what on earth are we going to do?'

'I don't know. I'm sorry, Connie, I'll have to ring you back. There's someone at the door. Look, don't worry. It'll sort itself out somehow. Frank's not a complete idiot.'

Edward rang off hoping he was right. What a day! Surely nothing else could go wrong? As he turned he saw who his visitor was. Verity stood in the hall looking forlorn and almost scared.

'Have I come at a bad moment?' she asked, seeing his face. 'Fenton's just been telling me that Miss Cardew – Maggie . . .'

'Yes, she wanted to put the scar back on her face,' he said brutally. 'Her brother had called her a whore for being friends with me. Oh, yes and Connie has been telling me that Frank has run off to America with Sadie Schuster-Slatt.'

Verity grimaced. 'That's terrible. Poor Edward, but your wound? Is that . . .?'

'Have I recovered from my wound to the heart?' he asked sarcastically. 'How *is* Adam, by the way?'

'Well, that's why I'm back in England. The fact is that he's been kidnapped – arrested, I suppose.'

'Oh God! I am so sorry, V. When did it happen?' Edward was immediately penitent.

'On January 16th. He had taken me to this concert . . .'

'I thought you didn't like music.'

'I don't but Adam was . . . is mad about Gustav Mahler. I had never heard of him, of course!' she said bitterly. 'He wants to teach me about music . . . He managed to get tickets for a performance of Mahler's ninth symphony which he had never heard. It was conducted by Bruno Walter. I hadn't heard of him either but apparently he's the nibs. Anyway, it was to be a sort of protest. You see, Mahler's music is no longer performed in Germany because he was a Jew. And, of course, if Hitler does what he threatens and takes over Austria, he won't be performed in Vienna either, despite the fact that he directed the Vienna Philharmonic in what Adam calls its golden age. You can guess how tense we all were. It was the most wonderful music I have ever heard and the saddest, too. It made sense of everything we are fighting for. Von Schuschnigg, the Austrian Chancellor, was there and, as we stood for the national anthem, I saw that he was weeping.'

'But who arrested Adam?'

'I'm not sure but Himmler's thugs, I think. Himmler has called him a traitor for refusing to join the Nazi Party. As we left the concert hall, several men jumped out of a big black car and seized Adam. Before I could do anything, the car had driven off. I screamed and the police came but they did nothing. They don't want to do anything which might annoy Hitler and, of course, Adam's a German citizen.'

'So you think he's back in Germany?'

'Where else can he be?' She shrugged her shoulders and a tear ran down her cheek. Impatiently, she wiped it away with her gloved hand as though this sign of weakness annoyed her.

Edward held out his arms and she came and laid her head on his shoulder like a weary child.

'What can I do?' he asked. 'I mean, you know I would do anything . . .'

'I was going to ask you if you could see your friend, Sir Robert Vansittart. If the Foreign Office made a fuss, they might let him go.'

'Too late for that, I fear, V,' he said regretfully. 'Sir Robert and Mr Eden have just resigned.'

'Then there's nothing to be done.' She seemed to have surrendered any little hope she had.

'Look, don't give up. They'd never dare send Adam to one of those camps. He has too many important friends. How long are you staying in London? We'll go round to the German Embassy tomorrow. And Weaver . . . if the newspapers . . .'

'I have to get the boat train tonight. I didn't want to leave Vienna but I thought . . .'

'Is there anything I can do . . . anything at all?'

Verity grimaced. 'I'm not sure . . . Well, there is one thing. Before Adam was arrested, he gave me a dog and I smuggled it back here. I couldn't leave him in Vienna. It's quite a small flat.'

'And this is a big dog?'

'Not that big.'

'How big?'

'It's a curly-coated retriever.'

'A curly-coated retriever! I'm sorry, V, but I can't have a curly-haired dog in Albany. In fact, I can't keep any animal here. It's not allowed.'

'I thought you could take it to Mersham. I thought Connie would like the company. I mean, Basil is very good-natured.'

'Basil?'

'Well, he was called Fritz in Vienna but, obviously, I can't have a dog called Fritz so I changed his name to Basil. Adam liked the name.'

'But V . . .!' he protested.

'He'll remind you of me.'

'But V,' he repeated, 'I was trying *not* to be reminded of you. Where is he anyway?'

'He's downstairs in the taxi.'

'In the taxi?'

'Edward – why do you say you want to forget me? We love each other, don't we?'

'But I thought Adam . . .?'

'I told you I might take lovers but that I would always love you. Isn't that enough?'

Edward started to say that it wasn't enough but he found, after all, that it was.

Also available from Constable & Robinson

No. of copies			
	The Quality of Mercy (hardback) – Available 26 October 2006	£17.99	
	The More Deceived	£6.99	
	Dangerous Sea	£6.99	
	Hollow Crown	£6.99	
	Bones of the Buried	£6.99	
	Sweet Poison	£6.99	
	P&P and insurance	£ 1.00	
	Grand Total £		

Name: ....

Address: ....

.... Postcode: ....

Daytime Tel. No. / Email ....
(*in case of query*)

Three ways to pay:

1. **For express service telephone the TBS order line on 01206 255 800 and quote 'ROB1'. Order lines are open Monday – Friday 8:30am – 5:30pm**

2. I enclose a cheque made payable to **TBS Ltd** for £ ....

3. Please charge my ❏ Visa ❏ Mastercard ❏ Amex ❏ Switch

    (switch issue no. ....)

Card number: ....

Expiry date: .... Signature ....
(*your signature is essential when paying by credit card*)

Please return forms (*no stamp required*) to:
Freepost RLUL-SJGC-SGKJ
Cash Sales / Direct Mail Dept
The Book Service
Colchester Road
Frating
Colchester
CO7 7DW

Enquiries to readers@constablerobinson.com
www.constablerobinson.com

Constable and Robinson Ltd (directly or via its agents) may mail, email or phone you about promotions or products. ❏ Tick box if you do not want these from us ❏ or our subsidiaries.